FOUR

BOOK TWO IN THE HIGHWAYMAN SERIES

M.J. PRESTON

WildBluePress.com

FOUR published by:
WILDBLUE PRESS
P.O. Box 102440
Denver, Colorado 80250

ISBN 978-1-952225-00-0 Trade Paperback
ISBN 978-1-948239-71-4 eBook

Cover design © 2020 WildBlue Press. All rights reserved.

Interior Formatting/Book Cover Design by Elijah Toten
www.totencreative.com

FOUR

AUTHORS NOTE

This novel is a work of fiction. Any resemblance to persons living or dead is purely coincidental; however, the author has taken the liberty of using historical characters, references and places to enhance the reader experience. References to known and convicted criminals, along with political figures, have been added to lend realism to the fictional tale contained in this story.

Kirkland Island does not exist, although it is modeled after islands which float in the Ohio River in the Pittsburgh area. I have taken many liberties with the region, including inserting fictitious towns, like Henessburg, Pennsylvania, and I respectfully acknowledge that this story and the depiction of these regions do not reflect the reality of those communities.

M.J. Preston

This Novel is for
my brother, Tony Preston.
You always kept me safe.

TABLE OF CONTENTS

PART I

VIRTUAL TAKEDOWN

"They got me on this one... They've got DNA.
I was gonna do another one, make it an even
50. That's why I was sloppy. I wanted to do one
more, make the big 5-0."—Robert Pickton

HIGHWAYMAN SERIES – BOOK II

The following crimes occurred between
19 September and 17 November 2008

PROLOGUE – COMPENDIUM OF EVENTS

1

5 September 2007

"He's setting me up, Julian," Maxwell said in a phone conversation prior to the release of an Identi-Kit composite. He was speaking of his boss, Special Agent in Charge (SAC) Hugh Bailey.

"How do you know?" Carswell asked.

"He wouldn't supply me with a sketch artist, so I had to use Identi-Kit. Then he makes himself unavailable during crucial times. He brought in Ferguson without consulting me. Now he's sending me signals to leak the Identi-Kit composite, while saying that he isn't authorizing it, and essentially will deny any such insinuation if asked."

"Max, that's a pretty bold indictment. I assume this conversation was between the two of you?"

"Yeah, cell phone conversation."

"He said, he said. His word against yours?"

"Except for one thing, Julian."

"One thing?"

"I recorded our call."

"You what?"

"I recorded it."

"Jesus H. Christ, Max!"

"I didn't feel like I had much wiggle room."

Carswell took a deep breath. "So, now you want what from me?"

"I was hoping you could tell me."

Carswell groaned. "You're not taping me, are you?"

"You really need to ask that?"

"No."

"What do I do, Julian?"

"Okay. First, shut your pie hole and do nothing."

Maxwell listened.

"I want you to call me on my personal cell in two hours."

"Okay."

"That's it, two hours." Carswell hung up.

2

September 5, 2007

Dumfries, VA

Carswell was seated in a booth by himself in a Ruby Tuesday. He had deliberately picked a booth in the corner and made sure that no one was in earshot. His personal cell phone, one he rarely used, was an iPhone his wife had bought him. He'd told Maxwell to call him on it because he was almost sure that it wouldn't be monitored.

Almost, but not one hundred percent.

I'm about to enter into a conspiracy, he thought to himself. This troubled him, but loyalty to his friend overrode the angst he felt in the pit of his guts. It was clear that Bailey was setting Maxwell up. He also knew that there would be a complaint of favoritism by Bailey, even if he didn't intervene. That would be Bailey's move; asshole that he was. *Fuck it,* Carswell thought, and, *Bailey needs to go.*

Carswell glanced at his watch. Max would be calling in roughly two minutes.

"Can I take your order?" the waitress asked. She was a young woman, perhaps twenty-nine, glasses, had a round face, was a little plump, and friendly.

"I'll have a bottle of MGD and a menu," he said, smiling.

"Coming right up." She turned and headed for the bar.

Carswell's phone rang.

"Hey," Carswell said.

"Hey," Maxwell replied.

"You alone?"

"Yup."

The waitress was returning with his beer and menu.

"Hang on a second, Max."

"Okay."

The waitress set the beer down on a coaster and placed the menu in front of him. "Would you like to know the special?"

"Sure."

"We have a soup and sandwich combo on, pastrami on rye and green pea soup."

Carswell wasn't big on the soup, so he ordered the sandwich and a house salad. The waitress jotted down his order and left the table. When she was out of earshot, he picked up the phone and asked, "Still there?"

"Yeah, I would've gone for the soup."

"I'll pass. After I saw *The Exorcist*, when I was a kid, I can't even look at the stuff."

"Your loss."

"You ready to talk?"

"I'm all ears."

Carswell took a swig of beer, glanced around, and said, "Okay, this is what you're going to do. You're going to draft me three memos. The first will raise concern about Bailey. The second will question his leadership. Oh, and bring up the sketch artist. The third will be a letter asking for direction and authorization regarding the Identi-Kit composite. You with me so far?"

"Yeah," Maxwell said.

"I don't think I have to tell you about dates on those memos?"

"No, I understand."

"The first memo, crumple it up and photocopy it. The second, put a crease in it and leave the third alone. Put all three in separate envelopes, then FEDEX them to me at my home. I'll take it from there. I'll also want a copy of the recording you made of your conversation with Bailey. Send that separately, but also send it courier."

"What are you up to, Julian?"

"Later today, I want an email from you requesting a follow up on those three memos. Outline the issue with the Identi-Kit, further explain your issues with Bailey, and ask for direction. Did I mention I want you to scan those three memos and encrypt them in PDF with a password?" Carswell was being facetious.

"You did not." Maxwell laughed.

"Do that. I want all three of those memos drafted, copied, and attached to the email. I want the originals in my hand by tomorrow. I don't care if you have to drive five hundred miles to find a courier."

"What are you up to, Julian?"

"Don't leak the composite, Max. It's a trap."

"I know."

"Get that stuff to me. I'll obtain authorization for a leak from the director herself. I'll be going in with copies of the email and PDFs you send me. If the shit hits the fan, someone is going to go digging for the originals."

The new FBI director was named Alicia Watters. She'd been appointed by the president six months earlier. Her predecessor had stepped down for health reasons. The rumor was cancer, but in fact, he had an aggressive form of multiple sclerosis. Watters' style of leadership was being dissected by political detractors, but she balanced her duties between the politico and the Bureau quite well. Maxwell liked her. Thought she was innovative and forward-thinking. But at that level, Watters was still a politician. She and Carswell got along very well.

"I understand."

"Things are going to get ugly, Max. Even uglier if you don't catch the Highwayman."

"You don't have to tell me."

"If this works, Bailey won't be breathing down your neck anymore."

"I can only wish," Maxwell said.

"Careful what you wish for, Max."

3

9 September 2007

Quantico, VA

September would end with SAC Hugh Bailey taking leave of his duties, and Maxwell being promoted from Special Agent to Special Agent in Charge, making him the overseer of the Highwayman case. For Maxwell, the promotion was bittersweet. While he'd known that this day would come, he'd done everything he could to sabotage it. Deputy Director Julian Carswell had been both his savior and saboteur. No longer would he be in the field chasing the bad guys, but sequestered to an office. Carswell's spin on it was that he was moving off the battlefield and into the war room.

It didn't feel like a war room, it felt like a cage.

Maxwell had been given the option of picking a successor. Carswell asked if he trusted Ferguson. Maxwell thought about it. If they sent Ferguson packing, it would look bad, and Maxwell felt Ferguson had been straight with him after being brought in. So, Special Agent Evan Ferguson took over Maxwell's duties as field agent. While Carswell had saved Maxwell from certain reassignment, he'd also helped take the case away from him. A by-product of that was turning it over to his intended replacement.

Ferguson had been brought in as a reserve until Bailey could find a way to get rid of Maxwell. But Maxwell had been too smart, boxing him in and beating him at his own game.

A day after he spoke to Maxwell on the phone, Carswell went in and had a sit-down with the director. She authorized the leak. Before doing so, she asked if Bailey should be brought in and if a meeting was in order. Carswell said he didn't want him reprimanded, he just wanted him reassigned.

"You sure about this, Julian?"

"I think he'll go quietly. I want to give him that option."

She thought about it. "Okay, it's your call."

When the news broke about the body in Stafford, Virginia, Carswell went to Bailey's office. That was when he said he'd be joining him at the crime scene.

"Okay," Bailey said.

They got on the bird and flew out of Quantico together.

Both men had a secret.

Bailey thought he had it all in hand. He called Ferguson and told him to get on a plane for Stafford, Virginia.

"What about Maxwell?" Ferguson asked.

"Just get on a plane to Virginia. I'll explain when you get there," Bailey told him.

Maxwell had been ordered by Bailey to return to Quantico for debriefing.

By the time Ferguson was on the ground, Bailey and Carswell were both back in Quantico. At that time, Maxwell was flying in. Bailey wrote a recommendation for Maxwell's promotion and Carswell authorized it. Maxwell, thinking that Julian hadn't saved him, came in expecting to be reassigned. When he passed Bailey in the hallway, Bailey never said a word to him. Maxwell gave him a glance and thought, *tough day at the office.*

Maxwell's phone rang.

He answered it. "Maxwell."

"Report to my office," Carswell said.

"On my way." Maxwell looked back at Bailey, who was now entering the elevator. Bailey was gazing back at him. His face was expressionless, but his eyes were another matter. They burned with resentment. The elevator doors closed.

Bailey was out.

Maxwell made his way to the deputy director's office and sat down in the waiting room.

The secretary let Carswell know Maxwell had arrived. "You can go right in, Agent Maxwell."

"Thank you," Maxwell said and went in.

"Sit down, Max," Carswell said.

Maxwell sat.

"You're being promoted to SAC. From here, you'll oversee the Highwayman file." Julian Carswell came out from behind his desk and put out his hand. "Congratulations."

4

10 September 2007

Lawrenceville, PA

The FBI had come close, too close. Now there was just one question. How long before they circled back for another look? Lance knew it was inevitable. He hoped the others' work would keep them off his trail for a while, but how long did he have? Sooner or later it would be time to go underground.

He spent the day boxing up the computer downstairs, disposing of the burner phone he'd used to communicate with the others about Norris and the rendezvous. With the destruction and storage of those items, he thought he might have some time. The Web site, macabre.club.com, was gone. So were the digital transcripts of what had happened; and what would happen. The deep Web wasn't as safe and anonymous as he'd thought. In the class with the DEA agent, Lance had learned how they had eventually taken down a major drug supplier. So, the authorities were out there, hunters lurking in the dark net, searching for the predators.

"Nowhere is completely safe," he said to the forest.

He was walking, carrying the computer hardware in a box, the first of five boxes heading for storage. Approximately nine hundred yards into the wood line, he stopped and set the box down. Beside it was what looked like an unsealed crypt. What it really was, was his time capsule, made up with the same concrete used to pour the third room. The underground compartment was four-by-five feet in width and five feet in depth.

An afterthought constructed after reading about child killer John Wayne Gacy. When authorities discovered the secret Gacy had buried in the crawlspace below his house, they'd taken the entire building apart, stick by stick. The cottage and the place in Syracuse would fall under the same forensic eye. Technically, this wasn't even a safe place, but it would be harder to find. He set the box down into the capsule and went back for the others.

The third room had been stripped. It was empty. The photos, the computer equipment, the news clippings, and the maps all packed neatly into boxes. Lance even swept and wiped down the entire room, clearing it of Norris' presence.

Once all the boxes were stored, he sealed the crypt and shoveled dirt on top. He'd only kept one item above ground.

5

24 September 2007

Silver Springs, Florida

The latest body was found near the Ocklawaha River off Florida SR 40, almost three-quarters of a mile from the intersection of County Road 314 and SR 40. It was a man's body, naked, cut up into six pieces, limbs and head removed from the torso, and positioned like a starfish.

It was also where Ferguson and Maxwell met for the first time face to face. Ferguson was wearing surgical gloves and examining the body when Maxwell entered the scene. Without looking up he asked, "So, what do I call you?"

"Call me?"

"Yeah. Sir, boss, what?" Ferguson got up from the crouching position. Removing his blue surgical gloves, he said, "You've got friends in high places."

"Is that the word?"

"It's an observation. Bailey never saw it coming. The question is, 'Why am I still here?'"

"Why wouldn't you be?" But Maxwell knew.

"I figured you'd be wiping the slate clean."

"Bailey called you?"

"He did." Ferguson didn't mention that Bailey had warned him that Maxwell and the DD were in cahoots and he was next to go.

"Bailey was the problem, not you. I've been promoted to SAC. I need a good field man. You were straight with me, that's why you're still here."

"Did you leak that composite?"

"I did," Maxwell said. Then he added a lie he hoped would put Ferguson at ease. "After the director authorized me to do so."

"Uh-huh. So, what do I call you?"

"You call me Max."

Ferguson looked unconvinced.

"Look, I didn't want the promotion, but for my sins, they gave it to me. Is the deputy director a friend of mine? Yes, he is. But the only time I've used that friendship is when brainless assholes try to jam me up. Bailey got what he wanted. You're on the point, and I'm tethered to an office. I was given the option to replace you, but I think you're a stand-up agent."

"Ah, bring on the accolades."

"All I ever wanted was to chase down bad guys. I would've been happy to finish out my career doing that. I've never wanted to be a boss, but here we are. What I want from you is to help me catch the Highwayman." Maxwell stuck out his hand.

Ferguson eased up, then. He even smiled a little and took Maxwell's hand. "Pleasure to meet you, Max. I'm Evan Ferguson."

Maxwell smiled and shook.

"Congratulations on your promotion."

Maxwell released Ferguson's hand and looked down at the body. "Anything new?"

"Cut up and staged, just like the other two."

"The other two? Don't you mean the others?"

"Not quite," said a voice from behind.

Maxwell turned to see a tall, slim woman dressed in a neoprene suit standing there holding an evidence collection bag. "Hello, Max."

"Shirley." Maxwell greeted the woman and released Ferguson's hand. Maxwell had known Shirley Cain for years. She'd been with the Bureau for over a decade. "I thought you were in Memphis."

"I was, until last week. I'm back in Quantico now. I'm taking over Wilbur Simons' position." Simons had been the FBI pathologist assigned to the case under the original FBI investigator, Lewis Ash. Wilbur Simons had been forced into retirement for health issues. Lewis Ash had also retired before solving the case and becoming a victim of the Highwayman.

"Good to have you back," Maxwell said. "What were you saying when you came up?"

"Norris and the female victim in Stafford had a puncture lower on the spine, as well as this male victim. The other victims had punctures between the C4 and C6 cervical vertebrae." Shirley Cain paused to take a breath and continued. "From Norris on, the puncture wounds have moved into thoracic vertebrae between T2 and T4."

"Any thoughts as to why?" Ferguson asked.

"None that would make any sense," Cain replied.

"Could our killer have purposely changed the location of the puncture?" Maxwell asked.

"What are you asking, Max?"

"To be blunt, would stabbing them lower on the spine incapacitate them more effectively?"

"I don't think so, in fact, it might increase the victim's chances of overcoming complete paralysis. The lower the puncture, the less nerve damage."

Then Maxwell asked, "Do you think it could have been somebody else?"

"You mean a copycat?"

"Possibly, but that doesn't explain why Norris has the same puncture wound." Cain produced a notepad and leafed through it. "The Ironworks murders had no puncture wounds. Also, there was no sign of purposeful dismemberment."

"That's because it was an impulsive killing. Lewis Ash was attempting escape, the two victims found with him were helping him with that escape." Maxwell paused. "My thought is, had Ash not been found by those two workers, he would have been starfished just like the others."

"Starfished," Cain said. "Did you start that, Max?"

"No, it was before I was on the case. I can't remember where it originated. Maybe the Rhode Island Staties?"

"So, why the sudden change?" Ferguson asked this time.

"I don't know," Maxwell and Cain said in unison.

But Maxwell thought something was off. "Let's all get some lunch. We can talk about this some more."

"All right," Ferguson agreed.

"I'm afraid I'm going to be busy for at least another four or five hours. Crime scene has done their collection, but I have an autopsy to attend," Cain said. "I might be able to make supper."

"Okay, supper, then. Bring your notes, I want to go through all of this." Maxwell took a last look over the crime scene.

And that was the day the Highwayman case went cold for the second time.

But only for a while.

***

CHAPTER 1 – DATCU EFFECT

1

19 September 2008

Quantico, VA

Lance Belanger had never entirely left Dave Maxwell's thoughts in the year since he and Cole Abraham had interviewed him. Maxwell considered him a likely suspect, but the discovery of bodies in Virginia, Maryland, and Florida had weakened that suspicion. Even if Maxwell ignored the fact that there was no way Belanger could be involved and pursued him as a suspect, he wouldn't be able to get a warrant to follow up. No judge was going to sign off on a man who had an airtight alibi for four of the murders.

Maxwell, Ferguson, and Cain all discussed the possibility that there was more than one killer. A copycat theory had been floated but quickly discounted. Neither the presence of punctures in the spine or the dismemberment were released to the media. Both Ferguson and Cain had accepted the possibility that Highwayman had simply changed the area on the spine to incapacitate his victims. Maxwell didn't think so but kept his suspicion to himself. It was too outlandish.

In July, 2007, yet another highway killer had been apprehended in Chelmsford, Massachusetts. The killer was a long-haul truck driver. He was discounted after his travel schedule and methods were explored. There were others, but none matched the specifics of the Highwayman's modus operandi. The criminal investigation soon faded from the public eye as the media again withdrew and focused on other events.

By the spring of 2008, the world economy was beginning to collapse. Lending institutions were failing, Americans were losing their homes, and the new villains on the 24-hour news cycle wore three-piece suits. The Highwayman was still on the FBI's 10 Most Wanted List, but he'd fallen from the headlines. Louisville Detective Lonnie Perkins once generalized in a press conference by asking the media if they had attention deficit disorder. The backlash over this was swift but short lived. Perkins' statement was also spot on from Maxwell's vantage point. They were easily distracted, not unlike a dog that sees a cat or a squirrel. Focus shifted from a national manhunt to the record shortfalls and job losses at General Motors. Before long, the Highwayman story was almost completely forgotten, as were Lewis Ash and the other victims; replaced by war, scandal, Paris Hilton, or whatever else was trending on the wire. Maxwell was dismayed by this, but he'd seen it before.

There had only been one victim since the Florida discovery almost a year earlier. During the quiet time, Ferguson and Maxwell re-interviewed witnesses and consulted with law enforcement in the jurisdictions where the bodies had been found. They hoped that they might shake something loose. The Cavalier that the Highwayman and Norris had used to escape Louisville was dissected by crime scene techs and the VIN was traced back to a man named Vernon Husk in Frankfort, Kentucky. Husk was nowhere to be found and authorities feared the worst.

On the 17th November of 2007, those fears were realized when Husk's dismembered body was discovered off US Route 127, next to Elkhorn Creek in Peaks Mill in Franklin County. Husk would have been able to identify the individual he sold the car to. Unfortunately for him, the Highwayman had tied up yet another loose end.

27 October 2008

Bucharest, Romania

Andrei Gusa hadn't known that his world was set to come crashing down that morning. If he had, he would have fled to Chechnya. There, he had contacts who could set him up in Panama or Venezuela. A master preparer, Gusa had backed up all the sites his shadow company hosted from eight different countries. All websites were illegal, their illicitness ranging from child pornography to snuff and everything in between.

His clients were from the United States, Canada, Germany, Russia, Australia, the United Kingdom, Sweden, and Mexico.

He did receive a warning, and that was enough. "INTERPOL has arrested Mikolai in Serbia," Teodora Berić warned in a phone call that morning. She was the only woman in the group. She was calling from Croatia. "Burn everything, my friend, and get moving. It isn't safe!"

"How long?" Gusa opened a drawer, removed a large tin box, and placed it on his desk. Simultaneously, he opened his laptop and brought up a screen that linked him to the administration panel of the entire mainframe. He typed in his password and scrolled down to a button with the word: `Autodistrugere (self-destruct)`.

He clicked on it.

`Esti sigur? (Are you sure?)`

Below that.

`Da/Nu (Yes/No)`

"You have to leave! They could be on their way right now," Teodora said. "Good luck, my friend."

"Thank you, safe travels," Gusa replied.

She hung up. It would be the last time they ever spoke. Gusa placed his mouse over `Da` and clicked.

Then the screen read: `Autodistrugere inițializată` followed by an animation of file folders moving from the mainframe into an incinerator. With that done, he opened the tin box. Inside was a fake passport, two cell phones, and an envelope filled with traveling money.

Gusa glanced at the monitor.

`74% au fost finalizate (74% completed)`

His heart was pounding. The computer was shedding the mainframe files at a high rate. But it still wasn't fast enough for Gusa, who urged, *"Grabă! Grabă!"*

`89% au fost finalizate`

Outside his office, he heard clunking of numerous boots on the service stairs. They were coming. He placed the items back in the box and focused on the screen

`94% au fost finalizate`

"Grabă!" He groaned and set the tin box back into the drawer. He would not be going anywhere.

`99% au fost finalizate`

They were coming down the hall now, military boots clunking through the buffer of carpet that padded the hardwood floor.

`Auto-distrugere completă`

Andrei Gusa let out a sigh, closed the laptop and drawer. He then placed both hands on the top of his desk. His door exploded open, and several men dressed in paramilitary attire and toting assault weapons came through the door. They enveloped Gusa from all sides, guns pointed at him. He kept his hands flat upon the desk, and a short, round man wearing a dark charcoal suit with matching hat entered the room.

In Romanian, the man said, "I am Inspector Datcu, I work with the Romanian Branch of INTERPOL. Andrei Gusa, you are under arrest for numerous internet crimes, including human trafficking, child pornography, money laundering and..."

Gusa only said one word in Romanian, "Lawyer."

"Get him up," the inspector said.

Two of the assault force officers slung their weapons and lifted Gusa by his arms. He didn't resist. If he did, they would probably beat him. Best to stay calm until he talked with his lawyer.

3

30 October 2008

Syracuse, NY

It had been over a year since Special Agent Maxwell and the state cop had come calling. In that year, there were changes. Some good. Some bad. At least from Lance's perspective. He was standing in front of the mirror admiring the full beard on his face, and the hair that now veiled a third of his ears. Lance thought the physical change was good. The sketch that resembled his former self was no longer circulating, but he'd decided to change his appearance anyway. Lance liked the beard, thought it made him look Bundy-ish. He remembered a television interview from YouTube that showed Ted Bundy sporting a beard in jail. Bundy had been proclaiming his innocence. He would escape a few weeks later.

That was the only time Lance thought Bundy looked handsome. His beard, a thick, brown mane, gave him the appearance of a college professor — not a killer who sawed off women's heads for the purpose of necrophilia.

Lance was considering growing his hair long, like a rock star, but that would take some time. Before this new look, he'd shaved his head and face to avoid dropping hair at the crime scenes. After suiting up in white neoprene painter coveralls, he even coated his face with a thin layer of Vaseline. This was to avoid the shedding of skin. Tools of the trade, a vocational requirement of evading detection while committing serial murder.

After law enforcement landed on his doorstep, he was forced to abstain from his favorite pastime. He'd taken precautions, lying low and imposing abstinence on the hungry monster lurking behind the mask. He hadn't fed that monster in quite some time. Over a year. As a result, the pressure inside him grew. Night seemed the worst, a time of internal arguments raging as he considered setting out to find a victim. The problem was Lance had no idea if he was being monitored. If he were, they would swoop in and grab him. But even if he wasn't, a new string of killings presented logistical complications. He'd gone to great lengths to cover his tracks. Disposing of Norris and the car, the murders he had the others commit to create a credible alibi.

He brought his hand up and ran his fingers through the beard. "Where do we go from here?" he asked the Bundy-ish reflection. Sooner or later, the monster would have to be fed. It was inevitable.

The other three, Dusk, Steel, and Larry, had helped in shifting the attention of authorities. But he was now wondering if they presented a higher risk than a benefit.

Steel had a thing for young girls, he'd killed in the states of Michigan and Illinois. Steel had also shared a space with Highwayman on the FBI's 10 Most Wanted List. Lance remembered that, it seemed so long ago. He had been jealous of Steel's status, even though he hadn't known who he was at the time. Then fate delivered the schoolgirl killer to him via the Macabre Club website. When Larry had his baring of souls, Lance realized who he was, but never said a word. He didn't mention that he'd felt in competition with and had even pondered killing a couple of cuties himself to raise his own profile. It was a small fucking world, even for serial killers.

What he wanted was to use them for was to increase his numbers and further confuse the authorities. Maybe even add one or two more to the mix. But when the FBI ended up on his doorstep, that had been unnerving. A moratorium on the killing had to be imposed. He'd regularly communicated with them, via burner phone, over the last year. After the Stafford killing, he sent a message that it was time to lay low. He checked in at least once a week. Larry and Dusk had complained about the pause. Steel had not.

He guessed that was because Steel hadn't stopped. During the pause, the killings in Michigan started up again.

That made Steel a liability, but they were all a liability.

Leaving the washroom, Lance went into the living room and flipped on the television. Had he not done that, his providence would have been sealed. Some 7,300 kilometers away, in a Romanian jail, his fate was about to be altered. If not for a broadcast on CNN, he wouldn't have seen the impending danger of being caught himself.

Lance saw the short clip of Gusa on CNN in a teaser before a commercial break. "Up next. A major illegal internet ring has been taken down by police agencies from around the world," the news anchor said.

Then came a commercial about acid reflux.

"Shit," Lance said. His pulse was quickening. "Andrei."

He waited until the commercials ended.

The newscast came back on. "Officials from four European countries have executed a joint sting, bringing down an intercontinental internet ring they say has roots in Europe, the United States, and Canada." The clip showed Andrei Gusa being led out of the same building Lance had met him in to set up macabre.club.com.

"Fuck!" Lance felt panic in his belly as he turned up the volume. "Oh fuck! Oh fuck!"

The news anchor reported, "There have been multiple arrests and officials have given notice that there will be many more. Charges include child pornography, human trafficking, and sex slavery."

The clip faded to another, where another man was being led by police to a waiting motorcade of black military vehicles. Under it were the words, SECOND ARREST MADE IN BELGRADE, SERBIA.

Lance didn't have much time. He'd prepared for this eventuality. If Andrei Gusa gave up his name, the government would seize all of Lance's assets. He brought out his laptop, opened a browser, and switched on the cloak he'd used in the past. He found the link he was looking for and opened it. For the last four years, he'd been moving funds into an offshore account under the name Wilson Rogers. He had approximately three million dollars in that account.

But what would he do? And where would he go?

He could leave the country but ran the risk of being picked up at the airport. There was the possibility that Andrei would lawyer up, and keep his mouth shut. That was possible. He figured that Andrei Gusa was in a dangerous predicament himself. The people involved in this could have ties to organized crime. That would make Gusa vulnerable if he talked. But then, he might already be looking at a dead man.

In the grand picture, Lance's website was a small fish in a pond filled with far more dangerous predators. They were people who enslaved young girls, exploited children, andkilled online to appease the sexual urges of others.

Thankfully, Lance hadn't used Gusa's server to transfer the money. It had been a slow, methodical process. Funneling cash out of his investments in separate denominations under $10,000 so as not to be flagged by the IRS. This was his rainy-day fund, and there was a storm coming.

He picked up and unwrapped one of the four burner phones he'd purchased. He activated the account and sent a group text.

There could be trouble. We may have to meet.

The responses came in one after another.

Steel: Okay

Dusk: Alright.
Larry: Where and when?

4

2 November 2008

Bucharest, Romania

Andrei Gusa was in a holding cell usually reserved for state witnesses who needed protection from the Romanian mafia. In Gusa's case, it was the Vladimirsku family or, for short, the "Vlad family."

The Vlads had ties with criminal elements all over the world and were the most feared family in the country, invested in every facet of illegal activity: drugs, extortion, prostitution, pornography, human trafficking, and murder. The Vlads rubbed shoulders with the worst of the worst.

When Gusa was arrested, they, the Vlads, immediately dispatched one of their lawyers to meet with him. Gusa said nothing to authorities. Doing so was suicide. As far as incrimination went, he considered his options. The mainframe had imploded, so they had nothing there, and his backups were stored in a safe place known only to him. There was no evidence linking him to the "Vlad family," but that didn't mean he was safe. He was anything but safe.

Andrei Gusa had become a liability.

His cell opened mid-morning, and a tall, gaunt-looking guard said in Romanian, "Prisoner, stand up."

Gusa stood.

"Turn around, face the wall, hands behind your back."

Gusa turned around. The guard stepped in behind him, stinking of cheap aftershave, and slid a chain through the loops of his prison coveralls. There was a click. Then a voice from behind the cheap smelling guard snapped. "*Ține-*

ți ochii la prizonier!" which meant, "Keep your eyes to the wall, prisoner."

"Almost done," the first guard said.

"Where are you taking me?" Gusa asked.

"To meet your lawyer." The guard hooked cuffs around his wrists and they clicked. "Prisoner, turn around."

He was led down a dimly lit corridor to an interview room. Gusa knew his jailers were as corrupt as the men they incarcerated. At any moment, he expected to be pushed into a room and feel the cold steel of a gun barrel behind his ear.

Every step, every breath, and every thudding beat of his heart-felt like his last. They marched him bent over at the waist, yanking his cuffed hands upward, putting stress on his shoulder blades. He saw only floor, and knew if he turned his eyes left or right, they would hit him with a baton.

"Prisoner, stop!"

He stopped.

Keys jangled, then they were inserted, and there was a mechanical click to his rear right. The door creaked on its hinges and he was told, "Prisoner back up and turn right."

He did, finding himself standing in the doorway, seeing only more scarred concrete which led into a room. The pressure on his arms loosened, the stress on his shoulder blades relaxing. "Prisoner, stand straight up!"

He did. Sitting at a table was the man who had arrested him, Inspector Datcu. Gusa was marched to the table and seated.

"Good morning, Andrei Gusa." Inspector Datcu wore the same charcoal suit as the day he had arrested Gusa, but the matching hat was on the table.

Gusa asked, "Why am I here? Where is my lawyer?"

Inspector Datcu grinned. "The Vladimirskus' lawyer is waiting to see you. I thought we might have a little chat first."

Gusa grunted, "Fuck yourself. I want my lawyer."

The inspector frowned. "Okay, but first..." He reached into a briefcase and produced a photo. "Take a look at this." He slid it across the table and spun it around.

Andrei looked down.

The photo was color, the subject quite clear. It was a man, naked from the waist down. He was kneeling, bent over a radiator, and tied. His black and white-striped jumpsuit had been cut away from the waist down. His feet had been cut off and laid on their sides. But that was not the worst. His legs were soaked in blood. Not from the amputation, but from the sodomy performed by repeated thrusts of a prison blade taped to a broomstick. Gusa knew this because the assaulting weapon still protruded from the man's buttocks. Gusa closed his eyes, not wanting to look.

"I believe you know Mikolai Annikov?"

Gusa turned away but said nothing.

"This happened about three hours after he met with his lawyer. The same lawyer who is sitting in the waiting area downstairs." Inspector Datcu removed a second photo from his briefcase and slid it across the table. "I believe you know Teodora Berić."

Gusa looked at the photo and recoiled.

Teodora Berić had suffered a similar fate.

"The Croatian Policija recovered her body in a warehouse outside Dubrovnik, Croatia." Datcu sighed. "They probably would not have found her so quickly if they had not been tipped off." Datcu looked directly into Gusa's eyes. "I believe the tip came directly from the people who did this. What do you think?"

Gusa shook his head.

"You know what else I think?" Datcu said. "I think that if you do not cooperate, we will not be able to protect you."

Gusa brought his eyes up to meet Datcu. "You think you can protect me?"

"No, probably not. And why would I want to? You exploit children for money." Datcu stood up, producing another piece of paper from his pocket. He said, "After you meet with your lawyer, you are being transferred to the Penitenciarul in Giurgiu." Datcu gathered up the photos and the transfer, placing them into his briefcase. He turned and walked to the doorway.

"Wait," Gusa said. "I have information, but I want assurances."

Datcu turned around. "Okay, you talk and perhaps…"

"No, I have information. I also have evidence, but I will not simply turn it over." Gusa did not trust Datcu or any of the Romanian police. If he provided them with information, they would throw him to the wolves.

"So, you don't want to see the lawyer?"

"I want to be moved to a safe location."

"That is a lot to ask for nothing, Andrei Gusa."

"Okay, I will give you a name as a show of good faith."

"I'm listening."

"Belanger."

Datcu pulled out a notepad, thumbed through it. "I do not know this name. Is he French?"

"Contact the FBI. Tell them you have information on the Highwayman case. Tell them I know who he is."

"Okay."

"Once you have done this, I want a government lawyer here to draft a contract of protection and immunity," Gusa said.

Datcu looked at the two guards and waved them out into the hall. "Take him back to his cell. He is not to be mixed with the other prisoners. I will hold both of you responsible if anything happens to this man. Do you understand?"

"Yes, Inspector," said the gaunt-looking guard.

The other nodded. "Yes."

"Keep him safe."

***

CHAPTER 2 – EUR-FUCKING-EKA!

1

2 November 2008

Quantico, VA

The call came early in the morning. Answered by the duty officer, there was some confusion about who or what department to contact. Datcu's English was marginal at best.

"My name is Inspector Datcu. I work for the Romanian branch of INTERPOL. I have information that may be of use to the FBI."

"And what would that be, sir?" The duty officer's voice was tired. Datcu had heard this from his own officers after pulling a long shift.

"We have arrested an individual who says he has information on killings in America. He has given us a name and nothing else."

"Could you give me that name?"

"Belanger."

"Hang on, please. I'm going to put you on hold."

"Yes, thank you." Datcu waited, tapping his fingers on the desk, wanting a cigarette.

Two minutes passed.

"The name Belanger isn't bringing anything up. Do you have any other information?"

"Not at this time. I will call back." The inspector hung up.

2 November 2008

Bucharest, Romania

Inspector Datcu had them open the cell door. Gusa was lying on his bunk, his right forearm across his eyes. When the door swung open, he got up on his elbows and said in Romanian, "What?"

"The FBI knows nothing of this name Belanger. I am beginning to think that you are playing games with me, Andrei Gusa." Datcu's voice seethed a razor-edge of anger. "Perhaps we should ship you up to Giurgiu."

Gusa sat up. He knew he would have to tell them more. "You need to speak to someone in the FBI who is investigating a serial killer. They call him the Bandit. No, that is not right. He is called the Highwayman."

"The Highwayman Bandit?" Datcu asked.

"No, just Highwayman. He is a serial killer. Belanger is the Highwayman. Lance Belanger. You will need to speak to whoever their lead investigator is."

"What else, Andrei Gusa?"

"I give you nothing else, until I know I have a deal."

"If you are lying to me, stringing me along, I will wash my hands of you. You can meet your friends in Hell. Do you understand?"

Gusa did not answer the question. He said, "Lance Belanger is the Highwayman. He also goes by the name Devon Mitchell. He has killed many Americans."

"How do you know this?"

"I met him. I have viewed his communications."

"This is simply an accusation. You have no proof."

"I have proof, but I am not going to share that. Not yet. I want to ensure that my safety is secure before I divulge anything else." Gusa laid back down. "Call them back,

Inspector. If you say, 'Highwayman,' they will know what you are talking about."

The cell door closed.

3

2 November 2008

Warfield, VA

Wilson Rogers had rented a car the previous day in Syracuse, New York. He had no issues making the purchase. He used an American Express Gold Card that was issued by Citibank. He had a New York State driver's license that would have passed the scrutiny of a police officer. The counterfeit license, library card, and various other identifications were all generated from templates Lance had purchased years before.

On the 30th of October, he started the process of disappearing. He removed all evidence from the property in Syracuse, NY, and Lawrenceville, PA, while generating fake identification with fresh photos of himself with a beard and longish hair. Once the IDs were made and plasticized, he took all the equipment and disposed of it. He didn't dare take it to a landfill or a dumpster. He took the stuff into the woods, away from his own property in Lawrenceville, and buried it. Deep.

With that done, he went through each room and methodically wiped them down. He told himself that this was precautionary, that Gusa would probably keep his mouth shut, but he knew better.

Both properties would eventually be seized, a warrant would be issued for his arrest, and the media would be broadcasting his picture into households across America. His advantage was the beard, the longer hair, and the fact that he'd removed and burned every photograph of himself.

That wouldn't stop the authorities from seeking out college photographs, but everything else was gone. Lance Belanger was dead.

"Long live Wilson Rogers," Lance said and laughed nervously.

He almost hoped that Gusa would out him. It would increase his notoriety. Even better, it would untether the monster, and he would not have to worry about maintaining a double life. No more fear about DNA. And as a bonus, he still had the other three to confuse the investigators.

He wheeled the car off US Route 1, turning left on Old Stage Road in Warfield and into the parking lot of Davis Travel Center. The place was a mini truck stop with parking in the back for big rigs, fuel islands, and a Subway sandwich shop.

He parked the rental out front and scanned the parking lot for the others. He hadn't alerted them to what kind of car he'd be driving or his change in appearance. Best to surprise them and keep such information off any cell communication.

He went inside and ordered himself a sandwich. Sweet Onion Chicken Teriyaki. He scanned the restaurant and saw no one he recognized. Then he saw a familiar face come out of the washroom. It was Larry.

Larry was around thirty-five years old. He stood over six feet tall and was naturally muscular. Meaning, he'd evolved to this formidable build rather than achieved it in a gym. His blond hairline had receded up over his crown, and he'd grown it out shoulder-length on the sides. He bore a resemblance to Otis from Rob Zombie's House of 1000 Corpses. Lance had seen that movie at least five times.

Lance loved the film's unapologetic brutality.

Larry glanced his way and even made eye contact, but he didn't recognize him. He looked around some more and then pulled a phone from his pocket. He began to text.

Lance's phone chimed. He looked down at it.

Larry: Where are you?

Lance typed: `Looking at you.`

Larry looked up from his phone and scanned the room again. When his eyes settled on Lance, they were met with a big, Bundy-ish smile. He walked toward the counter where Lance finished paying for his sub.

"Hey," Larry said.

"Hey," Lance replied. "Let's talk outside."

They walked through the Subway and out to the front parking area where Lance's rental was parked next to a green 2001 Ford Taurus wagon. This was Larry's ride.

"Where are the others?" Lance asked.

"They haven't arrived yet. I was the closest. I think Steel will be here in about an hour. Dusk should be any minute." Larry stopped to think about it and asked, "You wanna know their real names?"

Lance already knew their real names. Like the late Norris Connelly, he'd researched the three before bringing them into the fold. Only he knew that, so he said, "Yeah, sure. What are their names?"

"Dusk is Brad. Steel is Jim."

"Larry, Brad, and Jim." Lance smiled. "Sounds like three-quarters of a barbershop quartet."

"You're hilarious. What the fuck is going on?"

"I think we've been compromised."

"You think? You're not sure?"

"The website. The people who hosted it have been taken down by police in Europe. The man who helped me set it up is in jail."

"You said the website was wiped out. That was last year?"

"I know."

"So, how could we be compromised?"

"I don't think we are, but the guy I met in Romania who set the site up has been arrested. If he wants to bargain for a deal, he might have backup copies of the sites." Lance opened the passenger door to the rental. "Get in."

Larry climbed in, and Lance went around to the driver side and did the same. He said, "It could be a false alarm. It shouldn't take long to find out."

"And how is that?"

"If he rats me out, my name and face will be all over the news. I'm on the FBI's Ten-Most-Wanted List, Larry. I killed a retired FBI agent. They're going to be turning over every stone in New York and Pennsylvania once word gets out."

"So, that's why you grew the beard and abandoned the neo-Nazi look?" Larry pulled out a package of cigarettes. "Do you mind?"

"Actually, I do. Cigarettes are bad for your health."

"Yeah, yeah…"

"You drop a smoke at a crime scene, and they can extract your DNA off the filter. Never mind what it does to your lungs and throat," Lance said.

Larry put away the cigarette pack. "Maybe we shouldn't be with you, then. I mean the beard and hair definitely threw me off, but if news breaks, you're going to be pretty hot."

"So will you three."

"How do you figure? We never gave our names on that site. Everything was fabricated."

"When I went to Romania and met with this man to set up the site, I used the name Devon Mitchell. He knew who I was and addressed me by my real name. He told me he made it his business to check out the people he worked with. I'm sure he knows who you are, who Brad is, and who Jim is."

Larry's face screwed up into a knot. "That's fucking awesome!" He banged a fist on his knee. "Jesus Christ! That's absolutely fucking fantastic."

"Calm down." Lance placed a hand on his shoulder. "Nothing has happened yet."

"Bullsh…"

Lance squeezed his shoulder. "And nothing may happen."

Larry tried to speak up, but Lance interrupted him again.

"But if it does, I've made arrangements."

"What kind of arrangements?"

"Let's wait until the others arrive."

4

3 November 2008

Quantico, VA

"Good morning," the voice on the line said. It was a foreign-accented voice, possibly Slavic, but Maxwell wasn't sure.

"Good morning. The duty officer said you might have information regarding a case I'm working." Maxwell had a steno pad and pen at the ready. "Could I get your name first, sir?"

"I am Inspector Nicolae Datcu. I work in Romanian branch of INTERPOL at Bucharest." Datcu paused long enough to give Maxwell a chance to write the information down. Maxwell asked for spelling on the name, and Datcu spelled it out for him.

"Okay, I've got that, Inspector. I'm Agent Dave Maxwell, FBI." Maxwell didn't think going into rank specifics mattered much. "What kind of information do you have?"

"Eight days ago, INTERPOL conducted a joint European raid on an organization that does the business of human trafficking and child pornography. They work in the dark net." Datcu again paused. "One of the suspects we took into custody, he's name is Andrei Gusa. He is allied with the Vladimirskus. They are an organized crime family. Please forgive, my English, it is not so good."

"Your English is great, please carry on."

"One other male was taken into custody, and known female also being sought. Both the man in custody and the fugitive woman have been murdered. We think that the Vladimirsku family made killing to silence them. Gusa is in protective custody, and he wants to make deal because he's fright that he will meet the same fate as his colleagues."

"Okay."

"Andrei Gusa gave us some information, to… Show of faith? He said this information tangled to an FBI case called the Highwayman."

Maxwell sat up, heart rate increasing, attention sharpening. "Go ahead, Inspector, I'm listening."

"I do not know if this means anything, but he said that he knows the identity of the man you are seeking. He says the man's name is Lance Belanger."

Maxwell's heart almost stopped. "Could you say that name again?"

"Lance Belanger. He also goes by the name Devon Mitchell."

Maxwell had to do everything he could to contain himself and remain professional. He counted to three before asking, "Was there anything else? How did this Gusa come across this Lance Belanger?"

"I believe that Gusa did some work for him in the dark net, but I am not sure what. He will not say anything else, not until we make deal with him." Datcu paused. There was a sound, like a match being struck. The inspector was lighting a cigarette.

"Do you have anything else that can connect this Belanger and Gusa?"

"No, just his word. When we raided Gusa's office, he was able to destroy the mainframe before we could locate the warehouse where they kept key information. We monitored them on the web, but our evidence gathering was only enough to access warrants."

"Inspector, do you think he has more information?"

"Yes, I do. We know that the Vladimirsku family conducts illegal business in many countries, including the United States. Gusa may have computer backups stored somewhere. May I ask you a question, Agent Maxwell?"

"Sure."

"Is the information I gave you of any help?"

"Yes."

"Do you know of this Lance Belanger?"

"Yes, he was a person of interest."

"So, Andrei Gusa could be telling the truth?"

"Considering that you're calling me from Romania and are telling me information that was never made public. I'd say, 'Yeah.' Gusa is probably telling the truth."

"What information is that?"

"The second name you gave, Devon. That has not been released to the public. I'd like to interview your prisoner, if that's possible." Maxwell was already thinking six steps ahead. Arrange surveillance on Belanger, go to Bucharest, interview Gusa, find out his connection to Belanger. And…

"Andrei Gusa is in great danger. The Vladimirsku family will want him dead. If you come to Bucharest, I cannot promise there will be anything to gain."

"Does Gusa speak English?"

"I have not conversed with him in your language, but I would say he does. Most educated Romanians know three or four languages. If he met with your person of interest, it is likely he speaks the language. Our crooks do not like to use interpreters," Datcu said dryly.

"Would you be willing to arrange an interview?"

"I could do that."

"Okay, Inspector. I'll talk to my bosses here, see what I can set up." He grabbed a sticky note from his desk and jotted down the number from the call display. "Is this the number you'll be available at?" Then he read it back to Datcu.

"Yes." Datcu gave Maxwell his cell phone number as a backup.

3 November 2008

Quantico, VA

Patti, the deputy director's secretary, saw Dave Maxwell and her mouth dropped. She liked Maxwell, liked how he handled himself. She also understood a bit about the friendship between her boss and this man, both of whom she thought were honorable.

Something's going on, she thought, and then buzzed the director. She listened to one ring. Meanwhile, Maxwell had picked up some steam. At first, he'd been walking fast, which evolved into a jog. "Something big," she barely whispered.

"I'm guessing this is important," answered Julian Carswell.

"Yes, sir. Maxwell is running toward me as I speak."

"Okay, send him right in." Carswell hung up.

"Go right in," she said to Maxwell.

"Thank you," he said, trotting by and to the double doors that Carswell was opening.

"Put on the brakes, Max," Carswell said.

Patti watched as Maxwell slowed almost to a stop and grinned a little at Carswell's joke. He stepped through the door and Carswell closed her off from what happened next.

But the walls had ears.

6

The doors closed behind him, and he waited until Julian was right in front of him before he said, "I just spoke to an inspector with the Romanian section of INTERPOL. He told me that they have arrested a man named Andrei Gusa on a bunch of internet stuff, child porn, sex slavery... Anyway, they've arrested this guy, and he wants to cut a deal. He says he knows who the Highwayman is."

Julian frowned, "Max…"

Maxwell was grinning ear-to-ear, unable to contain his excitement. "He threw a name. You know what that name is, Julian?"

"Tell me," Carswell said.

"Lance Belanger."

"The rich kid from PA?"

"Yeah."

"Anything else?"

"This Gusa says that he met with Lance Belanger for business dealings in the dark net. He also said…" Maxwell stopped, scratched his chin, grinned a little wider. "This Andrei Gusa said that Lance Belanger passed himself off as a Devon Mitchell."

The director's eyes widened, realization dawning as the puzzle pieces came together. "No shit. Anything else?"

"One last thing, Julian." He pounded one fist into the other. "Eur-fucking-eka!"

"Okay, tell me what you need."

7

4 November 2008

Over the Atlantic Ocean

Maxwell was on an Austrian Airline aircraft that had carried him halfway to his destination. He had roughly six and a half hours left, including the connector in Vienna. He'd called Datcu, told him he was coming, and that it would be a short visit as his investigation was ongoing. Datcu had agreed to pick him up at the airport and decided to brief him on the drive back to the jail.

Meanwhile, he worked through Ferguson, who was planning to carry out dual surveillance on both of Lance Belanger's properties with local law enforcement. The first was a no-brainer and Maxwell ended up calling.

"Cole, we're going to need 24-hour surveillance on Lance Belanger's property in Lawrenceville. My boss has assigned four agents who will be joining you guys," Maxwell said.

"Were you listening for the crazy again, Max?" Cole Abraham asked and chuckled.

"You bet. We heard it that day. The crazy was in Lawrenceville. Somehow, the worm wiggled out of it, but the crazy always delivers. Can you cover this until my agents get there?"

"You're not coming?" Cole asked. "I didn't think you'd want to miss out on this."

"I'm on my way to Bucharest to interview a witness who identifies Lance Belanger as the Highwayman. He also has some inside information that only someone who knew the Highwayman would have."

"Well, if you miss the barbecue, we'll save you a drumstick or a wing." Cole Abraham chuckled again.

"Not so fast, Lieutenant Abraham. I'm the Special Agent in Charge, which means I call the shots, so I say when the suspect gets taken down. I'll be at the fucking barbecue, once we figure out which place he's at."

"Shit. I was already thinking through my interview with CNN for being the hero who caught the Highwayman."

"Save the speech writing for later. I need eyes on Belanger's place. I just want him discreetly watched. We don't want to spook him. I want to box him in."

"We can do that."

"Thanks, Cole."

"You're welcome. Don't stay in Bucharest for too long."

"In and out."

"Talk to you soon."

Maxwell hung up and made one more call.

"Perkins," Lonnie answered.

"Hey, Perk."

"Hey, Max."

"Keep a secret?" Maxwell knew he could.

"You got him?" Perk asked.

"Not yet, but the net is tightening."

"Never heard a thing," Perk said.

"I'll call you when we've got more to talk about," Max said.

"Later."

***

CHAPTER 3 – PARTING GIFTS

1

4 November 2008

Henri Coandă International Airport

16 KM north of Bucharest, Romania

The trip took 15 hours. Maxwell was exhausted. He'd slept a little on the flight, but his mind was on fire, full of questions, and he kept waking up. He didn't know the extent of Gusa's connection to Lance Belanger. Speculative thoughts pulled him out of a series of micro-naps, bringing him back to the same question: How had Belanger arranged the killing in Stafford, Virginia?

There had to be an accomplice. Someone who committed the killings to throw investigators off. If Gusa had dealings with Belanger on the internet, it makes sense that was where he met Norris Connelly. So, was that where another accomplice came in? Had to be.

When they raided Norris Connelly's place, they'd found a home computer, but the hard drive had been pulled.

So, Belanger meets with Gusa, sets up a site, and makes friends with Norris Connelly. It was plausible, but he wondered what kind of place became an attractant to serial murderers? What Maxwell knew about Gusa was that he was hosting sites on the deep web. Datcu had called it the dark net.

At the airport he was met by an older man, who introduced himself. "I am Inspector Datcu."

"Dave Maxwell." Maxwell smiled and shook his hand. Datcu returned the pleasantry as they sized each other up.

Datcu then said, "Do you have other luggage?"

Maxwell held up his carry on. "This is it."

Datcu reached for the bag and Maxwell let him take it. "We should go. There will be much traffic."

Maxwell followed Datcu out of the terminal to a little car he'd never seen before. It was a small white hatchback, the make was one Maxwell had never heard of, Dacia. He thought the emblem looked like a bottle opener. The car was white and on the side was the word POLITIA in royal blue stacked above a triple pinstripe of blue, yellow, and red that ran the length of the car. The paint scheme reminded Maxwell of those used by the Royal Canadian Mounted Police.

Datcu put the luggage in the back and came back around.

"We should go," Datcu said and opened the right door.

"All right." Maxwell was confused and must have looked it.

"What is it?"

"It's nothing… I just thought everyone in Europe drove on the left side of the road." Maxwell pointed to the steering wheel.

Datcu smiled. "This is not England, Agent Maxwell, this is Romania."

"Okay." Maxwell laughed and got in.

"We will be there in ten minutes," Datcu said and closed the door.

Interpol Headquarters

Bucharest, Romania

"I am having him moved to an interrogation room," Inspector Datcu told Maxwell. "It will be a minute or two." They were outside Datcu's office, in the hall; both had a coffee in hand.

"That's fine. Do you have any evidence to back up Gusa's claim?" Maxwell glanced left and down. He stood at least six inches taller than Datcu.

"Not on your case. We have collected some evidence connecting him and his partners to a child pornography ring and another site that hosted killing. I believe the English term is snuff?"

"Mr. Gusa sounds like a model Romanian citizen." Maxwell laughed.

"He is scum." Datcu didn't laugh. "His life is in danger, and now we are forced to protect him. The Vladimirsku family has already killed two of his partners. If we do not protect him, he will be dead in no time."

"You said he destroyed the computer mainframe. Where did you get the evidence for the raid?"

"We had a man inside. Took us almost a year to get him there. The sites were encrypted. The only way to gather evidence was to take screenshots with a camera. The same went for video."

"But nothing about my case?"

"No."

"Everything is based on Gusa's word, then?"

"Yes. Gusa's organization is intertwined with the Vladimirsku family. That is who we want to take down. If we can keep Gusa alive, we will be able to file charges against the Vlad family."

"How many sites was Gusa hosting?"

"Hundreds."

"How did you get him to talk about my case?"

"I showed Gusa the photographs of his dead partners, and he brought up the man you call Highwayman. He told us to contact the FBI."

"How much evidence do you have through your own investigation?"

"Enough to charge Gusa. Not much else. But Gusa says he has backup files for the entire operation. He used your case to begin negotiating a deal. I am having the chief justice draw up an immunity deal. If you can back up his claim, we will proceed." Inside the office, Datcu's phone rang. He stepped inside, picked up the phone, and spoke to the caller in Romanian. After a second, he set the phone in its cradle and said, "They are ready."

When they entered the interrogation room, Gusa was seated behind a table that had two chairs. Maxwell sat on the right, Datcu on the left. Gusa sat perfectly in the middle across from them.

"Does he speak English?" Maxwell had forgotten to ask.

"Yes," Gusa said. "I speak, read, and write English. I studied at the University of Toronto in Canada."

"Good," Maxwell said. "My name is Special Agent Dave Maxwell. I work for the FBI. I understand you have some information for me."

Gusa looked at Datcu and asked a question in Romanian, to which Datcu replied in Romanian. Realizing Maxwell's ignorance, he said, "He wants to know about the immunity contract. I told him that it depends on how he answers your questions."

"Okay. Mr. Gusa, I don't have jurisdiction here in Bucharest. I was invited by the International Policing Agency based on the information you gave them. I have no sway with these people." Maxwell looked at Datcu. "I'm here because of a name you gave to the inspector. I would like to know everything you know."

"Can you take me back to the United States?" Gusa asked Maxwell. "It is not safe here."

Datcu was about to raise a protest, but Maxwell interrupted him. "I doubt very much that the Romanian government would extradite you to the United States. It would appear they're building a very damning case against you and want your help with the Vladimirskus." Maxwell turned to Datcu, who nodded approval.

Gusa sighed.

"I would say that if you're forthcoming, the FBI would be favorable in bringing you back to help with our case. But I can't promise anything. You're going to have to tell me what you know and then perhaps…" Maxwell paused. "Based on what you tell me…"

"I'm not saying anything until I have a deal," Gusa said.

"The chief prosecutor is drafting an agreement," Datcu said. "Agent Maxwell has come a long way, Andrei Gusa. If you don't help him, I will tell the chief prosecutor that you are playing games with us! I am not up for games. You tell Agent Maxwell what you know, or I will tell the chief prosecutor you are uncooperative!"

Gusa, notably frustrated, shifted his focus back to Maxwell and began, "I met him at my office in 2005. He wanted to set up a website in the dark net."

4

5 November 2008

Lawrenceville, PA

Just after 5:00 p.m., the sky had darkened to a charcoal gray, limiting visibility to a few hundred yards. Above, the wind swirled through the forest, carrying on its breath light confetti-like snow. It was brisk, temperatures dipping down to freezing.

Corporal Billy Leeman and Lieutenant Cole Abraham had come in on foot and set up in the woods to the north of Lance Belanger's property. Both were dressed in winter gear, settled into a nest-sharing sentry over the place through a set of binoculars.

"I don't see anything," Abraham said. "He must be up in Syracuse." He handed the them over to Leeman and logged the time in a notebook.

"Could be," Leeman agreed. "How do they know it's even him? The other murders gave this guy a pretty good alibi."

"That's a question I don't have an answer to. Belanger felt good when Maxwell and I interviewed him. But the other murders threw us off."

Leeman remembered. Maxwell had looked sick when the word came down about the discovery of Norris' body and the body in Stafford, Virginia. "You know what's kind of funny, Cole?"

"What's that?"

"I figured Maxwell was going back to Virginia to be fired, not promoted." Leeman brought the binos up and scanned the property. There wasn't a single light burning. Earlier, Trooper Joe Radcliff had done a drive-by, in his personal pickup, of the property frontage to see how many vehicles were in the carport. There was only one, a car covered by a tarp.

"FBI politics, Billy. Nobody's immune. I'm pretty sure that Maxwell's boss fell on his sword. Max has a friend in high places. That's what probably protected him from the fallout."

"When are the other FBI agents supposed to arrive?"

"They should be here by tonight. Maxwell is going to be flying straight back. He'll probably be on the ground by tomorrow."

"How long is that flight?"

"Oh," Abraham said, considering his flight into Europe when he was in the military. "Gotta be somewhere between fourteen and sixteen hours."

"He'll be like the walking dead with jet lag."

"Well, he'll probably catch sleep on the way back. Assuming Maxwell is right, and I think he is, this case is about to blow wide open." Abraham removed a thermos, unscrewed the top, and poured himself a coffee. Leeman had a travel mug which he uncapped for a top up. Abraham poured them both coffee and said, "I'm just not confident that it's going to happen here."

"You think he's gone too?"

"He ain't here." Abraham put the thermos away. "But he might come back."

5

5 November 2008

Syracuse, NY

It wasn't nearly as cold for Agent Ferguson's surveillance unit in upstate New York. They were set up in a minivan, with tinted windows and heat, that was parked three houses down from Lance Belanger's place, which was also dark. Accompanying Ferguson was a second agent named Gordon Rice. Ferguson was watching the front of the property. There were two vehicles parked in the driveway, a dark green Oldsmobile Intrigue and a red Jeep Sahara.

"Well, all of his vehicles are there," Ferguson said. "But where the hell is he?"

"He could be asleep." Rice looked through the night scope at the darkened place.

"Maybe." But Ferguson didn't think so. "You turn off all your lights at night, Gord?"

"I usually leave the light over the stove on."

"Me too. I fell down a basement stairwell in my house one night. I didn't break anything. Just shut out the light and walked off the stairs. Funny thing, falling in the dark. You feel utterly helpless. I'll tell you this, it cured me of trying to save a few bucks by not leaving a light burning."

Rice laughed. "The worst thing I've done is stub my big toe on the couch. But I completely understand what you mean."

Ferguson nodded and brought out his phone. He called Lieutenant Cole Abraham's number and asked if anything was happening down in Lawrenceville.

"Looks like nobody's home here." Cole Abraham was talking in a low voice. "We've been set up for about an hour. Nothing moving."

"Any cars on the property?" Ferguson stuck his eye in the scope and swung it onto the parked vehicles.

"Just the classic Impala. It's under a tarp."

"Both his other vehicles are in the driveway down here."

"Hmm," Abraham said.

"Hmm, indeed." Ferguson checked his watch. It was 6:30 p.m. "Any lights on down there?"

"Nothing."

"Where the hell is he?"

"Maybe he's out partying."

"On a Wednesday?"

"Yeah, well, maybe he's out doing the other thing he likes to do," Abraham said.

"Fuck, I hope not." Ferguson thought about it and added, "I'm going to make a couple calls. See if we're any closer to a federal warrant for both places."

"Any word from Maxwell?"

"Not yet."

"I don't think he's here."

"I'll get back to you, Lieutenant."

"Okay."

05 November 2008

Warfield, VA

Leaving the country would have been Lance's best course of action. Mexico was the best option. Canada would be looking hard at his identification. But Lance was already well past that. He filled the three in on the dilemma. Larry sat quietly, as Lance explained about the arrest of Andrei Gusa. "My thoughts are that he'll be looking for a deal."

"How would he get our names?" Dusk asked.

"If he didn't destroy the site, our log chats will be accessible. Sooner or later, they're going to connect the three of you to me."

"That's fucking fantastic," Steel barked.

Lance sighed. It didn't matter what Andrei Gusa was going to do. He'd already set the ball into motion when he fed his neighbor, Donny Williams, to the monster. An immense pressure had been building inside Lance since the Gusa arrest, setting a fire in him of fatalistic abandon.

When the news broke on Gusa, so too did Lance's resolve to abstain from killing. On the day he cleaned up the cottage in Lawrenceville, he'd walked up to his neighbor's place just after lunch. There, he caught the old drunk half in the bag.

He should have turned and gone back home. Packed up his gear and ran for Mexico. Should have, but the grip he once held over the monster had slipped. Lance Belanger understood that he was now descending into a world of complete abandon.

"Lance," Donny slurred when he opened the door to his neighbor. "What's going on?"

"I thought I'd join you for a drink." Lance smiled. The ice pick was concealed in the pocket of his pullover.

"When did you grow a beard?"

Lance didn't answer; at least not directly. He said, "Fuck it!" Then he grabbed Donny Williams and pulled him into a bear hug. He thrust the pick into Donny's spine.

"Wha…" Donny started and then, "Ow, geez, ow!"

Lance held him tight. Cartilage popped, and then Donny Williams became heavy in his embrace. He removed the pick and said, "Hush, Donny."

Donny couldn't find his vocal cords. His mouth opened and closed like a fish out of water. Rye-soaked drool spilled from his lower lip onto the shoulder of Lance's pullover.

He lifted Donny and walked him back through the doorway into the house. The man was dead weight, but he was far from dead.

Instead of killing him in an outdoor setting with a creek or river close by to wash up in, he laid him out on the floor and prepped him for the next phase.

"I'll be right back, Donny." Lance exited the house and retrieved the machete he'd stashed by the stairs leading onto Williams' porch.

An hour later, he was finished. The floor in the living area looked like that of a slaughterhouse. Blood was everywhere, splattered up onto the leather recliner, the television, and coffee table. Donny Williams never said, or perhaps was unable to say, a word in the last portion of his life. But his heart worked feverishly, spouting blood out from the first amputation, which was his right arm. Then the second; his right leg. After that, he expired while Lance finished up.

Done, he took the one-sentence note and spiked it to the wall with the pick. He then staked Donny Williams' midsection with the machete and examined his work. There was no turning back. This was his destiny, he knew it now, and he embraced it with abandon.

"How do you know that they know who we are?" Steel said, breaking the recollection.

He gazed at all three of his partners. They didn't know about that. If he were a real partner in this, he wouldn't have chopped up his neighbor in Lawrenceville. But Lance Belanger had completed the metamorphosis. He finally said, "If he kept records from the site, our faces will be all over the news networks in no time."

"What are we supposed to do now?" Larry asked.

"I've got money. I'm going to drop the rental, and we need to find a vehicle. For now, we'll wait and see what happens, but I'm going to head west."

"What about us, Lance?" Larry asked.

Lance traced his eyes from one to the next. "The way I see it, you can either run or come with me. If you come with me, I'll support you until they find us."

"This is fucking bullshit!" Dusk banged his fist on the hood of Lance's rental.

"What are you planning?" Larry asked.

Lance smiled. "I'd say it's time we gave the FBI a run for their money. If we run and word gets out, we'll eventually be caught or killed."

"Run for their money? What the fuck does that mean?" Dusk again.

Lance didn't answer Dusk's question at first. Instead, he asked a question of his own. "How do all of you feel when you kill?"

This was met with silence, coupled with expressions of confusion. "So," Lance said, "when I kill, it excites me a great deal. It's like sitting down to a delicious meal. There's the anticipation. Then there's the act. And after that, the satisfaction."

Norris liked killing. He was defective because he couldn't control himself. That was why he had to go. But he was on his way, and he would have been a valuable part of our club. "I think that all of you can appreciate this. If we're caught, the one thing we enjoy most will be off limits. We'll be sitting in a cell waiting for judgment. Imagine years of hunger, with little to sate the appetite."

Larry nodded in agreement. "I don't even want to think about that." The others looked on, but Lance could see the intrigue on their faces. He had them.

"So, it means you get to keep doing what we're doing until they catch or kill us. I'm going west, back to Pennsylvania. You all need to make a decision whether or not you're going to come with me or go your own way." In his jacket pocket, he had a snub nose .38. He caressed the cold steel with his finger. It was his father's, one of many guns left to him. He didn't like guns. There was no sport in killing with a gun. But he was one against three. If they didn't want to come, he would kill them where they stood.

7

06 November 2008

Bucharest, Romania

The chief prosecutor brought in an immunity deal for Andrei Gusa, and he agreed to have one of the hard drives he had stashed retrieved. There was a caveat to that arrangement, however. He would call someone he trusted, and the identity of the individual would be withheld.

Inspector Datcu protested. He wanted all the hard drives, and the chief prosecutor, Marinda Vasile, was leaning that way as well.

"I will not risk the life of someone who has no part in this. I will retrieve the hard drive that has the information Agent Maxwell needs. Once I am moved to a safe location, I will retrieve the others." Gusa was firm. He knew the risks. Unbeknownst to the investigators, he would be asking his lover to retrieve the hard drive.

"You have a contract. It is witnessed by police and government officials, and it is also being recorded on video.

You want us to trust you, but you don't trust us," Chief Prosecutor Vasile countered.

"I trust no one. Bring a new cell phone. I will activate it and call for one hard drive to be retrieved. Once you have that hard drive, it will instill in you how important the others are." Gusa sniffed. "After that, I want to be moved to a safe location, far from the long arm of the Vlads."

"We need to talk," Maxwell said.

"Yes," Datcu agreed and knocked on the steel door.

Maxwell, Datcu, and Vasile stepped into the hall while a guard entered the interview room to watch over the shackled Gusa.

"I do not like this arrangement," Vasile said.

"Neither do I," Maxwell said. "What are the chances that the Vladimirskus will get to Gusa?"

Datcu said, "He will need to be protected under high security. Possibly a military escort. If he is telling the truth, the Vlad family will stop at nothing to silence him."

"Would they attack a police convoy?"

"Yes," Vasile said. "In fact, we will need protection for ourselves and our families once charges are made."

"Where would be a safe place?"

Neither Datcu nor Vasile had an answer.

"We are still looking at that," Vasile said.

"What if I could get clearance to bring him back to the United States with me?"

"No!" Vasile's face became hard. "Andrei Gusa is charged with many crimes here in Romania! This is not just about your case, Agent Maxwell. I am sure you would like to put him in an American prison, but we have a responsibility to the people of Bucharest and Romania."

"Not permanently," Maxwell argued. "Just to get him to a safe place. We could put him in a military jail. He could send word to retrieve the other hard drives. Once you've indicted the Vlads," he had trouble pronouncing their real name, "we could fly him back to testify."

"Extradition would be difficult. It could take a week or more," Vasile said.

"I'm not talking about extradition. I'm talking about protection until you build your case."

Then Datcu spoke. "And what if you take him back to America and he refuses to cooperate any further? You will have what you want, but we will be left in the cold."

"Look, I don't know if I can make this happen. It will be up to my boss. If we can get an agreement put together, I think that we can certainly incorporate a clause that if he fails to cooperate, he'll be immediately shipped back." Maxwell studied their faces, trying to gauge a reaction.

They appeared to be considering the proposal.

Datcu said something in Romanian to Vasile.

She nodded to Datcu and said to Maxwell, "Maybe getting him out of Romania would be the best way. How long would it take?"

"I don't know. I'll contact my boss, and he'll probably have to run it by the FBI director, and I assume the State Department will have to sign off on it. Maybe even the attorney general." Maxwell paused and thought about it. "The man we're looking is not just a serial killer, he also killed an FBI agent. We want this guy before he kills anyone else."

Datcu spoke then. "He also wants protection for members of his family. Romanian police are watching over them. The Vlad family will be watching also."

"That complicates things for your people. How big is Gusa's family?" Maxwell asked.

Vasile said, "He has a sister and a cousin."

"No parents or kids?"

"No. Gusa's parents are dead. Same for the cousin's parents and no children."

"Is the cousin involved in this somehow? Or the sister?"

"No. We have no evidence connecting either to Gusa's business," Datcu said. He turned to Vasile and said something in Romanian.

Vasile listened and eventually nodded in agreement.

Datcu turned back to Maxwell. "Sending him out of the country could ease the pressure while we investigate and build case."

"How would you like to proceed, Agent Maxwell?" Vasile asked.

"Call me Max, please. I say we go in and push him for the hard drive. Put an offer on the table that we will try and move him if he provides the hard drive. We can also put pressure on him that if he stops cooperating, he'll definitely be returned and all protection will be null and void, including your agreement."

Datcu still looked wary.

"Inspector, I understand how you feel. Guys like this should be put in a dark hole and forgotten. But from my point of view, you have a lot of bigger fish to catch. If you agree, I'll contact my boss to get the ball rolling once he delivers the first hard drive, and we get a look at what is on it."

Both Vasile and Datcu nodded in agreement.

They went back in to work the deal.

8

07 November 2008

Quantico, VA

"That's a tall order, Max," Julian Carswell said.

"I've perused the hard drive. We have a connection to Norris. We have three other individuals who I believe carried out the killings in Stafford and Florida as well as Norris to throw us off. We know it's him. Keeping Gusa alive is going to go a long way to getting the Highwayman and his accomplices."

"It's still a very tall order. I'm going to have to take it to the director. Also, the attorney general will have to be brought into the loop on this. You got anything else to make the pitch more palatable to the bureaucrats?"

"Well, this is speculation, and it will have to be worked out with the Romanians, but Gusa's business has international ties to the United States as well as other countries like Canada and the UK. You could tell the bureaucrats that bringing Gusa to America will open a floodgate of convictions. The Romanians only have peripheral evidence. So, getting those remaining hard drives is important for every country involved."

"Okay, I'm on my way in. I'll call an emergency meeting. On the upside, the attorney general has been following the Highwayman case. Also in our favor, she knew Lewis Ash. Leave it with me. No promises."

"Anything out of Syracuse or Lawrenceville?" Maxwell asked.

"Watching and waiting. No sign of Lance Belanger. With what you have now, I'm putting a call in to execute search warrants for both properties. Those will be coming in this morning."

"I'd really like to get back there."

"I know, but I need you in Romania. At least until we get support for your proposal."

"Something seems off, Julian. He could be out there killing or making a run for the border." Maxwell had an edge of desperation in his voice. He wanted Belanger behind bars. He wanted the others in custody.

"I expect by mid-morning we'll have a nationwide warrant for the arrest of Belanger. Maybe we'll grab him before he can do anything else."

"Maybe, but I still want to be there." Maxwell felt the tug of anticipation. This was his hunt.

"Remember what I said about the war room? You're in the thick of it now. We've got our best people on this. In the meantime, start formulating a plan with the Romanians for transporting Gusa out of Bucharest. If I can get this off the ground, I want you to be on a moment's notice to move."

"Yeah, okay."

"If it makes you feel better, put in a call to Lawrenceville and Syracuse." Julian hung up.

Maxwell made the calls.

Then he started on a plan.

***

CHAPTER 4 – SUICIDE SOLUTION

1

7 November 2008

Lawrenceville, PA

A nationwide warrant was issued for Lance Belanger, but the information was withheld from the media. Speaking by phone with IRS Special Agent Kendall Dickson, Deputy Director Julian Carswell suggested they monitor Belanger's assets, but not freeze them. The hope was that they would be able to track him using his bank card. Within the Treasury Department, a team was assembled to do a forensic audit of his accounts and purchases between 2000 and 2008.

They were now sure that Lance Belanger was their man, but to date, all they had was a witness from another country, a hard drive, and circumstantial evidence. But that was all about to change. The audit would reveal his comings and goings: the flights he took; the cars he rented; the proximity to the murders that plagued the districts and highways that stretched from coast to coast.

But the most damning piece of evidence against Lance Belanger would be discovered an hour before the execution of the warrants for both properties.

Lieutenant Cole Abraham decided to take a drive up the beaten, paved road that led to Belanger's cottage. Purposely, he drove past the Belanger place and on up to a neighbor's house. Abraham was dressed in civilian attire and behind the wheel of a subordinate, Trooper Radcliffe's, pickup. When he parked in front of Donny Williams' house, Abraham intended to question the neighbor about Belanger's whereabouts.

When he mounted the steps, he spotted two dime-sized droplets of blood on the porch in front of the door. This sent a shiver through Abraham's bloodstream.

His heart rate increased slightly.

He reached inside his jacket and unsnapped his shoulder holster. He was thankful to have not left it in the truck. He hadn't seen a threat in coming up here. Coming up in civilian clothing was meant to put the neighbor at ease.

But now…

He listened, trying to ignore the pulse now beating in his ears. Cole Abraham took a step back and peaked into the picture window. The window was obscured by a Venetian blind. There was a sliver between the window frame and the blind, so Cole gazed through it. That was when he felt a rush of fear. It was also when he saw what looked like a bare foot and blood.

A lot of blood.

2

7 November 2008

Quantico, VA

"We've got a body," Special Agent Karen Shelley said. She was the senior agent of the two assigned to the Lawrenceville stakeout.

"Is it Belanger?" Carswell asked.

"No, a neighbor."

"Where?"

"Just up the road from the Belanger place. We're pretty sure the neighbor was a victim of foul play. I went up for a look with Lieutenant Abraham, and there's an awful lot of blood."

"You been inside?"

"We haven't entered the dwelling, sir. I wanted to make sure we had the go-ahead."

"How are the state cops?"

"Ready. Chomping at the bit."

"You have my authorization to enter the house. Coordinate with the state police and get Crime Scene inbound."

"What about the Belanger place?" Shelley covered the phone and gave an inaudible order to someone. "Can we move on the Belanger place, sir?"

"Check the neighbor's house first. While you're doing that, I'll get on the horn and fast-track the warrants. I want a coordinated raid on both properties. Wait for my word, Agent Shelley."

"Yes, sir."

Carswell hung up and got on the phone to check on the warrants. They had been ready for almost a half-hour. He waited and called up to Syracuse.

"Special Agent Ferguson, this is Deputy Director Carswell. We've had a development. Do you have state police support in place?"

"We have two BCI agents on call. Five minutes notice to move."

"On call?"

"They're having breakfast two blocks over."

Carswell chuckled. "At least it's not a donut shop."

Ferguson laughed. "No. What is the development, sir?"

"Possible victim in Lawrenceville. You got your printer fired up, Ferguson?"

"Yes, sir."

"Get those BCI agents back and watch that printer. The warrant will be transmitted within the next half hour."

Ferguson turned to Agent Rice. "Get on the phone to the BCI guys and tell them to get back here ASAP." Then to Carswell, he said, "We'll be ready, sir."

"Good," Carswell said.

3

7 November 2008

Bucharest, Romania

"We don't have a choice. They're going in," Carswell said.

"Why?" Maxwell asked.

"Belanger's neighbor in Lawrenceville has been murdered. I guess Belanger must have known we'd be coming for him, and decided to throw caution to the wind," Carswell said.

"We know the neighbor was killed by Belanger?"

"Yeah. We also know he was killed by the Highwayman."

"How? I'm not getting you, Julian."

"He left a note after he cut up the neighbor with a machete."

Machete, Maxwell thought, and said, "A note?"

"Yeah. A note for you."

"For me? What did it say?"

"It said, 'Agent Maxwell, come and find me.' Then he signed it, 'Highwayman.' You were right all along, Max."

"Shit. I'm not going to get out of here until tomorrow at the earliest."

"Look, I know you wanted to be there, but we have competent people on the scene. Crime Scene and an FBI command post are inbound. They'll be raiding the properties in Pennsylvania and New York in five minutes."

Maxwell felt his heart sink. "I understand."

"Get your business taken care of, and I'll have agents ready to take Gusa into custody when you land. Then you can get on a bird to both scenes."

"Yeah, okay. You'll let me know what else they find?"

"Of course.

4

7 November 2008

Lawrenceville, PA

Warrants for both properties were executed, and coordinated searches occurred just before dusk. FBI Special Agent Karen Shelley and Lt. Cole Abraham were first to enter the cottage in Lawrenceville. They were backed up by Shelley's partner, Special Agent John Godfrey, and an assortment of Pennsylvania State Police officers.

Simultaneously, Ferguson and Rice, along with two BCI agents and eight uniformed members of the New York State Police, entered Lance Belanger's property in Syracuse, New York.

Unsurprisingly, Belanger was not present at either property, but what they found inside the dwellings was nothing less than enigmatic.

"Lance has been busy," Cole Abraham said.

"Jesus," Shelley muttered.

Both houses were clean and tidy, but what surprised the officers was the décor. After clearing each room, they were surprised to find that every photograph had been removed from their frames and replaced. Empty picture frames hung on the walls, sat on end tables, and on vanities. When they checked photo albums, they also found them empty.

Shelley got on the phone to Ferguson and asked, "Have you got anything?"

"Nope, nothing yet. He took all the pictures down and disposed of them. We found ashes in the fireplace, but nothing of use. He even burned his high school and university yearbooks. We found a couple of pages that didn't quite burn up." Ferguson paused. "How about you?"

"Same here," Shelley said. "Why, though?"

"I guess he doesn't want us posting his picture."

"Seems like a lot of effort for nothing. We can get a picture from Syracuse University."

Ferguson said, "That was eight years ago, Shelley. He's probably changed since then. Maxwell and Abraham interviewed him last year. I'll get a state cop to pick up a photo out of SU, and you can show it to Abraham. See what he thinks."

"All right, we're going to check out the rest of the property and see if we can dig anything else up. I'll talk to Abraham."

"Do that."

"Maxwell isn't going to be happy."

"No, he's not."

Shelley hung up and went outside to meet Abraham, who was coordinating a sweep of Belanger's property. He was addressing Corporal Leeman. "Lieutenant Abraham, when you got a minute, I need to talk to you."

"I'll just be a minute, Agent Shelley."

While she waited, Shelley put a call into Bucharest.

5

8 November 2008

Bucharest, Romania

The first official meeting between President-Elect Barack Obama and the press dominated headlines all over the world. America had elected an African American to the highest office, and everything was about to change. Many considered it a pivotal time for improving race relations in the United States.

Another story broke on AP News Bucharest, but that was as far as it got. It was not picked up by the world news cycle. A prisoner, charged with numerous crimes, had taken his own life in his cell. The suicide occurred between the hours of 1:00 and 1:30 a.m., during a shift change at the jail.

"This sets our case back significantly," Inspector Nicolae Datcu told AP News in a phone interview. When asked if Gusa had been under suicide watch, Datcu replied, "No." When asked if Gusa was cooperating with the authorities, Datcu would not comment. Datcu was irritable and did say that there would be a full investigation into the matter.

And that was where the story died.

6

08 November 2008

Bucharest Henri Coandă International Airport

Maxwell settled into his seat and waited for departure. He was happy to be going home. He wanted to get back to the investigation in Lawrenceville and Syracuse. He was also a bundle of anxiety and disappointment. He'd missed the raid on both properties. He'd been briefed by both Ferguson and Shelley and knew about the purging of photographs.

"There has to be a reason," Maxwell said. "Have you recovered anything from the neighbor's house?"

"Crime Scene has picked up clothing fibers and hair. We've also got fingerprints on both the pick and machete."

"It appears Lance has stopped giving a shit."

"But why bother with the pictures? Surely, he knows we can enhance them?"

"He must have changed his appearance. Dyed his hair or maybe grown a beard. We need to get his picture posted with Homeland Security, as well as Canadian and Mexican border officials in case he tries to cross the border." Maxwell thought that Belanger might have already crossed over. "What about his accounts?"

"We've frozen the accounts and are monitoring for transactions."

"Good, he's probably got some cash to carry around. But if he hits an ATM, we need to know about it. He's winding up. We need to get him before he completely unravels and kills more people."

"As far as I know, everything Lance Belanger touches will sound an alarm."

Just then, the flight attendant touched Maxwell on the shoulder and said in Romanian, "Sir, we are about to take off."

Maxwell didn't need a translation. "Shelley, I'm taking off. I'll see you, folks, tomorrow."

"Okay, looking forward to it."

Maxwell shut the phone down and smiled at the attendant. She smiled back and moved on as the plane began to reverse out of the dock. Overhead, the seatbelt light dinged as well as the No Smoking sign. Maxwell was already fastened in.

Three rows back, disguised and in the company of an undercover Romanian police officer, Andrei Gusa was seated. Maxwell didn't acknowledge Gusa or the undercover officer. Datcu had warned him that he was probably being watched. The officer had been brought in from outside Bucharest, and after they faked the suicide, Gusa was disguised with a beard and ushered out through a tunnel below the Romanian jail. There was even discussion of putting him on another aircraft, but it was decided that the risk was too high.

7

08 November 2008

Morgan County, WV

They were headed northwest, a new set of wheels beneath them and another body behind them. The MO had changed. The victim had been male, and the presentation was now outweighed by necessity. Larry, with the help of Dusk, had bludgeoned the man with a tire iron in an empty rest area. They drove both vehicles up US Route 1 to a place called Chandler Crossing, Virginia, and dumped the dead man's body in the North Anna River. The plates on the stolen car were from Los Angeles, leading them to assume that he wouldn't be missed for a few days.

They then drove up to Culpeper and got rid of Larry's car in a Walmart Supercenter. Lance returned his rental in Newport News, and Steel and Dusk's vehicles were left at the meeting place.

"We should've cut off his fingers and his head," Dusk said from the back seat. "Then they would've had trouble finding out who he is."

"Too late for that now," Larry said from behind the wheel.

"We can always get another car," Steel, who was riding shotgun, said.

"We don't need another car," Lance said. "We're right on track." He wasn't worried. Sooner or later, the authorities would have all their names. But they only had a little under three hours of driving left to do.

Then the fun would begin.

***

CHAPTER 5 – YARD STREET INTERRUPT

1

9 November 2008

Outside Henessburg, PA

They were stopped at a service station. Lance was checking out a map while Steel pumped gas. Larry and Dusk had gone in to get food. The station had one camera over the pump island. Lance didn't get out, but at this point, he didn't care if they captured him on video. Like a snake, he'd shed the old skin of anonymity and embraced his new self. He was already formulating what they would do, how the horror of their actions would instill fear.

Just then, a white Chevrolet van pulled into the lot and stopped in front of the convenience store. This caught Lance's attention, drawing his eyes from the map. A man got out of the van and walked into the store.

"Steel," Lance said.

"Yeah," Steel replied.

"Don't bother filling it up. We're not keeping this vehicle."

"Okay." There was an audible clunk as Steel shut off the pump handle. He put the cap back on and went in to pay, and then all three came back out.

Five minutes later, they were parked across the road, watching as the man came back out to his van and started it. When he exited the parking lot, they pulled out onto the highway and followed.

2

12 November 2008

Grand Acres Survey

Kirkland Island, Pittsburgh, PA

There were four houses already built and inhabited on the newly constructed street, and another five were under construction. Beyond that lay the beginnings of a new suburb — a reclamation of property that used to be home to a pulp mill on the west side of the island. Kirkland Island found itself floating in the Ohio River 17 miles northeast of Pittsburgh, Pennsylvania.

Once a booming industrial park, home to paper mills, steel plants, tank farms, and various water-borne industries, the island was quickly becoming a haven for young families just starting out. The lower property rates, low taxes, and the promise of renewal made the real estate an easy sell for property managers. As industry fell victim to the times and plants started closing their doors, developers bought up the land and began reclamation.

Above the murky water of the Ohio, a blood moon cut in and out, distorted by, but slicing through the haze of snow bearing clouds. There would be snow, a great deal in fact, but the red sphere didn't go quietly behind the curtain of winter. It loomed in a softer hue of blood orange.

Under the scarlet night, a white cargo van rolled silently through the gridworks of streets. One might think the vehicle transported a contractor, perhaps wandering the new survey, making some final adjustment or inspection, but the occupants of this vehicle had a more sinister agenda. It rounded the bend, yielding to a newly erected stop sign, working its way down to where the four completed houses sat. Once there, it parked at the end of the street, idling until the moon succumbed to the clouds and was gone.

When the van's back doors opened, three shadowy figures stepped out onto the street. For a moment, they were stiff and robotic. Then each was handed a carry bag, looking like a tool bag, by someone inside the vehicle. Each figure was a frozen silhouette against the darkening sky, standing side-by-side, waiting for something.

The doors closed and, as if on cue, they began to walk up the street together until they reached the first house. One of the figures stopped abruptly at the end of the drive, watching as the others continued. Then the second figure reached the second driveway and halted, and the third man took his place at the next. In unison, they turned their heads, focused on the vehicle, which began to glide back down the street past each figure until it reached the fourth house.

The engine shut off. There was a moment of pause, then again, the rear doors on the panel van opened and out stepped the fourth figure. This one placed his bag on the ground, closed the back doors, picked up the bag, and proceeded to the end of the driveway. The figure turned his head and nodded. All four started for the door of their assigned house. The lives of the inhabitants of each house were into their final minutes.

3

Cliff and Shawna Keene were on their way to Grand Acres to peek at their new house, but it really wasn't a house at all. The contractors had poured the foundation, and for now, it was only a concrete pad set into the dusty gravel lot. That didn't matter to Shawna, who could hardly contain her excitement. This was their first house, and she could not wait to move out of the apartment they were renting.

"Hurry up, Cliff, you drive like an old man," she prodded, but it was in good fun. She loved him so much, wanted to have his child, but for now, she wanted to start a new life in their new home.

"Listen to old lead foot," Cliff remarked and smiled back. "Don't get your knickers in a twist, Sweetie."

"Come on, come on." She hammered on his shoulder with the heel of her fist.

Just ahead, the four completed homes gave off light. Shawna looked at them, thinking to herself that it wouldn't be long before their house would be finished and ready to occupy. In five weeks, they would take possession. Cliff turned left, down Yard Street, away from the completed homes, Shawna spotted the panel van, but gave it little if any thought. The stonework of the fourth house was what had her attention, it was the same masonry she'd ordered for their place. She wanted to look at it, even touch it. Had she made the right choice? It was the only part of the process she was unsure of. Randy, the lady who had sold them the home, had rushed her on that, and picking everything had been a bit overwhelming. Now she was second-guessing herself, tempted to get Cliff to turn back, but he was off in his own world.

You can't change it anyway, she thought.

"Three, four, five," Cliff said, reciting the street numbers. "There it is." He pulled the Chrysler Sebring up in front of their lot and put it into park. Reaching across the seat, he placed his hand on her leg, his fingers running down the seam between her legs. "The first thing I'm going to do when we get the keys is fuck your brains out on the stairwell."

Shawna felt a shiver of sexual excitement run up inside her, but she took a breath and pushed it off as she pulled his hand from between her legs. "No, you won't," she whispered and kissed the back of his hand. "The first thing you'll do is

go down on me in the foyer, and when I'm satisfied, you can
fuck my brains out on the stairs."

She dropped his hand, opened the passenger door, and got
out into the night air. If she didn't, she might end up having
sex with him right there in the Sebring. That would be an
exercise in cramped futility. No, it would be better to wait
until they got home, and then they could rock that old bed
long and hard.

4

The door to the first house opened, and the figure stepped out
and paused on the doorstep, looking down to his left. Then
the doors to the second, third, and fourth houses opened, and
those figures also stepped forward. Like mute robots, they
proceeded down the walks and onto the driveways. Their
business here was done. Behind them, the front door of
each house stood open, light spilling out into the evening air
offering invitation to anyone with the nerve to come and see
inside.

The first figure opened the back doors of the van and
placed his bag inside as the others approached. He didn't
wait for them. Instead, he walked around to the driver's door
and opened it just as the second figure reached the back, then
the third, and finally the fourth climbed in and closed the
doors behind him. The engine growled, and with the same
stealth with which it had arrived, it glided down the street
and was gone.

5

"Turn right, Cliff," Shawna blurted. "I want to take a look."
She was bouncing up and down in her seat like an excited
child.

"Come on, Shawna, I want to go home. I gotta get up at
5:00 a.m.," he said. But he was already turning the corner

because arguing with her would be pointless. When Shawna got something inside her head, there was no turning back.

"Just for a minute, baby. I wanna look at the stonework, then we can go home." She reached over and caressed his leg, then smiled seductively, "I promise."

There was no arguing with that.

The fourth house was roughly three hundred yards up the street, but as they closed the distance, neither Cliff nor Shawna was thinking about how the stonework would look on their new home. Instead, both were wondering why the front doors of all four houses were standing open in the dark of night. They coasted up to the fourth house and stopped in front of it. Shawna suddenly felt uneasy, her stomach tightening as inexplicable anxiety rolled through her. Something was wrong, she could feel it. "Cliff?"

"What the hell," he muttered, opening the car door.

"Cliff, maybe we should go."

"Is that what I think it is?" He was stepping out now.

"What are you doing?"

"Is that?" He walked around the car, ignoring her, and started across the lawn toward the front door. For a second, he paused and looked back at his wife, confusion dawning on his face, uncertainty in his eyes.

Or was it fear?

Shawna suddenly felt anxiety begin to churn deep inside her belly. Something was wrong. She saw it in his face. He had his back to her, taking slow, methodical steps toward the doorway. She wanted to chase after him but was too terrified to unlock the car door. She pushed the button to roll down her window, but before she could call out his name, he disappeared through the front entrance.

Thirteen seconds would elapse from the moment he slipped through the doorway and re-emerged. For Shawna, it was an eternity. He was standing there, a silhouette against the wash of white light. She couldn't see his face, but she recognized how his shoulders so often slumped.

What is he doing? Why is he standing there, she thought and then said, "Cliff?"

His head cocked to the right, like a dog trying to comprehend language, and then he exploded into action. Sprinting for the car, he bumped up against the right fender, and there was an audible thud that should have been followed by a curse, but he just rounded the car and yanked the driver door open. As a matter of fact, he pulled the door so hard it creaked in protest as it swung beyond its usual arc.

"Cliff, what is it?" she asked.

He dropped into the car and turned the key without thinking that he'd left it running. The gear in the starter ground against the spinning flywheel. "Oh fuck, oh fuck, oh fuck," he blathered. He cranked the gear lever into reverse and punched the gas pedal onto the floor.

Shawna's neck snapped to the right, following the command of G-force created by the motion of the car. And if that wasn't enough, Cliff tromped on the brakes, sending her head back against the headrest. Before she could protest, he shoved the accelerator to the floor, and they were off and running.

"Fuck me! Oh God, fuck!" He was staring straight ahead. "Which way did they go?"

"Who, what?"

"The van, Shawna, that fucking white van! Which way did it go?" He was digging in his jacket, fumbling for something as he turned the wheel to the left. "Did you see it?"

"I don't know…" She started to cry.

"Here!" He pulled out what he was fumbling with and tossed the cell phone toward her. "Call 911, call them now!"

The cell phone bounced off her lap and onto the floor.

"What is it, Cliff? What did you see?"

"Call them, Shawna," he ordered, and then tromped on the brakes again. "Fuck me!"

Shawna grabbed the cell and looked up. Cliff was breathing in and out, in and out. She swore she could hear his heart hammering inside his chest cavity. Then she saw what made him hit the brakes.

The van was stopped four hundred yards ahead of them, idling at a stop sign.

Cliff never tore his eyes from the white van. "Call them now, Shawna. Tell them where we are. Tell them everyone is dead. Tell them to hurry." He clamped onto the steering wheel, his knuckles whitening. He swallowed and waited to see what the van would do.

"911, what is your emergency? Police, fire, or ambulance?"

Shawna gaped at her husband, then to the white van. "We're in Grand Acres. We need the police, everyone is dead. Please hurry, I think we're in real danger."

The brake lights on the van suddenly released, and Cliff reached across and took Shawna's hand in his. His palm was sopping with sweat but worse, it was shaking horribly. "Get ready to hold onto something."

"Cliff? What did you see?"

He expelled a breath, his eyes darting momentarily in her direction, then back.

Then the right signal on the van began to blink, and it turned the corner. After a second, it was gone, but Cliff didn't move an inch. He was locked on that corner, waiting.

"Cliff?"

He turned to her, his face chalky with shock, eyes wide and finally spoke.

"They killed everyone, Shawna," he whispered, almost as if he believed the vehicle they rode in might be bugged. "Everyone in that house was murdered." His voice hitched. "Everyone, Shawna, even the kids."

"Oh my God," she moaned.

He reached out, taking her hand in his.

Neither spoke. Terror filled the night, and it seemed an eternity before they heard the first distant call of sirens.

***

CHAPTER 6 – ENTER HALSEY

1

13 November 2008

Pittsburgh, PA

Detective Bob Halsey didn't usually party late. His motto was simple. Drunk by 10:00, bed by 11:00, and all is good. Especially on workdays. Unfortunately, the previous night, one thing had led to another, and here he was. Wet, heavy flakes of snow stuck against the window as he took a last cursory look around the bedroom to see if he'd forgotten anything.

The woman he'd picked up was sound asleep. And no wonder. After they closed the bar, they'd ended up back here. The grand finale lasted a long time. He was amazed at his stamina, especially after banging back shots of Jose Cuervo like water. He was still a little on the drunk side, and man, he was tired. What an animal she'd been. The crazy chick even bit his shoulder when they were in the full throes of sex. He'd been wondering if he was going to get off. Thought that maybe the booze had put his lower anatomy to sleep. After she bit him, he'd given a couple final thrusts and collapsed on top of her.

That was all he remembered.

Halsey guessed her age to be around thirty-four. She dressed like a younger woman, wearing low rider jeans and a camisole that clung to her still firm chest. She had raven hair that had probably seen a dye job or three. What really caught his eye was her smile. There was an imperfection, a crooked slant, that he found attractive. That smile reminded him of his ex-wife Kate.

Dressing, he surveyed the sheets wrapping over the curve of her buttocks, purposely pushed back to expose one leg. He did the same thing to regulate his body heat. Before their session, she'd also banged back several tequila shots. One-for-one in fact, and she was too small, to be matching drinks with Bob Halsey.

Buttoning his shirt, he reached down and caressed her leg. When he got up to go, she murmured, "Leaving?"

"Yeah," he replied. "I gotta get to work."

"Okay, I have to lock the door behind you." She rose, unabashedly naked, and followed him to the front door. She smiled, brought her hand up to her face as if to indicate memory lapse, and asked, "What was your name again?"

"Bob."

"Bob? Oh yeah. I had fun, Bob." She wobbled a bit.

Apparently, he wasn't the only one still feeling the effects of the night before. She unlocked the door, smiled sleepily, and he knew this would be the last time he saw her. Tomorrow there would be a new guy. With women like this, there was always a new guy, but then who was he to judge? He hadn't gone with the same woman for more than two nights steady.

Not since Kate.

He leaned down, kissed her neck, and said, "Me too," then stepped into the hallway. Behind him, the door closed, and as the deadbolt clicked over, he realized he didn't know her name.

Doesn't really matter, does it?

"No," he whispered, shaking his head, and started down the hall. It was dank, poorly lit, and smelled musty. He couldn't quite remember exactly where the stairwell was. He vaguely remembered climbing it. He thought he was going the right way, and then saw a red exit sign. As he trudged forward, he felt the vibration of his cell phone against his thigh. He knew who it was even before he dug it from his pocket and checked. The call display said OGGY. He pushed the green button and placed the phone to his ear.

"Yeah."

"You sober, Bob?" Oggy sounded disheveled.

"Halfway. What's up?" He shoved the exit door open and descended the stairwell.

"I need you to get over to Kirkland Island. On the east end there's a development called Grand Acres, we've got multiple homicides."

His footfalls echoed off the walls.

Multiple homicides? I'm lost. Fuck me, this isn't the way!

"Okay, what's the address?"

"Yard Street."

"You got a number, Oggy?"

"There are only four houses in the development, and all are on Yard Street. You'll know where when you get there. We have it sealed off. I'm on my way now. I'll meet you at the scene, and we'll go from there. What's your ETA, Bob?"

"I don't know, maybe half an hour? Forty minutes tops." He picked up his pace. *That is if I ever find my goddamned car.*

"All right, I'll see you there."

He ended the call and put the phone back into his pocket as he pushed out the exit door at the bottom of the stairwell. It was then that he realized he was on the wrong side. He was in an alley at the back of the building. Behind him, the door slammed before he could catch it. He gave it a tug. The crash bar had locked. "Fuck me and the horse I rode in on!"

Heavy wet snowflakes fell from above, their moisture darkening the shoulders of his suit jacket. There was roughly a foot of the stuff on the ground. He knew his car was parked a block away at the pub where he'd met the girl. He remembered the name of the pub, Chevy '57. Funny how he could remember that name, but not the name of the girl with whom he'd played so hard.

He touched his shoulder, the bite still stinging slightly, but not terribly. The truth was, when she bit him, he found it kind of exciting. Animalistic even. But he wasn't in any hurry to head on down to the local dungeon for some more abuse.

He worked his way north out of the alley looking left, then right. His head pounding, he decided that "right" was the way to go and wandered up the block.

Then he touched his gun purposefully to make sure he hadn't forgotten it. *Never forget your weapon, Detective. The day you forget that piece of iron is the day the charade ends, and they know that you are a drunk.*

"Fuck off, am not," he muttered.

The voice in his head fell silent. He didn't argue. He'd caught a case, and his priority now was convincing himself and others he was sober enough to take control of an investigation.

For him, that would be a hard sell.

2

Finding Grand Acres wasn't that hard. It was a burb among a declining industrial landscape. He could see the wink of reds and blues as he took the ramp that descended to Kirkland Island. As he wound toward the lights at the bottom, the snow clung to the scarred asphalt, making it greasy. He wondered what the story was. Multiple homicides usually only meant two things: gang or domestic.

Somehow, he doubted that the bangers were working in the north end of Kirkland Island. If this was fifteen years ago, he might have thought it was a mob thing. There had been a growing community of union organizers on the island during the boom in the '90s. But now? When the plants started closing, the surrounding neighborhood began to hollow out. The mob, for all its history, had lost its stranglehold after being forced to share its enterprise with gang bangers and bike clubs.

Besides, a house in this place was a bit out of their economic reach. Shit, it was out of Halsey's reach. Yeah, more likely it was some lunatic who freaked out because his dinner was cold. He'd seen that bullshit more times than he cared to remember. Ahead, the road came to a T-junction. He switched on the signal and turned right. His head was really thumping away now, reminding him what an idiot he was.

"Probably shouldn't be driving," he mumbled while rubbing his right eye in a futile attempt to soften the pulse of pain.

He'd broken his cardinal rule of three Tylenol and a large glass of water before bedtime. This rule had saved him, on more than a few occasions, from the monster that he now felt growing inside his skull.

There were only two reasons he might ignore this ritual, the first being that stupid invincibility one develops when they've had a few too many. "I'll be fine, no worries," the drunken moron that is his brain says. And oh, how convincing that idiot is. The second? Well, the second was the reason for this morning's chorus of pain, and that was some girl who'd wrapped herself around him. After a recipe of tequila shots, bump and grind with a dash of bite, he'd rolled off thinking about rummaging around her bathroom for some Advil or Aspirin, but instead, he drifted off.

"I'm a fucking idiot."

3

"Detective Halsey," he said, flashing his badge.

"They're expecting you, Detective. Go up the street, turn right, and park. I'll let Detective Ogden know you've arrived."

"Which house are they working?"

The young officer looked at him strangely and said, "All of them."

"What? What do you mean 'all of them?'"

"All four houses, Detective. All of them are crime scenes."

"Are you shitting me?"

"No..."

Then there was an uncomfortable silence. The cop's eyes fixed upon Halsey, nodding as the snow gathered on the peak of his cap and the shoulders of his overcoat. He could have asked him again, "Are you shitting me?" But he didn't, so instead Halsey said, "Up and turn right?"

"Yeah."

Four houses? What the fuck?

Maybe it is a gang thing after all. Maybe, Halsey thought but doubted it. He released the brake and rolled away, leaving the uniformed cop to man the roadblock. When word got out on this, they were going to need a lot more officers to form a cordon around the crime scene.

The street was lined with police cars on both sides. Bits of excavated mud sat in scattered clumps all up and down the snow-covered pavement. This was a byproduct of the construction. Halsey parked between the forensic van and another car that looked out of place. A Chrysler Sebring.

Oggy was standing on the edge of the drive at the first house, looking his way as he slid the car in behind the forensics van. His suit hung on him like a rack; he was tall, thin, once-red hair fading to gray. Across the street, a couple was with a uniformed officer. Both were in their late twenties. The woman was wearing blue jeans and a red pullover with PITT, the University of Pittsburg, emblazoned across it. Beneath that she wore hospital scrubs. Probably a nurse, he guessed. The U of P hoodie wasn't a part of her work attire.

The guy was wearing a suit; Halsey thought him a salesman or maybe an accountant. His skin was gray, almost white. Whatever this dude had seen had scared him white.

"Bob," Oggy called, drawing his attention away from the couple and onto the business at hand. Oggy was waving his arm, then dropped it when he nodded to acknowledge him.

He slipped the gear selector into park, let out a brief sigh, and unsnapped the belt. Climbing from the car, he felt his balance shift, a reminder that he really shouldn't have gotten behind the wheel. "Game time," he said grimly to himself.

4

"We have eleven victims: eight adults and three children. We believe each house had its own separate assailant," Oggy told Halsey as they made their way up the drive to the first house.

"How do you know that?" Halsey asked.

"Our killers left different shoe prints at each scene, and in the case of the first two houses, the methods were very different." Oggy stopped and looked into his eyes. "It's bad, Bob, worst thing I've ever seen."

He'd known Oggy a long time, both as a partner and a friend, and he looked spooked. He'd never seen him that way before. That's not to say that Halsey possessed some invisible armor that made him impervious to horrible things. It wasn't that way at all. The truth was, everything he saw affected him. To survive, he had to find a way to compartmentalize it. And it wasn't just the horrors of crime that influenced them. Sometimes their woes were of the homegrown variety.

"Let's take a look."

They mounted the steps and crossed the same threshold. Halsey would later learn what Cliff Keene had seen when he ignored his wife's call. What had drawn Keene to the house was exactly what they saw now. The body of a woman with long blond hair lay twisted, spread out in the hallway just beyond the cloakroom. The hardwood floor was sappy with coagulated blood. Her eyes were closed, and this caught Halsey's attention. It seemed unnatural, staged.

"She was the first to die," he said aloud.

"Best as we can tell, she met the perp at the front door as he was entering," Oggy said and added, "Her throat was cut."

Oggy reached into his pocket and produced two sets of blue surgical gloves. He handed Halsey a pair and they put them on.

That done, Halsey hunched down for a closer look, careful not to step in the blood, and used the tip of a pen to push back a lock of hair to expose the right side of the woman's neck. It had been sliced all the way to the windpipe. "That's a clean cut. Box cutter, maybe?"

"Well, I was thinking something similar. Box cutter or maybe a straight razor, it was definitely something with a very sharp edge." Oggy pulled out a pad. "Lucy Jones, twenty-nine years old, mother of two."

"Lucy," he said aloud and carefully replaced her hair. Just as he was about to get up, he spotted something. "Forensics finished their collection, Oggy?"

"Yeah, everything is done. Sweep and photographs, they're just waiting for us to do a walk through before they collect the bodies."

"Grab the photographer."

"Call Baden in here," Oggy barked at one of the officers.

"Baden," the officer parroted.

"What is it?" Oggy hunkered down beside him, and for a second, he seemed to recoil, then settled in. Halsey guessed he could smell the booze permeating from his pores but said nothing. "What you see?"

"Give me a sec, Og."

The photographer joined them, his camera at the ready. "What do you need, detectives? I've already shot the entire scene."

"Did you shoot her eyes?" Halsey asked.

"What? Uh, no… Why?"

"Ready your camera." He reached down a gloved finger and gently pulled back the woman's lid on her right eye.

"Mother of God," Oggy gasped.

"Sweet Christ," Baden added and began snapping pictures.

"Is that what I think it is?" Oggy squinted and brought his clenched fist up to his mouth.

Halsey reached over and pulled back the second eyelid, which gave a clearer picture. Burned neatly into the whites of both eyes were identical symbols. At first, he thought it was a shape, but when he pulled back the second lid, the symbol was easier to identify. "Looks to me like the number 4."

Oggy knelt, his mouth still covered, and leaned in for a closer look. Then he whispered, "What the fuck is this, Bob?" He peered over at Halsey, not entirely tearing his own eyes away from the victim's death stare. "What is that? A burn?"

He thought Oggy was right. It was small, but it appeared that someone had branded this woman. He wondered what could have been used to inflict such a mark. He brought his eyes up to meet Oggy's and said, "I think this is a calling card. Whoever did this wanted us to find it. We'd better check the rest of the victims for similar mutilation."

Above them, Baden sighed and snapped another shot.

They both stood. Oggy signaled Baden. "Better come with us, Baden."

They moved from the hallway into the kitchen where they found a male slumped backward in a kitchen chair. The linoleum floor and kitchen nook had turned copper brown. The puddles of blood were coagulating. The man's throat had been sliced wide open, his head pulled backward unnaturally, exposing the severed muscles and tendons in his neck. It was apparent he'd been killed from behind. Mindful not to step in the blood, Halsey positioned himself over the dead man.

"I don't think this poor fellow had a chance," Oggy mused.

"Yeah, he probably was bleeding out before he even realized he was cut." Halsey removed his latex gloves, placed them into an evidence bag, and then donned a new set. "Get ready to take another shot," he told the photographer. He pulled the man's right eyelid back, revealing an identical 4 burned neatly into the eyeball. Baden shot it and then the second eye.

5

They were standing in the doorway of the twins' room. Inside, two children, both boys, were laid out similarly to their parents. It was a horrific sight.

Now, more than ever, Halsey could feel the pull. He just wanted to get a bottle and climb inside.

"Cult killing," Oggy mused.

"Yeah, maybe," he replied. "Definitely planned."

"Yeah," Oggy croaked.

"Yep." Halsey took a deep breath and entered the room. *Who does this,* he wondered looking around the room. The walls were papered with the cartoon character SpongeBob SquarePants and his underwater world. It was a little boy's room. Cartoon wallpaper, two dressers, the drawers painted in alternating colors of red, blue, orange, and green. Both beds were covered with bedspreads to match the wallpaper. This was a place of innocence, a child's safe haven.

Until last night.

Last night evil had come, taken the innocence in the room, and turned it into a chamber of horror. The person who did this couldn't possibly have the capacity for love.

"The brutality doesn't make sense," Bobby said as he stood over the body of the first boy. "What are they, six, maybe seven? Why do this?" Both boys' throats had been cut with the same viciousness as their parents'. He leaned over and gently pulled back the lid of the first little boy who lay there and said, "Come on, Baden, let's get this over with."

The photographer didn't move. He was a statue, mouth hanging open, eyes glassy. The blood was draining from his face, turning him gray. He was a thousand miles away. In his right hand, the camera dangled like an anchor.

"Baden," Oggy barked.

The photographer snapped out of it and shook his head. "Yeah, sorry. Okay." He moved forward slowly and brought the camera up; his hands were shaking.

"What's your first name?" Halsey asked.

"Gene."

"Gene, we've got business to take care of here, and then we have three more houses. This sucks, I know. Everyone here feels exactly like you, but we owe them this." Bobby waved a hand toward the children. "The quicker we get through this, the quicker the coroner can get them out of here and restore their dignity." He did his best to look sincere. He didn't want Gene to feel like he was looking into a mirror. Bob Halsey's nerves were humming like a telephone wire.

The photographer studied him, digesting his words a bit at a time. He took one deep breath, then two, and shivered. Finally, as if rebounding from a sucker punch, he slowly regained his composure and straightened up.

"Okay," he said. "Let's do this."

Halsey pulled back the child's eyelid, and Gene Baden began snapping pictures.

Oggy watched, looming in the doorway, hanging on Bobby's discovery. A discovery he had initially missed.

Maybe he was beating himself up, Halsey didn't know. Oggy knew he had a talent for this, a skill he, himself, lacked.

Halsey appeared methodical and cold, but what Oggy didn't know was that he was shaking inside. Shaking was a poor choice of words. He was in constant quake mode, bits of his stability crumbling each day.

After Kate divorced him, it all began to unravel, turning him into a cliché. That was when what used to be tremors turned into a full-fledged seismic shift in mood and stability. When the shakes overtook him, there was only one way to relieve the pressure. Bob Halsey had a talent for this type of work, but that was just one of three. The second was boozing, and the third was maintaining his status as a functional closet drunk.

Oggy knew his secret, knew where he would be going to get away from the ugliness they were now basking in. By the look on his face, he might even join him tonight, but he wouldn't stay long.

Hanging around Halsey was like hanging around a poison control center, and he guessed his old pal Oggy feared that some of that poison was contagious. Tonight, he would find a pub, and before the poison inside him could find its way out, he would dilute it. Before haunting ghosts could inundate him with their accusations, he would escape into an alcoholic haze. That included the spirits of this crime scene. Tomorrow, when the work resumed, he would replace the mask of the methodical Detective Halsey.

6

Finished in the first house, they watched the ME enter. He would be readying the bodies for transport once the investigators completed their sweeps. An hour had elapsed since his arrival. In that time, the clouds broke up, and the now morning sun came out. Earlier a city plow had been brought in to scrape the street. Rising temperatures had aided in melting the snow, turning the asphalt of Yard Street a deep, reflective black.

The sun might have been up, but he still felt like shit. He was sobering up, the alcohol leeching out, bringing on the effects of a waking hangover.

"Anybody mind if I take a quick smoke before we move to the next house?" Baden asked.

"I'm going to get that couple out of here," Oggy said. "Smoke 'em if you got 'em."

Baden removed a pack of cigarettes from his pocket and offered one to Halsey.

"No thanks, I quit a few years back."

"You want me to step off?"

"Nah, hang about. I still like the smell of them." He watched Oggy cross the street to the car where the couple was and lean in through the window. He was sending them off. Oggy had filled him in as he examined the body of the second victim. He would have them in later for a sit-down. Halsey would be there for that, but let Oggy take the lead. Beside him, Baden exhaled, sending a cloud of smoke in his direction. He turned in Baden's direction, stuck out his hand. "Bob Halsey."

"Gene Baden." Baden switched the smoke from his right to his left and shook. "Nice to meet you, Bob, thanks for your help in there."

"Help?"

"I was losing my shit. Thanks for bringing me back."

"Oh, no sweat, Gene. It happens to the best of us."

"I got three kids, youngest is the about the same age as those little boys. Pretty hard." Baden took a draw on his cigarette; he was getting wired up again. "That'll be with me for a while, I suppose."

"Yeah," he agreed. "I can appreciate that, but the time to shake it out is after the job is done."

Baden shot him a wounded glance, but he understood, he'd seen the mask slip a bit. "Yeah, I get it. I'll leave it with the smoke."

Halsey nodded. He'd felt it overwhelm him, stalking him through every waking second, but even worse, it found its way into his dreams.

"Have you ever seen so many murders at one time?" Gene Baden asked.

"No, I haven't." And he hadn't, but there was a case that had been equally disturbing—one he didn't feel like sharing with a young police photographer he'd known only an hour.

Oggy started back across the road. Behind him, the couple pulled their Sebring away from the curb. Bob assumed they would be heading to the station house.

Baden took another puff off his smoke.

He asked, "Why do you call him Oggy?"

Halsey laughed. "His full name is Ogden Chartrand."

Baden snickered. "I guess you've been friends for a long time."

"A very long time," Bob said as Oggy came back into their group.

"I'm sending them home for now. They'll be into the station to make statements later this afternoon. The press is beginning to assemble at the barrier. Someone opened their yap. I guess it was inevitable." Oggy looked to both men. "I also got a call from downtown, and we should be getting a call from the FBI. They may be able to provide us with a profiler."

"Any idea who they're sending over?" Bob asked. He'd worked with a profiler from the Pittsburgh Office on a string of homeless murders that occurred back in 2003.

"No, not at this point," Oggy told him, "but I'm sure we'll know by day's end." Passing a glance between Baden and Bob, Oggy asked, "You boys ready?"

They moved to the next house.

At the second house, they were spared the stress of dealing with dead children. But there were still two houses left, and as Oggy had pointed out earlier, there were eleven victims all told. While Baden was a bit more at ease, Bob had no illusions that this was going to get any easier as they went on. He kind of hoped that they could get through the worst of it first.

The similarity between the first and second house was that the perpetrator had met the first victim at the door, but the execution had involved a blow to the head using a blunt object. Bob guessed it might be a large size hammer, possibly a ball peen hammer. The victim's skull had a perfect circular hollow in the side of her head. Peeling back her eyelids again revealed the branding on both eyeballs, but the numbers were slightly different. Smaller.

"Different brand," Bobby said.

"What the fuck does it mean?" Oggy asked.

"I don't know. It's definitely a message, and I'd say that it's directed at us. But I really don't know," Bob replied.

"Four," Baden added. "There are four houses. Maybe it's just that, four houses, four killers."

Bob thought about it for a second, could feel Oggy looming — wanting him to have an answer, but he had none. The best he could do was, "Maybe. Whoever did this is sending us a message. This was very well planned. I have a hunch that if we don't find the people who did this, we're going to get an encore performance."

The second victim was in the living room, also bludgeoned, the brand 4 burned into both of her eyes. She hadn't gone down on the first blow.

"This one fought back," Oggy said.

Halsey nodded in agreement. Next to her body, a single partial bloody handprint stained the floor. He looked at her right hand. It was very blood stained and deformed. The knuckle above her index finger was canted left. "He hit her, then she brought her right hand up. Probably to ward off another blow or maybe reach for the wound. Zoom in on the hand, Gene."

Baden began snapping pictures. First, the woman's head, then her hand, and then the spatters of blood. The DSLR whirred and clicked, whirred and clicked, mechanical declarations of its part in documenting the mayhem. Then something caught his eye, a picture hanging above the fireplace mantle — in it, both women shared a kiss. "Lesbians," he said, then took another shot.

Both detectives looked up, at first puzzled by the photographer's statement—then dawning realization as they followed his line of sight. Halsey leaned in a little closer, after spotting something on the left side of the victim's face. "What do we have here?" He pulled back a curl of her hair, revealing a flap of skin over her left temple. There was a wound that had been stitched closed; below the skin was a square roughly the size of a postage stamp. "Oggy, you ever seen anything like this?"

"Is that an implant?" Oggy asked.

Bobby touched the square with a finger. "It's hard."

"Looks about the size of an SD card," Baden interrupted, then exclaimed excitedly, "Shit, I bet that's what it is!"

On one side of the square was an incision which had been sewn up. "This was done postmortem."

"You sure?" Oggy was beside him now, close enough to smell the booze.

"How can you tell? It looks like a doctor did those stitches." Baden was hovering above them.

"Well, Gene, those stitches may have been done by someone in the medical field, but it was definitely done after this woman was killed." He ran his index finger over the neatly tied stitching, feeling the tips prick against the latex glove. "The wound is fresh, no sign of healing, and look,

there's a clean spot around it. I'd say our perp might have a medical background. Snap a close-
up of this, Gene. Where's that Quincy hanging out?"

"McCoy," Oggy yelled to the officer on watch. "Where's the ME?

"Car's out front, Detective."

"Yeah, I know where his car is, I want him. Get him in here!"

"You got a spare SD card, Gene?"

"Are you kidding? I've got fifty of the things." Gene reached into his bag and pulled out a wallet. He unzipped it and said, "I bet it is an SD card! Shit, this is freaky."

Halsey found it amusing that this was the same man who'd been in sluggish shock only twenty-five minutes earlier. Now he was giddy. He understood what was up. Earlier, the photographer felt like a bystander, now he was involved. "I just want to look at one and compare. Do you mind?"

"Be my guest, but if you touch it to that dead lady's skin, it's yours to keep."

"Nope, not going to do that, just want to compare it." He took the card in his left hand. "If it is what I think it is, Oggy, I want it removed here."

"Agreed." Oggy cocked his head over his shoulder. "Is he coming, McCoy?"

"Yes, Detective," the uniformed cop said.

Halsey placed his right hand on the protruding square in the victim's temple, feeling the edges while staring at Baden. Then he closed his eyes, his fingers on both hands working their way around, communicating comparison. A second passed, then two, then three. Halsey opened his eyes. "You know Gene, I think you're right."

The coroner came through the door. "Detective Ogden?"

Halsey didn't recognize him. "Over here, Doc."

Oggy stood up. "I'm Detective Ogden. We've found something on a victim. Something beneath the skin." He stepped out of the way, so the coroner could lean in for a closer look.

Halsey turned toward the ME. "Hey."

The ME was a thin man, lanky with gray hair and even grayer skin. He looked old to Bobby, and though he might be old, his voice was young, also deceiving. "Hey. What have you got there?"

Halsey lowered his eyes down to the victim, inviting the coroner to follow. "I think it's an SD card." He held the card Baden had given him up. "Like this."

The ME donned a fresh pair of gloves. "Okay, I'll make a note of it when I get them back to the morgue."

"I want to remove it now, Doc. I believe it was left for us on purpose. Seeing that it's electronic, I think we should take it out now. There might be something critical on it." Halsey was calm.

"What's your name, Detective?"

"Bob Halsey."

"Okay, I'm Jack Fraser."

"Good to meet you, Jack."

"Likewise."

"If it is an SD Card, it might be compromised by the body fluid."

Fraser considered this and nodded. "All right, Bob, I'll remove it, but it goes right into an evidence bag. You guys won't be getting your mitts on it until my technician swabs it for everything."

"Everything?" Baden mumbled.

"Anything foreign to the deceased. Hair, fiber, tissue. We'll pull it out, but nobody touches it until it's tested. I'm not having a DNA test overturned just because you want to know what's on that card. Assuming that's what it is." His face was stern as he set his gaze first on Halsey, then Oggy, and even Baden. "We understand each other?"

"It's your call, Doc," Oggy said.

"How long to get through the necessary testing?" Halsey asked.

"I can have a technician on it immediately. If you're worried about the possible evidence, I'll make it a high priority. But I guess we better make sure that's what it is." Fraser reached over and opened the metal briefcase he'd carried on site. Inside it were many surgical tools, scalpels, clamps, forceps, tweezers, along with four sets of scissors. Also in the case were rolls of surgical tape, plastic containers, baggies, and of course a box of surgical gloves.

"Okay, well, let's see what's below this young lady's skin, shall we?"

"Let's," Halsey agreed.

Fraser reached into the case and removed a fresh pair of gloves, enveloped in clear plastic. "Put these on."

Bob stripped off the old pair, passing them to Oggy, who placed them in an evidence bag. No quicker did he have the new set on when Fraser was passing another evidence bag across to him. "Hold this, Bob." He pointed down into the case. "I'm going to cut the sutures and place them in the bag you're holding. After I do that, I want you to seal the zip, grab another one, and have it ready for when I pull out whatever it is that the person who killed this poor girl saw fit to put inside her. Can you see the other baggies?"

Bob glanced down. "Yes."

"Good." He unsnapped two plastic containers. "The first is for the sutures. The second is for whatever it is we're about to pull out." He set a digital recorder on the box and pushed the record button. On the recorder, a green light blinked. In small letters below that were the words: Voice Recognition. Then he donned a fresh pair of gloves. "For the record: This is County Medical Examiner Jack Fraser. I am at the address 1 Yard Street in a suburb known as Grand Acres on Kirkland Island just outside Pittsburgh, Pennsylvania." He scooped up a set of scissors in his left hand and tweezers in the right. "The subject is a young woman, late twenties, the initial cause of death undetermined until a later examination. Under the consultation of Detective Ogden and Detective Halsey, I am going to extract a foreign body from beneath the skin on the left temple. It appears that a postmortem incision was made, and after the foreign body was introduced, fresh sutures were applied to seal the incision. The sutures appear to be 4-0 Vicryl, likely made with a PS-2 needle." Fraser paused. The light on his digital recorder began to blink again. "Here we go."

The procedure only took a minute. Fraser snipped each stitch, tugged them from the skin, and dropped them into the evidence bag. Once finished, he ordered, "Seal it and get me another, Detective Halsey. I am now going to remove the foreign entity." Using the tip of the scissors, he raised the flap of skin and went into the pouch with the tweezers. "Got it." The cut was just large enough to accommodate the little square object. Fraser pulled it from the wound, confirming that it was, in fact, an SD card.

"I knew it. I fucking knew it," Baden declared.

"Shut up, Gene." Halsey pointed to the digital recorder.

Fraser smiled at Halsey and held up the card. "Let the record show that I have removed what appears to be a... SD memory card from inside the victim's left temple. It appears to be wrapped in a thin layer of cellophane. I am now placing the card into a sealed evidence bag for further testing." He dropped the card into the bag, and Halsey placed it into the plastic container. "All right, I am now going to cover the incision with a medical-grade second skin to avoid contamination during transport." Fraser placed his tools into another bag and covered the incision. Then he snapped off the recorder.

"So, how long..." Halsey began.

Fraser raised a hand, removed his cell phone, and punched up a number. "Excuse me." He held the phone to ear, waited, and then said, "Shirley, I need a priority on a piece of evidence. Full workup, whatever you have on your docket takes second place, okay?"

There was a muffled reply.

"Yes, it's from the Yard Street crime scene. Priority one, Shirley. I'm sending you a computer card. I need everything done ASAP so that the good detectives can check what's on it."

***

CHAPTER 7 – CHAOS

1

Technical Lab

Quantico, VA

Maxwell was standing behind Gusa and a computer technician named George Feck, looking at two computer monitors. Gusa was on the left and Feck on the right. The hard drive had been copied in Bucharest and secured. They had since duplicated the copy as a backup and were now looking over the contents.

Maxwell wanted to get a closer look at what was on the hard drive. He'd only perused it in Bucharest, just long enough to confirm what Gusa was alleging.

When they opened the files, everything was in Romanian, but as Gusa navigated through the system and found the logs for macabre.club's chats, the script changed to English. The chat sessions between Lance and Norris read like a movie script. Maxwell noted how Devon (Lance) began grooming Barker (Norris), and he likened it to the same way a molester grooms a child.

Feck, who had just been brought in, knew very little about it. "I want a printed transcript of every page," Maxwell told Feck and rubbed his eyes. He hadn't slept the entire trip back. He was going to need to go to ground for a bit and recharge his batteries. Otherwise, he wouldn't be able to focus. There was so much to do. He wanted to get out to

Lawrenceville and check the progress of the investigation. He also had to get up to Syracuse. He said to Gusa, "Were you monitoring their chats?"

Feck wasn't on the case, but he understood what he was seeing. "Jesus Christ," he said. "This is pretty creepy stuff."

"Yes," Gusa replied. "In my business, I have to take precautions. There is also an attachment that passed between the two."

"An attachment?" Maxwell leaned in. "Show that to me."

Gusa scrolled up, changed the screen, and found another file folder that had Romanian writing. He opened it, and there were dozens of photographs gleaned from macabre. club.

"That looks like more than one attachment," Maxwell said.

"These files are pictures for temptation, for…" Gusa paused. "I don't know the word. Maybe decoration?"

"Decoration?" Maxwell chuckled. It was the fatigue; he was getting giddy. "I don't understand."

"When Lance set up the website, he made it. The pictures are not his." Gusa brought up photos of crime scenes, clicking from one to the next.

One of them Maxwell immediately recognized. "Plainfield," he said. "Ed Gein's barn." He was referring to the infamous black and white photograph of Bernice Worden's decapitated and eviscerated body hanging in Gein's barn. Maxwell had used the photo in several presentations he'd done for law enforcement when lecturing on serial murders.

"Leatherface," Gusa agreed.

"No, Leatherface was not real. That's from a movie, but it was inspired by Ed Gein." Maxwell said. "Gein was a grave robber and killer." He stopped, wondering why he was bothering to converse with Gusa about this. He switched gears. "You said they shared a file?"

"Yes."

"I'd like to see that."

"Very well." Gusa scrolled to the bottom of the file folder until he reached the ZIP file. "Here." He hovered the mouse over it. "It was encrypted and was made to go bad after a time, but I altered it before saving it." He looked up, a grin on his face, seeking approval.

Maxwell was annoyed at this but gave no indication. "Can you open it without damaging it?" Then to Feck, "George, have you got this backed up as well?"

"Everything is backed up, Agent Maxwell." Feck was following along on the second monitor, tracing Gusa's navigation.

"Okay, open the file on your computer." Maxwell placed a hand on Feck's shoulder.

"You got it." Feck clicked on the file and it opened, revealing another photo and a Word document. "What do you want to look at first?"

"The photo," Maxwell said.

Feck clicked on it, and another piece of the puzzle fell into place. Suddenly, there was a knock on the door, and Maxwell turned to see the deputy director looking through the small window. He nodded to Carswell and reiterated, "George, I want everything printed and copy it again. I'll be back in a minute."

"No problem, Agent Maxwell," Feck said.

Maxwell opened the door, and Carswell motioned for him to come into the hall. He stepped through the doorway and passed the two guards.

"Walk with me," Carswell said and began to move. Maxwell followed him down the corridor away from the guards, presumably to be out of earshot. "You look like shit. What are you running on for sleep?"

"Maybe a couple hours in the last four days. What's going on?" Maxwell ran his hand through his hair and tried to suppress a yawn.

"How are things progressing?" Carswell asked, but there was something else. Maxwell could feel it.

"I'd say there's enough on that hard drive alone for a solid conviction."

"All you gotta do now is find him." Carswell paused. "Something has come up."

"What?"

"Outside of Pittsburgh we have a mass killing. Four families were killed in their homes. The Pittsburgh cops are handling it, but we're sending over an agent from the Pittsburgh office. "Michelle Leigh."

"You think this is connected?" Maxwell asked.

"Probably."

"Leigh was pretty close to Ash. Wouldn't that present a problem?" Maxwell didn't have to ask that. He knew it would but left that to Carswell.

Carswell frowned. "Yeah, but we're strapped for people. The SAC in Pittsburgh is on medical leave for two weeks, he had his appendix out yesterday. The other agent I would've used is working on a homegrown terrorism case, which leaves me with Leigh. So, I authorized sending her in an advisory role. If it's connected, we'll deal with it."

Maxwell leaned into the wall for support. His eyes hurt, itchy and dry from fatigue. The trip to Romania had run his tank dry and his body was telling him he needed some down time, but he wanted to get back into the room with Gusa. "Okay. That's what you wanted to talk to me about?"

"That… and I wanted to see if all the political wrangling I did to get our Romanian guest here is worthwhile. Is it?"

Maxwell sighed. He was overwhelmed. He had so much ground to cover. Syracuse, Lawrenceville, Gusa, and tracking down Lance Belanger. "I think this guy may be a virtual goldmine for evidence. The shit he was into… has tentacles all over the world. I'm just going a little nuts here, trapped in a room when I want to be out hunting."

Carswell shifted gears. "How's Feck working out?"

"He's a pretty capable tech, but there's a lot of stuff to extract from this hard drive. And we haven't even scratched the surface." Maxwell rubbed his eyes.

"Max, you need to get some ground time and recharge your batteries." Carswell placed a hand on his shoulder. "Let Feck go through the hard drive and get it together. I'm going to assign a junior agent to extrapolate the information, to free you up with the field stuff. But remember, you're the SAC now, not a ground pounder. You go lie down for a while, a minimum of six hours. After that, I'll authorize a bird into Lawrenceville and Syracuse for the morning. By that time, maybe we'll know more about Pittsburgh and if there's a connection."

"What about Gusa?"

"Well, if he's as hot as you say, we'll put him in a hole to keep him safe. We're coordinating with our branch of INTERPOL, and they're going to provide a security detail to help out."

"Okay, who's the junior agent?" Maxwell asked.

"I haven't figured that out yet." Carswell stifled a yawn and rubbed his eyes using the thumb and index on his right hand. He blinked and said, "Go and get some sleep. I'll step in and talk to Feck. You'll have help in here before you wake up." Maxwell wanted to go back in, read the document in the ZIP file, but for the first time, Carswell was looking at him sternly. "You're no good to me if you're walking around like a zombie. Get your ass into a bunk, and I'll take care of it."

Fifteen minutes later, Maxwell was in what used to be Bailey's office. His office now. The blinds were pulled and the lights off. As he removed his shoes, random thoughts swirled in his head. This was chaos, and he hated it. The picture in the ZIP was from a Highwayman crime scene. Maxwell wasn't sure which. The Word document was probably...

Probably what, he mused. *A love letter between killers?* He lay back on the couch, sure he wouldn't be able to go to sleep. There was so much to do, and they had no idea where the Highwayman was or who he was with. *In Pittsburgh? Probably.* How was he going to put this all together? How did Julian keep it all together? How did…

Maxwell slept.

2

13 November 2008

Kirkland Island, PA

It was late into the afternoon, almost 4:30 p.m. The snow had stopped falling a few hours before. Above, the sun had emerged from the dispersing clouds, warming the air and melting the snow. From beneath the slush, patches of brown and black emerged. Before being blanketed in the November flurries, the street had been mud-soaked by the many contractor vehicles and equipment. Now, with the onslaught of police vehicles coming and going, the road was coated with the muddy brown of mixed snow and dirt.

They'd worked their way from house to house, rechecking each victim for foreign entities. The worst was revisiting the children. Halsey went over each with Jack Fraser until both were satisfied that no other calling cards had been left by the killers. During this, Oggy took care of the logistics of transport. Some food was brought in and there were rotating breaks for investigators to get a bite. Halsey ignored the breaks and continued until they were done. Then the bodies were removed one by one, taken in procession to the city morgue. Finished with the gruesome task, the investigators left the scene, and the techs from Special Investigations came and did a last cursory look before sealing the houses up.

Bob Halsey stood quietly in the background as Oggy addressed the reporters on the scene. For now, there was just a handful of them, three television crews, two newspapers, and a radio reporter gathered outside the barrier. Word hadn't got out just yet, but when it did, the crowd of curious minds would grow substantially. Oggy was good at handling public relations. Halsey, on the other hand? Not so good. It wasn't for the usual self-righteous reasons. He just found their presence to be a distraction. He would be second-guessing himself enough as the investigation progressed. He didn't need outsiders breathing down his neck. It was tough enough keeping it together with his superiors. Best to leave that stuff to Oggy. Then again, Oggy wasn't giving them anything to chew on.

"How many victims are there, Detective?" a reporter from Fox News asked.

"There are eleven victims," Oggy responded.

A hush fell over the crowd. Mumblings. Someone even said, "Shit." Another repeated the number, and then the questions and speculation rolled.

"Is this a gang-related crime?"

"I will not speculate on the nature of the crime until our investigators have had a chance to gather and evaluate all of the evidence." Oggy's tone was even, but authoritarian. He raised his right hand and pointed to the radio reporter. "Next question."

"Is it domestic?"

"I already addressed that," he snapped and then took a measured breath. This was all an act. Oggy called it "controlling the scrum." Halsey had seen him use this tactic time and again. Making them think you're pissed off, putting them on the defensive, and then laying down the parameters. "Look, what I can tell you is that there are eleven victims, that it is a horrendous crime, that our investigators will be working around the clock to examine all evidence, and that we will hold a formal press conference, once we have a better understanding of the evidence. Until then, I will not speculate and would ask you to exercise the same restraint."

Halsey thought about the SD card and its contents. It was a calling card; of this, he was sure. But what had they left and why? Pictures, most likely photographs, or maybe a manifesto, like the Unabomber or Zodiac.

Yeah, it was a message, no doubt about it.

The receding sun was beating against the snow and wet sheen of exposed asphalt, stabbing into his eyes. He squinted against the blur of Oggy's sports jacket. His mild drunkenness had receded during the hours of investigation, transitioning his state of mind to a waking sober hangover. He felt like shit.

Come on, Oggy, wrap this bullshit up, he thought.

But the conference continued, and Bob Halsey's pulse beat in his temples, doling out a well-deserved, post drunk headache. He squinted against the receding daylight, listening to voices far off, engaged in dialogue that sounded alien, while he continued his internal inventory of what he knew.

Four perpetrators? Could it be a cult thing, like the Manson family? Maybe, but for some reason, that didn't feel right. Cult killings were often about making a statement, pushing an agenda. He thought about the mass murders, the blood-smeared messages left by Charlie Manson's disciples: DEATH TO PIGS! Helter Skelter!

Well, maybe that was what they left on the SD card?

Maybe, but he doubted it. Four killers, four houses in a quiet suburban setting. This had been in the works for a while. While Manson might have groomed his disciples to commit murder, they weren't as organized or even as intelligent as this group.

Bunch of drugged-out hippies who were brainwashed into the killing by a complete psychopath. Bobby pushed the cult idea off. He didn't really think these eleven killings were cult-related, but then that left the question. If it wasn't a cult killing, then what was it?

I don't know.

A hand touched his shoulder. It was Oggy.

"We're all done here, Bobby," he said.

3

Police Headquarters

Pittsburgh, PA

They interviewed the Keenes separately. Cliff Keene told them about Shawna wanting to "take a peek" at the brickwork on the finishing house, about the open door and seeing the outstretched arm in the doorway.

"Did Shawna see it?" Bobby asked.

"No." Cliff Keene's eyes were unfocused, lost in the memory. He was hunched over, his shoulders broken by the weight of what he'd seen.

"Why did you go in?"

"What?"

"When you saw her arm, why did you enter the house?" There was no accusation in Bobby's tone. He asked the question for two reasons: one was to bring Cliff Keene back to the room and the other was interest. "Why didn't you just call 911 right then?"

"I don't know." He was focused on Halsey now, considering the question. "I guess it's like… I don't know… you see something like that, and you think to yourself, 'That isn't real,' so I stepped through the door. Even when I saw her, I still couldn't believe it."

"But you went farther into the house, Cliff. You went into the kids' room?"

"I did."

"Why?"

Cliff stared back at him, feeling the sting of the question. "Should I have a lawyer here?"

"Do you think you've done something that would require an attorney?"

"I didn't do anything," he spat. "Remember? I called you guys."

Halsey leaned over the table. "Yes, you did, and I don't think you had anything to do with this, but I'm still at a loss as to why you went deeper into the house. Your wife was in the car, there's a dead woman sprawled out in the foyer, and you kept going. Why? Weren't you afraid?"

"The picture," Cliff said.

Bobby leaned in farther. "What picture?"

Cliff Keene's eyes became glassy, tears welled up, spilled, and tracked down his cheeks, but his voice did not falter. "The two kids. There was a picture of them on the mantle just above her."

"Okay?" Bobby remembered it.

"I don't know, Detective Halsey, when I saw them, I just couldn't... You know... I couldn't leave until I checked. God knows I wish I hadn't. I wish we'd just stayed home last night." He buried his face in his hands, pushing his bangs up off his forehead, and then what little restraint he'd maintained came out in great coughing gulps. "We bought a lot there! Oh my God. How are we going to move in there after that? Why didn't we just stay home?"

Halsey reached out, placing a reassuring hand on Cliff Keene's shoulder, and squeezed it. "A lot of people would've run, and rightly so, Cliff. You went in because you're a decent guy. It's going to take some time to come to terms with this."

He then asked about the van.

"When did you first see the van?"

"When we arrived. I spotted it coming up the street. At first, I didn't, you know... give it much thought. I figured it was probably a contractor, but I saw the one guy walking up to that house. It wasn't until after that I put it together."

"Put it together?"

"That the guys in the van killed those people!"

"Can you describe the one you saw?"

"No, he was too far away. He wasn't fat."

"What about his height? Hair color?"

"He was so far away. I wasn't focused."

"Okay, what can you tell me about the van?"

"It was white. Looked pretty new. One of those cargo vans you see on job sites all the time. It was a Chevy, had the word 'Express' next to the logo on the back door. And the back windows on the van were covered with tin foil."

"From inside?"

"Yeah, when we rolled up behind it, I thought they were going to get out and kill us too. I've never been so scared in my life."

"But you never got a plate number."

"I didn't see a plate on it. Or maybe I just didn't see it. I thought they were going to kill us too. I was getting ready to bolt. So, I guess I wasn't really looking."

Bobby interviewed Cliff Keene for another ten minutes, covering the same questions, and when it seemed he had everything, he reached into his pocket and pulled out two business cards. One for him and one for Oggy.

"If you think of anything else you call me or my partner, night or day."

Cliff Keene took the cards, removed a business card holder from his pocket, and inserted them. "I can't understand."

"Understand what?"

"How do you guys do it? How do you go to work every day and deal with this horror? I'd go nuts." He was wiping the tears away with the back of his hand.

Oggy appeared at the window of the interview room. That meant he was done with Mrs. Keene as well. Bobby wanted to compare notes with him.

"It isn't easy, but we do what we have to. Please call if you think of anything else." He stood up and shook Keene's hand. "I think my partner is done interviewing your wife, so let's get you folks on your way."

They stepped out into the hall. Shawna Keene was sitting on a bench. "We're all wrapped up for now," Oggy said. "Could I get a uniform to drive you people home? You must be exhausted."

"That's okay. We'll manage," Cliff Keene said and wandered down the hall toward his wife. She also looked emotionally drained. Her makeup was pretty much washed away from the tears and subsequent smearing.

"Anything useful?" Oggy whispered.

"I've got a pretty good description of the van. No plate, but I'm guessing that it isn't registered with our killers."

"Yeah, you're probably right."

"What about the SD card?"

"Fraser hasn't called yet. I've worked with this guy before. He's a bit of a procedural hard ass. We don't want to push him." Oggy watched the Keenes push through the double door and disappear. "Did you ask him why he decided to go tromping through an entire crime scene before calling 911?"

"I did."

"And?"

"He saw a picture of the twins and went to investigate."

"Get the fuck out of here?"

"That's his story," Halsey said.

"You believe him?"

"Yeah, I do. Sometimes people do strange shit."

Oggy smiled. "Lucky for him he didn't walk in on the killing."

"Lucky for us as well. We made some gains on this. We're looking for a newer model Chevy Express panel van. Keene said the back windows were foiled over."

"Probably stolen."

"Most likely."

"You think they're all men, Bobby? Think it's a cult thing?"

"You been reading my mind, Oggy?" Bobby smiled.

"You're not hard to read, Detective Halsey. Tell you what. Let's get that description out over the wire. Check and see if there have been any thefts, and I'll give Fraser a call and gently nudge him regarding our SD card."

"Okay."

4

The Pittsburgh Mobile Crime Unit, MCU, buzzed with the activity of ringing phones, clacking keyboards, while officers moved in and about the room carrying paperwork. The story was now garnering international attention, which meant the upper echelon were already gathering in their offices to implement a plan to try and close the case as quickly as possible. The mayor of Pittsburgh was already promising that they would catch the perpetrators of "this heinous and disturbing crime," and that was being broadcasted across all the major news networks.

Bobby knew what was coming. They would be putting together a task force. It was inevitable; this was a front-page case now, and it would continue being the lead story for the foreseeable future unless something bigger came along, like a war or presidential assassination. A task force would be good, that would lighten the load and allow him to pass off some of the mundane tasks and focus on footwork. They already had uniformed officers canvassing the contract companies involved in the Grand Acres Development. He hoped they would get a hit off the stolen vehicle reports, known as 48s.

In the last month, twenty-seven vans in the greater Pittsburgh area had been stolen. Bobby was sitting at his desk crossing off vehicles first by type and then description, but not by model. Not yet, at least. He wasn't sure of Cliff Keene's assertion that the van was a Chevy. Witnesses made mistakes like that all the time. So, it would be best to keep all-white panel vans on the list and rule them out one by one. Thus far, he was down to six vans, knocking out all the minivans on the list and keeping three white Chevys, a white Ford, a white Dodge, and a light gray Chevy.

"What have you got?" Oggy asked, leaning over his shoulder.

"Six possible, if in fact our suspect vehicle was stolen. I kind of hope it wasn't, might be easier to track them down." Bobby moved his chair right; Oggy was a bit of a space invader. "You wanna sit in my lap, Oggy?"

"The chair would never support both of us." He grinned and moved into the cubicle and sat at his own desk which mirrored Bobby's. "I'm waiting on a call back from Fraser."

Bobby heard a commotion outside the maze of office dividers and poked his head up. The chief of police and the captain were entering the lieutenant's office. "Can you smell that?"

"Yeah." Oggy gave him a skeptical frown. "The upper echelon is now scrambling for cover thanks to a mayor who doesn't know how to keep his mouth shut."

"Task force."

"Yeah."

"So, while the suits are deciding who's in charge, I'm going to have Hicks track down these addresses, and see if we can get a hit. Who knows?" Hicks worked in the stolen vehicle division of MCU and had gotten Halsey the list.

"Better do it fast, because there will be changes coming."

5

A meeting was convened in a conference room at 6:00 p.m. In attendance were Chief Douglas, Captain Campbell,

Lieutenant King, Oggy, himself, and a female outsider Bobby guessed to be FBI. The chief came forward first, talking about the crimes and the immense pressure to find the perps, then he passed the mic off to the captain who parroted the same, and then passed it off to King.

"Thank you, Chief and Lieutenant. After a closed meeting which involved the mayor, it has been decided that we need to put together a task force. This meeting is a preamble to that announcement, which will convene tomorrow. Detectives Chartrand and Halsey, you have been selected to lead this force," King said. Oggy nodded and Bobby stared over at the stranger. She was FBI. And to confirm, King said, "Joining the task force will be Special Agent Michelle Leigh from the Pittsburgh Bureau Office."

The agent now has a name, Bobby thought as she nodded toward the lieutenant. She appeared to be in her early forties, dressed in a pants suit, her jet-black hair purposely cut short, exposing her ears which were tucked neatly against the sides of her head. She wasn't bad looking but appeared prim and proper, even uptight.

King continued, "I trust that you people will extend her every courtesy as she assists us in finding the perpetrators of this horrific crime. Agent Leigh, would you like to say a few words?"

She nodded. "Thank you, Lieutenant King." Then she turned her gaze to meet Halsey and Oggy. "I'll be brief. The Bureau has assigned me to your task force after the chief put in a request with the Pittsburgh office. My background is in forensic profiling; I served for five years at Quantico in the Behavioral Sciences Unit and will assist you in any way I can."

"Thanks," Oggy said.

"Yeah," Bobby chimed in. "Same goes here."

"Okay, well, I won't take up a bunch of time, except to say that I am a team player, and the Bureau is here to help. I'll leave it there."

"Thank you, Agent Leigh," King said. "Oggy, you'll oversee the task force and all reporting will be through the proper channels. You'll also be handling the administrative needs once we get this thing rolling."

Better you than me, Bobby thought. But it wasn't spiteful. Oggy was suited for this sort of work. This was the last rung on the ladder before stepping into his own command. King wouldn't give this sort of responsibility to Halsey. Diplomacy wasn't his high point, nor was toeing the political line when it came to dealing with the higher ups.

"All right, I'll be alerting the appropriate people and by tomorrow morning, I want this task force operational and on the hunt. Anything else, Chief?" King gave the floor to the chief of police.

He took in a slow, somber breath, removed his wire-framed glasses, and rubbed his eyes. Then he got up from his seat and moved across the room until he stood right in front of Oggy and Halsey. Chief Douglas was in his mid-fifties, a stoic-looking man with piercing blue eyes that had faded with age. He tapped his glasses against his leg and took another measured breath. "This is some really terrible business, Detectives Ogden and Halsey. This is mass murder. Do we have any leads other than the white van?"

"We're chasing down a few, sir," Oggy answered.

"Four perpetrators. That's what I'm to understand?"

"Yes, sir. Four perps."

"Eight adults and three children." This was not a question, it was reflective. He whispered this time, in a seething tone, "They killed three children."

"Yes, sir."

Halsey was mute, but he held the chief's gaze.

"People this bold are going to do this again." He replaced his glasses, then laid a hand on the shoulder of each man. "We need to put this one down very fast. I need everything you got, Detectives, and I'm counting on you to get it done."

And then the chief's voice lowered so only they could hear. "You get these fuckers."

"Yes, sir," Oggy said.

Halsey only nodded, but he knew that getting these guys before they struck again was going to be a tall order.

***

CHAPTER 8 – PADDLEFISH INCIDENT

1

Major Crimes Unit

Pittsburgh, Pennsylvania

It is well known, within any police organization, that the first forty-eight hours of a murder investigation are considered a crucial window for solving a case. Chasing down leads, canvassing for witnesses, and securing evidence is utmost on the mind of the investigators who catch the case. Failure to do so, especially with stranger killings, can lead to the trail going cold and the chance of conviction being minimized. Along with the fact that the murders were now garnering international media meant that Detectives Halsey and Ogden, along with Special Agent Leigh, would be pulling a long first night.

They were seated at a round table in one of the conference rooms at the Major Crimes Unit. This would be their base of operations, a place where they could convene and share information. After breaking away from the lieutenant's office, the three exchanged names.

"Okay, let's get right down to it," Oggy said. "Your specialty is behavioral science, Michelle, so can you work up a profile for us based on what we have?"

Leigh was rolling a ballpoint pen back and forth between her thumb and index finger. On the table sat a leather-bound folder emblazoned with the FBI logo. "It'll take a bit of research. Give me everything you've got, and I can do a workup once I've had a chance to review the files. You give me everything you've got, and I should have a full report for you within the next…" She looked at her watch. "Ten hours, but it will be a profile with moving goalposts."

"Sure, we get that," Bobby said. "You going to feed this information into Quantico?"

"Absolutely. I know everyone thinks that profilers are psychic crime fighters with superhuman powers, but you know that's all bullshit, right?"

"Like *Criminal Minds*?" Bobby smiled.

"Exactly, fucking television. So, yeah, I can get a profile based on what we feed through the database. Then I'll give you my opinion. How quickly can you get me crime scene photos of the bodies in place?"

Bobby smiled, pulled out his cell phone, and punched a number in. "Hi, I'm looking for Officer Baden." He nodded to Leigh and Oggy. "Yeah, I'll wait." He looked to Leigh. "What else do you need, Michelle?"

"Crime scene pics, the murder book, copies of all officers' notes from the scene, witness testimony…" Leigh answered.

"In other words, everything," Bobby said, and before he could laugh, he heard Baden announce himself on the phone. "Gene. Hi, how are you? Listen, where are you with the crime scene pics?"

"I'm categorizing them right now," Baden said.

"Can you bring everything up to conference room four? I have an FBI Agent here who is going to want to look at everything."

"Sure. Is it true they're putting together a task force?"

"Are you eavesdropping on the chief, Gene?"

"Uh, no. There's a rumor."

"Tell you what, Gene, get those pics up here, and we'll let you know."

"Is a half-hour okay?"

"Half hour?" Bobby asked Leigh.

"That'll be fine," Leigh replied.

"Okay, be there in thirty minutes, Bob." Baden cut him off.

"See you soon, Gene." He hung up his phone. Oggy was sitting across from him writing down names he wanted on the task force. Bob said to Oggy, "Add Baden's name to that. We can use him to shoot any other evidence and he can assist with…"

"He's already on the list, Bobby," Oggy said without looking up. Then his phone rang. "Detective Chartrand. Hello, Jack. Perfect. When can we send someone over to pick it up?"

Bobby already knew whom Oggy was talking to. He guessed the SD card must have been finished. He was antsy to find out what was on that card. Bobby strained to hear what the ME was saying.

"Not until morning? One more test? Okay, I'll have a man there first thing to courier it back."

"Shit," Bobby whispered and fell back in his seat.

"Sure, you can sit in, but I don't have to caution you about confidentiality, right?"

The inaudible voice was a bit more animated.

Leigh cocked her head sideways, grinning slightly. Bobby joined her, and Oggy, who was getting an earful, was smiling from ear to ear.

"Okay, so the lab will release it in the morning? That's good. We're going to be in a conference in the morning. We'd really like to get our mitts on that card and see what is on it before we sit down with the bosses."

Fraser continued his muffled reply.

"Okay, Jack, we're in the MCU wing, conference room four." He ended the call and set his phone on the tabletop. "We'll be here at 7:00 a.m. with bells on."

"I thought you said Fraser wasn't the kind you wanted to push?" Bobby said. Leigh was smirking as well. "Sounds like he didn't appreciate being lectured about confidentiality."

"I said he wasn't to be pushed, but I didn't say I couldn't give him a poke with a stick. I just love fucking with the crusty ones."

"You're a masochist, Oggy."

"I just hope there's something worth keeping confidential on that SD card. Something that will help us get these assholes."

"Amen to that."

"Okay, we've got half an hour. Let's get a list together, so I have something to pass on to the lieutenant before Baden gets here."

2

Ohio River

25 Miles Northwest of Neville Island

Greg Rollo was running his riverboat at a quarter throttle fifteen feet from the riverbank. Behind the flat-bottomed boat, two rods were set up on a trolling rig, skimming the river for paddlefish. Paddlefish were what some called the Ohio shark, a prehistoric thing that was very popular with Asian fishermen.

"Asians will eat anything," Rollo told his buddy Roger, who was keeping an eye on the rods and the bank, which was thick with scrub and low-lying trees. The engine on the riverboat engine cycled up and down as they ran against the current.

Both Greg and Roger had a can of Rolling Rock between their legs as they steered even closer to the shore. Greg had never actually pulled one of these supposedly prehistoric paddlefish from the river, which was evident by his method of trolling. A paddlefish would as much go after a trolling lure as a snail would play the flute. Roger knew this, had even looked the bloody thing up on the web, but he played along with Greg's hair-brained scheme because he liked Greg and didn't have the heart to tell him he was an idiot. Besides, Greg had an eighteen pack of Rolling Rock in that cooler, minus two, and Roger was more than willing to help him drink it.

The early evening was sizing up to be a nice one, the clouds were breaking up, and the sun was a glowing red ball dancing on the surface of the river. Roger looked back at the lures as they danced across the surface. He took a swig and grinned. Rollo sure didn't know shit about fishing. Roger took another swig, crushed the can, lifted the lid on Rollo's cooler, and reached for another. "You want one, Greg?"

Rollo turned back, crushed his can, and tossed it into the mouth of the open cooler.

"I'll take that as a yes," Roger said. He reached in, pulled out the first can, and set it on the empty seat behind him. Then as he bent over to grab a can for his buddy, he felt himself being catapulted forward into the floor of the boat. He didn't have a chance to put his hands out to break his fall and he went down on his belly. The ice and beer in the cooler banged miserably against the hard plastic edge of the cooler and then spilled over.

As the ice from the cooler spilled out, Roger could feel the air being knocked from his lungs. His ears filled with the sounds of the outboard prop as its whine pitched up and out of the water, and then through his confusion, he could feel the icy water running up along his sides. But that was the least of his worries because he'd felt the sickening taste of copper in his mouth, and there was a pop that he was pretty sure was the cartilage in his nose snapping. The prop whined even louder, then there was a hard clunk. The motor quit.

Apparently, Rollo isn't much of a boater either, he thought.

He thought they'd hit the bank, that Rollo had veered right too close to the shore. But when he lifted his head, he could see that they were still a good ten feet from the shore.

Maybe a rock then. He scanned the boat, and it took a second to realize that Rollo wasn't on board. What the hell had happened. What had they hit? He was up on his knees now, the boat listing beneath him. Where was Rollo? He grabbed the side of the boat and looked around.

"Greg, where the fuck are you, man?" The windshield was folded over, the plexus had splintered out across the bow. The chrome frame was twisted and bent. Roger looked left then right, panic beginning to invade his thoughts. He looked out across the Ohio, but saw nothing, then he turned his eyes back to the bank and felt his heart drop like a runaway elevator. "Oh Jesus fuck, Greg, how'd you get up there?"

3

Barely conscious, Greg stared back at Roger, his nose looked like it had been sculpted out of mashed potatoes and ketchup. He was still wondering, *how the fuck did I wind up here?*

He'd been turned around on the seat looking at Roger when he suddenly felt himself doing the backstroke through the air. Everything had slowed down as he floated through the air, and though he felt his right collarbone bend when he blasted through the windshield, that was minor. His ears were ringing and his left one sizzled with pain from being split in half. But that wasn't the worst of it. When he came to a full stop, there had been a snapping crunch of bone serenading to the vertebrae in his lower back. Greg wasn't dead, but he was in bad shape, and he would have to be cut down. Through the numb disconnect and muffled ringing he could hear Roger calling to him. "Mreb! Mreb! Mitts monna me mallmight!"

4

Roger was climbing over the bow, his eyes darting between Greg and the water. The boat shifted slightly, but it wasn't going anywhere. Once he reached the edge of the bow, he looked down and saw it. Through the chocolate milk haze of the river, he could see the outline. From up here, it looked beige. He reached into the water and four inches down he felt the flat steel roof and understood what it was they had hit.

"Roger," Greg called weakly.

Roger looked up.

"Get rid of the beer." Greg coughed, a grimace of pain in his face. Then he swallowed and his brought his gaze up to meet Roger's. "After you're done that, call me an ambulance."

"Myeah, mokay, man," Roger said.

Roger called 911 first and then started firing the beer cans into the river.

5

Major Crimes Unit

Pittsburgh, PA

Agent Leigh was going through the murder book when Baden arrived with a memory stick containing all the photos. "Murder book" was a nickname coined by law enforcement. It was a digital case file which would grow throughout the investigation. There would be a hard copy of this murder book, but the digital age made it easier for investigators to access information by logging into the MCU database. As she scanned the work in progress, notes were being entered in real time. At present, she was logged in under Halsey's account, but Oggy had already sought to get her an access name to log in on her own. By this time tomorrow, she would be one of six who would have full access to the file.

"These haven't been entered yet," Baden said to Halsey and turned to Leigh. "Hi, Gene Baden."

"Michelle Leigh." She shook his hand, not looking up.

"Special Agent Michelle Leigh," Oggy said.

"FBI?" Baden's voice was laced with awe.

"Yes." She smiled and glanced up. "Those are the photos? Can you upload them from here and add them to the file, or do I have to view them separately?"

"I'm still categorizing them. I have each set broken down by location, but before uploading them, I need to do a bit more cataloging. Detective Halsey said you guys needed them right away, so here I am." He couldn't take his eyes off her, but it wasn't sexual attraction, just professional fascination.

"When can you have them cataloged, Gene?" Bobby asked.

"By the end of my shift. I'm pulling some OT on this one. So, you guys are all the task force?"

"So are you." Oggy leaned forward. "You'll be notified tomorrow by the lieutenant."

Baden grinned.

Bobby leaned in. "But you don't know that, do you, Gene?"

"I'm on the task force?"

"I hear a peep about this, and you'll be shooting pictures down at the accident reporting center." Oggy pointed a finger without looking up. "You got that, Baden?"

"I got it. Fuck, this is cool!"

Halsey stuck out his hand. "Welcome aboard, Gene."

Baden shook his hand. "Thanks, Bobby. And you too, Detective Chartrand."

Oggy looked up from his notes. "Just remember what I said, Baden. One peep and you'll be out of MCU and into the traffic division, taking pictures of fender benders. All it will take is a phone call."

"I get it," Baden said.

There was silence then.

Leigh broke this by tugging at Baden's arm and asking, "Can you help me get these onto my laptop?"

"I'd be glad to." Baden dragged his seat next to hers and uncapped the memory stick. "May I?"

"Absolutely."

Bobby's phone rang. "Halsey."

"Bobby, it's Pete." Peter Gillis worked in the Auto Squad of the Investigations Branch of Pittsburgh PD. "I think I might have something for you guys."

"What have you got, Pete?"

"We got a late model Chevy panel van being recovered from the Ohio River. Might be the vehicle you're looking for."

"They already have it?"

"No, they're still trying to figure out how to pull it out of the river. If you get down there, you might catch them when they're still at it."

"Where are they at, Pete?"

Bobby took down the information and got out of the chair. "Auto Squad is recovering a van twenty-three miles northwest of Neville Island. I got a feeling it might be our suspect vehicle. Who wants to come for a ride?"

"I'd like to go, but I gotta get this manpower list made up," Oggy said. "Probably just a wreck anyway, Bob."

"Maybe. How about you, Michelle?"

She glanced up from the computer. "I better dig into this so I can have some semblance of a profile developed by morning."

"God damned office rats," Bobby sighed.

"I'll go," Baden said.

"Okay, Gene, bring your camera."

Gene Baden stood up. "Should I give my boss a call?"

"I'll call him," Oggy said. "You kids have fun on your field trip."

6

Bobby took the driver's seat, handed Gene the paper directions, and told him to keep an eye out for landmarks. They drove along Western Avenue and merged onto the PA 65, going north for twenty-three miles following the arch of the Ohio River. Highway 65, also known as the Ohio River Boulevard, snaked through the industrial outskirts of the city, offering occasional glimpses of the river. Once they got to the bend in the river, they crossed Beaver River and took the industrial road down to the riverbank.

"There's a sewage treatment plant just off the Mulberry Street Extension," Bobby told Gene.

"Is that where it is?" Gene asked.

"No, just a landmark, but that gets us in the grid."

"You think this is the van?"

"Probably not, but I gotta rule it out."

Gene spotted the sign: LAGER SEWAGE TREATMENT.

They followed the road which changed from broken, pitted concrete to worn asphalt and eventually became oily gravel. Even if Gene hadn't seen the sign, they smelled the pungent stench of methane and could have followed their noses.

Approximately thirty-five minutes after leaving the MCU, they found themselves rolling into a lot where two tow trucks, one State and two Pittsburgh patrol cars, congregated. An ambulance passed them on the way, and Bobby's heart sank.

Maybe it was a wild goose chase after all. Probably some dipshit who'd driven his rig into the river. "Fuck."

"What?" Gene was looking around. "What's wrong?"

"Maybe nothing."

They rolled up to the state police car and parked. Bobby got out and Gene followed. He swept his sports jacket back to reveal his badge and walked toward the officers who were assembled with the tow truck drivers and a scruffy looking fellow with a mashed-up face.

"Who's in charge?" Bobby asked.

A uniform police officer stepped forward. "That would be me. Are you Detective Halsey?" He put out his hand.

Bobby took it. "Yeah, how are you? You know Pete Gillis?"

"Sure, Pete's the godfather of my two daughters. Name's Ralph Clemmons, Detective."

"Okay, Ralph, you can call me Bobby. We can save all the rank stuff for the higher-ups." Bobby released his hand. "This is Gene Baden, he's our photographer."

Clemmons nodded. Baden nodded back. "Pete said you'd be coming. You're working the Yard Street Massacre?"

The other officers glanced over, and the scruffy-looking guy, who looked like he'd been talking when he should have been listening, glanced their way.

"Ralph, take a walk with me." Bobby didn't wait, he just walked, and though it took a second for Clemmons to understand, he picked up his pace and followed Bobby away from the gathering.

"Okay, what's the deal?"

"First, get the civilian into a car. Second, don't talk about the investigation again and, unless I ask you a specific question, you stay mum on that. Okay?"

Clemmons frowned.

"We've got eleven dead people and killers on the loose. You've got a bunch of civilians down there whom I don't want to see on *Fox and Friends* or that fucking *Situation Room with Wolf Blitzer*. We understand each other?"

"Yeah." Clemmons rubbed his nose. "Sorry."

"No problem, Ralph. This is how we're going to play it. You fill me in, and I'm going to dispute any connection between the vehicle you guys are pulling out of the river with Yard Street."

"Do you think it's connected?" Ralph looked him in the eye.

"I have no idea, but discretion is of the utmost importance."

"Okay, Detective."

"Bobby."

"Okay, Bobby."

"Fill me in, Ralph. What have we got here?"

"Okay, we got a couple local boys out for a few cold ones and running the river more as a social event than doing any actual fishing. Anyway, they hit a vehicle submerged approximately a foot below the surface and the guy driving the boat was catapulted ashore, hurt pretty bad, as a matter of fact. Probably broke his back. They had to pull him out of a tree and bring him out on a backboard. The other guy back there, he's the one who called it in. Follow me, and I'll show you what I've got so far." Clemmons led him back past the crowd and toward the riverbank. Two-wheel ruts led right down to the river and disappeared. "We think this is where they pushed it in."

Bobby looked down at the wheel ruts and saw weathered footprints on either side of those ruts. There were at least three pairs of footprints in the muck, possibly four, but the snow and fluctuating temperatures had practically destroyed the footprints and tread marks. Still, it wouldn't hurt to order a couple of plaster impressions to see if there was a match to the footprints they'd gotten at Yard Street. "Okay, this area is off limits."

"I'll get it taped up."

"Where's the vehicle?"

"It's about four hundred yards downstream. We think it probably floated down there on the current before it sank completely and settled."

"Can we access the van from shore?"

"No, the bank is covered in rocks, and there are way too many trees. We've really got two choices. We can try and recover it by water with a barge, or tug it back upstream and pull it out here."

"Where they pushed it in?" Bobby felt more and more that this was their van. "Give me a second, Ralph." He pulled out his phone and hit the speed dial. "Oggy, I need a dive team down here."

"You think this is our van?"

"Yeah, I'm not a hundred percent, but if I were a betting man…"

"Okay, I'll talk to the lieutenant and see what I can do."

"Call me back." He hung up and said to Gene, "Hold the tow truck drivers, and get that other guy out of here. Once you've done that, you can take me down the river, and show me the van."

They walked back up the bank. "Okay, well, looks like this is just an abandoned vehicle," Officer Clemmons said to the tow truck drivers. "Can you boys hang about? I'll have my boss put in an invoice for all your time."

"Any idea how long, Ralph?" the younger of the two truck drivers asked.

"Could be a while, until we figure out what we're dealing with here. We'll pay you boys for your time." He pulled out two business cards and handed them to the tow truck drivers.

"Is this about Yard Street?" asked the older one.

"No," Bobby said. "I'm looking for a pickup truck."

He didn't look convinced. The tow truck drivers strolled back to their vehicles to wait.

The state cop came forward, "If you like, I can run Roger back up to his pickup."

Clemmons went over to see Roger with Bobby in tow. "Roger, this is my card, and this is Detective Halsey's card. You think of anything, you give us a call."

Roger was pinching his nose, even though it had stopped bleeding. He was able to articulate better, but certain words were had. "Myeah, Yust another stolen vehicle, huh?" Roger gave him a skeptical grin.

Bobby reached out, placed an authoritative hand on Roger's shoulder. "Roger, I'm bringing a dive team down here to look at this vehicle. I'm going to get them to look around in the water and see what else they can find."

"Myeah, so?"

"So…" Bobby moved closer. "Drinking and boating is a chargeable offense in Pennsylvania. I see you on the news tonight, I'll make it my mission to dust whatever we find in that river for your prints and charge you." He hoped this guy was too dumb to realize he was bluffing.

Roger removed his fingers from his nose and his speaking improved. "We weren't drinking, and I wasn't even driving the boat."

"I can smell the beer all over you. You keep your trap shut. You hear me?"

Roger nodded.

Bobby pulled his arm back. "You okay to drive?"

"I'm fine."

"Bullshit," Bobby said and turned to the state cop. "Can you give this guy a ride to the ER?"

"If you're done with me. Sure," the state cop said.

"I'm fine," Roger protested.

"Shut up," Bobby snapped, then back to the state cop, "I'd appreciate it if you could give him a lift, I'm done with you."

"No problem." The state cop took Roger to his car, leaving Bobby with the two Pittsburgh uniforms. Before anything else happened, they taped the area off, and then Bobby read them the riot act.

Clemmons led Bobby and Baden down the bank; the terrain was rocky, and they had to move with great care not to catch an ankle in the many crevasses. The few spots where it was flat, mucky ground sucked at their shoes. Bobby's feet were soaked by the time they reached the spot.

From the shore, he could see the outline of the van fading in and out of the murk. It was parallel to the bank, nose down away in front of the current. "Gene, shoot this, will you?"

"Sure thing." Baden pulled out his camera and went to work.

"So, they push the thing into the water and before it sinks, the current grabs it, and it rolls down in here?" Bobby was looking up the bank, back in the direction from which they'd come.

"Yeah, that would make sense. Probably just rolled along the bank until it got hung up on something."

Bobby's phone rang; it was an unknown number.

"Halsey."

"Detective Halsey, my name is Officer Olshaker. I'm a master diver with the River Rescue Unit."

"You guys on your way?"

"We're in the river, Detective. Should be at your location within the next five minutes."

Bobby listened and could hear the distant drone of the boat. "Great, the vehicle is on the right bank, so come in slow. You know where the sewage treatment plant is?"

"The Lager Plant? Yeah."

"We're about four hundred yards downstream from there," Bobby told him. "What kind of boat are you bringing, Olshaker?"

"We're coming in a SeaArk."

"Pardon my ignorance, is that a big boat?"

"Big enough, thirty footer. Why?"

"Just wondering. See you when you get here." Bobby had an idea, but first, he wanted to make sure this was their vehicle. He put the phone back into his pocket and gazed into the murky water. It looked like a van. He stepped back from the bank.

Bobby, Clemmons, and Baden stood quietly on the bank as the drone of the rescue boat's twin motors closed in. While this went on, Bobby imagined the perpetrators rolling into the lot, turning off the lights, stepping from the vehicle, and pushing it into the murky waters as the snow fell upon them.

7

Recovery of the vehicle was a slow, cautious process. With the assistance of the divers, Bobby confirmed that the back windows of the vehicle were foiled over. They didn't determine if the van had anyone in it because Bobby didn't want it opened for fear of losing more evidence to the current. More, because they might have already, as the driver's window was wide open. What they learned was that the vehicle had not been pushed in in neutral, but driven into the river. The gear selector was in drive. After conferring with Olshaker, both Bobby and Clemmons decided the best way to get the van out of the river was to try and have the SeaArk tow it back the way it had come and then pull it out with the tow trucks. They hooked up the necessary cables and put the van in neutral. Getting it back to its point of entry took less than an hour.

By that time, Oggy had dispatched two more detectives to the scene along with a forensics team to make plaster castings of all the tracks. As Baden took pictures, Bobby walked the perimeter, looking for anything out of the ordinary. It was a fruitless search.

"This is the van?" Clemmons asked.

"Yeah, I think so," Bobby said. The winch from the first tow truck was pulling the vehicle from the river. As the muddy water receded, Bobby saw the foiled windows, then the logo with the word "Express" beside it. "Pretty sure."

The winch on the tow truck hummed mechanically. Downstream, the divers had recovered two unopened Rolling Rocks and little else. Once the vehicle was back on shore Bobby asked everyone, including the tow truck drivers, to gather around.

"Thank you for your help today. I'm sure the rumors have been swirling about the investigation into Yard Street, so that is what I'm going to address right now." He paused and brought his eyes to meet every man in the loose scrum, then he started. "Last night, on a quiet street, four families were brutally murdered. Among the victims, three children. This investigation has gained worldwide attention, and as it stands right now, we still have no idea who the killers are."

All eyes were upon him; they were riveted, hanging on his every syllable. Bobby cleared his throat and continued.

"All of you, police, EMS, and even civilians are now a part of this investigation, and with that comes the responsibility of conduct." He focused on the two tow truck drivers. "I need you not to talk to your friends and neighbors about what you saw here. Anything you say or do could compromise our investigation." He scanned the faces. "Do you understand?"

One by one, they nodded.

Bobby smiled. "Good. You folks did a bang-up job. I'll be contacting your bosses to thank them for sending you to us. Let's get this wrapped up."

Bobby stepped out of the circle and walked back to the car. By now, his shoes were soaked, his socks were spongey, and after standing around, his feet were getting cold. Gene caught up to him, camera bag swinging on his shoulder. It was suppertime, and Bobby realized he hadn't eaten anything all day. "Let's grab a bite on the way back, Gene."

***

CHAPTER 9 – STRAND THEORY

1

Being a functioning alcoholic had its drawbacks. It was all about keeping up appearances, and as much of Bobby wanted to find a bar, he wouldn't. Bobby wouldn't be doing any drinking tonight, maybe not tomorrow or even the day after that. He wanted to, but there was another drug that had him in its grip. The case had become his new girlfriend. He would be continuously focused on it as the pieces started to fall into place.

Bobby and Baden stopped off at a diner on the way back, and he called Oggy to see if they wanted anything.

Oggy said, "No," that he and Michelle were sharing a pizza. Baden was texting someone on his phone; Bobby assumed it was his wife. He looked a bit on the antsy side, but when they sat down, he ordered himself a double cheeseburger with fries and a side of gravy. Bobby got himself a clubhouse sandwich and thought some greasy French fries might absorb some of the hangover.

Or make me puke, he mused.

The waitress poured them each a cup of coffee and brought Bobby a tall glass of iced tea. He drank half of it as Baden finished his text message and put his phone away.

"Little woman?"

"It was my wife earlier. That was my daughter."

Bobby smiled and nodded.

"So, you think that's really the killers' van?"

"Yeah, I'm pretty sure."

"You think it's stolen?"

"On that, I'm almost pretty sure."

"You don't seem too disappointed by that."

"Should I be?"

"Well, yeah, if it's stolen it could be a lot harder to trace back to the perps."

"Yeah? And…"

"Geez, Bobby, don't you feel any pressure? I heard the president commented on the case today." Gene was smiling, but it was an incredulous smile, one that said, "I wouldn't want to be in your position." Before he could answer, the waitress swept in with two plates and set them down. She asked if Bobby wanted more tea, and he nodded, "Yes."

Bobby picked up the bottle of ketchup, squeezed a dark red blob onto his plate while showering the fries with enough salt to give someone high blood pressure just by looking. After the waitress set a fresh iced tea in front of him, he lifted a fry up, thoughtfully, as if there was some knowledge within the crisp shoestring. "I don't give a shit what the higher-ups think. I'm not going any higher up the ladder. So, the answer to your first question is 'No.' I don't feel any pressure from the bosses. Oggy deals with that shit, I don't." He stabbed the fry into the blob of ketchup, spun it, and tossed it into his mouth. The salt made his cheeks involuntarily contract.

"The first question…" He was holding two fries this time and paddled them through the ketchup. "Everything these guys touch leads back to them. They're like loose threads in a sweater. We pull on them, and they will lead us back to their originator. Each strand is significant, but all of them share a common denominator, and that is how we'll catch these guys."

"You seem pretty confident." Baden lifted his burger, took a large bite. The lettuce crunched. "This is good."

Bobby didn't respond to that. Instead, he pulled the toothpick from the clubhouse and bit into it. It was also very good. He was glad they'd stopped. He swallowed his first bite and popped the second half of the quarter into his mouth. Perhaps the turkey was a little dry, but it was real turkey. He washed it back with the iced tea.

"How's your food, boys?" the waitress asked.

Mouth full, Bobby gave a thumbs up.

Gene wiped his chin and said, "Good."

"Can I get you boys more coffee?"

"Two to go," Bobby said. "We'll be done here in about five minutes." The waitress smiled and went off to fill the order. Between bites, he kicked out short sentences. "These guys have left clues everywhere. Even more interesting, they did it on purpose." He was chewing the second quarter of the club. At this rate, he would be finished before Baden had even got in three bites.

"Okay, the branding, even the SD card, but you think they dumped the van in the Ohio on purpose?"

"I do."

"Why?"

"They could've parked that van anywhere. Off the road somewhere, in a park, there's plenty of places in PA where it would've gone unnoticed, but they dumped it in the Ohio where it would be spotted, either by boat or by air. Shit, the thing was only five or six inches below the surface. These guys are taunting us."

"Again, why?"

"They think they're smarter than we are." He went quiet again, eating like a man who'd been starving for several days. He gulped the iced tea, sipped the lukewarm coffee, and the clubhouse was gone. "Let me ask you something, Gene. Why do you think they burned a 4 into the eyes of every victim?"

"Well…" Gene was chewing on a large bite of burger. "I thought maybe they're a cult. Like the Manson gang, maybe?" He swallowed. "The 4 could signify something."

"Like what?"

"Shit, man, you tell me."

Bobby grinned. "Once we get a look at what's on that SD card, I'll give you my opinion. Until then I can only say that I don't think this is a cult thing. At least not in the traditional sense."

He was down to a small stack of fries.

The waitress returned with the fresh coffees. Bobby grabbed the bill, and Baden got the tip. Baden was still chewing when they got into the car. He sipped the coffee as Bobby started the car and asked, "You think these guys have done this before?"

"Possibly. They're definitely going to do it again." Bobby slipped the gearshift into drive and got back on the road. "We might as well get over to Auto Squad and take a closer look." He pulled out his phone and dialed.

"Chartrand."

"Oggy, I'm pretty sure this is our suspect vehicle. What's the chance of getting Cliff Keene in for an ID?"

2

The Auto Squad usually kept stolen vehicles in a lot two blocks over from the main building, but in the case of a violent crime where the MCU was involved, a warehouse was allotted so that investigators and forensics could give the vehicle a thorough going over.

Halsey and Baden arrived just as the van was being winched off the flatbed and onto the warehouse floor. The clubhouse sandwich and fries were now a sickening weight in the pit of Bobby's stomach. So much for food making him feel better. The only way he was going to improve was an uninterrupted stretch of sleep, but that was something he wouldn't be afforded for at least a few more hours, if at all.

A trail of river water stained the route the deck truck had taken back to the warehouse, and now that it sat stationary, the water trickled from every seam down onto the warehouse floor. Bobby walked around the van, careful not to get too close until the driver had finished his unload. Once it was off the ramp, the deck contracted, and the driver working the controls came around to disconnect. "Be done here in a sec," he said.

"Okay, thanks." Bobby got in a little closer and took a glance at the ignition. A set of keys dangled there. The rig hadn't been hotwired. That was strange. Maybe the van would lead back to the perps. He stared down at the floor, where papers and garbage floated in what water remained — which was about a foot.

"You want some shots before you crack it open?" Baden asked.

"Yeah, shoot the cab. The keys are still in the ignition. Make sure you get a clear shot of that." Bobby withdrew and worked his way around to the front of the vehicle. He gazed down and saw a new dent that marred the black paint on the bumper and cracked the plastic casing. Probably caused by a rock in the river when it came to a stop. He turned the corner, looking for some distinguishing marks. So far nothing. The plates were gone as well, front and back. "Gene, shoot the front bumper when you're done with the cab. There's some damage."

"Got it." Baden snapped a few more shots and came around. "I'll shoot the whole thing."

Bobby was about to say something.

"Detective Halsey," came a voice from behind.

He turned. Standing behind him was a man he recognized. He was the print man from Yard Street. They'd crossed paths a few times before. Bobby could never remember his name. "Hey."

"Detective Chartrand sent me over."

"Yeah, how long before you can dust this puppy?"

"Well, the doors are almost dried out, so I can go to work right away."

"Good. If possible, I'd like to get a look inside this thing before we call it a night." What he really wanted was to find out where it came from, trace it back to the owner. The keys in the ignition were nagging at him. They could have stolen it from a job site, but none of the vans on his list matched that, and there was nothing about keys being taken. But then, somebody who had their vehicle stolen might not report the keys for insurance reasons.

Sure, they could've been sitting in the ashtray or up in the visor.

"No problem, Halsey, I'll dust the driver side door first, if you like."

"Thanks."

"Stoughton."

"Huh?"

"My name's Stoughton," he said, smiling, and walked toward Bobby.

"Yeah, Stoughton. I remember." Bobby nodded. "Yard Street."

"Liar. You might remember Yard Street, but you don't know my name." His grin had a measure of contempt that put Bobby on the defensive.

"Okay, I didn't remember your name, but I'll remember it now."

The grin eased, and Stoughton nodded. "Okay, let me see what I can get off that passenger door." He pushed past Bobby toward the door and called to another officer, "Can you slide that table over here, so I have something to rest my gear on?"

Stoughton went to work on the driver's door first. He couldn't lift anything in or around the door handle. The perps might be taunting the police, but they hadn't left any prints at the scene at Yard Street. The only evidence they'd left unintentionally were footprints at all four houses. If the footwear could be recovered and connected to the killers, that evidence would be as good as a fingerprint.

Ten minutes elapsed, and Stoughton shook his head. "Not looking like they left much on the exterior."

Bobby crouched down beside him. The chemical smell from the print kit wafted up into his nostrils. "You think the river washed them off?"

"Possibly, but the vehicle wasn't in the water all that long. I've pulled prints off a vehicle that was submerged over forty-eight hours. How long do you think this was in the water?"

"I don't know," Bobby said, checking his watch. It was 7:06 p.m. "I guess somewhere between eighteen and twenty hours."

"Yeah, that was what I would estimate. If they left prints, I could probably get an impression. Maybe not a clear one, but the doors are clean. Nothing visible, but no latent prints either. They were probably wiped clean before the vehicle went into the river."

Bobby knew there were three types of prints usually found at a crime scene. Visible prints could be left in blood or some foreign substance, making them visible to the naked eye. Latent fingerprints were the invisible type; these were the ones that investigators dusted for and most commonly used as evidence. Latent prints could be lifted from all sorts of surfaces, even a human body. The third kind of prints were impressed prints, or as some called them, plastic prints, which were left in pliable surfaces like clay or wet paint.

"Yeah, I'd agree. They probably wiped the surface clean. Did you get anything useful from the houses?"

"Hard to tell. There were hundreds of latent prints, but they gotta be processed. If you wanted me to speculate, I'd say we won't get any incriminating prints from the crime scene. The ones we lifted probably belong to the victims." He paused to rub his nose. "We'll feed them into the computer and see if we get a hit. Who knows, maybe we'll get one."

Gene Baden, who was standing back, came in to join them. "Hey, Bill, you mind if I take a couple shots?"

"Fill your boots, Gene," Stoughton said and replaced a brush in its case. "Nothing but a blur of powder, but knock yourself out." Then back to Bobby. "Maybe we'll have a bit more luck inside the vehicle."

"Maybe," Bobby said.

Before opening the vehicle up, they decided to pump the water using a contraption that consisted of a filtered sump pump that was lowered to the floor through the driver window. They couldn't open the doors and allow the river water to drain out onto the warehouse floor. Rather than wait the hours it would take to drain slowly, they brought in a pump that fed into forty-five-gallon drums. The pump was being run at a slow rate, and Clemmons estimated that it would take between two and three hours before the vehicle was drained. Coupling that with the fact that Crime Scene would be doing their bit, Bobby asked Clemmons to alert him if anything came up, and he and Baden went back to MCU.

3

Major Crimes Unit

9:20 p.m.

The VIN was recovered from the vehicle and run through the stolen vehicle database. It did not match any of the stolen vans on Bobby's list. And for a brief moment, that kindled a glimmer of hope. While they chased down the ownership through the DOT, Bobby took a nap on the couch in one of the adjacent offices. Oggy told him to go lie down.

"I'll come get you if anything breaks," Oggy assured him. Before this, he told Baden to hit the road as well and to be back at 7:00 a.m., when the ME was set to arrive with the SD card. During that time, notices would be sent out to the officers on the task force list, notifying them of a meeting set for 9:00 a.m.

Bobby didn't argue. He was exhausted. Both physically and mentally. He needed a power nap to recharge his batteries, and he figured it might be a long night. There was still quite a lot to do. He had a spare set of clothes in the MCU locker room, street clothes, but what he had on now had the pungent aroma of stagnant water. His feet had dried out from the river, but his socks were crusty and rank. He didn't bother to shower before he put his head down. A shower would spike his energy, and he really wanted an uninterrupted nap. He kicked off his shoes, loosened his belt a notch, and bundled his jacket into a makeshift pillow. He closed his eyes, pushing away the things he'd seen, and sank into sleep.

4

November 14, 2008

"Bobby, time to get up," Oggy said. Bobby ignored the stir of his partner's voice at first, thinking it might be a dream. "Come on, it's 5:00 a.m., Bob, get up."

5:00 a.m.? He felt like he'd just laid his head down. Bobby opened his eyes to see Oggy standing over him. He looked fatigued, as though he'd just gotten up himself. His eyes were puffy and tired, lines of age stretching below those eyes. "I'm up, Oggy."

"Coffee's on, and I figured you'd want a shower and a change of clothes. I'm heading down for one myself. Once you got your shit together, we can look over a few new developments." Oggy closed the door.

Had he really slept eight hours?

He took in a deep breath and sat up. The headache was gone, as was the hanging strain in his guts. Yesterday had been a long day, and now a new one had begun. He breathed in again and got a whiff of the moldy stench of his socks. Yeah, a shower and a change of clothes would improve the situation. He pulled off his socks, rolling them together and placing them in his overnight bag. He slipped on his shoes and made his way down to the locker room to get his shower gear.

Half an hour later, he was dressed in his street clothes and sitting at the table with Oggy, sipping a coffee. "You all set?"

"Yeah," Oggy replied. "I finished up an hour after you sacked out. Got up about an hour before you."

"Where's Leigh?"

"She went back to her place. She'll be here in about an hour."

"How was she?"

"Thorough investigator. She said she was going to make a few calls to the Quantico lab to process our evidence. The president is talking about it on CNN, so now the FBI has made the case high priority."

"Hmm, I wonder how long that means before they come in and take over completely." Bobby sipped the coffee and held it in his mouth before swallowing.

"I'd say the clock is ticking, partner." Oggy was matter-of- fact in his tone. A case like this was a double-edged sword. It could launch your career into the stratosphere, or send it plummeting into the abyss. Media and political attention meant scrutiny. Oggy could handle the media. He had a talent for that sort of thing. He reminded Bobby of General Norman Schwarzkopf. Hell, he even looked a little like him — same receding hairline, same chubby cheeks - but Oggy was thinner than Stormin' Norman. Schwarzkopf knew how to handle a press conference like no other, but Detective Ogden Chartrand wasn't that far behind.

"What's the new development?" Bobby asked.

"They've traced the van back to a contractor who lives in Henessburg, Pennsylvania. The company's called George's Conduit and Electric. It's registered to a Walter George."

"Anybody tried to contact Mr. George?" Bobby already knew the answer. They would want to pay a visit in person, just in case Mr. George was somehow involved. "Never mind, Og, I already know the answer to that one."

"Once the task force meeting is over, I'd like you to head out to Henessburg, check it out in person. Maybe you can drag Leigh or Baden along." Oggy stood up and grabbed the coffee pot. "Refill?"

"Yeah." Bobby joined him, and he poured. "You know, partner, it would be nice if you could come along. Not that I have anything against Leigh or Baden."

"Yeah, I'd like nothing better than to get out of this office, but I'll be up to my ass in delegation. If Leigh isn't busy, take her along. We're adding two more detectives to the task force. Jobin and Harmac have been brought on board to assist."

"Harmac? Oh, fucking great. That guy is a complete dick."

Oggy grinned. "Yeah, he's a self-righteous a-hole, but he's a good detective, and we need some guys to help with the footwork. We need door knockers."

"Fine, but I'm telling you this, Oggy, if Harmac starts quoting Bible scripture, I'll punch him in the face." He didn't like Harmac at all. He was one of those do as I say not as I do types. He was a kiss-ass as well. "Try and keep him away from me."

"Who you going to punch in the face?" Agent Leigh entered the coffee room with a briefcase under her arm. She was dressed in a new pantsuit today, hair pulled back, and very little makeup on.

Bobby grinned. "Not you. Morning, Michelle."

"Morning and that's good. I'd probably kick your ass." She smiled back, but Bobby guessed that she just might. Michelle Leigh looked like she was in good shape and based on her background, he thought she'd probably thrown down a time or two. "Coffee. The lifeblood of every investigator."

Bobby got Leigh a cup, and the three went over the evidence that had been gathered as they waited for Baden and Fraser to join them. A laptop with media had been set up, and Leigh suggested they make a couple of copies of the SD card before they viewed it. Both Oggy and Bobby agreed that it would be a good idea. One copy would be sent to Quantico for analysis. Another would be used for the task force briefing. Baden arrived at 6:30, and as they waited for the arrival of the ME, he went over the photographs he'd taken the night before. A call also came in from Crime Scene to alert them that the van had been completely processed, and no prints had been found. Fibers had been collected along with a steel toolbox, but it looked as though it was just a part of the van's kit.

At 6:50, Jack Fraser showed up carrying a case in which the SD card was contained. As Leigh made two copies of the card, he told them that they had found traces of DNA within the cellophane wrapping, and that it had been forwarded on to Quantico for testing.

The size of the SD card was sixty-four GB, and the contents came in at twelve GB. On it was a single folder; inside that was an AVI video. As they copied the contents of that file over from one SD card to the next, Halsey and the rest anticipated what would be on it.

***

CHAPTER 10 – WHILE MAXWELL SLEPT

1

PPD Task Force

Pittsburgh, PA

When they slid the SD card into the laptop's reader port, they had no inkling of the horror they were about to witness. On the wall hung a forty-two-inch LG flat panel television.

Baden ran an HDMI cable from the laptop to the big screen, and set it up so they could watch it without huddling around the computer. "Okay, we're ready to go," he said and snapped off the lights.

"Run the video," Oggy prompted.

For the moment, there was not a word uttered. The five of them were fixated to the screen as the video slowly came into focus. At first, what they saw was distorted, a small blue light winking on and off. Bobby guessed it might be the digital clock on an appliance of some sort. For the first ten seconds, there was nothing, just black and that blur of blue light blinking away in the far-right corner of the screen. Then he heard it, and he leaned forward to listen more carefully. Breathing. Labored breathing, on the edge of hyperventilation. In and out. The dry click of the person swallowing. Fear. Then more breathing.

In, then out.

In, then out.

The camera panned slightly, losing the blinking light, and came into focus.

"Shit," Fraser whispered.

At first, Bobby thought there was only one. A single panic-stricken man perched before the camera, his eyes darting left and right, perspiration trails beading down his face. His nose was bloody. It appeared that he'd been in a fight. He wasn't looking at the camera but above it, which led Bobby to the conclusion that there was someone behind it. The man's face filled the screen, close enough to see the droplets of sweat welling up out of his pores. Close enough to see the brush strokes of hazel in the iris of each eye. The man on the screen was terrified.

"Speak," the voice behind the camera said.

He looked up and then down. He cleared his throat, a liquidy sound full of phlegm. "This message is for the Pittsburgh Police and all law enforcement. You are hearing a message from us only because we wish..." He stopped, gulped, strained his neck to look back.

"Continue," the voice said.

The man cleared his throat again. "You have already witnessed what we are capable of." He was reading from a script, like a hostage being held by a terrorist organization. "You cannot run. Nor hide. You are only seeing this because it is what we want." The man stopped reading, addressing his captors. "Please," he begged.

Then from behind, there was a cry.

He turned left to look back, his horrified face still filling the screen, then he paused, took a couple of hard gasps, and continued. "This... will not stop... nor will any... any of you be safe." His voice quivered, on the edge of tears. The camera refocused, zooming out, revealing two more people. On the man's right was a woman, her face smeared with the tears of running makeup. Her mouth had been taped shut with a foil-type duct tape. Bobby realized that it was the same foil used to cover the windows of the suspect van. On the left sat a young girl, maybe fourteen, also gagged with the same foil tape.

"It's the Georges," Bobby whispered just under his breath.

Leigh was silent, studying the screen.

"Yeah," Oggy agreed.

Fraser was mute. He just covered his mouth and watched.

Back on the screen, behind all three, stood menacing silhouettes, dressed all in black, one for each captive, looming over them like angels of death.

The man stared down at the unseen script and continued. His voice hiccupped in shrill chirps. "No one is safe… You now know… what we are capable of, and we will not stop. You cannot run." He sniffed; a mixture of bloody mucus dribbled from his left nostril. "Nor can you hide…" Finished, he looked up from the script.

"Good," the voice said. "You did well."

"God!" Gene Baden was standing now, visibly uncomfortable.

The silhouettes began to move. The one behind the young girl raised a hammer. The woman, presumably her mother, screamed mutedly through her covered mouth. Then the man began to beg. "No, please. I did what you said! Please… please… please. No!" The darkened figure behind him closed a gloved hand over his mouth, and then a blade was raised to his throat.

They all knew what was coming, not that it made it any easier to watch. Each stared in horror as the trio was executed. The pleading, the terrified cries, met with fatal blows — lethal cuts, and then — muted, hollow silence. Bobby looked at the woman. Her throat had been cut, but she wasn't quite dead. She was bleeding out, her eyes staring into the camera, slowly losing concentration, fading, fading, and then she was gone.

The silhouette came around to face the camera. His head was covered in a black stocking that hid his facial features.

He leaned down beside the dead man's slumped head and said, "This is just the beginning."

The video stopped.

There was a long silence, almost a minute long, a quiet in which the audience digested the horror of what they had just seen.

"What the hell kind of monsters are these?" Fraser asked.

"Oggy," Bobby said, ignoring Fraser's comment.

"Yeah?"

Gene turned on the overhead light. Everyone winced reactively.

"You better tell King that I won't be at his task force meeting." Bobby looked around the room. "What's that address in Henessburg?"

"You really think that was Walter George?"

"Who is Walter George?" Baden asked.

"Shut up," Oggy told him and turned to Bobby. "You think that, Bobby?"

"Yeah. I'm about ninety-nine percent."

"I'm going with you," Oggy said.

"So am I," said Leigh.

2

The task force meeting was pushed off until the afternoon. Lieutenant King wasn't too happy about it, but given the circumstances, he said that he would make the necessary arrangements, and alert the upper echelon regarding the new development.

Henessburg was approximately thirty-nine miles west of Pittsburgh. Sitting just off US Route 22, the little township had a population of six hundred, a sheriff, and two local officers, one being the deputy who also happened to be the chief of Henessburg's volunteer fire department.

The sheriff seemed a bit standoffish when Oggy spoke to him on the phone. They hadn't told him anything other than they were tracing down a stolen vehicle. "Well, I'm pretty tied up this morning. Maybe you could come down this afternoon sometime?"

Oggy took a deep breath and exhaled. He didn't know the sheriff and worried he might be a local yokel with a big mouth and a fetish for media attention. "What's your first name, Sheriff?"

"Mark, Mark Robinson," the sheriff said.

"Folks call me Oggy, which is far better than what my dad christened me with. My real name's Ogden."

"Shit." Robinson chuckled. "I guess."

"Anyway, Mark, we're in a real jam here. This is a suspect vehicle in a case we're working here in Pittsburgh. We need the support of the Henessburg PD." Oggy paused, looked across his desk to Bobby, and rolled his eyes.

"Now I recognize the name. You're working that nasty business on Kirkland Island, aren't yuh?"

Oggy raised his hand to his forehead. "Yeah, and we really need to keep it quiet until we chase down this lead. Can you help us with that, Mark?"

"Sure, sure I can. I'll clear my morning slate, and you boys come on up, but this ain't Pittsburgh, Oggy. This is Henessburg, and I'm the governing law around here."

Oggy gritted his teeth together. "Well, I'm not one to trample another man's jurisdiction, but then I'm not running the show." Oggy switched his gaze from Bobby to Michelle Leigh. She was sitting on the edge of the desk they had provided her.

"Who is running the show, then?"

"FBI," Oggy said. "You watch the news, Mark?"

"Yeah."

"Then I don't have to tell you that the president has taken an interest in this case, and the FBI is overseeing the entire operation. I'm doing the briefings, but I'm really just a liaison officer. I handle media, make calls, but the Pittsburgh Bureau has sent over a special agent to keep us on the straight and narrow."

"What's his name?"

"Leigh, Special Agent Michelle Leigh."

"A woman?"

Oggy grinned. "I hear you, but this agent has the ear of the president himself. So, we need complete discretion until we chase this down." Oggy motioned for Leigh to come over. "Oh look, here she is right now. Would you like to talk to her?"

Leigh was working her way over, a smile on her face.

"Well, uh, I…"

"I'll put her on," Oggy said and put the phone on speaker and handed it over.

Leigh locked eyes with Oggy and got down to it. "Sheriff Robinson?"

"Yes."

"On behalf of the Bureau and the President of the United States, I would like to thank you for your cooperation. We can be up there within the hour if that works for you." Leigh was all business.

"Umm, sure."

"Perfect, I'll let Detective Chartrand know that our team has the full cooperation and discretion of the Henessburg Police Department." She was getting ready to hand the phone back.

"What's he like?" Robinson asked.

"Who?"

"The president?"

"Oh…" Leigh grinned. "He loves knock-knock jokes. See you in an hour, Sheriff." She handed the phone back to Oggy, and he hung up before the sheriff could finish whatever his retort was. Leigh glanced at Oggy. "I've been promoted."

Oggy stood up and Bobby said, "I'm willing to bet that you guys will be in charge by this afternoon anyway."

Leigh said nothing. On the way out, they picked up Baden.

3

US Route 22

Henessburg, PA

They arrived at the small police department in two vehicles. Leigh rode along with Bobby, and they talked the whole way out. They bounced ideas off each other. She gave him her impressions of what they'd seen so far. Oggy had been right, she was thorough. Oggy and Baden barely spoke a word on the way out. Oggy made Baden uncomfortable; it was an authoritarian thing. Baden had wished he'd jumped in with Bobby or Agent Leigh, but when she said she would ride with Bobby, he felt inclined to ride with Oggy.

Sheriff Robinson was standing outside, smoking on the steps of the little police department. He was short, five-foot-six inches and balding, a rotund little man who Bobby guessed had a big chip on his shoulder. He was decked out in a khaki uniform, and on his head, he wore a black ball cap with a gold-lettered inscription: HPD. Below that: Protect and Serve. When the two cars parked out front, he took a couple more puffs and stubbed the smoke out in a battered, old steel coffee can.

"Mark Robinson," he said as he came down the steps to meet Ogden first.

"Hi, Mark, I'm Oggy. These are Detective Bob Halsey and forensic photographer Gene Baden." The usual pleasantries were made, handshakes exchanged, the insistence that first names be used, and then the introductions came around to Leigh. "Special Agent Michelle Leigh."

Sheriff Robinson took a moment, his eyes roving all over Leigh, her shape, her breasts, and eventually her face. She stood there and said not a word. This was too important, let the little troll have a look. He put out his hand. "You can call me Mark."

She shook his hand. "Thanks, Mark, you can call me Agent Leigh. Maybe we should go inside and talk about our situation."

"Right this way." He motioned with one hand, and Leigh led the way.

Bobby entered the conference room and looked around. Apparently, the HPD didn't have much of a budget. The conference room was made up of a folding table, the kind you get at Home Depot and what looked like old plastic school chairs.

"It ain't much," Robinson admitted.

"It'll do just fine," Leigh said, and they sat down. "Who wants to fill the sheriff in?"

"Well, if you're not going to delegate, I guess Bobby can fill him in regarding the stolen vehicle," Oggy said. Robinson was staring at Leigh, mesmerized. "Sheriff Robinson?"

He turned. "Yeah, I'm all ears."

"Sheriff, do you know a man named Walter George? Electrical contractor? George's Conduit and Electric?"

"I don't know him personally, but I know the company. He's a small-time operator, works for himself. Got a farmhouse halfway to Monroeville off 22, I think." Robinson paused. "I'd have to look it up."

"So, you've never had any trouble with Mr. George?"

"Not until today. How about we quit playing footsy, and you tell me what's going on?"

Bobby looked to Oggy, who nodded, then as an afterthought gave Leigh a glance. She nodded as well. "The murders—on Kirkland Island—we recovered a suspect vehicle. A Chevy van. We're pretty sure it was the van used to perpetrate the crime. That van is registered to Walter George, but it doesn't come up on any stolen sheets."

"Nope, first I heard of it. We get the odd stolen vehicle out here in the country, but it's usually some kids on a joy ride."

"So, if Walter George got his van stolen, you would have heard?"

"Yeah. You think he's involved?"

Mark glanced over at Oggy.

"You got three officers on your roster, Mark?" Oggy asked.

"Three, including myself. My deputy is at home, he works four until midnight. I have a patrolman who works the midnight to eight shifts. I handle the day shift. We don't have the budget for more officers. The state troopers handle most of the traffic. We act as peace officers, do domestic disputes, impaired driving, that sort of shit."

"You're going to need to call them in."

"For a stolen vehicle?"

"For a murder investigation."

Sheriff Robinson leveled his gaze on Oggy. "Murder investigation? Okay, I know you think I'm just a local a-hole, but what you're telling me isn't adding up. Are we talking about the Kirkland Island murders? Or additional murders?"

"We have reason to believe members of the George family were killed by our suspects." Oggy's face was like stone.

"Jesus," Robinson gasped. "What would lead you to that conclusion?"

"We have in our possession a video of three people being murdered. A man, a woman, and a teenaged girl. We know that the van used in the murders on Kirkland belongs to Walter George. If he isn't involved, which we suspect he isn't, he and his family likely fell victim to our suspects."

"Okay, I'll call my people in," Robinson said.

The house was set into an orchard two hundred yards off US 22. In addition to the three local cops, two state cops had been called in. Bobby studied the house through a pair of binoculars. There were two cars parked beside it, a Chevy Cavalier and a Ford Taurus wagon.

Oggy had his phone on speaker for the rest of them to hear. It rang four times before going to voicemail. "You have reached George's Conduit and Electric. Please leave a message, and we will get back to you as soon as possible."

Was that the same voice they'd heard on the video? The man who was executed? Bobby couldn't be sure. Oggy didn't leave a message. Instead, he ended the call and first looked into Bobby's eyes.

"Looks like we're going in, partner," he said.

"How you want to play this?" Bobby asked.

Oggy took a deep breath, then spread out a rough drawing Sheriff Robinson had done up of the farmhouse. Robinson had downloaded ten different Google Earth images of the property. In doing so, he'd located all windows, entries and exits, and the layout of the property. He and Robinson would enter by the front door after knocking. Bobby and Leigh would cover the rear. Baden would stay back with the state cops while the deputy and the constable covered the driveway.

"I don't have a great feeling about this, folks. I don't suppose there's much of a threat, but let's approach as if there is," Oggy told them. "Any questions?"

There were none. The team readied their weapons and moved in.

Leigh trotted in front of Bobby, moving in great, purposeful strides, and he had to stretch out his pace to keep up with her. He took long, deliberate breaths while exhilaration coursed through his veins. With each step, he could hear the faint crunching of the frozen grass below their feet as they moved into position. They flanked the west side of the house, far ahead of the others who came forward at a more deliberate pace. When they reached the rear, Leigh ducked below the windowpanes, and more or less monkey-walked to the back door. Bobby did the same, sucking in small breaths as he brought up the rear.

I'm out of fucking shape, he thought.

Leigh got on the other side of the door and turned to face him. She had her gun pointed upward, finger along the trigger guard. Bobby followed suit and they faced each other, waiting if someone would come crashing out in an attempt to escape. Bobby was huffing in and out, and Leigh smiled at this. Bobby smiled back.

All they could do now was wait.

5

Oggy and Sheriff Robinson mounted the porch and got on either side of the door. They took up a similar position, and Oggy nodded to Robinson, who knocked loudly on the door and then pulled back.

They listened.

There was nothing. Not a footstep, nor an echo from a television or radio. A minute passed.

"What now?" Robinson whispered.

Oggy got up and looked through the glass pane at the top of the door. He couldn't see anything, but then there was a repetitious pulse of light against a darkened door frame down the hall. It was blue. He turned to the state cops, motioned for them to get ready, and pulled back on the screen door.

"We don't got no warrant," Robinson said.

"We won't need one," Oggy replied and kicked at the front door. It gave after two hard wallops and crashed against the wall. Oggy pulled back, gun at the ready, and raised his fingers.

One, two, three, and he went through the door.

6

From behind the house, both Leigh and Bobby perked up when they heard the door crack at the front of the house. They tensed, waiting for something or someone. It only took Oggy and Robinson a minute to clear the house, and then they heard Oggy's voice. "Come to the front door!"

They moved back around front.

Sheriff Robinson was as white as a ghost; his eyes were wide and lost. Bobby looked from him to Oggy, who already had the phone to his ear. "Lieutenant, we're going to need everyone. Yeah, it's the place. We'll get it sealed off for Crime Scene."

"My God," Robinson said. "Who does this sort of thing?"

Leigh peered inside, careful not to touch anything. Down the hall and around the corner was where it had happened. A single bloody footprint marked the carpet in the hallway. She holstered her weapon and turned back to Bobby.

They were going to have to wait until Crime Scene gave them clearance before they could go in. Robinson looked stunned, and Bobby guessed this was the worst thing he'd ever dealt with. Bobby leaned into him. "Mark, how about you get your people to tape the area off while we take care of things here?"

He looked up.

Bobby smiled reassuringly. "Can you send Baden here?"

"Yeah, okay." The sheriff thumped down the steps and out across the field toward the waiting cars. Bobby felt sorry for the guy. He was out of his element.

Oggy ended his call and joined Bobby. "In case you haven't already figured… It's them."

Bobby wanted to get inside. Wanted to get on with this. "Michelle, what are we dealing with here?"

Leigh turned her attention back to Bobby. "Spree killing. These guys are just warming up. We'll get them, but I wonder how much damage they'll do before that happens."

"What did you see, Oggy?"

"Same… more of the same."

"Worse than Yard Street?"

Oggy didn't answer.

***

PART II

FUGITIVE GHOSTS

"You constantly think about getting caught, but the rush is worth the risk."—David Alan Gore

CHAPTER 11 – THE HAND OF DEATH

1

15 November 2008

FBI Headquarters

Quantico, Virginia

The knock at the door came at 6:00 a.m. Maxwell barely heard it, a soft rapping through the padding of a deep slumber. He felt himself coming back, but had no idea from where. He'd expected that his sleep would be full of speculative vignettes about the case. Transitioning from one scene to the next. But there was nothing. Just a black void in which his mind shut down completely.

Coming back, surfacing from the blackness, he was still putting his thoughts together, remembering bits and pieces. Had he really gone to Europe? Had Belanger really pinned a message to the wall inviting him to come and find him? He hadn't even considered the hard drive, or if the murders in Pittsburgh might be related to his investigation. But Maxwell knew they were. Otherwise, he would have to accept them as coincidence, and that was unlikely.

The knock came again, followed by a female voice, "Agent Maxwell, the deputy director sent me to wake you."

Maxwell sat up and shifted his feet onto the carpet. "I'm up, thank you." The woman, whoever she was, hovered outside the door, perhaps trying to decide whether to stay or go. Maxwell said, "Is there anything else?"

There was a pause, contemplation, and then, "No."

"What's your name?" Maxwell stood up and put on a pair of sweatpants.

"Boyden. Agent Linda Boyden."

"All right, Agent Boyden. Thanks for the wakeup call. I've got it from here." He put on a shirt, peering down at the shadow breaking the pencil-thin line of light at the base of the door.

"Okay," Boyden said, and the shadow departed.

Maxwell flipped the light on and squinted simultaneously to shield himself from the bright. He inventoried Bailey's office, his office now, and wondered if he would ever get used to it. Maxwell didn't think he was boss material. He didn't address people by rank, asked for their first names, and insisted they call him Max. He'd almost called Agent Boyden, Linda. This would have been fine, superiors did that all the time, but they didn't say, "Call me Max." That didn't happen in the FBI, there still had to be a chain of command. He also had a disdain for the notion. Once, he'd responded to a senior officer who told him, "You can't call me Bob. Not in front of the troops, Max." To which he'd responded, "Okay, sir, if that's the case call me Agent Maxwell." That had gotten him in some hot water.

The memory faded.

He grabbed his duffle bag, which contained a change of clothes, and headed for the shower.

2

"There's three more dead in the Pittsburgh area," Carswell said to Maxwell. Both were in Carswell's office. In a few minutes, a meeting would be convening in the adjacent boardroom and everyone involved, FBI-wise, would be present, many via satellite uplink. "You're going to Pittsburgh," Julian Carswell said to Maxwell. "That's where the Highwayman is."

Maxwell didn't say anything. He was still processing what Carswell was saying to him. All his thoughts and intentions were being wiped from the slate. "Max, there's going to be shit to pay when this is over, and we've got to knock this bastard and his accomplices down as soon as humanly possible. This could easily be turned on us as a major fuckup."

Now, Maxwell looked up at Carswell and did speak. "Whose fuckup, Julian? Mine?"

"It never works like that, Max. This will be on the FBI. The media will be kicking the hell out of us if we don't bring immediate closure to this. Never mind the politicians. They'll be running for cover. The attorney general called me this morning, she's watching this thing up in Pittsburgh."

"What about the evidence gathering in Lawrenceville?" Maxwell asked.

And for the first time, during their long friendship, Julian Carswell stiffened. "Dammit, Maxwell, you're a fucking SAC now, get used to not having your fingers in every pie! Your objective is to knock this asshole and his accomplices off the game board. As soon as possible." He took a breath, looked at his watch.

Maxwell said, "Okay. Who's taking the lead in the briefing?"

"You are."

"You're kidding? I have nothing prepared."

"Max, I'm the deputy director. I don't kid. We go in, have your people report, take notes, give direction, and then you get your ass to Pittsburgh."

Maxwell said nothing.

"Welcome to leadership 101," Carswell said and gave him a light punch in the shoulder. He glanced at his watch and added, "Time to go in."

Highwayman Task Force Brief

Quantico, Virginia

The conference table was at least thirty feet long, lozenge-shaped at the ends. There were settings for six people seated neatly in front of laptops and at the head was a placeholder card which read: FBI SAC DAVID MAXWELL.

Welcome to leadership 101, Maxwell thought with an inward sigh, taking his seat while Carswell stepped up to a podium and prepared to read an introduction. He looked at Feck and asked, "We ready to go, George?"

"Yes, sir. Everyone is standing by," Feck replied.

"All right, let's get this show on the road."

"Yes, sir." Feck clicked on the computer and keyed up the conference video. The screens on each laptop came to life, breaking into multiple windows: Agent Karen Shelley, Lawrenceville; Agent Evan Ferguson, Syracuse; Agent Michelle Leigh, Pittsburgh.

Then there were the others in the room. Maxwell read the nametags at each seat: FBI technician George Feck, IRS Special Agent Kendall Dickson, Special Agent Linda Boyden, and recording the briefing was Carswell's secretary, Patti.

Carswell sat down behind his laptop and glanced from the screen to the people seated before him. "Good morning, everyone. I am going to do a brief introduction, and then I'll be turning it over to Special Agent in Charge Dave Maxwell."

Meanwhile, Maxwell stewed, internally nervous about how he was going to handle this. They were all looking to him now for direction. He was going to have to depend on many of these people if they were going to catch the Highwayman and his accomplices. On a pad, he jotted down the names of each investigator, putting them in an order in which to address them. As Maxwell considered this, Carswell gave a short overview of the case and Maxwell's background. All eyes moved from Carswell to him. They weren't dissecting, but probing. Then, after the introduction, Carswell said, "I will now turn this over to Special Agent in Charge Dave Maxwell."

Maxwell cleared his throat, looked around the room and then into the monitor. He'd spent plenty of time with strangers during investigations and he knew that other police entities could be standoffish to FBI interference. Sometimes it was the assigned agent or the Bureau itself that created the indifference. He'd always been able to break through those barriers to forward the momentum of an investigation, so why not now?

"Good morning," he said and paused. There was a collective response of murmurs returning the greeting. That done, he said, "Look, I'm a no BS guy, so I'm going to lay it out for you. I've been on this case since the end of August in 2007. That was after the murders in Louisville that led to the death of retired FBI agent Lewis Ash and two local contractors who were attempting to save his life. Some of you know me. Some of you knew Ash. All of you are an intricate part of this investigation that has now stretched out beyond the borders of the United States to Europe. As some of you know, I have returned from Romania with a witness who has connected our suspect, Lance Belanger, to the Highwayman murders. What you may or may not know is that I am dependent on all of you.

"You are the ones who are going to help us close this case, and bring a murderer and his accomplices to justice. I have never worked a case that has so many intricacies and unknown agendas. Our main suspect is young, intelligent, rich, and up until recently, had one up on us. But the evidence gathering of all of you is what is going to bring him down. What I am going to ask of each of you is an individual briefing on how your piece of the investigation relates to the

Highwayman case, not only to bring me up to speed, but for the rest of the team. In doing this, I want everyone to listen to the briefs for possible crossover. After everyone has had a turn, we will then move to the next phase; a comprehensive plan to take down the Highwayman.

"So, here's the breakdown, and you will forgive me for using last names to expedite the process. First up Ferguson, then Shelley, Feck, and we will finish with Dickson and Leigh. Any questions?" He paused, glancing from the monitor then to each person seated in the room. Boyden had been the one who had woken him, and he had no idea who or what her purpose was. Julian Carswell had said they were getting him more help; he guessed she was it. "Evan, whenever you're ready."

Evan Ferguson gave a briefing on the Syracuse property which had been stripped and wiped clean by the departing Belanger, except for some furniture. Forensics had found an old blood drop on the sofa in the living room, and it had been matched to hairs that they surmised belonged to Belanger. Ferguson stated they were digging around the property to look for evidence relating to the murders.

"What are you looking for specifically?" Maxwell asked.

"Based on the patterns of our killer, I doubt we'll find anything in the way of victims, but we did find a computer power plug he'd left behind, from a Toshiba Satellite A205 series. We think he may have buried it somewhere on the property. It's unusual that he would forget the power adapter if he were planning on taking it on the road."

"Let's check local Syracuse dealers to see if anyone has purchased a power cord for that model," Maxwell said. "We could also check the Lawrenceville area, as that seems to be his last known position before meeting up with the three accomplices." He gazed at Shelley, who nodded and jotted the model number down.

"We'll keep digging in Syracuse, but it doesn't seem like he spent a lot of time up here. We do have a moving truck rental on 05 September 2007. We think this vehicle was used to dispose of the Cavalier they used to escape Louisville. Castings from the tires are being matched to partial castings taken at the scene of the Cavalier's recovery. Also, we found another drop of blood inside the cargo box of the rental. It has also been sent to see if it matches the blood drop at the Syracuse property."

"Good, we need everything to strengthen the case." Maxwell gave Ferguson a few seconds and asked, "Anything else to add, Evan?"

Ferguson glanced at his notes. "That about covers it for now."

"Thank you, Evan." Maxwell glanced down and said, "Okay, next up is Shelley."

Shelley briefed them on the murder of the neighbor, the discovery of the copied Highwayman file which they believed had come from the hands of Lewis Ash. When this was said, Maxwell gazed at Leigh for a reaction. Other than extreme interest, he didn't see anything that would indicate that she had previous knowledge of the copied case file. That was good. Leigh was a wild card, but they needed her on point in Pittsburgh. Shelley also spoke of the "Come and find me" message pinned to the neighbor's wall that was directed at Maxwell personally.

Maxwell made a note of that.

Belanger had starfished his neighbor.

"We're using ground-penetrating radar on the Lawrenceville property. Thus far, we haven't found any victims, but we have found bones of larger animals, including a dog in the southwest corner of the property."

"What other animals?"

"A mandible from what is presumed to be a raccoon or possum and there's plenty of small, unidentified bones that are in the adjacent woods. Going back to the underground room which had been stripped of everything but a glass desk and the previously referenced Highwayman case file, we believe that Belanger used this as his command post, and we also believe it was covered with news clippings by the vast number of pinholes in the north wall. We're actively looking for a computer, printer, and monitor. We have local and state police checking the dumps and are venturing deeper into the woods to see if there's a hiding place. If there's anything on the property, we will find it, but it will take time. We've extracted DNA from inside Belanger's dwelling that matched Norris Connelly's DNA taken from his Louisville dwelling. So, we have a clear connection between the two, although it seems moot, considering that Belanger has already outed himself with the neighbor's murder."

"What are your thoughts on that?" Maxwell asked.

"I don't know. Here we have a killer who has gone to great lengths to cover his tracks, and then on a whim, he kills a neighbor and leaves a damning note? It doesn't make much sense," Shelley replied.

"We have to keep in mind that Lance Belanger is not a normal human being. He's a master planner, but he's driven by his cravings for murder. I'm speculating here, so if any of you think otherwise, feel free to interrupt. I think Belanger is degenerating. Our visit last year pushed him underground. Even though he threw us off the trail with the killing in Stafford and the discovery of Norris Connelly's body, he was forced to do something he didn't want to do." Maxwell looked around the room and into the monitor. "Anyone want to hazard a guess?"

"Stop killing," Leigh said.

"Exactly. I'm sure all of you are familiar with the Ted Bundy case. Bundy was a meticulous planner. But he was incarcerated from 1975 to 1977 after being charged with kidnapping. When he escaped in early January of '78, Bundy fled to Tallahassee, Florida. There, he melted into the college scene, and all he had to do was lie low." Maxwell paused and took in his audience. Most of them knew this story, so he gave them a condensed version. "All he had to do was lie low. But Bundy hadn't killed in years, and his inner craving to take life was overwhelming. Within a week, he embarked on a spree killing at the Chi Omega sorority house, murdering two women and severely beating and raping two more. But even that wasn't enough. That same night he beat another woman almost to death after raping her. Those five attacks, perpetrated in one night, fed his murderous craving for roughly three weeks. Then, at the beginning of February, he abducted a twelve-year-old girl and brutally raped and killed her. Bundy was degenerating, losing control of the inner monster, making mistakes, and taking huge risks. That is what I think is happening with Lance Belanger. He's degenerated from meticulous planner to reckless, homicidal maniac." Maxwell again paused — they were all looking at him, making him realize that he'd gone off on a tangent. He cleared his throat and asked, "Have you got anything else to add, Agent Shelley?"

"No, not at this time," Shelley said.

"Okay, I'm going to move on to you, George. Tell us what you've learned from the computer hard drives." Maxwell turned his attention to Feck, who cleared his throat.

"What we've been able to determine from the hard drive is that Belanger set up a virtual website intended to draw in killers, a forum for murderers to exchange and share ideas. He started with Norris, grooming him as the first, but there were three others who came later, and it appears that they conspired to do away with Norris after he was outed in Louisville for the murder of his coworker."

"Is there evidence of this on the hard drive?" Maxwell asked.

"Yes, but it's circumstantial. Belanger and the other three referred to Norris as the problem child. And there was a consensus that he would have to go. We've found an awful lot of discussion about starting a killing club. There was mention by Devon – Belanger - of something called the Hand of Death."

"Jesus Christ," Carswell interrupted.

"The Hand of Death?" Boyden this time.

"A killing cult," Carswell said. "Henry Lee Lucas and Otis Toole claimed to be part of such a group that encouraged killing, mutilation, and cannibalism. To our knowledge, it was fabricated to raise their serial killer rock star status. So, you're saying that Belanger wanted to start such a cult?"

"That's how it appears from the chat exchanges, sir," Feck said. "The site is a spider web of fetish, murder, and torture. The discussions were all geared toward the subject, and ideas were exchanged. Belanger initiated a lot of these discussions. And we've only scratched the surface. I'm still working with Gusa, I have hours of text exchanges, and we even have photos that can be linked to the Highwayman murders."

Maxwell again. "I want you to comb through that hard drive and reconstruct a timeline, George. We're going to need everything you can extract, no matter how insignificant it may seem."

"Okay," Feck replied.

"Have you got anything else?"

"No, Agent Maxwell."

Dickson was next. He was the epitome of a stereotypical accountant: thick glasses, deadpan face, weak chin, and a receding hairline. He also had an aura of awkwardness he was going to great lengths to suppress. Maxwell guessed that IRS Special Agent Dickson wasn't much for people. His briefing was dry, recounting Belanger's financial records, income tax returns, and then there was an interesting tidbit. "We've frozen all of his accounts, so he can't access any money. However, there are irregular withdrawals dating back a couple of years, cash that cannot be accounted for."

"I'm not following you," Maxwell said.

"He was withdrawing amounts just shy of $10,000 on a regular basis, but there aren't any major purchases on record to substantiate the withdrawals," Dickson said.

"How much?" Maxwell asked.

"Roughly $3,100,000 is unaccounted for."

"You think he was building a rainy-day fund?"

"That's what I was thinking." Dickson smiled for the first time during the briefing. "The real question is where did he put that money? You can't just carry $3,100,000 around with you."

"Why not?" Maxwell asked.

"Because it's heavy, Agent Maxwell," Dickson said.

Everyone, except Dickson, laughed.

"So, what do you think he did with the cash?" Maxwell asked.

"He could have it in an off-shore account, but given his present situation, I doubt it. I'd say he's set up a shadow bank account with an alias."

"Will you be able to trace it?"

"Yes."

"Good." Maxwell laughed, surprised by Dickson's certainty.

"It will take time. We must follow the dates of the withdrawals and correlate them to new investments around that time with similar transactions. I'm confident enough to say with great certainty that we will find the account unless Belanger really is carrying it around with him. But I doubt it. The only thing that will slow the process is the sheer numbers of accounts. But we'll find it."

"Any idea how long?"

"I don't speculate, Agent Maxwell."

"Agent Dickson, if you can find out where that money is and we can connect it to withdrawals, that may help us catch our killers." Maxwell sighed. "You're an intricate part of this investigation, and even if what you bring to the table doesn't secure the capture, we're going to need you for building a case of conviction."

"I understand." Dickson looked intrigued, and perhaps even a little excited. "I will leave no stone unturned." The slightest grin creased his lips. "I have nothing else for you at this time."

Maxwell then moved on to Agent Michelle Leigh.

Leigh gave a complete brief, starting with the Yard Street killings. She covered the branding of the eyes, the SD card and its content leading to the discovery of the family murdered in Henessburg, Pennsylvania. "I'm working with the Pittsburgh Major Crimes Unit on this. We were thinking this was a cult killing of some sort until…" She paused to gaze down at the notes she'd been taking. "Agent Feck mentioned the three accomplices and the Hand of Death. Also, I wrote my thesis on Ted Bundy, and I think your theory that Belanger is breaking down is a distinct possibility. But he has an issue, Agent Maxwell."

"What's that?"

"He has three other personalities to clash with. They will certainly have their own designs on survival. There's a possibility of power struggles within the group."

"I'm hoping that's the case," Maxwell admitted. "How far is Henessburg from Pittsburgh?"

"Roughly forty miles."

"That's where they got the van?"

"Yes."

"You think that was the first killing? Before Yard Street?"

"I can't say for sure. I would certainly hope so, but the attacks are brazen. The Pennsylvania countryside has a lot of little burgs and rural farms. There could be more."

"Why do you think your killers decided to strike on Kirkland Island, Michelle?" Maxwell asked.

"The Highwayman wants the notoriety. This has turned him into a national figure. Kirkland Island has all the elements of a major killing, like the Manson murders. I think the killer is well-read in true crime and is emulating serial killers, and even attempting to surpass them. The grooming of Norris, the contact with the others, and the online discussion surrounding The Hand of Death all point to admiration and ambition."

"So, you're confident that the Highwayman killer is directly connected to the 4 killings?" Maxwell locked eyes with Leigh. It was her opinion he wanted most of all. She'd been on the Highwayman case, knew Agent Ash well, and had already drawn up the psychological profile before Maxwell was brought in to take over.

"Yes, Agent Maxwell, I believe that we're looking for the same killer, albeit he's now a killer with three accomplices."

"How are the people at Pittsburgh Major Crimes?"

"Chomping at the bit. This is in their backyard. They want to get these guys. I'm working with two seasoned investigators named Ogden and Halsey, both very capable. But we need more resources."

Maxwell turned his attention to Julian Carswell, who said, "You have everything the FBI has to offer at your disposal, Agent Leigh."

"Thank you, sir," Leigh said.

The Pittsburgh brief wrapped up and Maxwell looked at Boyden, who hadn't brought anything to the meeting except a lined pad on which to jot down notes. "Do you have anything to add, Agent Boyden?"

She opened her mouth to speak, but Carswell cut her off. "Agent Boyden will be assisting you as you proceed with the investigation, Agent Maxwell."

Maxwell nodded, then he addressed them all collectively. "What I see is solid investigative work on the part of everyone here. These are some horrible people we're chasing, and we need them put out of commission. So, I'm going to ask you to give this investigation everything you've got. That is not to diminish the work you've already done. It's solid. But I'm asking for more."

There were collective nods of acknowledgment.

"On a personal note, I can tell you that I'm not a glory hound nor a politician. You bust your ass for me, and I will give you everything you need to get it done. The deputy director can attest to my investigative style." He smiled at Julian.

"Can I ever," Carswell said, and there were a few laughs.

"So, I'm not going to leave you high and dry for personal gain. There'll be no bullshit. I want the Highwayman and the other three taken down. The president and the country are watching, and we need to show them who and what the FBI is about. Let's get these bastards."

The meeting wrapped up, but not before Maxwell asked Leigh to stay online. He also asked Boyden to give them a moment of privacy. Boyden stepped into the hallway with the others. Carswell remained, as Maxwell would have expected. Once the door closed, Maxwell said to Leigh, "Investigative protocol would dictate that you should be removed from this case because of your connection to Lewis Ash."

Leigh's face tightened. "Yes, sir."

"I'm not pulling you, Agent Leigh. I need you." Maxwell turned to Carswell, who nodded.

She relaxed slightly. "I understand, sir."

"I'm coming to Pittsburgh. I want to meet your investigators, and I want your assurance that you'll put your personal feelings aside until after we catch these guys."

"You have that, sir," Leigh said.

"Good," Maxwell nodded. "I'll have my assistant send you the details of my arrival as soon as I figure them out myself."

Carswell got up. "Max, I'll leave you to it."

"Yes, sir." Maxwell nodded.

"And don't forget about Boyden." Then he was gone out the door, closing it behind him.

Maxwell turned his attention back to Leigh. "I read up on Lewis Ash, he was a hell of an agent."

Leigh blinked. "He was the best."

"When I get to Pittsburgh, there will be optics to consider. I'll be assuming command, but I'm counting on you to be my right hand, and if you can do that for me, I promise you that I will back you all the way."

"Thank you, sir."

"Michelle, I'm a hunter just like you, been around a little longer, but I read your file. So, cut the 'sir' bullshit, and call me Max."

"Yes, okay, Max."

***

CHAPTER 12 – BLOOD TRAIL

1

15 November 2008

Off State Route 218

Near Brave, PA

They were holed up in a farmhouse in a county south of Pittsburgh and very close to the West Virginia state line. The lives of the three inhabitants of the house, a husband, wife, and preteen boy, had been extinguished two nights before. Their bodies were now stored in a spare bedroom at the south end of the house.

The killing had been good, but Lance felt that the location had been a mistake. It was too remote, and he hadn't calculated the same way he had with Henessburg. Henessburg yielded all sorts of advantages. There, they'd accessed a video camera and the white van used for the Kirkland Island killings. Here? They could probably hide out here indefinitely, unless a friend, neighbor, or relative came wandering up the mile-long drive. Beyond that, it held no significance.

But there had been no one, and the now-deceased Fowlers offered little advantage other than the fact that they increased his kills by three more.

There had also been discord in the ranks. Steel had started making comments to the others. Comments about what they were doing. About Lance. Larry had alerted him to the comments.

"He's saying shit," Larry said.

"What kind of shit?" Lance asked.

Steel had become despondent. Their online alliance that had translated into real-time murder now seemed to be wavering. Steel made comments like, "What kind of suicide mission have we signed onto?" And, "I should have stayed in Michigan." And on this day, "I think it's time to get the fuck out of here."

"It's a little late for buyer's remorse, Jim," Lance said, placing a hand on his shoulder.

"Don't call me that." Steel shook him off.

"Don't you like what we've done so far?" His reassuring hand retracted like a moray eel retreating into its lair. "Aren't you having fun?" he asked with an edge of sarcasm in his tone.

Larry and Dusk watched the exchange with carnivorous fascination. Their faces were intense and hungry. They were less skittish about the risk. They enjoyed the killings, Larry especially.

"I shouldn't have come out here, gotten involved in this insane kamikaze mission of yours," Steel said, not looking any of them in the eye. "The whole fucking world is looking for us!"

"That's not quite true," Lance said. "They're looking for me and three accomplices. I haven't heard any of your names on the news."

Steel stood abruptly. "Yet!"

"Well, what do you want to do, Jim? You want to leave?" Lance turned his attention to all three. "Who wants to leave?"

Larry and Dusk lowered their eyes like commoners standing before nobility. Steel held his gaze and said, "You're going to just let us leave?"

Expressionless, Lance said, "I'm not holding you prisoner, Jim. You want to bug, that's up to you."

Steel stared into Lance's eyes, as if trying to gauge them, to decide whether this was a test or a bluff. "Just like that?"

"Well, no. I would want assurances that if you're caught, you'll keep your mouth shut. Sooner or later, Jim, you're going to get caught. Because killing's in your blood, and just because you leave our little quartet doesn't mean you'll want to stop."

"I won't say anything."

Now Lance stood up. "How can we be sure?"

"Because I'd be connecting myself to this."

"So, you won't say a word?"

"Of course not."

"Grab your gear then, but you'll be walking out." Lance smiled. "We need the van, and the truck will tie you to this place, so you'll be using your shit-kicker Cadillacs."

Steel thought about it. "Okay, I'm going. Nothing personal, Lance."

"No offense taken," Lance said. His voice was even, and he looked completely sincere… but… inside he was a rage of sweltering bile. *How dare him! How fucking dare!* "Grab your gear, Jim. Nobody is going to stop you."

2

Hesitant, Steel took another cursory glance around and went to get his gear. He marched into a bedroom where the bags were stored and began gathering up his things. He had an old army duffle bag which carried his clothes, and a cache of trophies he'd taken from his victims. There was a driver's license, a pendant, two rings, a lock of hair, and from his other life of killing, seven swatches of plaid taken from the schoolgirls he'd murdered. Those, he cherished most of all. He brought the Ziploc bag out and examined them. He shouldn't have left Michigan, shouldn't have hooked up with Lance or the others. There he'd had anonymity.

This? This is a disaster waiting to happen.

He replaced the swatches in the bag and before zipping it up, he removed and unfolded a Buck knife and slid it into his boot. The steel tip danced above his ankle, prodding it as he shifted up onto his feet. He would have to refold it once he got out of here, but for now, he had to get away before Lance changed his mind. He slung the bag over his shoulder and exited the bedroom.

He half-expected that they would be standing there ready to restrain him, but no one had moved. Dusk and Larry were still seated, albeit watching him. Lance had his back to him, seemingly interested in something in the Fowlers' china cabinet. "You're sure about this, Jim?" Lance asked.

Steel set the bag down. If they rushed him, he would have to be fast with the knife. "You going to let me leave, Lance?"

Lance turned, a gun in hand, and said, "I can't."

Steel took a knee, fumbling for the blade.

Dusk and Larry stood up.

Lance said, "Do you know who Karla Homolka is, Jim?"

His fingers grazed the handle of the Buck knife, and when the hands clamped onto his forearms, he felt it pull away, and knew that there would be no retrieving it. "Huh?"

"Karla Homolka. She was part of a Canadian duo who kidnapped and killed two schoolgirls. The schoolgirl part made me think of you, Jim. Karla testified against her husband, Jim, and she got a reduced sentence…"

"I said I wouldn't…"

Then there was a crack and the smell of cordite, followed by ringing in everyone's ears. Dusk and Larry dropped like Steel out of surprise, but that did nothing to expedite his chance of escape. Muffled, but still audible, even through the intense tinnitus of ringing, Lance said, "She testified against her husband, called him an abuser and got a reduced sentence. They called it a deal with the Devil. After they cut a deal with this woman, videotapes surfaced showing that she was an active participant in the girls' murders."

Steel barely heard; his left foot was on fire with pain. He felt like a red-hot poker had been stabbed into the top of his foot and was now twisting its way through the tendon and bone. That was what he felt, but the bullet had passed through his foot and boot sole, and was now embedded in the hardwood floor. He struggled and in broken words, he said, "I… said I… wouldn't talk… Lance."

Then Lance shot him in the other foot.

Steel screamed.

"Fuck, a little warning, Lance," Larry barked, hands over his ears.

Lance turned his attention to Larry and used every ounce of self-control to keep the monster inside him tethered. He had to, because it was roaring at the top of its lungs, "Kill them all! Kill them all!"

Steel was curling up into the fetal position, letting out a discordance of agonizing moans. The second bullet had been closer to his ankle, exploding it out onto the floor in fragments of bone and flesh. He begged, "Please… Please…"

Lance took a deep breath and knelt. "She got out in 2005, Jim. She's married again and living somewhere in Canada. And her husband, Paul Bernardo, is in solitary confinement." He tapped the gun against the ankle wound, which made Steel scream and recoil. "I'll tell you what, Jim, I'm going to let you leave. I'm going to give you an hour to crawl out of here and if you make it, we won't pursue you. It's about five miles to the highway, Jim, but I doubt you'll make it that far. I think your best bet is the woods, you could disappear out there."

Dusk and Larry were standing over them.

"What time is it, Larry?" Lance asked.

"Twenty past eight," Larry replied.

"You best get going, Jim. The clock is ticking," Lance said and smiled. At 9:20, we'll be coming for you." He looked up at Larry, who smiled back and gave Steel a light kick. Then they retreated and Lance opened the front door, letting in a gush of frigid November air. "The clock is ticking."

Steel lay motionless, trying to control the pain with his mind and failing miserably. Outside, daylight faded, and the cloak of night solidified. He took a couple deep breaths, gathering himself.

"Fifty-nine minutes remaining," Larry said.

"Giddy up, little Jimmy," Dusk chimed in.

Lance leaned down and caressed Steel's leg, crawling down his pant leg like a tarantula until it found the Buck knife. "You won't be needing this," he said and pulled it from the boot. "Now, get moving before I change my mind."

Steel gathered his strength and began to crawl toward the door. As he did, the others didn't move or follow. Outside, the freezing air beckoned him into the boney embrace of night.

3

FBI Field Office

Pittsburgh, Pennsylvania

Maxwell landed in darkness, happy to be off the plane, his relationship with aircraft strained. He wasn't much of a flyer, but being compacted into a tube with so many others made every trip claustrophobic. Leigh picked him up at the Pittsburgh International Airport. They drove back to the FBI Field Office in Carlson which, if one was in the proper section of the building, had a view of the Monongahela River.

Leigh was attractive, tall and athletic, and Maxwell wondered if she was in a relationship. She didn't have a ring on, but a lot of people didn't wear wedding rings these days. In fact, marriage seemed to be in decline.

"There will be a joint press briefing in the morning with Pittsburgh Major Crimes and the Bureau. I was originally slotted to cover that brief. I assume you'll be taking over?" Leigh asked.

"Yeah, I'll need to look at your notes. Tell me more about the two detectives, Halsey and Chartrand." Maxwell brought up his phone and saw there was an email from his new assistant, Boyden. He ignored it for the time being.

"Chartrand is a bit on the conservative side. He's good with the press and briefings. I haven't got Halsey figured out completely. There are rumors he might be a drunk, but I can't substantiate that. He's been in the game for a while, and he's taken some FBI courses over the years."

"Is he a wannabe?"

"No, he has no interest in joining the Bureau, he's just boning up on investigative techniques. He's got a good track record for closing cases. Word around Major Crimes is that he has authority figure issues, and that's why he hasn't advanced from detective to the next level."

Maxwell smiled at this. "Maybe he just likes hunting."

Leigh gazed over at him. "Like you?"

Maxwell didn't say anything else, but the smile remained.

"So far, I'd say he's a solid investigator. We've also got a tag-along named Gene Baden."

"Tag-along?"

"Sorry, he's a forensic photographer. He's been added to the task force as an asset. He's been in it since the Yard Street killings and has been very effective from a techy point of view."

"So, we need him?"

"It certainly won't hurt."

"Any assholes in this bunch?"

"The sheriff up in Henessburg is a sexist pig, but he's being kept in check by the state cops. Honestly, he's harmless, a civil servant completely out of his depth when it comes to homicide. He was with us when we found the last crime scene, and it kicked the hell out of him." Leigh turned onto Hot Metal Street and after that, hooked a left on Sidney Street.

Maxwell's phone beeped again.

Another email from Boyden.

He ignored it as Leigh turned again and entered the parking garage below the field office. "Okay, so Halsey is a possible drunk, Chartrand is stand up, and the tag-along is Baden."

"Yeah." Leigh backed the car into a spot, and they got out.

"What time are we doing that briefing?"

"It's scheduled at 8:00 a.m."

Maxwell looked at his watch. It was two minutes past eight.

Maxwell removed his bags from the trunk and said, "I want everyone gathered in a briefing room for 6:00 a.m. You contact whoever you want, and if anyone gives you any shit, tell them they are off the task force."

"Seriously? That's gonna piss a few people off."

"We gotta crack the whip on these guys. Let them know that we're in charge. I think everyone will fall into line. Who is your main liaison?"

"Captain Campbell. Above him is the chief." Leigh shook her head. "This is going to piss people off, Agent Maxwell."

"Max," he said and smiled again. "We need people pissed off. We need to show them we're in charge and kick a bit of ass. Once we've done that, we'll motivate them to really start hunting."

"You sure this is the right approach?"

"First, we kick a little ass, then we show them we're not really bad guys, and then we get them moving. The bosses back in Quantico want this wrapped up as soon as possible. I don't mind telling you that this is a career make or break moment for everyone involved. Personally, I didn't want to be in charge, but an idiot back in Quantico was fucking it up so badly I had no choice but to take over."

"Are you saying I'm doing the same?" Leigh's face flushed.

"You caught the Beekeeper?"

"Yes, I helped catch the Beekeeper."

"Tell me about that? But let's walk as you do."

They started moving across the underground parking lot toward the elevator. Leigh began. "We didn't have enough evidence for a warrant. We were sure he'd abducted a young girl and taken her out to a slaughterhouse. Ash had applied for federal warrants to search the property, but we had nothing."

"So, what did you do?"

"I went on Google Earth and found a still of a man leading a child out to one of the buildings. When we approached the judge with that, he signed off on a warrant."

"Was the girl alive?" Maxwell already knew.

"Sadly, no, but we got him, and he had a twelve-year-old girl bound and gagged in the back seat of his car."

"You saved her."

"I didn't. I wasn't there when they took him into custody."

Maxwell grinned. "That's why you're still here, Michelle."

They entered the elevator, and Leigh pushed the button for the fourth floor. "I was lucky, that's all."

"No, you were innovative, and you probably saved the lives of more little girls, even if you didn't save the one on Google Earth." Maxwell turned to her. "We need to finish what Ash started."

Her face hardened, a minute scowl tugging at the corners of her mouth. "Yes, I agree, Max."

"I told you that you're going to be my right hand. I meant that. When you have questions or concerns, don't hesitate to raise them. There is a method to my madness, and now the Highwayman has made it personal for me as well."

The elevator door opened, and they stepped out.

Leigh turned right, and Maxwell followed her.

Had Ash been sleeping with this woman?

He doubted it, but stranger things had happened in the past. She was attractive and quite possibly eligible. Some women were about power, rather than sex appeal. Some were willing to lie down with a man a decade their senior. He wasn't sure if Leigh was that way. He wasn't ready to judge her for it, wasn't sure about many things, but he was going to find out.

4

Off State Route 218

Near Brave, PA

…57 Minutes later

Steel's fingers had lost feeling, and fortuitously so, because on seven of his ten digits, the nails had peeled right off. His kneecaps were also ragged from repetitively scraping against the frozen earth.

And that was the easy part.

His feet were the worst. Worse than anything he'd ever felt in his life. Once, when he was a kid, his back was burned by boiling water. His foster mother, number four to be exact, had dumped a boiling kettle onto the lower part of his back. It wasn't intentional, just the aftermath of too many vodka martinis, minus the olive and vermouth. The initial scalding spill wasn't even the worst part, it was the aftermath of having his skin turned into the jelly found around a canned ham. The burning was constant, coupled with an agonizing itch, buzzing hornets burning their way beneath the layers of skin. He wanted to roll over and die. Succumb to the night and fall asleep.

But he had to keep going.

If he didn't…

Overhead, the moon was obscured by the silhouettes of tree branches clawing at the night sky. Steel blinked — he was losing it — thinking things best not thought of when you are the hunted.

Time was running out.

The light of the house behind him, he crawled for his life over the frozen ground, into the canopy of forest, and into the awful dark. He would probably bleed out, and perhaps it wouldn't be so bad. The alternative to being found offered an endless supply of horrific possibilities.

Momentarily, he stopped to look back through the treeline, and he saw them coming off the porch down the steps. The distance couldn't have been much more than six hundred yards. He'd thought he'd made it much farther. His hope began to dissolve.

"There's a blood trail," a voice said. Steel couldn't make out if it had been Larry or Dusk. It wasn't Lance. A beam of light cut across the long drive, slicing through the darkness, first left, then right. "This way," the voice insisted. The light traversed, finding Steel's direction.

"Ah fuck," Steel whimpered, pushing his body a little farther until bumping into a partially uncovered tree root. That was when he knew he was going to die. When the drive that had kept him going the last hour ran out of him. He turned onto his back and pulled himself along the root toward the towering tree it stemmed from. He got himself up onto his butt, pushing his back against the tree trunk. Under the moonlight, he could see the knees of his jeans were worn entirely through. Beneath that peeked ragged pink flesh, numb from the abuse and frozen ground.

Then he heard Lance.

"Where are you, Jim?"

The flashlight beam swung across the woods, back and forth, inevitably finding him propped against the tree, and there it stopped, pinning him to the spot.

They were fifty feet away.

"Jim," Lance, who was the middle of three gray approaching silhouettes, said, "you made it pretty far."

They closed in, and he could hear the crunching footfalls, snapping twigs, and even the breath expelling from their lungs.

Steel tried to think of a response. He was beyond begging for his life. This was payment for his deeds. The devil had come to collect a debt for the lives he'd extinguished. Once they were upon him, the light probing him, he said something he might have heard in a movie. "Where the hell is Michigan?"

Then their hands were upon him.

As they lifted him, he heard Lance say, "Not yet."

Then he passed out.

16 November, 2008

10:04 a.m.

Route 218, Spraggs, PA

The stolen Suburban rolled north toward Waynesburg, leaving behind a slew of bloody carnage. Larry drove, Dusk rode shotgun, and Lance sat in the back seat considering his options. On the seat next to him, the snub nose .38 lay at hand's reach, two of its six chambers spent. The three were exhausted, having spent hours prepping the site before leaving.

Steel was just the beginning. Lance knew this, perhaps had always known. Their coalition of murder was unraveling, survival trumping comradery. And that was fine by Lance. The other two were only a means to an end. He reached over and touched the cold steel of his father's gun with two fingers. It gave him comfort.

"Where now?" Larry asked.

"We're going to Waynesburg," Lance said.

"What's in Waynesburg?" Dusk asked.

Lance smiled at Larry, who was watching him in the rear-view mirror. Larry's expression was opaque, impossible to read, and Lance wondered what must be going through their minds.

"Lance?" Dusk again.

He shifted his eyes to Dusk, who was looking over his shoulder, eyes darting down to the gun, and then back up at Lance. "Yes?"

"What's in Waynesburg?"

"Infamy."

***

CHAPTER 13 – STEELY DAN

1

16 November 2008

10:30 a.m.

Over Brave, PA

The aircraft was a Cessna Skyhawk named "Steely Dan" and the pilot, Hank Small, had turned over the controls to his trainee, seventeen-year-old Mathew Goff, twenty minutes before. Hank Small's flight school catered to people seeking their private pilot's license. He had ten clients, and if he had to rate them, the kid sitting next to him was the best. Mathew Goff was on his thirteenth lesson, and Hank was impressed. The kid's father, Mathew Goff Senior, had paid for the lessons in full with a certified check for $15,000, a pittance for an investment banker worth over twenty million.

They had been cruising at 12,000 feet, 2,000 below the service ceiling for this aircraft, but Hank decided to have the kid descend to 500 feet and do a little low-altitude maneuvering. During their thirteen lessons together, Mathew had said he wanted to be a fighter pilot in the USMC. Hank doubted the boy's father would sign on for that, but the kid had an ability. And Hank had flown an A-10 Warthog with the 354th Tactical Fighter Wing in the first Gulf War, so he had a soft spot for those who wanted to serve their country.

Below them, the trees and farm fields rolled by on the earth's endless conveyor belt. Blanketed in snow, the countryside was beautiful this time of year. In the distance, Hank could see a plowed field and to the southwest, there was a barn and a farmhouse. "Mathew, I want you to bank twenty degrees to the right until we're lined up on that barn, and once you're leveled off, I want you to ascend to six hundred feet."

"Okay," Mathew Goff said and began to apply his rudder and turn the controls. The maneuver only took a few seconds to align them with the barn. The kid climbed to six hundred feet.

"This stays between us, kid. If your dad caught wind that we were playing around at these altitudes, he'd have my ass." Hank smiled at the kid from behind his aviator glasses. "What happens in the air stays in the air."

"Sure thing, Hank." He leveled the single-prop airplane off at six hundred feet on a direct course for the barn.

"What's your cruising speed?" Hank asked.

Mathew gave a quick glance to the controls. "One hundred five knots."

"Now, without looking at the gauge, convert that to MPH," Hank said.

Mathew Goff stared out over the nose of the airplane without looking down at his controls. Most of his students tried to steal a glance at the airspeed indicator. Mathew Goff didn't cheat, he was doing the conversion in his head, and that made Hank happy.

"Umm, I think it's 120 MPH," Mathew said, and before Hank could compliment the kid, he said, "What's that?" Hank was looking at the kid, but when he turned his attention toward the approaching barn, the kid interrupted the question he was formulating with another question. "Is that a mannequin?"

Hank saw it then and knew almost immediately that it was not a mannequin but a human body. Having seen the horrors of war, he recognized it from his low-level missions in Iraq. "Matt," he said, "I want you to return the controls to me."

"Did I do something wrong, Hank?" And again, before Hank could answer the question, the kid interrupted him with a revelation. "Holy shit, that looks like a real body."

Calmly, Hank repeated, "Turn the controls back over to me, son."

Mathew Goff sucked in a deep breath and held it, then he returned control of the airplane to his instructor as they passed over the barn and the dismembered body in the driveway. "What did we just see, Hank?"

"I'm not sure, kid." But he was. "Take a look at the map and see if you can pinpoint the location of that farm." Then he was on the radio. "Waynesburg Tower, this is Skyhawk 67-Charley."

"Skyhawk 67-Charley, tower."

"Yes, sir, reporting information India, 67-Charley, we're about ten miles for a full stop." Hank's voice was steady.

"Skyhawk 67-Charley, Roger. Continue straight in. Report at three mile final."

"Roger, Tower. Is Alpha Papa Uniform on site?"

"Skyhawk 67-Charley, do you have an emergency?"

"Skyhawk 67-Charley, no mechanical, but will need to meet with Alpha Papa Uniform immediately at full stop."

"Skyhawk 67-Charley, yes. Alpha Papa Uniform available. Tower will advise."

"Roger." Hank turned to the kid. "Looks like we'll be cutting your lesson short, but I'll throw in an extra hour on your docket."

"That was real?" Mathew Goff's mouth hung open.

"Yeah, I'm pretty sure it was."

They were silent for the last leg of the trip until Hank Small called on the radio, "Skyhawk 67-Charley, reporting three mile final."

"Skyhawk 67-Charley, clear to land on runway two-two. Additional India, Alpha Papa Uniform has been advised of your request and awaits final stop."

"Roger, clear to land runway two-two."

2

16 November 2008

Major Crimes Unit

Pittsburgh, PA

The task force briefing was wrapping up. Maxwell was meeting with Detectives Chartrand and Halsey, discussing the Yard Street and Henessburg killings. Plans for Maxwell to visit the crime scene at Henessburg were being discussed when a call came in from the state police. Oggy took the call.

"Detective Ogden," he answered.

"Hello, Detective, my name is Staff Sergeant Lucas Jackman," the caller said.

"What can I do for you, Staff Sergeant?"

"This morning, we were alerted by a pilot out of Waynesburg, that he and his student might have spotted a body on a farm outside Brave, Pennsylvania."

"Student?"

"The pilot runs a flying school. He had a young kid with him." Jackman sounded a little irritated that he had to explain this but carried on anyway. "They were on a training flight when they spotted a body on a farm approximately five miles southeast of Brave. We dispatched a patrol car to the scene, and our crime people found the body and three others in the main dwelling."

Oggy put his hand up to alert the others, "What's the status of the crime scene now?"

"We've got the area cordoned off, state police investigators are walking through, and our Crime Scene people are on the way."

"Can you hang on a second, Staff Sergeant?"

"Um, yeah, I guess."

Oggy turned to Maxwell. "We've got another one near Brave, Pennsylvania. Four victims. State police are on the scene."

Maxwell turned to Bobby. "How far to Brave, Pennsylvania?"

Bobby pulled his phone out, but Leigh beat him to it. "It's about eighty miles."

Oggy said, "Can you send me the coordinates for that farm, Staff Sergeant?"

"I can do one better. I'll patch you into the scene. I've got the state investigators on the other line. Can you hang on a sec?"

"Yes, I'll hold." Ogden kept the phone to his ear and said to them, "Looks like they struck again."

3

Then Maxwell's phone rang. It was Boyden. "Maxwell."

"Agent Maxwell, Special Agent Boyden. I'm calling to alert you that we've made a couple breakthroughs on this end."

"What have you got?"

"Feck has the names of the three accomplices."

"Excellent," he said and repeated the news to Leigh. "We've got the three accomplices' identities." Then back to Boyden. "Email me everything; we're dealing with a new crime scene."

"I'm already sending it. Also, Agent Kendall Dickson from the IRS wants you to contact him. He says he may have found where Belanger shifted the missing money."

Maxwell smiled. "Agent Boyden, if you were here, I'd hug you and probably kiss you too."

Boyden paused momentarily, then let out a small laugh and said, "Okay. Guess I'm glad I'm not there."

Maxwell turned his attention back to the others. Everyone had a phone stuck in their ear; concurrently their eyes darted in the direction of others on the team. "We're going to need a bird."

"I'm working on that now," Leigh said.

4

South of Waynesburg, PA

A chopper was dispatched to Pittsburgh by the Pennsylvania State Police to carry investigators to the scene. The FBI could have chartered one, but Director Julian Carswell had a friend in the upper echelon of PSP who greased the wheels.

Maxwell was filled with anxiety. They were getting close, but now there were more victims, and if they couldn't close the net, there would be even more dead. He knew the Highwayman was going to be arrested or killed, that was an inevitability, but he worried how much damage he would do before they took him down?

"How long until we touch down?" Maxwell asked the pilot.

"About seven minutes," the pilot replied.

"Thanks," Maxwell said. He dialed the number for Kendall Dickson and pressed it hard against his ear to suppress the sound of the props.

It rang three times.

"Agent Maxwell, I've got some excellent news for you."

"You got the account?" He found himself shouting to hear his own voice.

"I've got a name."

"I'm not getting you, Kendall."

"I've found a name that I'm sure will lead us to the account or accounts." Kendall was clacking away on a keyboard. "The name is Wilson Rogers. We should have a lock on the account or accounts by late this afternoon."

"That's great! What kind of surveillance could you do on the transactions on those accounts?"

"We'll need warrants, but given the urgency of the situation, I'm pretty sure we can fast-track them." Kendall paused. "I haven't got them yet, but I'm confident, Agent Maxwell."

"Let me know when you've got it locked up. I'm flying into another crime scene with the Pittsburgh task force. The quicker we can put this together, the better chance of taking these guys off the board before they do more damage."

"Understood, Agent Maxwell."

"Kendall, do me a favor and call me Max."

"Okay, Max."

"Two minutes," the pilot said.

"Got to go, Kendall. Touching down. Great work!" Maxwell was looking over the email from Boyden. The heading read: SUSPECT IDENTITIES AND PHOTOS.

"I'll be in touch," Kendall said, and added, "Max."

Maxwell brought up the email. His phone rang again. This time it was Deputy Director Julian Carswell. "What have you got, Max?"

"New crime scene, in the area of Brave, Pennsylvania. We were told four bodies. We'll be landing in about a minute and a half. I'll update you once we've done a walkthrough and have a better understanding of what we're dealing with."

"Have you been reading the international news?" Carswell asked.

Datcu, Maxwell thought. "What is it?"

"The chief prosecutor, Marinda Vasile, was shot dead outside her home in Bucharest yesterday morning."

"They got anyone in custody? Suspects?"

"No one in custody. The suspects are the same people who want our guest in Quantico very badly."

"I've got to tell you, Julian, it wouldn't bother me a whole lot handing Andrei Gusa back over to the Vladimirskus. He's such a fucking scumbag." Maxwell sighed. "What about Nicolae Datcu?"

"He's okay. He's the one who called me this morning with the news. Hang on, Max." Carswell covered the phone and conversed with someone else, then came back on the phone. "You got the profiles of the other three suspects from Boyden?"

"Yeah, haven't opened them up yet. I was just going to do that when you called."

"I've already seen them. If it doesn't mess up your investigation, I'd like to get their faces on the news and turn the screws on them hard. Maybe we'll get a sighting from a concerned citizen."

Maxwell thought about this. "Okay, Julian, let's do that."

"I'll have Boyden get a hold of the big three in Pennsylvania and arrange a press conference. You haven't read the profiles yet?"

"No, not yet."

"Well, here's a strange tidbit for you. One of the four suspects is a person of interest in a string of schoolgirl murders in the Ann Arbor, Michigan, area. James Parch, aka Steel."

"Prepare for landing," the helicopter pilot warned.

"We're touching down, Julian."

"All right, keep me advised."

"Will do. Bye for now."

5

Leigh was the first to recognize the starfished body of Jim Parch. She held up her phone and compared the email photograph to that of the dismembered man in the driveway. She murmured, "And then there were three."

"What?" Halsey asked.

Leigh gave Bob Halsey a sideways glance and said to Maxwell, "This is one of our suspects." She held the picture on her phone up, and Maxwell looked from photo to body.

"James Parch," Maxwell said. "I guess they figured him for a liability."

"Maybe he wanted out," Bobby said.

"Maybe," Maxwell agreed. "Maybe they were worried he might try and cut a deal."

They were standing in a group around the first body. Maxwell, Leigh, Halsey, Ogden, and a state police investigator named Aurora Brown.

"DMV has three vehicles listed to this residence. A 2004 GMC Sierra, a 2006 Chevrolet Suburban, and a 1979 Ford F150," Brown said.

"Are they all accounted for?" Oggy asked her.

"The Suburban is missing," Brown said.

"We got a BOLO out on it?"

"Statewide."

"Good. If they're driving it, we'll get them."

Maxwell listened tentatively, taking in the severed head of James Parch. His eyes and mouth were wide open. The eyes had fogged with gray ice crystals while the mouth twisted into a grimace that had become frozen in time. "What happened that made them turn on you?" Maxwell asked the corpse.

"I think they're breaking down," Leigh said.

"Maybe Jim realized that Lance was using him," Maxwell mused. "Maybe he tried to turn the others." He examined the rest of the body. Both of Jim Parch's feet were shot up. "Lance was putting down a revolt."

"Where are the other three?" Halsey asked.

"In the house," Brown said.

"Cut up like this?" Oggy asked.

"No, burned with a brand."

"What was the brand?"

"The number 4."

"What are you trying to accomplish, Lance?" Maxwell mused. "First Norris, who proved to be a liability, now these three who are proving to be a liability. What is your endgame?"

"Good help is hard to find," Halsey said, which got Maxwell's attention. "Belanger isn't just a serial killer. He's a megalomaniac with visions of grandeur. He wants the notoriety. Craves it. But look at the fuckups he's working with. None of them meet his standard. Norris was photographed in a truck stop, bringing the heat to Lance's door."

"You think he's going to kill the other two?" Leigh asked.

"Just a matter of time," Oggy agreed.

"Then what was the point of all this?" Maxwell waved a hand over the body. "Why bother chopping him up?"

"That's for your benefit," Leigh said.

Maxwell thought about this, his face contorted into a scowl.

"Do you want to see the other bodies?" Brown asked impatiently. "My Crime Scene folks need to close off the scene, so if you folks want a walkthrough… We should probably get moving."

Maxwell got up and nodded, "Let's go for a look."

6

State Route 28

Summerville, PA

For most of the ride, they were silent, searching the gray-white landscape for an easy opportunity. The snow was beginning to fall and stick to the secondary highway, turning black to gray. The Suburban was going to be hot once the Fowler farm was discovered. But Lance had miscalculated how quickly the scene would be found.

The decision to go to Waynesburg was changed to Summerville, and the one hundred sixty-seven-mile ride was extended by route and weather.

Lance had replaced the snub nose .38 in his jacket pocket, trading it for a virtual map. The other two were settled now, no longer focused on what they had done, instead on the mission at hand. They had to find another vehicle, one that wouldn't be reported stolen and placed on a BOLO list.

The radio reception in the area wasn't all that hot. Lance scanned through the dial looking for a news channel and was unsuccessful. He bounced from country station to evangelical, and eventually settled on a static-filled classic rock station that was doing a Led Zeppelin tribute. As the snowflakes danced, Robert Plant chanted about sitting with the elders of the gentle race.

It was unraveling. The goddamn plan was unraveling. Lance had made several mistakes. The monster had been in control, and he was losing his grip. He had to push it back down, had to figure a way out of this mess.

They're going to turn on me, he thought. *They might've agreed to take down Jim, but they're looking at me sideways now, and if they're alone, they're going to turn on me.*

Larry, who was driving, reached down and adjusted the radio, trying to tune it. "Fucking Quaker state."

"What?" Dusk had been nodding in out of consciousness.

"We've gotta find another vehicle and ditch this one," Lance said.

"Where are we going, exactly?" Larry asked.

"Yeah," Dusk said. "We can't go back to Pittsburgh. Maybe we need to get out of the state. We should've headed into Virginia or North Carolina."

Lance said, "First we're going to find another vehicle and…"

Robert Plant was abruptly interrupted by a news bulletin. "The Pennsylvania State Police and FBI are asking for public assistance in locating a fugitive vehicle connected to a string of murders in Brave, Pennsylvania. The vehicle of interest is a 2007 mint green Chevrolet Suburban. The license plate number is YYC9750, registered in the state of Pennsylvania. Police are warning that the occupants of this vehicle may be armed and extremely dangerous. They are cautioning the public not to approach the vehicle, but to contact police using 911 or by calling..."

"Fuck!" Lance felt his heart jump a beat.

"We better ditch this truck," Dusk said.

"No shit, Sherlock," Larry barked. "But I'm not walking into butt fuck nowhere in the middle of a snowstorm. We need another set of wheels."

"Slow down," Lance ordered. "And everyone shut up and listen!"

The news announcer continued with their names and descriptions, and connected Lance and the others to the Highwayman killings along with the Yard Street murders. There was even a soundbite from Agent Maxwell.

"Jesus Christ, they're going to have roadblocks everywhere! We gotta get the fuck off this road," Dusk complained.

The light was draining from the sky. Snow was swirling in torrents through the cones of the headlights. That was when an opportunity presented itself.

***

CHAPTER 14 – EPIPHANY

1

16 November 2008

PA Route 28

Outside Summerville, PA

The storm had worsened. The snow collected in drifts along the highway, some as high as three feet. Lance knew that there would be police checks on all the major roadways. And he figured they must not have found the Fowler farm because there was no mention of Jim Parch in the news broadcast.

The net was tightening, and it now looked as though he would have to abandon his plans and start thinking about self-preservation. He gave Larry and Dusk a stealthy glance. Like Norris, like Steel, they would have to go. He was disappointed that the plan he'd spent so much time, money, and effort on was falling apart.

Fucking Gusa!

The opportunity came in the form of taillights glowing in a rest area outside Summerville, Pennsylvania. The car was barely visible in the blowing snow, and they might have missed it, had it not been for the news broadcast and weather slowing them down.

"Pull in there," Lance said. "Right behind the car and kill the lights." He tightened his grip on the .38.

"What's the plan?" Dusk asked.

"You really have to ask?" Lance was shaking his head.

"Maybe we ought to find out how many there are," Larry said. "We don't need anyone taking off, giving up our location." He pulled in about five feet behind the snow-covered Ford Taurus wagon and killed the lights. The car was idling, and judging by the sheath of snow enveloping it, the vehicle had been there awhile.

"We gotta drag them out. We don't want any blood in the car. Over there." Lance pointed to the woods beside the rest area. "We walk whoever's in the car into those woods and dispose of them."

"What about the Suburban?" Larry asked.

"That'll have to go too," Lance said.

"Enough talk," Dusk said, reaching for the door handle. "Let's get this done."

They exited the Suburban at the same time, Lance and Dusk moving up the right side of the wagon, while Larry came up the driver's side. The windows were blanketed except for the driver's side window. The snow was wet, flakes as big as quarters plopping upon their shoulders, sticking and accumulating like icing sugar. Larry glanced inside the vehicle, first the front seats, and then the back.

He shook his head, "No."

Lance backed up, wiped two fingers of snow from the hatchback, and could see a lump beneath a sleeping bag. He raised a finger on his right hand to his lips while pointing at the hatch with the left.

Larry nodded and waved them away. They gathered behind the Suburban. "I've got an idea," Larry said.

2

Twenty-one-year-old Carolyn McIntosh was sleeping when she heard the vehicle pull in behind her wagon. An hour earlier, she'd parked in the rest area to get out of the storm. Three miles back she'd almost gone into the ditch. That had been enough to convince her to get off the road. She'd been making her way back to Waltham, Massachusetts. More specifically, Bentley University, where she was into her third year of accounting and finance.

She'd dropped the back passenger seat and spread out her sleeping bag in the cargo compartment. The back of the wagon wasn't as warm as the front, but she couldn't sleep upright. She was cocooned inside the bag, using her breath to keep warm, feeling the cold, flat, hard carpet beneath her. She should have bought a foam pad to make things more comfortable, but she hadn't. She was drifting in and out of sleep, the faint noise of the car radio and idling engine suddenly joined by the new vehicle pulling in.

She tiredly wondered if it was a state trooper or just another weary traveler. An hour before, a rig had pulled in, its big engine rumbling obnoxiously. Thankfully, the driver was only there for a few minutes. Probably updating his log book or taking a pee, she guessed.

Then she heard the faint crunching of snow beneath the feet of more than one person. She didn't move, didn't peek from beneath the bag, and then the feet, at least two pairs, maybe three, moved away. It was quiet then, except for the dual idling engines and faintly, The Eagles singing "Peaceful Easy Feeling" on her radio.

Then there were vehicle doors opening and closing.

Cachunk... cachunk... cachunk.

Three of them, she thought. *Probably got out for a pee.*

She barely heard the gear selector clunking from park to reverse, neutral, and then drive. The vehicle wheels turned, crunching the snow.

She poked her head from the beneath the covers and said, "Good. Go away. I'm trying to sleep." That was when there was a mild thump and the wagon lurched forward. They had hit her car. "Damn it! Oh, damn it!" She popped up wearing a Bentley University sweatsuit. Her hair was short, cut like a boy, ears exposed. She put her sneakers on without lacing them. The car was brand new, didn't even have a thousand miles on it. A gift from her father.

There was a tap on the passenger window.

"Hello, is anyone in there?" said a voice, then another tap. "I'm afraid I bumped into your car."

Sneakers on, she climbed between the seats and back into the front. She saw a hand wiping away the snow.

The silhouette said, "Oh my God, this is embarrassing." She hit the power unlock, and the doors opened on both sides. From behind, she felt hands clamp down on her shoulders, and suddenly she was being dragged out. Before she could inhale, she heard the same voice behind her say, "If you scream, I'll cut your throat."

She exhaled, feeling the backs of her sneakers filling with snow, thinking, *I'm going to be raped and murdered.*

The other two were still looking in the car.

One of them said, "This'll do nicely."

The one who had dragged her out was now spinning her around to face him. He said, "What's your name?"

"Carolyn. Please don't hurt me."

From behind another said, "We're not going to hurt you. We just want your car." She turned to face the man who said that. He was in his mid to late twenties, shoulder-length hair and a scruffy beard. He looked sort of like Kurt Cobain. "So listen, Carolyn, keep your cool, and everything will be all right."

What are they? Escaped convicts? Robbers?

Then she remembered the news broadcast from earlier, and she felt the panic overwhelm her. She let out a scream and began to fight for her life. "Nooooo!"

If they take you, they're going to kill you.

The man holding her almost lost control, then the other one, the one who didn't look like Kurt Cobain, came around and punched her in the stomach, doubling her over. She hung there in his grip panting, trying to breathe.

The puncher leaned down and growled, "Shut up, bitch, or I'll cut off your tits and force feed them to you." He brandished a big hunting knife and pushed the flat part of the blade against her left breast. "You pickin' up what I'm saying?"

She froze, thinking, *I gotta get away or I'm dead.*

She was a small girl, five-foot-four inches, easily controlled by the two men who held her by each bicep. The guy who looked like the lead singer of Nirvana came around and faced her. "Do you know who I am?"

She knew who he was, who they were, she'd heard the news bulletins, their names. But she didn't want to admit it. To acknowledge who they were would seal her fate. She shook her head. "No."

He grinned. "Do you know what a tell is?"

She didn't answer.

"A tell is something cops look for when questioning someone who they think will lie to them. It can be a darting of the eyes, a mannerism, but it's an unconscious physical reaction, and you just gave me a tell. So… I'm going to ask you again; do you know who I am?"

She brought her eyes back up to meet his. "Yes."

"Thank you for being honest," he said and looked at the others. "Over behind the restroom should do it. Maybe one hundred feet." Then he stopped and looked at the console of the car, apparently spotting something. "Grab her cell phone, Dusk."

Dusk leaned in and snatched the cell phone, pulling the charging cable with it. It glowed in his hand as if waking to the violence.

"Give it to me," the Kurt Cobain guy said, and Dusk handed it over and he dropped it into his pocket. Then he brought his eyes up to meet hers.

In that finality, she knew she was going to die. The phone was her lifeline. These men were killers. Everyone in the state was looking for them. She'd listened to a special report about it on the news just after lunch that day. The certainty soaked in a little deeper, and she scolded herself. *I've been so damned stupid. Killers running around and...*

They tightened their grip. The big one who had pulled her out said, "All right, let's get this done."

"Sure thing," the one with the knife agreed.

Then they were dragging her backward through the snow, and she watched Kurt Cobain following casually behind. That was when she began to beg. "Please! Please! I... I don't want to die!" Her pleading was a mixture of stutters and coarse sobbing, sounding almost childlike. "Just take my car, I won't tell anybody. P-please!"

One of her sneakers came off and now her bare heel dragged through the snow, her Achilles tendon beginning to tighten and numb. The long-haired guy held eye contact with her, his face emotionless. He picked up her dropped sneaker, continuing to follow. Behind him, the car was getting farther and farther away. The vehicles disappeared around the restroom she'd used only an hour earlier.

They're going to kill you, her mind screamed. Then there were trees slipping past, silent witnesses to the horror of it all. *This is how it feels when you know you're going to die. I don't want to die! Please God, please.* The trees became thicker, her abductors weaving between them, the man behind following along.

"How much farther?" the big guy asked.

"Fifty feet should do it," Kurt Cobain replied.

"Why are you doing this?" Carolyn whimpered.

He smiled, brought out a small handgun, and said, "This is what we do best." Then he turned his attention to the one holding her on the right. "Dusk, do you see that stump over there?"

"Yep," the one named Dusk acknowledged.

"Take her there, and we'll get this done."

They cut on a diagonal. Carolyn couldn't see the stump, but she knew its purpose. They would probably repeatedly rape her and when they were finished… "I don't want to die," she said. "Please let me go."

Cobain watched them line up on the stump. "That'll do it," he said. "Grab her by the wrists and hold her."

"Wait," Dusk said. "Aren't we going to at least have a little fun?" They grabbed her by each wrist and pulled her arms out until she thought the joints might pop.

"We don't have time for that," the big guy said. "We gotta get moving. Everyone is looking for us," he scolded. "Come on, Lance, let's get this over with. We still gotta get rid of the Suburban."

She was screaming now, "Please… please… please…"

"Lance, are you listening?" the big guy pushed.

"Yes," Lance said and brought up the .38, aimed, and fired, twice.

The screaming stopped after the shots, which were dampened by the storm and woods.

3

Task Force Pittsburgh

Pittsburgh, PA

The winter storm beat down mercilessly on Pennsylvania, upstate New York, and the southern part of Ontario, Canada. Checkpoints were set up on all major highways by state police in three states, Pennsylvania, West Virginia, and New York. Even local cops were alerted to keep an eye out for a Suburban carrying three male occupants. In all, there were one hundred seventy checkpoints in place within hours of the Fowler farm massacre. CNN, MSNBC, and FOX reported the manhunt as the most extensive scale cooperation by police forces ever conducted.

Maxwell was sitting in an office looking over emails, filing reports, and waiting to hear that the perps had been grabbed by authorities. He called Inspector Nicolae Datcu in Romania, and they discussed the murder of Chief Prosecutor Vasile.

"It is bad," Datcu told him. "Chief Prosecutor Vasile was my friend, as well as my colleague. She helped me put many bad people behind bars."

"Maybe you should get out of Romania. You could come here until things cool off a bit," Maxwell said. He liked Datcu. He was the embodiment of what he imagined a foreign detective to be like. "I've got a place in Virginia. You could stay there."

"That is very kind, Max, but I will not be leaving Bucharest. I will not be stopping until the Vlad family is behind bars or dead." He paused. "No matter what they do, they now have the full interest of INTERPOL and the Romanian police." He exhaled loudly.

"Have you gained any ground?"

"We have three hard drives now and the cooperation of the Czech Republic as well as the Serbian government. But I do not want to go into detail. Phone service here is easily compromised."

"I understand," Max said.

"It appears that you have your hands full there. The Highwayman is still on the run, no?"

"Yeah, it's a shit show."

"Shit show?"

"A mess."

"Mess, yes, this I understand. I read up on you on the internet before you came to Bucharest. You are good at what you do. You will get him." Datcu took another drag off his smoke and exhaled. "Soon, I think."

"I wish I were as confident as you, Nicolae. He's on the run with two other killers. We will eventually get him, but how many more people will he kill?"

"Some things are beyond our control, Max."

"I know," Max said and thought, *that's what drives me crazy.*

"Please hold, Max." There were others with Datcu now. Romanian voices chattered back and forth. The phone line became muffled and Datcu said something in Romanian as well. Then he came back. "I must go, Max, I have business to attend to."

"Take care and stay in touch."

Datcu said goodbye and Maxwell's cell rang once more. He looked down at the caller I.D.

It read: K. Dickson.

"Kendall," Max answered. "Tell me you got something good for me?"

"We're now monitoring the account of one Wilson Rogers." Kendall sounded less stiff, even delighted. "The account is not offshore, that was a misdirect."

"Where is it, then?"

"The Royal Bank."

"In England? I thought you said it wasn't offshore?"

"The Royal Bank is a Canadian institution."

"Canadian? Really? How the hell would he do that? Never mind, can we track him?" Maxwell was simultaneously looking over an email from Boyden. Attached was information on Jim Parch and his possible, now likely, involvement in the murders of eleven schoolgirls in Michigan.

"I've already made arrangements with the Mounties and the Canadian Revenue Agency. There are approximately two million dollars in investments and another million in soluble cash. If he needs walking around money, it can be accessed through an ATM."

"All he has to do is make a withdrawal." Maxwell chuckled.

"Exactly," Kendall said. "He makes a withdrawal, and I'll call you on speed dial."

"What about a teller? If he goes into a bank, will we have the same advantage?"

"That would be even better. The ATM alert could be minutes. There's an alert on the bank computers. If a teller brings up the account for Wilson Rogers, a prompt will tell them to cooperate but notify security immediately."

"That's good news, Kendall. Everyone in the state is looking for him, but Mother Nature is being a bitch right now."

"I see that."

"You call as soon as he punches in his PIN, and I'll have an army of cops ready to swoop in."

"I will."

"All right, I gotta get back to the more mundane part of my job. Filing reports for the bosses. I'll talk to you later, Kendall." Maxwell hung up after Kendall said goodbye. He returned to the Parch file and the schoolgirl killings. He kept thinking about the Hand of Death, and how so many had bought into the bullshit that Henry Lee Lucas and Ottis Toole were slinging. There was no Hand of Death. It was concocted by the two drifter-killers to raise their status and keep investigators asking questions. Lucas and Toole were both dead now, old men who had falsely confessed to hundreds of killings, but the Hand of Death was a thing of lore.

Except the Highwayman wanted to make it a reality, Maxwell thought, perusing the crime scene photos from the schoolgirl killings. *The son of a bitch was trying to start his own little murder club, for Christ's sake. But now he's killing them? Why?*

A knock came at the door, breaking Maxwell's train of thought.

"Come in," he said.

The door swung open, and there stood a tall drink of water named Detective Lonnie Perkins. "How are you, Max?"

"Holy shit, Perk?" Maxwell got up from the desk and came around. "What the hell are you doing here?" He was shaking his hand now, happy to see his old friend.

"I've got four weeks of accumulated vacation time. I thought I might come out and offer a hand, if I'm welcome. I'm not looking for pay. I just want to be in on the hunt." Perk smiled.

"Oh boy, that could be a real tough one, Perk. Right now, I'm dealing with state cops, local cops, and the Bureau. Are we talking independent? Does your boss even know you are here?"

"My wife? Yes, of course."

"Funny guy. I'm serious. Does your boss know?"

"I believe his parting words were, 'Perk, stay the fuck away from those goddamned Quakers. Or at least, I better not hear about it.' So, he's not going to hear about it." Perkins uncoupled his hand from Max's. "What do you say, Max?"

Maxwell thought about it. This would ruffle the feathers of the bosses, but Perkins could be useful, and Max needed a friendly face. "Come with me," Max said and led him out to meet the others.

4

PA Route 28

Outside Summerville, PA

When the two men went down, they dragged her with them into the snow. The guy with the gun was a frozen silhouette against the night, standing over the madness of murder for which he was responsible. Breathing in and out, puffs of vapor left his body like a machine winding down after a hard workout.

Carolyn expected the guy who looked like Kurt Cobain to shoot her dead, but he just stood there, robot-like, holding her sneaker in his left hand, gun in the right. Her survival instinct hadn't kicked in. The fear held her to the ground, kept her from finding something to defend against him, or as a last resort, running into the forest.

5

Lance was coming back, trying to focus. He hadn't wanted to shoot them, not yet anyway. No point in arguing honorable intentions. He had to kill them and would have. But killing them now? No. That had been an impulse, and it hadn't made his situation any better.

It had been the monster again, rearing its ugly head and fucking things up. Clouding his judgment and fucking things right the fuck up!

Fuck off, you're the monster, it growled from within.

"No," Lance spat back. "I had a plan!"

But the internal voice was relentless.

You are the one fucking up.

"I had a plan!" Lance gripped the gun harder.

6

You had visions of grandeur.

"No."

Necrophiles and Vlad the Impaler!

"It was you. You screwed up the plan. I was careful!"

You could have gotten away last year.

"I wasn't done!"

But you had to taunt him!

"That's not my fault! You and your goddamned cravings!"

Come and find me!

And suddenly the conversation stopped.

His sense of equilibrium had become unbalanced. It had all started to unravel back in Lawrenceville, thanks to "Fucking Gusa!" He cuffed the gun against his thigh, growling first and then into a maniacal rant, "Fucking Gusa! Fucking Gusa! Fucking Gusa! Fucking Gusa! Fucking Gusa!"

Carolyn McIntosh couldn't feel her hands anymore. They were buried in the snow, propping her up in the position of a sunbather. The man above her was losing his mind, raving at some unseen force. She could think only of Norman Bates and his rantings, "Mother, what did you do? No Mother! No!"

But for Lance, the storm was passing.

7

Insects buzzed inside his ears from the gunshots… he could hear his heart beating… downward, slowing, calming. His breathing eased. His eyes focused and before him, she stood pleading with her eyes. He took a breath, then another, and brought up the gun to meet her face.

"Please," she cried. "Please don't, I'm pregnant."

He cocked the hammer on the .38. "What's your name?"

"Carolyn… Carolyn. Please don't hurt me."

He swallowed, listening for the monster's protest or approval, and then realized the separation of his other half was what had led to the plan coming apart.

You're the monster, the voice echoed.

Had they switched places? Was he the monster? Was the methodical Lance buried down there in the purgatory, tethered by the same restraints that held the creature who now held the gun? Or had he simply not embraced the darkness that lurked in his heart?

"Yes," he said. "That has to be it."

He looked down at the bodies of Larry and Dusk. Dusk never knew what hit him. The bullet hit him square in the back of the skull. Startled by the shot, Larry had turned his head slightly before the .38 slug penetrated his head just behind the right ear and exited, demolishing the bridge of his nose. The dead bodies bookended the girl, Carolyn, who looked as though she was going to say something, but she wasn't privy to Lance's epiphany. She was just a loose end, another hapless victim. He embraced the darkness and became one.

"Please let me go," she begged.

He came back then, holding his aim and her shoe, a strange smile on his face. Yes, he'd done it all wrong, but now he would embrace the darkness and allow full access. No more bondage. No more restraint. He accepted everything.

Then there was the issue at hand. Carolyn.

"We've got a problem, Carolyn. You know who I am. You just witnessed me killing two of my three partners. Killing you just makes sense."

"Please, I'm pregnant. I won't tell anyone. I promise."

"That doesn't really matter to me, and yes, you will."

"I can help you."

"Help me?"

"The roadblocks, they said on the news they're looking for three men. If you ride with me, we'll be able to get through, and you can escape." Her pitch was hurried, desperate. "It can work, but you need me to make it happen."

Lance grinned then. This was a stark contrast to the spitting, ranting maniac Carolyn had seen only seconds before.

He said, "Well, I wouldn't want people to think I'm a baby killer," and tossed her the shoe. "Better put that on."

She reached out furtively with an icy claw and snagged the sneaker, struggling to get it onto her equally frozen foot. With the shoe on, she looked back up, expecting him to pull the trigger, sending a bullet crashing through her skull.

"Come on, Carolyn. The clock is ticking." He used the gun to motion her to get up.

She rose, her foot numb except for an itching pain that pricked numbly on the surface of her skin. She felt something warm and wet on her left hand and realized it was the big guy's brain matter. She was about to wipe it off on her pants when the man with the gun said, "Ah, no, wipe it in the snow or on him. I want your clothes clean for our ride."

She shuddered. "I don't want to touch him."

"May as well get used to it. If you want to live, you're going to help me hide the bodies." He pointed at each with the gun and said, "And we'll need to get rid of the vehicle as well."

Carolyn knelt slowly, wiped her hand on Larry's jacket, and got back up. She thought at least that if this man killed her, maybe her DNA would turn up, and her parents would know that whatever happened to her had started with these two men.

"Come on," he invited. "I think there's a shovel in the Suburban."

"The ground is frozen," she said.

"You'll just cover them with snow." He waved the gun toward the vehicle. "Let's go. We need to get moving while the storm is on. We'll need to get you cleaned up for our trip." He jammed the gun into his jacket pocket, keeping it trained on her, but out of sight. He felt good. He was complete now, no more internalizing, no more hiding the other side. And he still had a plan, and but for the grace of God, it might just work.

It took Carolyn roughly twenty minutes to cover the bodies of the two men with snow. At first, the blood seeped through the burial blanket, but with each heaping shovelful of wet snow, they simply became white lumps that disappeared in the interlocking eastern hemlocks shrouding the landscape.

The Suburban was a little trickier. There was nowhere to hide it in the pull-off, and Lance didn't want to leave Carolyn alone with either vehicle. Even if he tied her up, a car could roll into the rest area, and he would find himself without wheels or a hostage.

The two got inside the Suburban and drove about a half a mile down the highway, where he found a forestry access road. Luck would have it, there was no gate, and the trees were even denser here than at the pull-off. They drove in and parked it beneath a tree that towered roughly one hundred thirty feet. Its branches provided cover from anyone who might be searching from the sky. Not that there would be any helicopters out in this weather. He had her gather deadfall and place it over the vehicle. This took about 15 minutes.

"Let's go," Lance ordered, and they trudged back up the road against the blowing snow and onto the shoulder of the highway.

Carolyn prayed that a highway patrol car might come along, scanning the road for motorists stuck or in distress. Even a snow plow would be enough. She could shove her captor down and make a run for it. Her feet were wet and cold, but her core temperature had improved drastically after the physical exertion of burying the bodies and gathering branches to help camouflage the Suburban.

By the time they reached her little hatchback, she had no illusions about her fate should she not escape. For now, she'd become a tool to get Lance through the roadblocks. But once she outlived that usefulness, he would kill her, probably dumping her body in a ditch or burying her in much the same way they had buried his two partners.

They got into the car and he said to her, "Okay, Carolyn, I want you to listen very carefully to me. What you do will determine whether I kill you and your unborn child. Do you understand?"

She nodded. "Yes."

"No, say it."

"Yes, I understand."

"We're going to see my family up in Plattsburgh, New York. I'm your boyfriend. Understand?"

"Yes. I understand." She wiped her runny nose. She wanted to ask a question which she was sure would get her killed. Something like, "What if the cops ask you for identification?"

But she left it alone.

"If you mess around along the way, I'll shoot you in the guts and leave you in the snow. Being gut shot is extremely painful. I read about it somewhere. So, there's that."

"I won't mess around."

"Checkpoints. Not only will I kill you, but I'll kill the cop, and if I get away…" He smiled. "I'll make a point of killing your family. Even the kids. You got a little sister, brother, a cousin? I'll kill them." He brought the gun out to show her he meant business. "Understand?"

A single tear spilled out of her left eye, over her cheek, down to her lip, and into her mouth. "I understand."

"There's good news, Carolyn." He nodded his head. "Do you want to hear the good news?"

"Yes."

"You do what I say, and you will be remembered as the only person the Highwayman ever spared. I promise you that. I need you to get through the roadblocks. If you help me with that, I'll let you go. You understand?"

"I understand."

But she didn't believe him.

***

CHAPTER 15 – THE DEVIL IN INSPIRATION

1

16 November 2008

They routed north on Highway 28 through Summerville without meeting a single roadblock. The travel was slow, Carolyn driving against the full brunt of what had now become an all-out blizzard. The Taurus wagon never got over 35 MPH, anything more and she began to lose control of the car. Beside her, the Highwayman shifted his focus back and forth between the road and her. He was quiet for the first hour. Then he pulled her cell phone from his pocket and unplugged the charging cord. Winding it around his fingers, he said, "If we're stopped, you call me Will." He opened the window and tossed the charging cable. "Understand?"

"Yes, Will," she said and added, "You're my boyfriend, and we're going up to see your parents in Plattsburgh."

He then went to work on the phone. He pulled a knife from his pocket, speaking as he cracked the shell of the phone. "We've got lots of time, so don't do anything stupid like run us off the road. If you do that, I'll kill you and just hitch another ride. I'm not screwing around."

"I won't, I promise." She held the wheel in a death grip, both hands. The highway was completely snow-covered, no tracks to keep her position on the road.

"You better not." He pulled the battery from the phone, tossed it, then a little farther down the road, the remainder went out the window.

The next town was Brookville, Pennsylvania, and still no checkpoints. But they'd been traveling at a snail's pace, sometimes as slow as 10 MPH. Sometimes less.

It took forty-five minutes to reach Brookville, a mere eight miles away, and on the other side of the town, police strobes cut through the night, turning the falling snow red and blue.

"This is it, Carolyn." He pulled the gun out to show her and replaced it in his jacket. The checkpoint was roughly three hundred feet away. "This is where you earn your right to live."

There was a single police car, parked in the middle of the road. Carolyn couldn't make out if it was a sheriff or state cop. The officer was tall and lean, dressed in winter gear, shoulders sugared with snow. In his hand, a flashlight with a red cover waved them forward. Carolyn eased the car forward through the driving snow. Her heart was jackhammering, her hands clamped down on the steering wheel. She was hyperventilating.

Then she felt a hand reach over and touch her leg. She turned toward the man who had not only threatened her, but her family. He said in a calm voice, "Relax. They're looking for three men." He smiled. It wasn't a charming smile. It was predatory, voracious, hungry. His eyes shifted between her and the fast approaching police car. "I'm your boyfriend, Will. We're going up to Plattsburgh to see my parents. Take a deep breath."

Sixty feet away now.

Carolyn took a deep breath and exhaled. "Okay."

"I'm going to lie back like I'm sleeping."

Forty-five feet now.

The cop was a local.

Carolyn had no idea what she would do. Her mind was churning through the possibilities. She could open the door and dive out of the car. *But what if he kills the cop?* She could do what he said, and talk her way through the checkpoint. *And what will become of me?* Would he really let her live if he got her to the border? *Of course not! Don't be foolish!*

Thirty feet now.

The headlights lit the police officer's face in the night. He continued to summon them forward. He was looking into the car, checking the number of occupants. He cocked his head right and spoke into the radio mic attached to his lapel.

Twenty feet.

"I'll kill him. Make no mistake, Carolyn, and I'll kill you and find your family."

Fifteen feet.

"I'm a bad guy," he whispered while leaning back and closing his eyes. But he was watching.

"I know," Carolyn said.

Ten feet.

"No, you don't, but if you fuck this up, you will."

For Carolyn, the last eight feet were a series of frozen moments. She took a final breath and made her decision. Reaching down, she touched the radio, resurrecting the volume up to a level of background music.

The Alan Parsons Project sang, "Games People Play."

Giving a sideways gaze to her abductor, she rolled down the driver's window, inviting a cold blast of air.

The cop began to lean into the window.

She could see the cop's overcoat was pulled back, and his left hand was resting on the butt of his gun.

I can do this, Carolyn thought.

"Good evening," the cop said and shone his light into Carolyn's face while checking out her passenger. "Where are you folks headed?" Then he put the light on Lance. "Just the two of you?"

"Yes," Carolyn said. "Wake up, Will."

Feigning sleep, Lance opened his eyes, "What's going on, Carolyn? Was there an accident?" Then he looked directly at the cop or rather, into the blinding light of his Maglite. "Evening, Officer, what's going on?"

The flashlight came down to the coat that Lance had used to cover himself, following his legs to the floor, then swung back onto Carolyn. "Pretty lousy weather to be out on the road," the cop said.

"We're heading up to Plattsburgh to spend time with his parents." Carolyn shrugged, while her mind screamed, *please help me.*

"Plattsburgh, eh?" The cop grinned, leaned down on the window, and probed the back seat and hatchback with the Maglite. "I played ball up around Johnstown. Nice area." He snapped off the light. He was bored, probably from standing out there for hours.

"Is the highway closed?" Lance asked.

"No, it's open. But you kids might wanna be careful. This storm is going to be hitting us for the next forty eight hours. It would probably be best to turn you around and send you back to get a room."

"We've been sleeping in the car," Carolyn said. "Saving money on hotels."

"Yeah, I saw your sleeping bag." The cop smiled a little wider. "How far are you folks planning on going tonight?"

"Probably up to Warsaw, if the weather gets worse, but we'd like to make it to Brockway."

"You got family in Brockway?" the cop asked.

Then the police radio intervened.

"Dispatch to Car 4. Bob, you got a copy?"

He brought the mic up. "Copy, Car 4, go ahead?"

"We've got a head-on at the junction of Alaska and Highway 36. Two fatalities. Can you go up and give Jammer a hand in securing the scene?" the dispatcher asked.

"10-4, I'll be there shortly." The cop got up off the window and said to Carolyn and Lance, "We're looking for some bad people out here. Three men. You folks don't be stopping on the highway. Get up to Brockway, or if you're tired, stop in Warsaw."

"What kind of bad men?" Lance asked innocently. "Bank robbers?"

"Worse." The cop started swinging the light, motioning for them to get moving. "If you're going to sleep in your car, do it in a public place. Stay out of the rest areas." He was backing away, edging toward the cruiser.

"Okay, we will," Lance called after him.

And then they were rolling.

2

FBI Field Office

Pittsburgh, PA

A thin net was cast out across the states of Pennsylvania, West Virginia, and New York, Brave, Pennsylvania being the center of that net. FBI Director Julian Carswell had coordinated with state police in all three states, but they weren't getting the coverage they wanted. Not by a long shot.

By estimation, Jim Parch hadn't been dead for more than six hours, which meant that the killers couldn't have gone much farther than one hundred miles. That was Maxwell's contention.

"The storm will be slowing them down just like everyone else," Maxwell said to Julian on the phone. "They may be looking for another lair. In six hours, they could be almost three hundred miles away, but they won't be moving fast."

"We've got them on a nationwide lookout. The director got approval from the attorney general herself for us to coordinate with the state cops, and we've got a team reaching out to local law enforcement," Julian responded.

"The storm's going to be a bitch for us too. Those same state and local cops are going to have their hands full with traffic and accidents. How long until we get this going, Julian?"

"It's already started, Max. Now, what I need from you is a plan to take these three down."

"Yeah, well, I want to assign a special task force now that we're on the hunt, which will include Detectives Ogden Chartrand, Robert Halsey, and Lonnigan Perkins."

"Perkins? The Louisville cop? What the hell is he doing in Pennsylvania?" Julian didn't sound angry; in fact, he chuckled a little.

"He was passing through on holiday," Maxwell said.

"Oh yeah? Does his boss know?"

"Probably. But in denial."

"That seems to be a symptom of bosses."

"Yeah."

"Belanger's going to try and head for Canada. That's where his money is. He's probably thinking that if he gets across the border, he can disappear in the north. There are lots of places to hide in Canada."

"Okay, what's the plan?"

"I want to send each of those three out to places in proximity to where I think he'll cross. That is, if the weather gives us a break. I'm thinking two hundred miles. Halsey and Chartrand, myself, Leigh, and Perkins. But if they slip through, I want to be waiting for them at the most likely crossing."

"They'll be conspicuous. Three men in any vehicle will be of interest at the checkpoints," Julian said.

"Conspicuous." Maxwell thought about that. "I don't think the other two have much time left to live. He's going to kill them sooner or later. If they take another house, he might just do it after that. Take a vehicle and run for Canada. But we've got a bug in his money pot. Agent Dickson of the IRS and our very own Agent Boyden have coordinated with the RCMP and the Royal Bank of Canada. Even if he gets across the border, once he goes for that money, they'll be waiting."

"Okay, where will they cross?"

"I've got a friend in Homeland Security who tells me that there's about a one hundred twenty mile stretch of border between Alexandria Bay and Akwesasne. This would be the area we'd want to focus on. Smuggling on the Saint Lawrence River has been a long tradition in these regions."

"You think he'll pay someone to smuggle him?"

"Possibility. Lance Belanger is pretty intelligent."

"So, if he breaks through, he hires a smuggler to take him into Canada… What smuggler is going to take a serial killer across the river into Canada? Seems far-fetched."

"Probably. But, that's where I think he's going to try and cross."

They were silent then while Carswell digested each of Maxwell's theories, all born of marrying speculation with facts. Maxwell was extraordinary at speculation, but 120 miles was still a long piece of river to watch. He hoped with some evidence they might pare down the amount of ground they were covering. Phone pressed to his ear, Maxwell was looking at the map when something caught his eye.

"There's a Mohawk reservation up around the Cornwall crossing. My guy says they smuggle everything up around that area. Used to be cigarettes, then guns and drugs. ATF picks off a few, and a few more step up. Plus, the territory is restricted to outside police. They've got their own police force. They don't like outsiders. Word is that they aren't afraid to strip a cop of everything, and make him walk out naked."

"Kind of cold time of year for a nature walk."

"Yeah, but if we could get them on board to help, it might be another obstacle for Belanger. Sooner or later he's going to trip over one of them."

"I'll have Boyden get someone onto the Bureau of Indian Affairs, and see how we can arrange a meeting and cooperation with them."

Maxwell chuckled. "Good luck."

"Fuck you, Max." But Julian laughed as well.

It would be a tall order, trying to establish cooperation from people who generally thought the FBI and state cops were nothing but shoot first ask questions later cowboys.

"I need a favor. Can you call Perkins' boss? Sound all official and cook up something to make the Louisville P.D. happy. Say we're requesting him for a special interstate task force."

"Yes, and I'll try and sound like the deputy director of the FBI. And to sound all official, please refer to my immediate answer."

"Thanks, sir."

"Yeah."

"I don't think we're going to get anywhere tonight, but neither will they. Hopefully, they'll stumble into one of our checkpoints, or meet a nosey local cop with the brains to not get his ass shot," Maxwell said. "But if the weather clears and there's still no sign, I'd like to move some people into place as early as tomorrow. I'll need to work out the locations. We'll have to fly, and then rent vehicles to try and cut them off at the pass."

"Get your plan together tonight. You have my permission to add those people to your docket and use them as you see fit. With any luck, it won't come to that. Hopefully, we snag them up in the net before they kill anyone else, but put it together, consult with the other members of your team, and have it in my inbox by the morning."

"All right." Maxwell hung up.

Pittsburgh had become Louisville, another debris field of murder and mayhem, but a debris field, nonetheless. The Highwayman had moved on and they, the task force, would have no fixed base of operations. They were going to need everybody. He would be calling the cavalry, suspending his agents on the Lawrenceville and Syracuse crime scenes.

The hunt was on, and they had a day, maybe two.

3

US 219

14 miles south of Brandy Camp, PA

They went past Warsaw, bought fuel in Brockway, and even went through the drive-thru at McDonald's. There were no police checkpoints any farther up the line. The updated BOLO for the Suburban was recirculating through ViCAP.

Bad information had allowed them to pass through, but phones were ringing all over three states in a wide array of police stations and detachments. The federal agents, under the direction of the attorney general, were requesting state assistance, and the state cops were reaching out to local and jurisdictional police for support.

They pushed up the US 219 against the snow, which in the headlights of the Taurus stabbed at their eyes. They drove out of Brockway, two Big Macs, fries, and Diet Cokes heavier, fighting growing fatigue from the day and the battle against the elements. Against the recommendations of the Brookville cop, Lance began looking for a remote place to park. Given that he was the fugitive they sought, the officer's warning became moot.

Lance stared down at the burner phone and tried to get a signal. Nothing. This angered him, but that was Pennsylvania for you. They still hadn't figured out the cell tower or repeaters that seemed to have become the norm in other states. He had internet boosters at his place in Lawrenceville that he'd purchased from a manufacturer in France. Suddenly, it occurred to him that the properties in Lawrenceville and Syracuse would never be his again. The

Feds would seize them, and probably bulldoze both houses into the ground.

"Fuck," he grunted.

"What?" Carolyn asked.

"We need to get off the road. Find a place to sleep."

This brought about a physical reaction in his prisoner. An upheaval of fear. Her knuckles whitened on the steering wheel; her cheeks hardened from clenched teeth. She was terrified and he could see she was falling apart. He'd seen this before in other victims and in those cases that was fine. But he needed this woman. "Stop it," he snapped.

"What?"

"You know what."

"No," she whimpered.

"Carolyn, I'm not going to kill you." He was chomping down on the last of his fries. "That is if you do what I tell you."

She took one hand off the wheel and used the back of her hand to wipe away the tears.

"There," Lance said, pointing to a sign on the highway: CAMP INSPIRATION – Christian Study Camp. Below that, 5 MILES, and taped across it in a diagonal slice: CLOSED FOR THE SEASON.

This didn't ease Carolyn's concerns. The idea of going to a remote camp with this man only heightened her terror.

Lance finished his fries and said, "Let's hope the road is plowed, and we can access it." Then he yawned. "It's been a long day."

Carolyn laughed nervously. "It sure has."

Lance let out a small chirp of laughter himself. "Best to get off the road for a few hours and grab some sleep. Maybe the storm will let up a bit." But he knew this wasn't true, the weather guy on the radio had said the storm might last as long as three days, and that it was hammering everything from New Hampshire right down the eastern seaboard and stretching as far west as Ohio.

Bad weather was going to slow him down, but it would also give cover. Right now, the girl wasn't missing. The bodies of his dead colleagues were freezing in the snow, cloaked from public attention quite possibly until spring. Even if they found the Suburban, they probably wouldn't find the bodies right away, and he only needed a couple days to get up into Canada. He'd prepared for this, but not intentionally.

Lance didn't need a boat to get across the river into Canada, although he knew where there was one. It was in the woods along the shore of the Saint Lawrence River east of Massena, New York, across from the Long Sault Islands, at a place called Hopson's Point. He'd spotted the twelve-foot Lund there, one August day in 2005 when he was scouting the area as a potential killing ground. It was a childhood place that had drawn him back. He'd accompanied his father and three of his friends on a fishing trip up there on five occasions that hadn't involved a lot of fishing. The men drank, leaving twelve-year-old Lance to wander the landscape looking for animal prey, which he found in both the wild and domestic.

The boat intrigued him, but the Massena shoreline would never become a killing ground. The area was remote enough, but there'd been too much traffic. And there weren't a lot of private places to park. People, campers, park officials, and even the odd border guard moved through the area like spawning fish.

Hopson's Point was one of many road trips he'd made in preparation to ply his trade. He had a few places around the country that hadn't worked for killing.

He'd camped on the site, and though he would never return, that boat never left his mind. He didn't think he would use it, but he never thought about things going this haywire. Never thought for all his planning that things would have turned into such a goddamned shit show.

There was a possibility that the boat wasn't even there anymore. But that didn't matter because, at this point in the year, the boat would be completely unnecessary. It had only served as a reminder of the location and became the location where he intended to cross.

According to an article in FIELD AND STREAM, this late into the year the Saint Lawrence would be frozen, and the ice would be solid enough to support an average man or woman. Ice fishing was common in the area.

He shook the last shoestring fry from the box and crunched down on it.

"Hopefully, that road is plowed."

4

Camp Inspiration

Near Brandy Camp, PA

They drove up into the camp and found it deserted. The buildings were locked and presumably, the plumbing would be winterized. On the bright side, a plow had come in and made a pass on the road, making their travel uneventful. Lance had Carolyn drive around the crescent drive and park on the far side of the camp next to an old gazebo.

They would be sleeping in the Taurus. But there was an outhouse and she, Carolyn, had a case of Nestlé bottled water and some canned goods in the back of the car, if they needed it.

Lance waited for Carolyn to finish her McDonald's meal before discussing the logistics of going to the bathroom and sleeping arrangements. Carolyn went to the outhouse and did her business while her abductor stood vigil with the gun in hand. The outhouse also doubled as a holding cell while he, Lance, took care of his own bathroom business in the nearby bushes.

They did a walk around the camp to see what they could scrounge. In the gazebo, Lance found a stack of gunny sacks. He pulled one off the top and handed it to Carolyn. "If we find anything, put it in here."

"Okay." She shivered and took the sack from him. They slogged from one building to the next, her in front, him behind, always watching. Carolyn was beginning to believe that he wouldn't kill her tonight. She was still useful to him. They would be driving tomorrow, and there would be more roadblocks. He needed her.

But sooner or later he wouldn't.

As they moved from one building to the next, he had Carolyn pick up found items and place them into the sack. Outside the counselors' quarters, he found a half-used roll of duct tape. It was frozen cock-stiff, but it would thaw in the warmth of the car. She also deposited a dull hatchet and three boxes of strike-anywhere wooden matches into the bag.

They checked out the rest of the camp and found a tool shed with a wealth of items. A bag of large, black plastic zip ties. Five cans of Sterno camping jelly, a sharpening stone, and to Lance's surprise and amusement, the same style of machete he'd used to perpetrate killings all over the country. The blade was flecked with rust and dull, but he had a sharpening stone.

The three items, hatchet, zip ties, and machete, all went into the sack, along with the camping jelly and stone. Carolyn felt her heart and hopes sink with each deposit. Equally troubling was the robotic smile on her abductor's face as she placed them in the sack.

They found one more thing on the way back to the car, a small wooden cross fashioned from the forest wood and created by a talented carver. Perhaps a counselor who preached scripture. But this was not the vestibule of God's playground, no matter how tranquil or beautiful the surroundings.

"Do you want it?" Lance asked.

"Yes, please," Carolyn said.

Lance picked up the cross and used a piece of meat cord from the tool shed to fashion a crude necklace. Then he handed it to her. "For the vampires," he mocked. Carolyn didn't smile. She set the sack down and placed it around her neck.

When they returned to the car, she prayed to God for protection as Lance used the zip ties to bind her wrists behind her back. Silent tears streamed down her cheeks. She wanted to be home, and away from this horrible nightmare.

"Carolyn," Lance said.

"Yes," she whimpered, wishing she could hold the cross which hung there reassuringly. It was maddening.

"If you try anything while we're supposed to be sleeping, I'm going to chop you up like the others. Understand?"

"Yes," she said, but she really didn't. She wasn't privy to the gory details of Lance's exploits.

Then his face came up, a looming specter of the madness she'd seen when he killed his partners. He said, "But before I do that, I'll gut you like a fish." Then he smiled. "Now get some sleep."

He popped the hatchback, and she sat on the tailgate as he laid her down and placed the sleeping bag over her. "Get as much sleep as you can, because tomorrow is going to be a long day."

"Okay, Lance," she said, submitting. "Goodnight."

It was the first time she'd used his name.

"Goodnight," he said, and after a minute, he went about sharpening the machete and the hatchet. Inside the warmth of the car, Carolyn listened to the stone grating against the dull metal, its resistance lessening with each pass. She prayed harder, trying not to think about the crazy man sharpening tools with one intended use.

This is a holy place, she assured herself. *God will protect me.*

For the most part, she was right, Camp Inspiration was where Christians gathered each summer to teach scripture and inspire young minds to turn their backs on the evils of the world.

There was only one problem.

Today, the Devil had come to Camp Inspiration.

***

CHAPTER 16 – SPIDER HOLE

1

17 November 2008

Near Summerville, PA

The Suburban was located just after 3:00 in the morning when a snowplow driver turned down a forestry access road to take a leak. The plow driver's name was Peter Schoonover. He'd been driving for three years. He liked the work and didn't even mind the hours. He spotted a glint of light in the amber of his strobes. Tucking himself away, he walked a few feet in and understood immediately what this hidden truck meant.

"Probably stolen," he whispered.

His heart kicked up a beat as he approached. Only hours before, the lead hand, Harvey Van Tassell, had come out and made an announcement.

"Listen up! The police are looking for three fugitives. These men are killers and considered extremely dangerous. Ladies and gentlemen, when you're out cleaning up the highways for the good people of Pennsylvania, I want you to keep a keen eye. If anyone spots a 2007 mint green Suburban carrying three men, I want you to call in the location immediately and then get the hell out of Dodge." Harvey didn't stop there. "These men are killers, folks, they killed a bunch of people over in Pittsburgh. Even kids. Don't pick anyone up. Don't approach anybody for any reason, because I need all of you back here safe at the end of your shift."

He was in front of it now, the vehicle partially obscured by branches and a fresh dusting of snow. Peter Schoonover reached down and pulled back a branch from the grille, and his chest tightened. Suburban.

He twisted his head left and right, then spun completely around. "Fuck," he croaked and began running for the plow. On the way, he tripped and came up with a beard full of snow. "Get out of Dodge! Damn straight." He pushed off from a kneeling position like an Olympic sprinter. As he bounded forward, he heard a vehicle off in the distance. "Fuck, that could be them!" and then, "Who the fuck am I talking to?"

Then he had the door to the plow open, and was climbing inside when he slipped and grated his shin against the steel step. "Fuck me and the horse I rode in on," he yelped and scrambled inside the truck, slamming the door behind him. Peter didn't call it in, because he had a redefined directive. Get the fuck out of Dodge, and then call in your position. He jammed on the clutch, slammed the truck in gear, and released the brakes.

The plow lunged forward, and he was rolling. He hit the auto door lock. "Just in case." He could see the lights coming down the road from the opposite direction he'd come.

From that goddamned rest area.

He turned in the direction of the oncoming vehicle, his mind an eruption of speculation and intermingling terror.

That could be the killers! They could've stolen a car from the rest area! They might see my tracks coming out of the forestry road!

For this reason, he turned on his high beams and moose lights. He slowed the plow to a crawl. The car was coming at him, flashing its own high beams to signal that he was blinding them. Peter ignored it, creeping the plow along, listening to his pulse pounding in his temples.

They stop, I'll ram them.

The car passed, horning screaming in disgust, and was gone.

Peter shifted up and got the fuck out of Dodge.

Then he called it in.

2

Camp Inspiration

Near Brandy Camp, PA

Lance slid in beside her only minutes after he stopped sharpening his tools. He was spooning against her; absent was having her arms wrapped around him because hers were bound. But her breasts were bunched against his shoulder blades, and his butt pushed back against her nether regions. Carolyn worried he might rape her, but he cooled that with two comments. "Get some sleep," and, "I want you fresh for the road."

She lay quiet then, and before long, exhaustion took her.

3

Lance listened to her breathing as she slept, considering his options. They would leave when it was still dark. He set the alarm on the phone for 5:00 a.m. That was all the phone was good for. He couldn't get a signal out here, or Wi-Fi.

At least it will wake me up in the morning, he thought and saved the alarm. The car radio wasn't picking anything up but some Bible-thumping station out of Blue Ball, Pennsylvania, and even though the town name's humor was not lost on Lance, he didn't feel much like laughing. He was an information junkie — he needed to know what was going on, and not knowing was driving him nuts.

He was overexposed.

The killing was the ultimate, but another part of the kick was following the case. Making notes, gloating over the mistakes the cops were making. Lance was a celebrity now, soon to be a household name, just like Ted Bundy. Granted, he was still a newcomer to the table, but after this, he would be among the top discussed serial killers of all time.

"Infamy," he barely whispered into the darkness.

Carolyn's warmth was soothing.

Given the proper amount of time and attention, he could turn her onto his side. But that would involve many nasty things. Beatings, rape, psychological terrorizing. Of those three things, the third gave him an erection, and on cue, the monster inside him began salivating.

Behind him, she stirred, pushing against him.

"No time," he whispered, even lower.

Grudgingly, the monster relented.

And with that, the erection began to melt away. Lance closed his eyes, and before drifting off to sleep, he eased his finger from the trigger on the snub nose .38.

I'm almost out of bullets, he thought.

From there, he surrendered to sleep's embrace.

4

FBI Field Office

Pittsburgh, PA

State troopers from F Troop descended on the forestry road and the Suburban called in by Peter Schoonover. It was confirmed to be the one stolen from the Fowler farm. This lit up the phones, and the task force agents found themselves being wakened one after another.

Lieutenant Cole Abraham of the Montoursville State Police Barracks called Maxwell with the news. "We found the stolen Suburban."

"Where?" Maxwell stood up and flipped the light on. He'd been catching an hour, before an upcoming operational briefing. He'd worked late into the evening, finishing off the presentation and forwarding a copy to Leigh and Julian.

"Off PA 28, on a forestry access road."

"Bodies?"

"None that they could find, but they're still sweeping the area. By the way, good morning, Max."

"Morning, Cole. This presents another challenge."

"One of many. The highways are a mess. There have been over twenty-five accidents in our jurisdiction alone, two of them involving big rigs. Now we've got a new vehicle with no identity. We'll have to look really hard at every vehicle with three men inside."

"We have to get these guys before they kill again."

"And that's why we're out here," Cole said. "Life sure would've been a lot simpler if we could've ground Belanger down before he hooked up with this bunch."

"He was already hooked up when we found him. That's how he threw us off."

"Yeah, I forgot about that." Cole Abraham hadn't. He was just musing how close they'd been, right inside Belanger's house grilling him over a year ago, and now there were twenty-three people dead. This wasn't Cole or Max's fault, it hadn't even been entirely the fault of Maxwell's predecessor, Hugh Bailey. But Bailey had helped Belanger with his attempt at fucking Maxwell. "Why do you suppose he took all the pictures out of his house, Max?"

"I'm not sure. Maybe he's altered his appearance, and there were photos of that alteration. Belanger isn't doing things in his usual methodical way. He's erratic and extremely dangerous. I think he's losing control. We've got to get them."

"We'll get them. It's just a matter of where or how."

"Yup. Hopefully, sooner rather than later."

"So now I guess we just listen for the crazy, eh Max?"

Maxwell laughed, thinking about one of the state police calls that involved a dildo-wielding disgruntled customer in a Pennsylvania sex store. Part of Maxwell's tragedy that involved checking crazy calls that might lead them to Highwayman. "I think we should stick to the checkpoints, and hope they don't find a hole and slip through. I don't have to tell you how important this is."

"No, you don't. I'll keep on my people. You going to come out for a look at the vehicle?"

"I can't, I'll send Agent Shelley out there. I'm putting together some stuff here that I hope will help us get the jump on them. Hopefully, if the weather clears, I'll be on the move in the late morning."

"You going to a BBQ?"

"I wish. More like a reconnaissance."

"Well, if you do get out my way, I'll buy you lunch or breakfast." Cole sounded doubtful and with good reason. "I like Shelley, but the offer still stands."

"Thanks, Cole. Maybe once we have these three in custody. Hopefully, your boys snag them in a checkpoint. If they do that, the drinks are on me." Maxwell had another call; it was Leigh. "Sorry, Cole, I've got an incoming call and a meeting. I'm going to have to get off; I'll be in touch."

"Happy hunting, my friend," Cole said.

"Happy hunting to you as well," Max said, hanging up and getting Leigh on the line. "Hey, Michelle. Is everyone ready?"

"Everyone is ready and waiting."

"I'll be down in a minute."

5

Operational Briefing

FBI Field Office, Pittsburgh, PA

The meeting was closed to the rest of the task force. In attendance were Detectives Ogden Chartrand, Robert Halsey, Lonnigan Perkins, and FBI agent Michelle Leigh. They gathered in a conference room located on the second floor of the FBI field office. Maxwell had Leigh set up a PowerPoint projection on the wall. He also had her place a release form in front of the three men sitting there. Once everyone was seated, he turned on the projector and got started.

Lonnie Perkins picked up the release form.

"Good morning, what you have there is a form authorizing your attachment to the FBI as special deputies. All of this has been cleared through your bosses by the deputy director of the FBI, but you will need to give final authorization by signing it and returning it to me," Maxwell said.

Lonnie Perkins gave Maxwell a nod, pulled out his pen, and signed. Bobby and Oggy did the same and handed the forms back to Leigh.

"Good, so everybody's in. Now, let's get down to it. I just received notice that the stolen Suburban from the Fowler farm has been located."

"Great," Halsey muttered and turned to Chartrand.

Maxwell ignored the comment and tried to stay on track. "The Pennsylvania State Police are on the scene, and a representative from the FBI will be bringing in a forensics crew to check the vehicle. But there is no sign of the suspects, and it would only make sense that they've hijacked another vehicle and have either killed or kidnapped the owner or occupants of that vehicle."

"Well, that's going to make things tougher," Oggy said.

"It certainly is, but it's sort of expected too. With the media broadcasting their names and faces across America, it was only a matter of time before they discarded the vehicle." Maxwell flipped the page on PowerPoint presentation from the FBI logo to a map of upstate New York. "We have a few things on our side now. We know that Lance Belanger is heading for Canada. I was informed by Special Agent Kendall Dickson of the IRS that they've located Belanger's money in the Royal Bank of Canada. It's being monitored for transactions. Once he tries to make a withdrawal, we will be able to pinpoint his location."

"Don't you mean their location?" Halsey asked.

Maxwell turned his attention on Halsey, "Bob, I'm doubtful that the other two are going to be around much longer. They have, like their predecessors, Norris and Parch, outlived their usefulness. He's going to kill them. Parch was killed by a .38 caliber bullet. Ballistics says the bullet likely came from a snub nosed six shot revolver. Belanger's father was a hunter/collector, and in the inventory of his home, we found a case and owner's manual for a 1929 Colt Detective Special. We believe this was probably the weapon used to shoot Jim Parch, and is likely being carried by Belanger now."

"Effective weapon to conceal and carry," Leigh said.

"And deadly," Halsey agreed.

Maxwell cleared his throat and brought everyone back into focus. Using a laser pointer, he traced it along the Canada/U.S. border and said, "Somewhere in this span of one hundred and twenty miles, Lance Belanger is going to attempt to cross into Canada. I think he will kill his remaining partners before he does that, probably using the .38."

"I wonder how much ammunition he's carrying," Oggy mused. "With the media coverage, I doubt he'll be sticking his nose into a local gun store to replenish."

Maxwell agreed. He'd been in and out of hundreds of gun stores over the years, and he thought that eighty percent of them were owned and operated by people who really wanted to shoot somebody. Those same concerned, armed citizens would be regular news junkies, and on the lookout for everyone from Osama bin Laden to Lance Elmer Belanger. "A box or two wouldn't be that hard to conceal. He shot Parch in both feet, so the others know about the gun. Hazarding a guess, he probably has at least one box of ammo. If not more."

Halsey turned back to the map. "So, you think he's going to try and sneak across the border?"

"Yeah. But I doubt Belanger will risk doing it at a crossing. It's more likely that he'll try and cross in a less monitored area of the border."

"So, you want us to patrol a hundred and twenty miles of border?" Halsey was shaking his head. "That's like looking for a minnow in the ocean."

"Not exactly. I want the five of us to relocate to upstate New York and be in proximity to potential crossings. The Department of Homeland Security, the New York State Police, and even the Royal Canadian Mounted Police are going to be looking for that minnow. If he gets picked up in a checkpoint, which will be the most likely outcome, then it won't matter. But if he breaks through, I want us to be waiting for him." Maxwell's face hardened. It was personal now. "He's not going to get away this time. Whatever he does, we're going to be waiting." He gave Leigh a glance, who looked back approvingly.

Maxwell turned the slide and below an FBI logo emblazoned in bold letters: OPERATION SPIDER HOLE. "From this point forward, nothing further will be released to the media about the comings and goings of our investigation. We will be splitting up into two teams and relocating to upstate New York. The teams will be as follows: Halsey, Chartrand, and FBI Special Agent Evan Ferguson, who will be joining you after we get upstate. Ferguson will be the ranking officer. The second team will be me, Leigh, and Perkins. Once we reach Syracuse, we'll split up. Team 1 will head for the Akwesasne Reserve and marry up with local and state police in that region. Team 2 will head for Alexandria Bay and do the same. The deputy director has given us authorization for air support from the New York State Police Aviation Unit out of Rochester. The've put one of their Huey IIs at our disposal. In fact, they've already staged a chopper in this region." Maxwell pointed to the area of Watertown, NY on the map. "The chopper can cover the span of our target area in under an hour. So, if something happens up in Akwesasne with Team 1, the second team can be there in less than an hour. If Belanger doesn't get picked up at a checkpoint, he'll be heading into an ambush."

"Where do you think he'll cross?" Perk asked.

"At first, I thought he might hire someone out of Akwesasne, but I'm sort of doubtful now. There's a long tradition of smuggling up there, and helping Lance Belanger would be extremely bad for business. He doesn't need a boat now; the river is frozen. After consulting with the DHS, this seems the most likely crossing."

Maxwell blew up the map, showing several islands and the Saint Lawrence State Park. "He'll be drawn to the woods. He feels protected by the forest. He'll probably cross at night either on foot or with a small, fast craft, like a snowmobile. But more likely on foot. Clues to his direction will be dictated by the alarms he sets off. If he kills his partners, it won't be long before their bodies are found. If he steals a car or kidnaps someone, it's only a matter of time before they don't check in. Sooner or later, he's going to need money, and that is where he'll out himself. When he does, we'll be waiting to meet him."

6

17 November 2008

Camp Inspiration

Near Brandy Camp, PA

Lance opened his eyes to darkness. It was early, 4:58 a.m., just minutes before the alarm on the phone was set to go off. Sleep had been dreamless but undisturbed, and that was good. As he gathered himself, silent panic suddenly gripped him. He reached around, blindly searching for the .38. He tried to do so without waking his passenger. He must have released it sometime during the night. And then…

He felt the cold gunmetal against the tips of his fingers and the panic withdrew. She couldn't have gotten the gun anyway; her hands were bound. He sat up and said, "Carolyn, wake up. The snow has stopped. We have to get moving."

"Can you untie my wrists? I need to use the bathroom." She struggled to sit up and Lance grabbed her forearm, lifting her into a sitting position beside him. Through the night she'd cried almost silently, and though he'd pretended he hadn't heard, her makeup had run down her face, making her nocturnal tears obvious.

He crawled between the seats, popped the hatchback, which lit the interior light, and came around to help her out of the car. He cut the zip tie binding her wrists using a toenail clipper from her shower kit. When he did, she brought her wrists up and massaged the indentation from the ligature. He marched her over to the outhouse and said, "Make it quick."

Carolyn went inside the cold outbuilding and did her business. But while she sat on the cold wooden seat, she considered her options. She heard the grating of stone against metal.

Who is he sharpening those tools for? For me?

Beside the outhouse to her left, she could hear him urinating on the ground. If she ran now, he would find her and kill her. If she waited until they were at a checkpoint, that would probably go horribly wrong as well. And he said, he would find and kill her family. Carolyn was unconsciously clenching her teeth as she thought about these things. She defecated only feet from the man who would likely kill her, but not before he stripped away every dignity of her privacy.

The sound of the urine stream began to slow, and she heard him pull his zipper up. "Come on, Carolyn. I want to be out of here in two or three minutes, and we still gotta clean you up for the road."

She felt frantically around the darkened shack for something she could use as a weapon. Nothing. And then… She ran her hand over something sticking out of one of the wall supports. She pinched it. It was a large nail, pounded halfway into the wood at a forty-five-degree angle, pointing skyward, strategically placed so that visitors to the throne could hang a piece of clothing not relevant to the business conducted here.

She reached up.

"Let's go, Carolyn. My patience is wearing thin."

She stopped and said, "Lance, I have to shit. I can't help that! Let me finish what I'm doing, please." She stopped there, withholding further comments about how pulling over on the road to finish her business would be bad for the fugitive business.

Outside, there was brooding silence.

Carolyn reached for the nail, touching it, but not twisting it out. Instead, she was waiting for the maniac to react. To come crashing through the doorway with his machete or hatchet, or both, ready to chop her into pieces.

Then he said, "All right, but make it quick."

She didn't respond. She reached up and wiggled the nail, twisting it left and right, not wanting to bend it. She worked it out of the gray, weathered wood and into her palm. It was four inches long, hard steel with a large, flat head and a four-sided point on the other end.

She finished cleaning up and hid the nail in the back waistband of her panties. She pulled up her jeans and straightened herself out. Before she opened the outhouse door, she reached back and felt through her jeans to see if the nail was noticeable.

It wasn't, and now she had a weapon.

She pushed open the door, and he was waiting there for her in the darkness of winter morning. The wind was still blowing, but the snow had stopped. The morning air was crisp and biting against her cheeks, pinching them in its icy grip.

In Lance's hand, he held a bottle of water and a piece of paper towel. The gun was tucked into the kangaroo pocket of the Syracuse University hoodie he was wearing. "We need to clean up your face before we get rolling," he said, and without waiting, he began wiping her face down. As he did this, he spoke calmly to her. "I won't be able to put makeup on your face, and you won't have time either. But you know what, you're pretty without makeup, so it won't matter." He stopped and smiled at her. Then he continued to wipe away at her face. The paper towel was abrasive, rubbing her skin raw with each swab. She imagined it must be an irritated pink. "You're a natural beauty, Carolyn."

"Thank you, Lance," she said.

"Just do what I say, and this will be over before you know it," he said and pulled back. "There, much better." And then, "Okay?"

"Yes," she said.

They mounted up at 5:17 and began to pull out when a set of headlights met them coming up the drive. It was a pickup truck. On its roof a single amber strobe twisted, lighting the morning darkness ablaze in mustard yellow.

"Fuck," Lance said to himself and to Carolyn, "Stop the car, and don't do anything stupid. Move to the right to let him pass."

Carolyn moved over and the pickup truck kept coming. She could see the driver window lowering, and she whispered, "What do I do, Lance?"

"Keep quiet and let me do the talking."

"Okay."

***

CHAPTER 17 – COUGAR SPIRIT

1

17 November 2008

Camp Inspiration

Near Brandy, PA

Oscar Johnson wound his service truck up the snowy road unaware who he would be meeting that morning. He was angry; it was his day off, and they had called him after pulling three hours of overtime the previous night. He didn't mind the extra money so much, *who doesn't after all*, but he was exhausted and needed a day off to recharge his batteries. The other thing that had him steamed was the hour that they had called him at home; *which was just after 2:55 in the goddamned morning!* His supervisor, John Ahearn, said that one of the guys had caught the flu and couldn't make it in on his callout shift. Oscar knew who had fucked him. *That malingering fuck, Philip Webster.*

Oscar agreed to come in, but he was still pissed. The last thing he did to bring on the mood was spilling his coffee all over the seat of the service truck. And that was because the county had bought the lowest end trucks they could. "Apparently, cup holders are a fucking option," he grumbled, mopping up the mess with his scarf. "Not even a sip. Ahh, shit."

The coffee had been an hour ago, and he was almost done with his rounds except for checking Camp Inspiration. His mood hadn't lightened much since the coffee; he was still thinking about how Webster had fucked him on his day off. As he wound up the drive to the camp, he saw something that surprised him.

"What the fuck," Oscar said as headlights filled the cab of the truck with milky fluorescence. Thinking it was kids, he said, "You little shits better not have broken into the place!" That would mean paperwork, reports, something Oscar Johnson didn't want to deal with today.

The oncoming car stopped as he approached. His own headlights illuminated the interior of the car, lighting up the faces of kids. He relaxed a little. *Probably just kids, out here smoking a little weed.*

He lowered his driver's side window, the snow crunching beneath wheels drowning out the idling engine of the waiting vehicle. The girl behind the wheel really was a kid, early twenties. He reached for the clipboard and pen sitting on the seat and pulled it closer. *I'm going to have to do something, don't want this biting me in the ass.* He took note of the car's license plate and scribbled it on the pad. *Just in case they're thieving bastards.*

He rolled up next to the driver's side window and it opened, revealing a pretty girl behind the wheel and the silhouette of a hippie kid in the passenger seat.

"Hi," the hippie kid said, but he didn't sound so much like a kid, but someone a little older.

Maybe later twenties, early thirties, Oscar thought, and said, "What're you kids doing up here? This is private property."

"We got hung up in the storm and came up here to sleep in the car for a few hours," the passenger said.

The female driver had a look on her face that Oscar couldn't quite put his finger on. He only knew that it was unnerving. Her face was expressionless, but her eyes told a different story.

Was that fear in her eyes? Pleading?

"We didn't know we were trespassing," the passenger said. "We were just looking for a place to get out of the storm. You can understand that, can't you?"

And Oscar could, but the girl's eyes said something else, something was wrong. Then she smiled, and whatever lingered in her eyes was gone. He turned his attention back to the passenger and said, "Yeah, sure, I can…"

"Carolyn, sit back," the passenger said.

She leaned back in her seat robotically.

"Huh," were the last words Oscar Johnson said.

He never heard the shot. He felt something hit him just above the right eyebrow. After that, nothing.

2

Carolyn sat there stunned, ears ringing, the rotten egg stink of cordite nesting in her nasal cavities, the horror of seeing another murder melting over her.

There was a voice calling, muffled by the ringing, but insistent. "Carolyn, look at me. Carolyn, look at me." But she didn't want to turn in the direction of that voice. Didn't want to see him raise the gun yet again and kill her the same way he'd killed the innocent man in the service truck. She couldn't stare into the face of death, because to look into that infinite evil lurking behind the mask her abductor wore was to acknowledge it, and with acknowledgment came only one thing.

Death.

Suddenly, he had her wrist and she felt something cutting into it, then heard the zipper clicks of the plastic ligature fastening it to the steering wheel.

"Don't move," the voice, suppressed by ringing, barked. Then she heard him snatch the keys from the ignition, and there was the distant sound of the door being opened. Only three feet away, but far off, like it was in a warehouse.

He crossed around the front of the car, absorbing each headlight as he did, deflecting the beam upward and catching the monster in its spotlight. For only a second, their eyes locked, and she thought, *that is the face I will see before he kills me.*

She brought her unbound left hand up to touch the right side of her nose. She felt a bump that had not been there before, and understood that something had dislodged during the firing of the gun and embedded beneath the skin of her nose.

Gunpowder residue, she thought. *I have the gunpowder residue of a murdered man under my skin. Does that make me blameworthy? Did I help kill this man?*

3

Lance was at the driver's door of the truck. He held the gun out and away from the window as if the dead man inside might grab it from him. He inventoried the cab. The driver was slumped over, hanging from his seatbelt. There was a pencil eraser-sized hole just above his eyebrow, scorched skin pushed inward into blackness. Blood had seeped only a final heartbeat before the pump stopped. Below the hole, a spongy eyebrow slowed the trickle. Below that, one eye contorted to the right while the left was fixed forward.

Lance marveled at how quickly he'd extinguished this man's life. The gun was a useful tool for killing, but it lacked the raw, visceral, psycho-sexual high he got from killing with a machete. The gun was like a vibrator, a mechanical replacement for carnal, physical gratification.

He saw the clipboard and on it, a hastily scribbled license plate number. With his right hand, he reached in and pulled the clipboard out. He gazed back over his shoulder at Carolyn, pondering whether to kill her and just take his chances on the highway.

"What a fucking mess," he whispered to the dead man. "Now, someone is going to come looking for you, and they'll know I didn't get far." He looked back over his shoulder at Carolyn, who was touching her face and staring off into space like a zombie.

She alerted them, the monster insisted. *We should take her out into the snow, cut her up like the others, and leave her for that fucking Maxwell and his task force.*

He couldn't.

The monster continued its homily. *Come on, just think of how good it would feel. That is how this all became a mess in the first place. We stopped being pure of heart, our hunger for celebrity outweighed our common sense. We did fine before we started playing with other people. Let's just have a little fun. A little foreplay with the gun should end with an orgasm of dismemberment.*

He glanced back at her.

4

Two Hours Later

Coudersport, PA

It had been Lance's original intention to shoot straight up the US 219 through Ridgeway, Pennsylvania, all the way up to Salamanca, New York. These were his roads, his states, he felt safe in Pennsylvania and New York. Up until the recent madness, it had been his sanctuary after each killing expedition, the place where he melted in.

Not anymore, the monster said.

Nope, not anymore. The enemy was no longer at the gates, it was now an occupier that was actively looking for him.

What a goddamned tragic comedy.

The radio no longer played the "Blue Ball Fire and Brimstone Power Hour." It had been traded in for Rod Stewart singing, "Have You Ever Seen the Rain?" Lance was trying to decide if Rod Stewart should be killed, or just horribly tortured and then killed, for singing John Fogerty's classic melody.

"The Ramones did a better version," Carolyn mumbled.

"The Ramones," Lance said. "I didn't really follow them. They're a punk rock band." He turned to face her, no longer transfixed on the secondary highway they were driving. "I never figured out what anybody saw in punk rock."

Carolyn was silent.

He waited to see if she would say anything. After a moment, he shifted his attention back to the road. They were at the end of PA 872 and merging onto US 6 West. They didn't meet anyone on fifteen miles of the US route that could well have taken Lance home had he stayed the course until he reached US 15 and pointed north.

Instead, they drove right through Coudersport, and turned north on PA 44 until they were out of town. Lance didn't want to run up against law enforcement. The vehicle stank of gunpowder and Carolyn would probably give him up. The last thing they passed, once leaving the town limit, was a curiosity called Jim's Coffee and Bait Shop. It still hadn't opened. That was too bad because Lance could have used a cup of coffee. But what to do about Carolyn?

"Keep going north," he said.

"For how long?" she asked.

"Until I say otherwise."

17 November 2008

PA Route 28

Outside Summerville, PA

The belief in Pennsylvania is that the last cougar in the state had been killed somewhere back around 1874. Sightings of cougars in the state are on par with spotting flying saucers, alien abductions, and sex crazy sasquatches. People who report a cougar encounter are met with nodding heads, rolling eyes, and a big cup of skepticism.

But there is a cougar rumored by the people in the region to be the embodied spirit of all those killed into extinction. Local lore says that such a creature rises when a man kills one of his own, to consume the body and spirit as revenge for the genocide visited upon its species.

Glen Underwood had never heard about the myth or the cougar reports, but when he parked his 2006 BMW 3 Series in the pull-off of PA Route 28 for a smoke, he saw something extraordinary in the array of his headlights.

He was just lighting up, using the open driver's side door to shield himself against the abrasive wind cutting into him from the chest up. He cupped the lighter, stabbing a cigarette between his teeth. The sky overhead was still blotted with darkness from which white flakes fell almost miraculously into the blue halogens of the BMW.

Glen Underwood sensed something moving out of the corner of his right eye, as he inhaled his first taste of a cigarette he'd been savoring for over an hour and a half. He turned his head and there it was, the biggest cat he'd ever seen coming out of the woods in complete silence. The beast seemed uninterested in Glen Underwood or his BMW, and the event happened so fast that it took Glen a moment to process the encounter moments after it ended. The cougar walked out of the rest area, down the bank, and across the highway, then was gone.

Glen stared in that direction for a while, trying to understand what he'd just seen. And little by little it began to register, although he didn't particularly like what his mind was telling him. Cougars are aggressive animals, bold enough to attack a hiker - or some dumb mope who decided to park his BMW in a rest area for a smoke. He watched until it was gone, then he followed the animal tracks backward with his eyes and the drizzling of blood that had been warmed by bone-crunching teeth and salivation. Glen only wondered one thing. Who was the owner of the arm that the creature had been carrying in its mouth?

Carrying a flashlight in his left hand, he went around to the trunk of the BMW and opened it. Inside there were two duffle bags, one filled with meth, the other with guns. He opened the gun bag and pulled out the 9 mm. He made sure it was loaded and closed the trunk. He knew he should just get the hell out of here and get his ass off the road, but he had to know.

The tracks drew him into the woods until he stopped, making the decision it really was time to get out of here. As he scanned between the trees with the flashlight, he settled on a large stump and two blood-soaked lumps in the snow. The one on the right had been opened right up. Entrails and ragged flesh spat upward out of the cocoon.

Then there was a screech and an impatient owl landed upon the lump, using its talons to tear at the opened cocoon while pivoting its accusing eyes up at Glen. The owl scared the shit out of Glen, causing him to react without thinking.

Glen Underwood shot the owl before he even knew what it was, and as Dirty Harry used to say, "He blew its head clean off." Then he turned to run, but halfway back he stopped and grunted, "Fuck." He went back, grabbed the headless owl, and took it with him.

He drove south to Alcola, Pennsylvania, where he met his brother, and they unloaded the guns and drugs into a barn. He met no checkpoints along the way. When they were done, he said, "I just wandered into a dumping site."

"Like a body dump site?" his brother Danny asked.

"Two of 'em. And get this, I saw a cougar with an arm in its mouth," Glen said.

"Bullshit!"

"I'm not kidding, Danny." Glen lit a cigarette and exhaled. "The question is, what to do about it?"

"Do about it?" Danny turned, eyes wide and incredulous. "You do nothing, big brother. That's what you do. Whatever happened in that rest spot, that's their business, and this is ours." He swept his hand toward the hiding place where they'd stashed the guns and drugs destined for a buyer in Newark. "Honestly, big brother, I can't believe you'd even be thinking such a thing."

Glen nodded his head, considered this. They'd been purchasing meth from a distributor up around Ridgway, Pennsylvania. Glen reached into the trunk, pulled out the dead owl, and handed it to his brother. "May as well throw this away."

"What the fuck?"

"Dead owl," he said. "I shot it."

Danny never asked why he shot the owl; he carried it over to a forty-five-gallon drum they used as a burn barrel and tossed it in. "What a fucked-up night you had, big brother."

"No kidding."

6

Four Hours Later

Near Summerville, PA

The morning light was revealing a gray sky when the state patrol car found its way into the rest area, and the officer, named Keith Thatcher, got out to relieve himself. He only made it three steps when he spotted the tracks and blood. He also saw a set of footprints following alongside what he thought were probably wolf tracks. It never occurred to him that the culprit might be a cougar because there were no cougars in Pennsylvania, hadn't been for over one hundred and thirty years.

The drizzling of blood also didn't worry Thatcher all that much. He figured it was probably from a freshly killed rabbit or some other rodent prey. But it still interested him, and it had deterred him from a piss that seemed a much higher priority only minutes before. The Pennsylvania State Police were on high alert for three fugitive killers and during his shift briefing, they had all been told to keep an eye out for anything suspicious.

Rabbit or not, it warranted checking out.

The young officer kept at least three feet to the left of the tracks, just in case it amounted to something other than a wild animal chowing down on a fresh kill.

Closing in on the woods, he noted the second set of human tracks that came chaotically back in his direction. This made him stop, unclasp his holster, and place his hand on the butt of his gun. He looked back at the return footprints and followed them with his eyes to a set of windblown tire tracks in the snow.

"Shit," Keith said. His heart began to race. He pulled out his service weapon and resumed his investigation. He was going over what could have happened here. *Someone else has walked this path,* he thought. *Someone who might have been involved. Or maybe someone who didn't want to be involved?*

A minute later, he found the bodies.

30 Minutes Later

Allegheny County Airport

West Mifflin, PA

The Cessna Grand Caravan was just lifting off with six occupants: the pilot, two FBI agents, and three cops. Maxwell was sitting shotgun when his cell phone chirped, and he checked the number. It was Cole Abraham again. Before he could answer, a second call came in. It was Agent Boyden, and then a third, the deputy director, Julian Carswell.

He looked up from his phone and said to Leigh, "I think something big just happened." Then he held it up for her to see. "Who do I answer first?"

"The deputy director, of course," Leigh said and added, "I'll call Boyden back."

"No, you call Deputy Director Carswell and tell him I'm on the phone with the Pennsylvania state cops. I'm going to answer the call from Cole Abraham. He's probably closest to whatever the hell happened." Then to the pilot, who was still in a climb, he said, "Once you level off, I need you to put us in a holding pattern. We might be going somewhere else." He answered the phone.

"Hey, we can't just change a flight itinerary in mid-flight," the pilot said. "You booked a flight into Syracuse. That's where we're going, or I'm putting this lady down."

"Hey, Cole, I'm up in the air. I need you to hang on for a second." Maxwell reached into his jacket, pulled out his shield, and stuck it in the pilot's face. "This is an FBI operation, and I'm the ranking officer. If I tell you to fly this craft to Kalamazoo, Michigan, you'll do as I say, or I'll start laying obstruction of justice charges. Do we understand each other?"

"Yes," the pilot conceded.

"Now, put us in a holding pattern until I figure out what the hell is going on," he barked, and said into the phone, "What's going on, Cole? Tell me you got them."

"Might have found two of 'em," Cole said. "One of our troopers discovered two bodies in the woods next to a rest area off Highway 28 about a mile south of where we found the Suburban. Identities haven't been confirmed yet, but I've already dispatched the Crime Scene guys onto the site. We've got tire tracks and footprints, and soon we'll have prints from the bodies."

"Could they just be more victims?"

"Could be, maybe the owners of the vehicle that replaced the Suburban, but both the victims are male, and I think our friend from Lawrenceville is making good on his plan."

Simultaneously, Leigh was talking to the deputy director and getting the Reader's Digest version of the same events. Perk, Bobby, and Oggy were all leaning forward in their seats, trying to listen in over the drone of the single prop airplane.

Leigh reached across and tapped Maxwell. "The DD wants you on the crime scene."

Maxwell nodded. "Cole, what's the closest airport to the crime scene?"

"Hang on, Max," Cole said.

Then the pilot said, "Dubois Regional Airport."

Maxwell asked, "How far is that from Summerville, Pennsylvania?"

"Umm, let me check my map," the pilot said.

"Between twenty-five and thirty miles," Cole came back. "I'm on my way to the crime scene. I can pick you folks up."

"There's five of us, Cole." Max then said, "Perk, can you check if they have a car rental service in Dubois?"

"I'm on it."

Then to the pilot, "Get this bird pointed toward Dubois."

The pilot nodded and did as he was told.

The Cessna banked out of its holding pattern and headed northeast. That was when Bob Halsey leaned over and said to his partner, "I guess we won't be hitting any bars up in Akwesasne."

"Not yet, at least," Oggy said.

***

CHAPTER 18 — RAGE AND ABANDON

1

17 November 2008

Off PA 28

Near Summerville, PA

The rest stop was buzzing with police cars, cops on foot, and a white Chevy forensics van emblazoned with the State Police logo. From that vehicle, men in white neoprene suits carried equipment up a snow-beaten path to where a tent had been erected over the bodies.

Maxwell's mini task force, now married up with Lieutenant Cole Abraham, was standing at the scene being briefed by an investigator named Paul Cheswick, from the Pennsylvania Bureau of Forensic Services. "We've got two adult male victims, late twenties to mid-thirties. Both bodies have been mutilated by local wildlife. One of the bodies is missing an arm, chewed off at the elbow. As far as we can tell, both were killed by gunshots to the back of the head and then buried with snow to conceal them."

"Are the faces recognizable?" Maxwell asked.

"One is. The other one must have been tastier because the animals took his arm, nose, left eye, and the right cheek has been chewed down to the bone," Cheswick said.

Maxwell held up his phone. "I'd like to go in for a look. How long until your people are finished processing the scene?"

"We'll be here all day, but if you suit up, you can come in for a look." Cheswick was speaking of the white neoprene throwaway coveralls he was wearing.

"You got my size?" Maxwell asked.

"Yeah, we got every size imaginable."

"Good, let's do this then. I'd like to bring my team up there if possible." Maxwell looked around to see if anyone had a complaint. No one did.

Cheswick led Maxwell to the forensic van and opened the sliding door. He climbed inside, leaving Maxwell outside, and rooted around until he found what he was looking for. "Try these." He tossed Maxwell a set of coveralls.

"Thanks," Maxwell said and unwrapped the coveralls.

"If those don't fit, I got two sizes larger."

Maxwell shook the coveralls out and put them on. He then smoothed them out and said, "This'll work."

"One sec," the investigator said, and picked up a handheld radio. "Mike, you have a copy?"

"Go ahead, Paul," the forensic investigator replied.

"Where are you at with the collection process?" Cheswick asked. He stared up at Maxwell and the others while waiting for his guy to reply and lit a smoke.

"The footprint castings are setting. We should have them off the ground in about fifteen minutes," Mike, the forensic tech, replied.

"Okay, I have a group of investigators here from the FBI who want to come up for a look. Does that work for you?"

There was a pause, then, "Yeah, give us twenty minutes, and we won't have to worry about anyone walking all over the crime scene." Emerson sounded irritated by the request.

Cheswick shrugged. "His full name is Mike Emerson. He's a thorough tech, just not a people person."

Maxwell grinned. "You guys got a job to do. We get that, and we'll try not to be in your way for too long. We just want to get a look at the faces and compare them to the guys we're chasing."

Cheswick said, "We'll get yuh in for a look, Agent Maxwell. We want them just as bad as you do."

Maxwell doubted that, but still said, "Thanks." He didn't think anyone wanted them as badly as he did. Except maybe Michelle Leigh, who had her own axe to grind.

2

It was cold, but the skies had opened, paroling the sun from its wintery purgatory. While the sun offered some relief, warming the shoulders and faces of the investigators on the scene, they still stamped their feet to stave off the cold. The distance from the parking lot to execution stump was more than one hundred and fifty feet but seemed longer as the six investigators followed the path marked with the blood of one or both dead men.

As they walked, Leigh was at Maxwell's side, keeping pace, giving him brief glances. He was deep in thought, sure that he would find the bodies of the two killers, which would bring a whole new dynamic to the hunt. He was sure Lance was heading for Canada, but with whom was he riding?

Leigh broke his thoughts. "You think it's them?"

Surprised, he turned to her and said, "Yeah, pretty sure."

Behind them, Lonnie Perkins and Cole Abraham walked side by side, lawman mistresses of a nomadic FBI agent. Cole and Lonnie were both tall men, both smokers, although Cole had a decade and a half on the Kentucky investigator.

"I saw you on the news." Cole smiled.

"That so?" Lonnie said.

"Yeah, and by the way, I got a granddaughter with attention deficit disorder." Cole paused for effect, and Lonnie looked over, expressionless. "But what you said to the press, accusing them of having ADD; that was goddamned funny."

"My boss didn't think so." Lonnie grinned. "I'm not allowed to talk to the press anymore."

"That bothers you?"

"No, not really."

They both laughed.

Behind them, Bobby and Oggy conversed.

"Oggy," Bobby said.

"Yeah, Bob?"

"This has got to be the most fucked up case I've ever worked in my career."

Oggy laughed. "I agree with you there, partner."

"I mean it," Bobby said. "One minute we're investigating a massacre in suburbia, and now we're bombing around the state like we're in a posse. Can you think of a more fucked up case?"

"No, Bob, I can't. It's pretty fucked up."

"You think it's them?" Bobby asked.

"I'd bet a beer on it."

They filed into the woods, chatting away, listening to the snow crunching beneath their feet. The posse began to slow as the barrier of yellow tape marking the execution site came into full view. The cold had suspended the decomposition but as they closed around the dual grave, there was still a faint familiar odor lingering up into the nostrils of each investigator.

Maxwell looked down at the frozen bodies and knew before he brought up his phone to compare the wanted photos. The cyanotic hue of their skin made them appear more like wax figures than real people. He brought up his phone and showed the pictures to Leigh.

"The one on the left is Bradley Todd, and the one on the right is Lawrence Jarvis," she said.

"Fuck," Maxwell whispered. "He'll probably have a hostage. Or he'll have killed someone else… God damnit." And then to the rest, "It's them."

The tech named Emerson came up, a little friendlier than on the radio. "Hi, I'm Emerson, is there anything I can help you with?"

"Any tracks to indicate a third person?" Maxwell asked.

"Well, there are the tracks next to the animal's, but those are fresh. I'd say they're from someone who discovered the bodies and ran away. The tracks of these two men and whoever killed them were wiped clean by the storm."

"What about vehicle tracks?"

"Same thing. The winds were high last night and the night before. Mother Nature didn't do us any favors," Emerson said, and then paused… trying to remember something. He blinked and said, "We did find something. Could be nothing."

"What was that?"

"A receipt from a store."

"What store?"

"Come with me."

Emerson led them into a tent where the Crime Scene guys kept their equipment as well as both plastic and paper evidence bags. He reached down and plucked up a baggie. In it was a four-day-old receipt for a scarf bought at Old Navy. It was a debit purchase.

Maxwell didn't shop at Old Navy. "Anyone have any thoughts on this?"

Bobby reached out and said, "Can I take a look?"

Emerson handed him the encased receipt. "Sure."

Bobby gave it a look. "It's a woman's scarf."

"How can you tell?" Perkins asked.

Bobby pointed at the top of the receipt next to the date, and said, "The department is Women's Apparel. That's what WA means."

"Can I get a scan of this?" Maxwell asked Emerson.

"Sure, you want to run the debit card? Because we've applied for a warrant to run it, but it might take a day or so, depending on the bureaucrats." Emerson took the receipt from Bobby and handed it to Maxwell.

"I'd like to get some cops down there to question the cashier, see if they remember anything." Maxwell pulled his phone out and called Boyden.

She answered on the first ring. "Agent Boyden."

"Linda, it's Max, I'm going to send you a scanned receipt. Can you get some cops down to interview some folks at the Old Navy in Harrisburg, Pennsylvania? I also want you to see if you can grease the wheels for the Pennsylvania state cops to get a warrant on the same debit card purchase. I have a federal judge named Poe on call, he helped us in Louisville. He's probably the man we want to get this moving. This is a top priority. We may have an abduction in progress."

"I'll get right on it," Boyden said.

"While I've got you on the line, anything from the IRS agent?"

"Not yet."

"Okay, get those cops in for an interview ASAP, and give them my number and email."

"Anything else?"

"No, but if anyone gives you the gears, call immediately, and I'll sic the deputy director on them."

Boyden laughed. "Will do."

Maxwell hung up and looked at Emerson. "We should be able to expedite your warrant on the debit card. What's the deal with the animal tracks?"

"They look like cougar tracks," Oggy said.

Bobby gave him a strange look. "Oggy, how the hell would you know that?"

"I grew up in Washington state. Did some hunting when I was a kid. Bear tracks and cougar tracks are something I saw a lot of."

Emerson said, "There aren't any cougars in the state of Pennsylvania."

"I'd say there's at least one," Oggy said.

"Cougars aren't in these parts."

"Okay, we can debate that later," Maxwell said. "Emerson, you got anything else that we can chew on?"

"We don't have any tire tracks, except for the tracks from whoever followed the animal prints. We think it's from a high-end car, maybe a Mercedes or BMW. But right now, that's an assumption."

"Could the car be owned by the abductee?" Leigh asked.

"I'm doubtful, the tracks are pretty fresh. These two have been dead over twenty-four hours. It would seem unlikely that the killer would hang around that long," Emerson said.

"Somebody that didn't want to be involved," Maxwell said.

"That would be my guess," Emerson agreed.

Bobby looked around at all of them. "So, Belanger comes into the rest area, then executes his accomplices… And what? Waits for someone to arrive?"

Abraham spoke up. "Most likely, they got rid of the Suburban, and then came back here looking for another set of wheels."

"I don't know." Maxwell looked down at the two bodies and said, "Maybe they were dragging the abductee out into the woods and got shot in the process."

"If there is an abductee," Oggy interjected.

"There is," Maxwell said and looked around.

They all nodded in agreement.

Maxwell pulled out a business card and handed it to Emerson. "If you come up with anything else, don't hesitate to call me."

Emerson took the card and looked at it. "Okay, we'll do that, Agent Maxwell."

"Anybody got anything else?" Maxwell asked the rest of the group. No one spoke. He turned his attention back to

Emerson. "You've been a big help. Keep gathering evidence. I promised we'd get out of your way, and that's what we're going to do. Thanks for the walkthrough." Maxwell began to walk off when Emerson called to him.

"Agent Maxwell?"

Maxwell turned.

"You folks get this bastard."

Maxwell nodded. "That's the plan."

3

PA Route 46

5 miles southeast of Rew, PA

Carolyn was stealing intermittent glances of the man who had killed three people in her presence as they drove north in the daylight. He was quiet. His facial expressions kept changing from blank to scowl and back again. They had been traveling for five hours after he shot the man in the work truck. Roadblocks hadn't presented a problem. They had been running secondary highways since leaving Camp Inspiration. Staying off the state routes and the interstate system had given them freedom of movement, but it also slowed their progress considerably.

Three hours before, they got lost on a secondary road, taking them at least thirty-five miles into a nature preserve that had no turn around when they came to a barrier that blocked a bridge. She placed the car in park and Lance mumbled something incoherent beside her, and she wasn't sure how to respond because it didn't make any sense. He stared through the windshield at the barrier for a long time. He was angry. That was quite clear.

They would have to go back. On either side of the car, the road had two and a half feet of shoulder. It was going to be challenging to turn around. They should have been in New

York by now, but the weather and choice of back roads had proved to be a significant miscalculation.

"Should have been in New York," he said and, "Fuck."

"What?" Carolyn asked mildly.

His head traversed like a robot, and he lost his mind. "I said that we should be in fucking New York by now. Are you deaf as well as stupid?"

"No... I..."

"We need to turn this car around without getting it stuck. Do you think you can pull that off, Carolyn?" His eyes were an inferno of rage.

Afraid that he might kill her if she got the car stuck, she said honestly, "I don't know."

He exhaled loudly and said, "We need to turn this car around and drive back to the main highway. If we get stuck, I'll have to find another vehicle. Chances are that won't be likely, because we're in the middle of fucking nowhere. So, we can't get stuck, Carolyn." He paused for a second. "Now I'm going to ask you one more time. Do you think you can turn us around and not get stuck?"

4

If she said, "Yes," he would get on with the business of turning around. If she said, "No," he would take her onto that bridge and use the machete on her. Then he would walk to Canada if he had to.

She said, "Yes."

His thin smile widened. "That's the team spirit. Now, let's get to it."

"Okay," she said. "Please just tell me what you need me to do."

He said, "I'm going to need you to make a bunch of really short corrections, back and forth until we get the car turned around. I'm talking like a foot forward, a foot and a half back while turning the wheel. I'll direct you from outside."

"Okay," Carolyn said.

"If you listen to me, we won't get stuck." Lance kept his voice even and gaze deadpan. "But if you don't, and we do get stuck, or if you try anything stupid… I will take you into the woods, strip you naked, and dismember you. By the time they find your body, the forest animals will have had a real feast."

"I won't," she whimpered.

"They usually eat the genitalia and the breasts on a woman first, and then…"

"I won't get stuck! I'll listen to you, Lance." She was sobbing. "I won't get stuck, I promise. You just need to tell me what to do. Please don't hurt me, Lance."

He stopped. She was trying to connect with him. Calling him by his first name. And now she'd done it twice. His eyes drilled into her.

Patronizing little bitch, the monster growled.

Lance pushed the monster down. He needed the car to get north. He needed to stop and find a new set of wheels, and get his ass to Canada.

"Do what I say, and I won't hurt you," he said, bringing the gun up. Outside, the sun showered them in an illusion of warmth, but it was going to be cold. "Roll down all the windows."

"Why?" she asked.

"So you can hear what I'm telling you to do." He pulled the passenger door open and began to ease out while keeping the gun trained on her. The outside air made his skin prickle. "Don't do anything until I say." Then he closed the passenger door and came around the front of the car, keeping her in his gun sight.

At that moment, Carolyn considered snapping the car into drive and lunging forward, but the gun was pointed right at her and his finger was on the trigger, probably already applying pressure. She wanted to run him down but couldn't find the nerve to take the gamble.

He came around and leaned on the driver's window jam. "Give me your left hand," he said, and as she lifted it out, he put the gun on the roof of the car, grabbed her wrist, and zip-tied it to the driver's side mirror. Then he picked up the gun and said, "You'll have to steer one-handed, Carolyn."

"Okay, Lance."

He brought the gun up to her cheek and pushed it hard against her. "Stop fucking calling me by my first name." Then he eased back. "You're creeping me out."

"Okay," she said.

He stood then and said, "Okay, let's get this done."

The three-point turn is a vehicle maneuver used to turn a vehicle around in a confined space. What Lance and Carolyn were about to do would amount to a twenty-point turn.

He stepped back, walked to the back of the car, and said, "Turn your wheels hard to the right." She did and he continued, "Now put it in reverse, and back up with your foot on the brake." She did for a foot and a half until he said, "Stop!" He came up the side of the car, got out front to her left, and said, "Turn your wheels all the way left, and come forward." She did as he said, and twenty minutes and fourteen, not fifteen, turns later they got the car turned around.

He came back up and said, "Give me the keys." She reached down with her right hand and pulled them from the ignition. She was sure this was where he would drag her out and kill her.

But he didn't.

Instead, he took the keys, put them into his pocket, and then cut the zip tie that bound her now frozen left hand to the mirror. She pulled it back inside, tucking her hand into her armpit to warm it.

The passenger door opened, and he climbed back in. "Very well done, Carolyn."

"Thank you," she said mechanically, and they got moving.

6

Only three hours before, he'd been ranting about not getting to New York by now, but Carolyn believed that wasn't a bad thing. As they rolled sluggishly north, she was watching her life expectancy slipping into a chasm of unknowns.

Ever since they dragged her out of her car, she'd been in a perpetual state of terror. Passing wooded areas presented conceivable locations to kill her, and then dump her body. She'd seen the emptiness in this man, not only as he presided over her after killing those three men, but in the disconnects he exhibited while they drove.

She believed that somewhere up the road was the end of the line, the juncture where she would become a dragline to be cut.

Where will that be, she wondered, *at the next stop?*

As far as Lance went, she couldn't gauge him. Aside from being a homicidal maniac, he was sinister, like a robot rather than a man. The only emotions she'd seen in him were rage and abandon. She could connect him to three murders. She knew he was a serial killer, the one they called "the Highwayman." She didn't know everything about him or the men who had been with him, but she knew enough to expect that he would kill her.

She had to get away.

Or die trying.

She kept the car rolling up the secondary highway. They were almost into mid-day and had driven a little under one hundred and seven miles. The lack of roadblocks meant less chance of rescue, which meant that she had to find a way out of this.

Or die trying, she thought again.

"Why are you smiling?" Lance demanded, snapping her back.

"Huh?" She gawked at him. *I was smiling?*

"What were you thinking about, Carolyn?"

"My baby," she lied. "If it will be a boy or a girl?"

"And that makes you smile like that?"

"Like what?"

"I don't know, contemptuously. You were smiling like someone thinking evil thoughts." He raised his eyes to meet hers, studying her reaction. "You weren't planning on doing something that would affect our business arrangement, would you?"

"No," she blurted.

She felt him dissecting her, but she didn't lower her eyes. His face was expressionless, but behind those gray-blue eyes, anger and violence was waiting. The thing that he became when he killed was itching to get out.

Never wavering, he said, "Eyes back on the road."

Then he withdrew into himself, turning back to stare out the window as if some long-sought answer awaited him out there in the fading morning.

7

Lance was brooding over what a disaster this had become and his own missteps in the affair. They wouldn't make Canada by tonight as he hoped, maybe tomorrow. He was still safe. They hadn't found the other two or the workman. They were still looking for three fugitives, or so he thought.

But in all directions of their position, a gathering storm of law enforcement wove pieces of evidence together.

The net was tightening.

***

CHAPTER 19 – MAXWELL'S POSSE

1

17 November 2008

US 219

Outside Reynoldsville, PA

Lieutenant Abraham was the only one who stayed behind at the crime scene. Maxwell's posse was on the move again, headed for the airport in Dubois, Pennsylvania.

Without Abraham's truck, the five of them were crammed into the rental vehicle. Perkins was driving, with Maxwell riding shotgun while Leigh was in the rear with Bob and Oggy.

"You think he's made it up to New York yet?" Oggy asked.

"Maybe," Maxwell said. "If we can get a name off that receipt, we might be able to narrow the location down with a make and model on the car."

"You think the girl is dead?" Bobby asked.

"Could be," Maxwell responded. "But who knows? She'd be a good decoy to use at checkpoints while we were looking for three guys."

"She's alive," Perkins said.

"Probably," Maxwell agreed.

"But for how long?" Leigh interjected.

"Yeah, for how long?" Maxwell stared out the window. He needed the make on that car, the sooner the better.

"The clock is ticking," Oggy said.

Twenty minutes out of Dubois, Boyden called to say that the Pennsylvania state cops had cracked the receipt. The purchase for the scarf was made by Carolyn Catharine McIntosh of Chapmanville, West Virginia. Miss McIntosh owned a 2003 Ford Taurus wagon, and she included the license plate. A BOLO was issued for the car, covering the states of New York and Pennsylvania.

"What about a cell phone?" Maxwell asked Boyden.

"She has one, but the folks at Verizon haven't been able to ping it," Boyden said. "Maybe he pulled the battery and destroyed it."

"Maybe. Could be lying in a ditch somewhere along the side of a highway," Maxwell said. "We need to keep this off the news. If he gets wind that we know who she is, he'll kill her for sure."

"I already pushed that with the state cops. They agree. But we can't control every little police force," Boyden said. "The West Virginia state cops are visiting her parents and they're going to ask for an up-to-date photo to circulate to all the checkpoints."

"Do your best to keep a lid on it, Linda."

"I will."

He ended the call and said to the rest of them, "He's got a hostage, driving in a 2003 Taurus wagon. Girl's name is Carolyn Catharine McIntosh, age twenty-one, college student."

Bobby spoke up first. "We can't just go north and wait. I mean, how would that look? That girl gets murdered in Pennsylvania while we're lying in wait at the Canadian border."

"He'll probably get picked up at a checkpoint before we even see him anyway," Perkins said. "We got a make and plate, and right now, the press doesn't know anything."

Maxwell listened.

"We're in a horse race now," Oggy said. "But not with Belanger."

"I know," Maxwell said.

"The press gets wind and broadcasts it, they'll be signing that girl's death certificate," Oggy continued.

"I think our mission just took a left turn, Max," Perkins said. "We gotta rethink this."

Maxwell was listening intently.

Then Leigh said, "Her name is Carolyn McIntosh."

Perkins stopped. "Yeah, Carolyn." And then, "Let's pull over and talk about this."

"Why do we have to stop?" Leigh asked.

"Because Perk is jonesing for a smoke," Maxwell said.

"You know me too well, Max." Perk clicked on the right turn signal as a ramp approached. "Ten minutes, tops." They turned up the ramp and Perkins removed the cigarette pack from his pocket, steering with his left hand and tapping the smoke with the other, catching it methodically between his teeth.

Leigh watched in disbelief. "Try not to get us killed, okay, Lonnie?"

He glanced in the mirror, cigarette bouncing on every syllable. "Call me Perk, Michelle, and don't worry, I'm a professional." He rolled the car through the intersection at the end of the ramp without stopping and got onto the shoulder of the onramp. It was wide enough so that everyone could stretch their legs while Perkins had his smoke.

"Hey, Perk, you just blew a stop sign," Bobby said. "What kind of message are you sending to the children?"

"You Quaker cops obviously have a different policing style than a Kentucky lawman," Perkins said.

"Oh yeah, how's that?" Bobby asked.

Perkins raised his middle finger and smiled. "We do what we want."

Bobby laughed.

The car stopped, and they bailed out.

2

As it turned out, there were three smokers in the pack, one hardcore Kentuckian, one reborn Pittsburgh detective, and the FBI agent running the whole dog and pony show. Leigh and Oggy watched outside the perimeter of smoke.

"So, what do you wanna do?" Bobby asked.

"They could already be in upstate New York," Maxwell said. "We don't have a proper timeline to determine how far they've got or even if Carolyn McIntosh is alive."

"We have to operate on that assumption," Leigh advised.

"I know." Maxwell took a drag off the cigarette and eased it slowly into his lungs. He wasn't a constant smoker; his throat and lungs were virgin. "Perk is right, that he'll probably get picked up in a police checkpoint. I understand your concerns, but we don't know where the hell he is. He could be one hundred miles from the border right now. They've had over thirty-six hours since Belanger killed his accomplices. Even with a storm, it doesn't take a day and a half to get up into northern New York State."

"It would if they're traveling secondary roads, trying to get around the check stops. He's had a great cover to this point, but would he really want to expose himself with his face being broadcast all over the country?" Oggy stepped a little closer and said, "Listen, you're the boss, but wouldn't it make sense to sit tight just in case something shakes loose?"

Maxwell thought about it and said, "What do the rest of you think?"

Leigh, Bobby, and Perkins agreed with Oggy. The discussion was one of frustration. They needed more evidence of the Highwayman's movements. A collective spirit of helplessness plagued all.

Then Maxwell's phone rang as he was stubbing out his smoke. It was Abraham. They'd found a murdered highway worker up in a place called Camp Inspiration.

"You up there now, Cole?" Maxwell crushed out the cigarette and put the phone on speaker while Perkins lit up another smoke.

Abraham continued, "On my way. Local cops have secured the scene. You might want to turn tail and come on up for a look. I talked to the county sheriff, and he thinks the workman was killed early in the morning."

"Why does he think that?"

"Because the truck was still idling when they found him, and his boss had sent him out on the call. If that's the case, they couldn't have gotten far. The workman has one shot to the head, they're thinking .38 caliber."

"You got a location?"

"Yeah, you're less than an hour away. Directly north of you, straight up the 219 past Brockport. If you leave now, you'll probably beat me to the crime scene." Abraham paused, as if doing something, then said, "I just texted you the coordinates."

"Are you texting and driving, Cole?" Bobby asked.

"You been told to fuck off today, Halsey?"

"I have now," Bobby said.

"Yes, you have," Abraham said and got off the phone.

They got into the car and turned north.

Maxwell said, "Michelle, give the pilot a call and tell him we're going to be late."

She did.

3

US 219

5 Miles North of Killbuck, NY

They only crossed one checkpoint where the I-86 and the US 219 intersected, but the BOLO had not been fully distributed, and the picture they were circulating of Lance was that of a young man with a buzz cut. Almost, but not quite militant-looking. The man sitting in the passenger seat of the Taurus wagon had shoulder-length hair and a full beard. He looked like a hippy college student. Like the boyfriend parents don't entirely approve of but tolerate in the hope that he is simply a passing phase.

The state cop manning the checkpoint held up the photos, and hardly gave them a second glance before waving them through. But he would remember them, or rather, the car and that it had a female driver and a male passenger. Not that it would matter. By that time, the shit would have already hit the fan.

4

The route Lance had picked would take them off US 219 and onto State Route 98 toward Farmersville, New York. He wanted to stay off the main highways, away from the probing eyes of law enforcement. By his estimation, he had roughly three hundred miles to go. A six-hour drive on a regular highway, but more like ten with their chosen route. They wound up the NY 98 into the Great Valley region of New York state. The landscape morphed into a turmoil of hills and forest broken by contrasting basin farmland. The snow on the hills, trees, and farms looked like they were covered with icing sugar in the opaque daylight.

"I have to go to the bathroom," Carolyn said.

"Keep driving," Lance muttered.

"I need to go bad."

"There isn't a rest area for miles."

"I can go in the bushes."

"Too chancy."

"I won't do anything stupid."

Lance looked at her hard. "One or two?"

"Two."

He curled his nose and looked out the window. About two miles up the road, the forest was becoming denser. "Up there," he said. "You better be quick."

"I will."

Ten minutes later, he was leading her to a spot in the woods where she could conduct her business. The car was pulled as far onto the shoulder as Lance dared. He'd allowed her to put on her coat after checking all the pockets and finding nothing more than a pack of Kleenex tissue. He left it for her to use. When they were far enough from the road, Lance took her left wrist and attached two zip ties to a sturdy branch on a young tree. "Get on with it, Carolyn. We have places to be."

"Can I have a little privacy?"

"Are you kidding me?"

"Please."

He sighed and turned his back. That was when he heard an approaching vehicle and grunted, "Damn it." He would have to go back to the car and check it. He called back to her, "Have your shit, and make it snappy. You make a noise, and I'll come back with my gun and silence you."

"I won't make a sound." She was holding the button on her jeans with her free right hand, waiting for him to turn around.

"Not a sound," he said, and plodded back through the snow toward the car. He stumbled once, dropping the gun into the snow, and then frantically searched for it. When he picked it up, the barrel had snow in it. "Fuck."

The car was getting closer.

He jammed it into his pocket and came up the bank.

About half a mile south of him, a vehicle approached. Lance couldn't tell if it was a car or a truck. Or if it was a local or a police car.

"Hurry the fuck up, Carolyn!"

"I'm working on it," she called back.

He focused in on the vehicle, squinting against the reflecting white light, trying to identify it. It might have been a pickup truck. He brought his hand up as a visor and tried harder.

It's a pickup.

But was it a police vehicle?

It wasn't, just a farmer, probably traveling between farms, or to friends or family. As it got closer, Lance stepped onto the passenger side of the Taurus and unzipped. The pickup was almost on top of him now. He began urinating and raised a free hand to give a wave to the driver when it passed without incident.

Once it was up the road a bit, he called, "All right, let's go, Carolyn."

There was no answer.

"Carolyn?"

Nothing.

"Fuck!"

5

When the zip tie gave way to the tourniquet force of the twisting nail and came off her wrist, the plastic dug into her skin. It made a snapping sound and tumbled into the snow, a speckling of her blood clotting the white. For a second, she stared dumbly down at it.

She listened to the passing vehicle.

Then he called to her, "All right, let's go, Carolyn."

And again.

"Carolyn?"

Then he said something that sounded so very foreign, but only

because it was something she'd heard on television as a
kid. "Stop or I'll shoot!"

By the time Lance had barked, "Fuck!" she'd begun to
run into the forest. It wasn't easy. She bumped her shoulder
on a tree trunk and fell, but recovered quickly when she
heard him thumping down the path behind her.

Carolyn didn't stop. She knew that this was do, or die
trying. She dodged behind a tree when he pulled the trigger.
She heard the crack, but it didn't sound the same as when he
shot the others, and there hadn't been any screaming.

Screaming?

6

Lance raised the gun, cocking the hammer, squeezing the
trigger, and then there was a detonation accompanied by the
rotten egg stench of gun powder. He felt a stinging in his
face and blooming of scarlet fire in his right hand.

At first, he thought that it was all a trick of the eye, and that
somehow, she'd flanked him with a tree branch and smashed
his hand upward. But through the haze and growing agony
he caught a glimpse of her running between the trees while
letting out a howl of agony and falling to his knees.

"Fuck," he screamed, then fell onto his side, still clutching
the mangled piece of steel in his right hand, seeing its barrel
splintered and smoking. For some reason, he couldn't let it
go. He jammed his hand into the snow, the gunmetal sizzling,
while inhaling and exhaling like a woman in labor doing the
breathing method.

7

He brought his right hand up and examined it. The
trigger guard was crimped over his index finger, the flesh

surrounding it scorched and lacerated. He tried to work through the pain.

Using his left hand, Lance meticulously began to work the mangled .38 out of his numb right hand. He cried like a baby as he did this. "Fuck…" He managed to extract his index finger, which was thankfully still intact along with his other digits, from the gun. His hand was in one piece, but it was covered with lacerations and peppered with powder burns. He dropped the .38 into the snow and tucked his hand protectively under his left forearm.

Before he turned to go back up the trail, he yelled into the forest. "I'm going to kill your entire family for this! Do you hear me, Carolyn? Do you hear me, you little cunt?"

He listened over the hum of pain.

No response. She was gone.

He had to get out of here. She could identify him; he didn't have much time. "Fuck!" Lance turned and stumbled back up the trail to the waiting car. He opened the door with his left hand and climbed awkwardly into the passenger seat. Lying on the seat was a scarf, her scarf. "Fucking bitch-cunt!" He wanted to smash something, to light the car on fire. To unleash the monster, but the pain controlled him.

We've gotta get the fuck out of here!

"Okay, okay, okay! Gotta go," he blubbered. He picked up her scarf, winding it loosely around his hand, and the pain in his hand lit up with each wrap.

Done, he leaned back in the seat, took a couple of gasps, exhaled, and whimpered.

Let's fucking go, the monster demanded, *before she finds a cop.*

"Okay." More deep breaths.

He pushed the pain down as best he could, and got on with it.

Every left-handed task was a nightmare, inserting the keys, turning the keys in the ignition. The only thing that wasn't hard to do was put on his seatbelt.

He eased off the shoulder and onto the road, pointing the car north, leaving the escaping bitch behind. He vowed to go back and kill her and her family if he ever got out of this.

Once up to a manageable speed of 55 MPH, he held the steering wheel with his knee and carefully unwrapped the scarf from his hand. He moved his digits, one at a time. They weren't broken, just burned and lacerated.

He couldn't look at it. Not now. He rewrapped it.

He would need a first aid kit.

***

CHAPTER 20 – SINGING ITALIAN SONGS

1

17 November 2008

NY State 98

8 Miles Southwest of Franklinville, NY

He was on fire with rage, left hand clamped on the steering wheel like a vice, teeth clenched so hard that every muscle in his cheeks hardened, turning his face into that of a lifeless golem. But from his lower lip, drool spilled down in twin tendrils, puddling on his chest and darkening the front of his hoodie. Beside him, the source of that rage felt like it had been attacked with a blowtorch and pliers.

He was right-handed.

For fuck sake!

Lance's eyes were transfixed on the road, barely blinking, but when they did, they opened and closed as if in slow motion. He was meditating against the pain, trying to pigeonhole it. He had to calm down and figure something out with that hand. It hurt way worse than the stab wound Norris had inflicted on him before the others had taken him away.

The others.

The radio was barely on, Chicago was singing "Saturday in the Park." They were just at the part about the man selling ice cream and Italian songs. Lance hated that song but couldn't bring his right hand up to turn off the radio. He frothed, bits of drool swinging off each syllable like corn syrup. "Doesn't that just fucking figure! One more 'fuck you' from the great beyond. Norris, Steel, Dusk, Gusa! Fucking Gusa! That prick! He had to get himself caught. It wasn't supposed to be like this! The plan was supposed to be: Leave a mark and disappear."

The plan had turned out to be a disaster.

I forgot about Carolyn, he thought, and that only inflamed the burning in his hand up into his arm like ants, filled with fiery venom, biting as they went.

"I'm going to make her pay for that."

"You're going the wrong way to do that," the Highwayman said. The waterfall of drool stopped, forwarded to lubricate the dual rantings of a madman.

"I had to leave!"

Then he heard his father's voice inside his head. *"How many times have I told you that the barrel of a weapon is like a bomb if it gets plugged?"*

"Fuck you too, Dad."

Piling on, Chicago sang, "A bronze man still can tell stories..."

"What a fucking stupid song," Lance screamed.

Stop!

The advancing insects on his arm halted, something kicked in, hushing them, compartmentalizing, moving each issue back into its own place. Norris in the first room. Door slams. The Pittsburgh three in theirs. Door slams, and on and on, even Gusa. Slam! It took approximately ten minutes to get each chaotic thought locked in its own cell. Silenced by a barrier. Then came hard, staticky white noise, buzzing like electric insects.

Then silence.

Focus!

He brought up his scarf-covered right hand and cautiously wiped the drool from his chin. His hand throbbed. A new song came on the radio, one he liked quite a bit, one he'd seen in a bad television movie when he was a kid. The song was called "Don't Fear the Reaper." He couldn't remember the film, just that it starred actor Gary Sinise.

"Time to man up," he said, then clamped down on the scarf with his teeth and slowly unraveled it from his injured right hand. Once on the last wrap, the veil fell away, exposing the wound which didn't look nearly as bad as he'd imagined. Projecting on his part. He examined his hand. It was swollen around the webbing of his thumb and index finger, but it felt like molten lava wrapped in the scarf. He moved his pinky, then his ring finger, until he got to his index. The index finger was the worst, tugging painfully at the lacerated and scorched skin when he wiggled it. Then his thumb, which felt even better than its neighbors.

Lance smiled. "Not so bad."

He attempted a fist, and his index protested painfully.

He turned his eyes back to the road, working his hand, opening and closing it. Biting down on the pain. He was going to need that hand. He was going to need it very soon. *Sooner or later, they're going to find that little bitch, and they'll be looking for this car.*

Then something caught his eye.

In the distance, he could see a farmhouse. On the left of the road, about a mile up in a field, was a man riding a tractor. Lance unclamped his hand and tightened it again and again.

He was going to need that hand.

2

17 November, 2008

Camp Inspiration

Near Brandy Camp

They were standing around the work truck, looking over the scene. The victim's body was still leaning over, as if in a strange slumber for the audience of cops. There was very little blood, a dime-sized hole in the forehead of the man, and as far as they could tell, the bullet had not gone all the way through.

A Crime Scene perimeter tape had been set up along both sides of the drive. The investigators were standing outside the taped- off area, peering in, as the forensics people took photographs and gathered evidence. There were two sets of tire tracks, those from the work truck containing Oscar Johnson's dead body and to the right, wheel tracks from a much smaller car. There was a single set of footprints crossing from one set of tire tracks to another, and two sets going from one cabin to the next, then circling back. There were also footprints from the parking spot up to an outhouse.

"Looks like they camped out here," Leigh said.

"Met him in the morning, maybe Carolyn tried to make a break for it," Perkins said. "Lance shoots him and gets her back under control."

"I don't see any tracks other than the ones from the vehicles," Bobby said and pointed to the truck. "Maybe he surprised them and was killed to eliminate him as a potential witness."

"That's what I'm thinking," Maxwell said. "They can't be too far ahead of us."

"Five hours, maybe," Oggy said.

Maxwell left the others, walking around the perimeter of tape and following it to the outhouse. There, a Crime Scene tech was taking pictures of the inside. "Anything interesting?"

The tech said, "At a glance, no. But…"

"But what?"

"There's a small hole in the wall."

Maxwell craned his neck, but the crime tech was in his line of vision. "Would I be able to see it from here?"

The tech was dressed in white neoprene, wearing blue rubber gloves, and donning clear safety glasses. The man stood and turned around to face Maxwell. There was a momentary pause as they exchanged eye contact, and then he smiled and said, "Sorry," moving to one side.

When he stepped away, Maxwell saw the hole he was photographing. "Is that a nail hole?" There were splinters protruding from it, as if it had been wiggled and pulled.

"Looks like it. And it's a big hole. Probably a two-and-half-inch construction nail, I'd say. But I found something else." He reached over and lifted a Crime Scene baggy, and said, "I found a strand of dark hair beside the toilet seat."

Maxwell craned his neck. "I can't really see it from here."

"You wanna trade places?" The tech smiled.

Maxwell laughed. "I'll leave the evidence gathering to the professionals."

He stood up and came out to meet Maxwell. "You must be Agent Maxwell?"

"I am, and you are?"

"Mike Perry. I work for the Bureau of Forensic Services."

"I didn't know my name was being circulated through the BFS."

"Cole Abraham is a drinking buddy and sometimes hunting pal." He handed the evidence bag over, and Maxwell lifted it up. "That's not a very long hair."

"It's a female hair. I'd bet on it." Perry said.

Maxwell looked closely. "Why do you say that?"

"There's dye in it. A touch of red, or pink."

Maxwell scrutinized the hair. "I can't see anything red or pink."

"Hold it up to the light, and try and look through it."

Maxwell held it up. "You've got better eyes than me, Mike."

He smiled. "I've also got some corroborating evidence."

"What's that?"

"There's a feminine scent in there. Perfume or body spray, maybe hair spray, but it's a female scent."

Maxwell handed back the evidence bag, brought his hand up, and scratched his chin while taking in the hole where the nail had been. "I think our hostage has a weapon."

"Hopefully, she knows how to use it."

"Hopefully."

Maxwell moved down the line where two BFS techs were casting several footprints using dental stone. Maxwell had taken a course on casting and remembered the instructor telling them to always take pictures along with the castings as a precaution when doing it in the snow. "One might offset the shortcomings of the other," the instructor suggested. The two techs were doing just that.

"Looks like they did a walkabout," Perk said, coming up from behind.

Max turned to face him. "Yeah, they spent a night here for sure."

"Michelle and Bob are talking to the state cops about likely travel routes." Perkins lit a smoke and continued. "If anyone knows these roads, it'll be the troopers."

"Yeah." Maxwell looked on, distracted by thoughts best not thought. Time was running out for the girl, and they were still only in evidence gathering mode. He was struggling with what to do now. They couldn't just go into upstate New York and hunker down. They needed a tip, something to get them back on the scent.

"They got anything?" Lonnie asked.

"She might have a weapon. There was a nail pulled out of the wall of the outhouse. A woman's hair not far away." Maxwell said.

"A nail. Not much of match for a .38."

"It's something." Maxwell turned and began walking back to the others, and Lonnie followed him. Simultaneously, Abraham was pulling up in his vehicle. "Hopefully the state troopers can give us some ideas about which way they'd be going."

"Yup, that would be good."

They huddled over the hood of Abraham's vehicle, a map spread out, north toward the windshield. Abraham had marked all the spots where the bodies and the vehicle had been located, including this one. He traced those locations back using secondary routes only. "Speculation," he said. "But I'd say that this was his route." He ran his finger along the highway from Brave all the way up to the rest area in Summerville, Pennsylvania, and then on to the location they now stood in. "The only question is, where are they going now?"

"Upstate New York," Maxwell said. "Probably the Canadian border."

"New York is out of my jurisdiction," Abraham said.

"Mine too," Lonnie.

"Good luck with the troopers up in New York."

"Why's that? You saying they ain't no good?" Perkins asked.

"No, they're capable enough. They just aren't trained to the high standard of the PST."

"It'll be tough losing your support," Perkins said.

Bobby laughed, while Michelle and Oggy focused on the map along with the silent Maxwell. He traced his finger north along Route 28 and whispered, "How far?"

"He could already be over the state line," Oggy said. "Have we had any reports of them going through a roadblock before the BOLO?"

"No," Abraham said.

"We need to box them in," Maxwell said. "Come at them from the north and south."

"We have to know where they are," Michelle said. "Or at least have proximity."

It was late afternoon, and soon the light would be draining from the sky, offering dark shelter to their prey.

"We need a goddamned break," Maxwell cussed.

3

17 November 2008

NY State Route 98

7 Miles Southwest of Franklinville, NY

The man on the tractor was named Perry De Jong, and he saw the oncoming car coming up the road through the right-side view mirror of the John Deere. De Jong was a slim, balding man whose clothes hung on him like a coat rack. Behind the tractor, a derelict wagon carried two large round bails of hay intended for his sheep. He didn't pay much mind to the car, expected it would pass by, but it decelerated and aligned itself with him.

The two carried on this way for a few seconds until De Jong turned his gaze onto the driver, who was staring straight at him. When they locked eyes, he could see the driver was trying to get his attention. De Jong stopped the tractor, cut the engine, and slid the glass door open. In turn, the driver stopped his car and opened his window.

"Can I help you?" De Jong asked.

"Hi there." The driver smiled, but it was patronizing. "I was wondering if you could help me?"

"Help you?" De Jong wondered if the driver was looking for some gas. It wouldn't be the first time a traveler or some guy down on his luck had sought help. "What do you need?"

"A hospital. Is there one up in Franklinville?"

Hospital?

The driver held up his right hand, and De Jong saw cuts and abrasions. "I feel foolish. I was checking my oil, and I dropped the rag down into the fan shroud, and when I stupidly tried to retrieve it, the electric fan came on."

"Ouch, that looks like it smarts some," De Jong said and climbed from his tractor to take a closer look. The man in the car opened his driver's door and eased out as well.

"It looks worse than it is, but I'd like to get it looked at."

De Jong met the young man at the roadside and brought his hand up, beckoning. "May I?" The young man surrendered the injured right hand to De Jong, who carefully turned it over and examined it. "It doesn't look too bad. A bit of peroxide and some bandages should fix you up. If I had my Ford, we could wrap it up here. There's a first aid kit in the Ford."

"Ford? Pickup?"

"No, Ford tractor. They make great tractors. I'm a Dodge man when it comes to pickups." He smiled, revealing teeth that were neatly aligned and well maintained. "Trouble is the tractor is at the other farm. I'm pretty much wrapped up here. If you follow me back to my place, we'll get you fixed up and on your way."

The young man looked embarrassed. "Really, I don't want to impose."

"No problem." He grinned. "That's my place down there, drive on up. There's a big dog there, but he's friendly to strangers and the coyotes as well, I think."

"The coyotes?"

"The ones that keep stealing our eggs. The dog's a lousy guard, name's Jake, friendly but stinks at his job." De Jong let his hand go and turned to go back to his tractor. "It'll take me a minute to get there."

"Thank you."

"We are our brother's keeper."

4

Lance waited in the car for the tractor to make its last leg into the farmyard behind the three main buildings at the farm. They were a brick two-story, post-war home and a traditional barn scaling itself of the dried red paint chips that were probably set on its aging bone wood at least two decades before. The barn wasn't quite as old as the house, but certainly not far behind. Then there was the poultry house, the newest and most modern building. Made of corrugated steel, it was roughly fifty feet wide and at least five hundred feet long. Along its sides were four great big air exchange fans circulating the air for the thousands of chickens housed inside.

Lance had worked at four different chicken farms when he was a kid after his father insisted he get out among the commoners and learn a little about why he needed to get an education. The poultry barns hadn't been this modern, but they were similar, albeit a little more beaten. He thought about those days, swamping chickens from the building into the waiting cages on a truck transporting them to their eventual demise.

After the first encounter on the farm, bearing witness to the terror of the birds as his fellow workers gathered three up in each hand, walking them out to the waiting death truck, Lance was hooked. Moving in the darkness, he gathered up three horrified birds, one leg in each hand, and every other capture he would feel a leg break. The stink of ammonia only added to the exhilaration, and Lance actively sought three more chicken catching jobs until the season was out. He thought it was comparable to the Nazi death camps he'd read about in the school library, and that jacked him up.

The dog, Jake, an overweight golden Lab, who probably had diabetes, came out to meet him. On the side of caution, he stayed in the car. Bad things came in threes, and as far he could tell, Carolyn's escape and the gun blowing up in his hand were two. There was no point in chancing getting mauled by a lying dog.

There was no sign of anyone else, no kids or woman came out to investigate. While he waited for the farmer to park the noisy diesel contraption in the barn, he looked for places to store his own car out of sight of the road. He would leave it here for now, but not for long, and the barn would be the best option.

The engine on the tractor capitulated to an encore of echoing minor clangs and ticks until it fell mute. Lance watched the man approach. They were of similar height, but the guy was about seven years older, and his hair was similar even though it was thinning on top.

"Jake," the farmer called, and the dog left its spot by Lance's driver's door. "Don't worry. Like I said, he's friendly," the farmer assured Lance.

Grudgingly, Lance pushed the car door open and stepped out onto the compressed snow on the farm drive. The farmer patted his dog on the head and closing the distance, he said, "My name's Perry De Jong."

Lance looked at the farmer and said, "Devon Mitchell. And thanks for this."

"No problem," De Jong said, and placed a hand on Lance's left shoulder and squeezed. "Come on into the house, and we'll take a look at that hand."

They started for the house.

The dog watched them go.

***

PART III

PREDATOR AND PREY

"Come and find me."—Lance Belanger

CHAPTER 21 – THE
RULE OF THREES

1

Raecher Hill State Forest

Great Valley, NY

There were five of them winding through the forest, accelerating, slowing, passing, the engine calls throttling into the night like a pack of mechanical wolves baying to a full moon. The group consisted of seven kids on five snowmobiles, three girls and four boys, ages ranging from fourteen to sixteen, the oldest being a boy named Anthony Hartley.

Anthony was the leader of this group for a couple of reasons. Being the oldest didn't hurt, but he was well liked, and much sought after by the girls his own age and younger. And if that wasn't enough, he was straddling a brand new F1000 Arctic Cat snowmobile, which made him the fastest and the coolest. But even that wasn't the balls of it, because wrapped around him was the prettiest, most popular girl in his class.

Her name was Kristine Powell, a slender blond fifteen-year-old who could have had any boy she wanted. Anthony knew this because his school chums commented on her all the time. He was crazy about Kristine, loved holding and touching her. They hadn't gone all the way yet; there had been plenty of touching and petting, but he held it back. He wanted to have sex with Kristine, but he was afraid of rejection and the possibility her dismissal would end their relationship. That dulled his courage to ask. And it wasn't just because he really liked her, because he did, but there was his reputation to consider. Most of his friends assumed that he was already sleeping with her. Even though he'd never said it, he never denied the gossiping of his four male friends in the pack.

She held him tightly, as he twisted the throttle on the snowmobile and pulled away from the group. Ahead, a daylight moon hung above the trail. He felt Kristine hug him and lay her helmet-encased head against his shoulder blades. Just over the drone of the snow sled he heard her say loudly, "I love you, Anthony Hartley."

He reached down with his gloved left hand, squeezed her thigh, and said, "I love you too, Kristine."

She hugged him even tighter.

For Anthony, this was so fucking cool.

And it was about to get cooler.

Anthony saw a blur he thought was a deer stepping from the forest. Realizing that he might collide with the creature, he got off the throttle, and when he realized it was a woman, he got onto the brakes a little too hard and almost lost control. "Whoa, whoa, shit…"

Simultaneously, Kristine lifted her head. "Huh? What…"

He steered hard left, just missing her, passing and stopping after twenty feet. Anthony popped up the visor on his helmet while Kristine removed hers. They took in the spectacle only seconds before their approaching friends were on the scene.

The woman looked like a frozen zombie, dressed in a coat that hung open. She was wearing jeans and running shoes that were soaked and frozen. She had frostbite on her face and her wrist was injured, but her eyes were the worst. They were maniacal, darting left and right, then up and down the trail. She finally turned to look at them, and amid the madness, her voice was calm, mechanical. "My name is Carolyn. I just escaped from a serial killer. We need to get to the police. We need to leave now. Please help me. Please help me. Please don't leave me. Please don't…"

Kristine's eyes welled up with tears as she climbed from the seat and moved to comfort the women. "It's okay," she said, her voice soothing. "I promise. We won't leave you."

"Yeah," Anthony chimed in. "We won't leave you," and thought, *Serial killer?*

She turned toward the approaching snowmobiles and said, "My name is Carolyn. We have to go. We have to go right now."

Kristine closed in embracing her. "I'm Kristine, and we're going to get you out of here."

Carolyn started to cry.

"Hey, it's okay, don't cry. My name's Anthony," he said, pulling a first aid kit from the saddlebag of the snowmobile. He held it for a second and tossed it back in "We've got a cabin east of here. I'd like to take you there, and after we quickly get you warmed up, we'll jump in my truck, take you to a hospital, and call the police."

The others were there, cutting the engines on their machines and raising their visors. Kyle, Anthony's best friend, called, "What happened?"

Anthony raised a hand to silence Kyle and asked Carolyn, "What did you say about escaping from a serial killer? How long ago was this?"

Carolyn ignored the question. "We have to get out of here."

Kristine leaned in. "We're not going to leave you, Carolyn."

"No one is going to mess with seven people. You're safe," Anthony added.

"What the hell is going on?" Gordy, Anthony's other best friend, asked.

"Shut up, Gordy, and listen."

"He killed three men," Carolyn said. "Right in front of me."

Anthony's heart was jackhammering in his chest. "Okay, I got the biggest sled, so she'll have to ride with me."

"I'll ride with Kyle," Kristine said.

Then Anthony said something that would seal his fate as a hero in the eyes of his friends and the girl who thought she loved him. "Listen up, this woman… Carolyn, says she escaped from a serial killer. We need to get her back to the cabin and warm her up, then we need to get her to a hospital and call the cops."

As soon as Anthony said, "serial killer," the others were looking left and right, up and down the trail, faces blossoming with fresh fear. "Let's get out of here," a girl named Brandy Popovich said.

"How long have you been in the woods?" Kristine asked.

"I don't know," Carolyn said. "Maybe hours, he was up on the highway when I escaped."

"What's he driving?" Anthony asked.

"My car. He has my car."

"What kind of car?"

"We need to get out of here," Brandy urged.

"Shut up, Brandy," Anthony barked. "What kind of car, Carolyn?"

"Ford Taurus, a wagon."

"Okay." He leaned in and zipped up her coat, and said, "You're going to need to hold onto me. You don't have any gloves, so I want you to put your hands inside the pockets of my snowsuit to keep them warm. Okay?"

"Give me your scarves," Kristine called to her friends.

They turned over four scarves, three from the girls, one from Kyle, who had an authentic Arab Keffiyeh Shemagh scarf his dead brother had given him as a souvenir before dying on his second tour in Iraq. Kyle wore the scarf in honor of his brother. "Here," he said, handing it to Kristine. "Please take care of it."

"Thank you, Kyle," Kristine said and went back to wrap up the poor woman's legs.

Kyle followed her and helped. The woman's ears had little white, waxy dots of frostbite around the lobes. "We can use the Shemagh to protect her face and ears."

They got her onto the back of Anthony's F1000 and did the best they could to wrap up her legs, neck, and head.

They didn't have a helmet for her.

"How far to the cabin?" Carolyn asked.

"Thirty minutes," Anthony said.

"Do you have a gun there?"

Anthony smiled. "I've got a gun in my saddlebag. A .357 Magnum." His smile faltered slightly as he added. "It's mostly for bears. But some asshole in a Taurus who gets in our way can qualify as a target."

Kristine looked on, in awe of her boyfriend, as did the others.

Carolyn said, "You're very brave. Can we please go now?"

"Absolutely." Anthony said, and then to the others, "Let's roll." He was scared, but he saw how his friends looked at him, how Kristine had looked at him.

They were going to be heroes.

2

De Jong Farm, NY

The house was disorderly, a bachelor's home that had once had a woman's touch, but long ago. Empty boxes of many different things were stacked against walls. Boxes that contained household appliances, a toaster, an oscillating table fan. There were boxes from Amazon, and there were also newspapers piled up. Lance was sitting at the kitchen table which was a clutter of dishes, empty glasses, stained coffee cups, and candles. The man, Perry De Jong, was opening the first aid kit and seemed not to notice Lance inventorying the room.

"Where's your family?" Lance asked. "You don't live here alone, do you?"

"My wife decided farming wasn't her thing last year and left with my son," De Jong said and turned to face Lance with a bottle of hydrogen peroxide and some cotton swabs. "Let's get that cut cleaned up."

That's going to make things a little simpler, Lance thought.

He sat quietly, as the farmer swabbed his hand with a hydrogen peroxide-soaked cotton ball, watching the clear liquid bubble in his cuts, but it didn't sting like the iodine his father had insisted on using. "Thank you," he said.

De Jong paused to look at him, smiled, and went back to wiping.

Lance watched as the superficial powder burns from the exploding gun dissipated and rubbed off with the pass of each applied swab. Some burns went deeper into the skin and wouldn't wipe away. They looked like tiny grains of pepper or, as Lance thought, fly shit. The farmer soaked a fresh piece of gauze and rubbed a little harder, causing Lance to flinch and pull his hand away.

"Sorry," De Jong said, "this is where it stings a little."

"It's okay." Lance surrendered his hand again. "That did sting quite a bit."

De Jong gingerly took his hand. "I'll try to be more careful."

"I appreciate that."

De Jong continued to clean the hand, adding to a pile of gauze stained with copper and gunpowder. If he'd seen a gunshot wound before, he made no mention. Then out of nowhere, he said, "I was upset at first, about my wife, I mean, but she and I weren't happy for the longest time. Sometimes people just don't belong together. We were incompatible. You know what I mean?"

Lance did. He felt incompatible with everyone. In a sense, he felt alone in the world, unable to comprehend others' feelings. He wanted to ask the farmer about the kid, whether he didn't fit, but pushed it away and decided against it as the man finished cleaning his wounds. He only said, "Yeah, I know what you mean."

De Jong studied him for a second, then turned his eyes back to the business of first aid. Ten minutes later, Lance held up a freshly bandaged hand. De Jong had done an excellent job and had even left most of his hand exposed to the air after applying some ointment, only putting a bandage on his index finger and a smaller one in the webbing between thumb and index. His hand felt better; he was even able to make a loose fist. "Wow, not bad at all."

De Jong said nothing; just smiled.

Lance wondered what he was thinking. He had a strange look on his face.

"Would you like a cold drink or some tea?" De Jong offered. "Maybe some food?"

"I don't want to be any trouble." Lance was hungry and thirsty.

"No trouble at all."

"Okay, then."

De Jong gave him a Pepsi and heated up some leftover lamb stew. Lance liked the stew; it was nice to eat something that didn't come out of a drive-thru window or a microwaveable wrapper. The light outside faded as they ate. There wasn't much conversation. De Jong queried about where he was going and when Lance told him that he was headed for Plattsburgh, New York, he nodded.

But something felt off.

De Jong was stealing glances of him, when he thought he wasn't looking, a strange half-painted smile on his face. He'd seen that look before, and it made him wonder if this man was who he said he was.

Lance finished the stew and took a second helping when offered. He ate every bite. He couldn't believe how hungry he was. And tired. He was tired. It had been a long day of driving, and Carolyn's escape and his loss of self-control had proved exhausting.

I can't stay here too long, he thought.

De Jong took the empty bowl and asked, "Can I get you anything else?"

"No, thank you. That was more than enough. I'm stuffed."

"Okay," he said and rinsed the dishes in the sink.

"Can I use your bathroom?" Lance asked.

De Jong turned off the tap and said, "Second door down the hall on the left."

"Thanks."

Lance got up out of his seat and felt a momentary loss of balance. He caught the back of the chair and steadied himself, waiting to see if the farmer would turn around.

He didn't.

That's when the paranoia began to seep in.

I need to get out of here.

He wasn't sure if he was intoxicated, but something felt wrong. Had the farmer put something in his food or drink? He wasn't sure. If he had, why? "I'll be right back," he said and moved down the hall toward the bathroom.

Maybe I've stumbled into another killer's lair, he thought.

He pushed down the hall, stepped into the bathroom, and closed the door. Then he lined up on the mirror and began considering his situation. *Is it possible? Have I stumbled into the lair of another? What are the odds?* He'd read somewhere that there are as many as 2,000 operating serial killers at any given time. It seemed like a high estimate, perhaps one concocted by police forces looking to pad their budgets. But there were a lot of people out there of like mind. Macabre.club had shown him that, drawing in Norris and the others. Never mind the applicants who hadn't made the cut.

The ones who played footsie with the idea, but hadn't and possibly wouldn't cross the line from fantasy into reality.

Yeah, it's possible.

How many farmers lived alone without a family? There was the pig farmer up in Canada who had killed almost fifty women and fed them to his pigs. *No family there.* There was the Beekeeper killer, Sammy Rudolph, who had murdered six girls in Virginia. There were plenty, when he thought about it. Juan Corona out of California and crazy Edward Gein up in Wisconsin. All of these men had been single, as far as Lance could remember.

So, this is my fate, to be killed by one of my own. It would certainly be poetic justice and a hell of a way to end my sordid tale.

To his surprise, he smiled at the thought.

Maxwell would keep searching after I disappeared into the earth.

Then from outside De Jong called, "Everything okay in there?"

Lance stared into the mirror, holding up his shaking hands, and his voice cracked when he said, "Yeah, I'm good, be out in a minute."

"No pressure," De Jong said and laughed.

He's laughing.

He knelt, opened the doors beneath the basin, and rummaged through the cabinet. There had to be something he could use. Then he found the magazines and that decided it.

He pulled them out, one by one. *Drummer, Bound & Gagged, Dungeon Masters…* They were BDSM mags geared toward male on male domination. Now he knew why his wife left.

If there ever was a wife and kid.

He set the magazines aside and looked deeper into the cabinet. Behind a bottle of Scope and a bottle of Toilet Duck, he found a basket filled with sex toys.

Fuck.

Most of the toys were dildos, but there were other things, including a set of handcuffs and nipple clips. After grabbing a wad of tissue, he curled his nose and pushed the toys, which had been God knew where, aside, and found what looked like a makeup bag.

Maybe there was a woman?

Or maybe he did his makeup after he dressed up in the skin of his male victims after torturing them sexually for days with his basket of toys.

He unzipped the little makeup bag and was happy to find that there had been a woman, or at least someone who used an eight-inch nail file. He held it up. Not a great weapon, probably cut the shit out of his hand in the process, but it was better than grappling with the man.

He *could be out there waiting with a knife or a gun.*

Lance felt the fear percolating in his guts.

Bad things come in threes.

He picked up the handcuffs in his left hand and flushed the toilet to cover himself as he replaced the items in the cabinet. He would have to be fast.

Don't let him have a gun.

He reached for the doorknob and turned.

3

De Jong was washing the dishes, stacking them on a tea towel he had laid out, oblivious to what was coming down the hall. Lance's outstretched right hand clutched the nail file, while the left held the cuffs, ready to incapacitate. De Jong never saw this; had he seen the expression on the face of his would-be killer, he would have climbed out the window to escape.

Lance wore a glower of rage and lust. His eyes were distant, hungry like a junkie looking for a fix. This was the monster. There would be no negotiating his position. Perry De Jong's fate was sealed.

He only got a glance of movement, before he felt the blade go into his spine just above the shoulder blades. "Oh…" he tried, but then felt his senses, touch, and balance suddenly evaporate. Then he was falling, unable to throw out his arms and protect his face. They were useless, flippers of meat without cause. He went down on the linoleum hard, smashing his cheekbone, flooding his vision with freshly squeezed tears.

He didn't even connect his present situation with the young man to whom he'd fed dinner. But it was clear who had stuck him when the ranting man got right into his face.

"What did you put in the stew?" he said and snapped a cuff first on De Jong's right, then left hand, locking them behind his back. "I asked you a question."

"Uh, uh… I don't understand." De Jong honestly didn't.

"Answer me," Lance barked. He stood up and opened a counter drawer. Then he returned with a meat cleaver. "What did you put in the stew?"

"It's lamb stew," De Jong said.

"Every time you lie, I'm going to cut off a piece!"

"Why are you doing this?" De Jong lay there, barely able to turn his head. "I fixed up your hand. I fed you. I didn't put anything in your stew. I swear!"

Lance thought about it.

He might be telling the truth. This could all be a big misunderstanding. But there were the magazines. The sex toys. The handcuffs he's wearing.

"Fuck it!"

Lance raised the meat cleaver and brought it down hard. There was a pop as the blade sliced into De Jong's tracheal cartilage. The blood was minimal. He hadn't severed the main artery.

Lance straddled the man, then lowered his head down on his chest. He listened to the beat of life fading from this world, taking with it the man's spirit…

Lance looked down at his own hand and saw the fresh cut across the palm from holding the nail file. "Fucking DNA," he said and laughed.

***

1

17 November 2008

De Jong Farm

Once Lance was sure the farmer was dead, he went outside and moved Carolyn's car out of sight. The west side of the poultry barn was shaded by an equal length of American beech trees that hid anything from the road. Even without their summer bloom, the trees' interlocking branches cloaked the car. He made sure of this by walking the drive, out onto the road, and looking back. The farmhouse and an old apple tree, that looked like an upturned claw, also helped to block any view.

"Good," he said, and looked up into the darkening sky. He didn't think that driving at night would be wise. Traffic would be thinner, and they would be looking at all single males at any given checkpoint. It would be better to leave early in the morning. The volume of cars on the road would make it easier to blend in.

He was roughly two hundred and fifty miles from the crossing. A five-hour drive to freedom, but that was the most direct route. He would have to keep on the secondary highways, and that would add hours, possibly even double the driving time.

"I have one day left," he said aloud. "One day and then I'm gone." He smiled. He was sure if he got across the border he could melt right into Canadian society. He had the money. He could bide his time, keep a low profile. Stay out of trouble, and when things cooled off, he could go back to killing. Even if he was caught, the Canadians didn't execute their murderers. And, as a bonus, they didn't deport prisoners facing the death penalty. "Tomorrow."

The evening temperatures were dipping below freezing, and Lance only just then realized that his coat was inside. The cold air pinched at his exposed arms like tiny crabs, and his skin had become rigid beneath his thin shirt.

Jesus, I can't believe I forgot to put on a jacket, he thought. *Something so simple, and now I'm freezing my ass off.*

He hadn't blacked out. Not exactly, anyway. He'd just become disconnected from himself, like watching himself in a lucid dream. This was happening more frequently, as the monstrous side of his personality surrendered to its need.

When he placed his fingers on the farmer's neck to check for a pulse and determined there was none, a voice told him he had to get the car out of sight, and he'd marched out the door without thinking. No jacket. He went out into the yard and started the car, and drove it over the freshly plowed drive which encircled every building on the farm. He parked, got out, and walked around the car, trying to see through to the road. He couldn't, but it wasn't good enough, so that was why he'd gone up onto the road and checked. What he wasn't aware of was how long these actions had taken. If not for Old Man Winter pinching his arms, would he have stood out here until he'd frozen to death?

That was a troubling prospect.

Am I losing my grip on reality? Will I become a rabid animal in the end? One without any sense of self-preservation?

Then it occurred to him that he was still standing there mulling all this over. He would need to warm up and start making some plans. He walked back up the main drive, past the house, and back to the poultry barn. On the north side, the closest to him, he found a man-door and opened it.

Immediately, he was slapped in the face with the hot ammonia stench of chicken feces. Then he heard them, clucking and purring in the darkness. Hundreds of them warehoused for the pleasures of man. He wasn't that different; farmers committed horrific acts, and there'd been the chicken farms from his past. The breaking bones in his clutch, the terrified birds screeching for their lives. What made the farmer any different, other than that his motive was monetary, while Lance's was…

He didn't know what his reason was. Hunger? Lust? He was driven to kill, just as a painter must paint or a singer must sing. "I was born with the Devil in me," he said, quoting H.H. Holmes, and giggled.

He was warming up, the smell of terrified prey in the darkened barn exciting him. He thought how nice it would be to go and find a house with more victims. He stiffened, felt himself wanting to slip. Maybe that's what he should do. Go out into the night and unleash the monster. But that would probably lead to his capture.

Who cares?

He was too close. Two hundred and fifty miles.

But I want to!

Ten hours of driving.

The farmer was too quick. Anti-climactic.

Ten hours to freedom.

He relented and left the barn.

2

New York State Police Troop

Ellicottville, NY

The evening was bitter, the night sky wide and bright with a half moon and pinpricks of white dotting the sky.

They arrived at the police station in three vehicles: the first, a Ford F150 driven by Anthony, carrying Carolyn, Kristine, and Brandy. Behind them came a Toyota and Chevy pickup. Every one of the kids had come, none wanting to wait at the cabin with the possibility there might be a serial killer skulking around. All of them had seen enough slasher movies to dismiss the idea. Besides, they all wanted to be a part of this story.

They parked their vehicles in the visitors' parking lot and assembled in the lot.

"Now, what's all this?" the duty officer said when he spotted them coming for the front door. It slid open, and they came through into the lobby. "Can I help you?"

"Yes," Anthony said. "This woman says she escaped from a serial killer. We need your help."

3

Three Hours Later

Ellicottville, NY

They had driven the almost two hours out of St. Mary's, Pennsylvania, up to Ellicottville, when the news of Carolyn's escape reached them. They'd checked into the Holiday Inn Express in St. Mary's because it was the closest place they could find a decent hotel. Maxwell needed somewhere besides a rental car or an airplane to formulate their next move. He had Boyden cut the pilot out of Dubois loose and charter an on-call flight out of the St. Mary's Regional Airport if they needed it.

Flying would have taken longer, given the pilot was at least an hour and a half out from the airport and the lateness of the evening meant the roads would be mostly clear. That prompted them to get rolling and head north. Maxwell drove.

The others were tired from the day and looked lazily off into the night. Not Maxwell, he was wired up. What he hoped to glean from an interview with Carolyn McIntosh would, at the very least, be a location and a timeline. The New York and Pennsylvania state cops had been alerted that a vehicle carrying five agents would be traveling north up US 219, destination Ellicottville. The vehicle plate and description were distributed along with an order that it was not to be stopped for speeding.

Maxwell was speeding, averaging between seventy-five and eighty miles per hour.

They hit their first speed trap between Ridgeway and Johnsonburg. Maxwell was doing eighty when he spotted the state police car sitting on a ramp in his rear-view. It didn't move, but the officer inside flashed his interior. Maxwell didn't know if that was a signal of good luck or if the cop was just doing paperwork.

There were two more along the highway. Neither gave chase nor lit up their interiors as the first had. Maxwell smiled. "Just doing paperwork."

Maxwell had to slow down when passing through the many towns that make the US 219 a less preferred route for travelers wanting to make good time. But the countryside and winding road through the Allegheny Mountains was a forgivable trade-off.

"How far?" Lonnie mumbled.

"Ten miles," Maxwell said.

"I need a smoke."

"We'll be there in about seven minutes," Maxwell said. "But you best smoke on the move, Perk, because I'm not taking a break before we go in." He turned to look at Perkins, and there was a strange smile on his face. One that was barely visible, a smirk being born. "You might even want to crack your window and light up now."

Perkins grinned, reaching for his smokes.

"I'd prefer you didn't," Leigh said.

He sighed.

They took the fork left in the Great Valley, no longer unwittingly following the Highwayman's trail, but unaware that they were roughly twenty miles from the killer they sought. They wouldn't find that out until much later in the investigation when they retraced the Highwayman's movements. Then they would see their own missteps.

Five minutes later, they pulled into the state police lot in Ellicottville, New York. Perkins had a cigarette between his lips and was lighting up as he opened the door. They were all up and out, weary travelers stretching and waking for the task ahead.

They met with the very young male trooper working the desk, who immediately buzzed them in. "The senior investigator is Joy Bentley. She's been waiting for you."

She met them halfway up the hall.

Joy Bentley wasn't what Maxwell would call an attractive woman. She was rake thin, her hair salt and pepper, hanging like dusty curtains two inches above her shoulders. Her face lacked makeup or want of. She looked like a tired investigator.

Maxwell had talked to her briefly on the phone.

"Agent Maxwell, I'm Joy Bentley." She extended a hand.

Maxwell took it. "Nice to meet you. How is she looking?"

"Banged up. Her wrist is the worst. It has a deep ligature cut. Doc came in and took care of that while you folks were on your way." She turned to the others and put out her hand. There were further introductions. Then she said, "She's extremely traumatized. She claims that he murdered three men in her presence."

"Where is she now?" Maxwell asked.

"She's in the lieutenant's office. There's a couch. Didn't feel right leaving her in an interview room after what she's been through." Bentley frowned. "She wants to go home to her parents tonight."

"Well, the quicker we interview her, the quicker that can happen," Maxwell said, and realized how condescending he sounded. "No offense meant, it's been a long day, and we've got a lot of miles to go yet."

"None taken." She smiled. "Everyone gets bitchy once in a while."

The others laughed.

A tight smile was the best Maxwell could manage.

They moved Carolyn into an interview room, and the decision was made to have Leigh take the lead, with Maxwell and Bentley in the room while the others observed through the mirror.

Carolyn sat on one side of the table, Leigh on the other, flanked by Bentley and Maxwell. Bentley made the introductions, and once done, Leigh took over.

"I can't tell you how happy we are that you're sitting here right now, Carolyn. You're a courageous young woman. We want to get you home as soon as possible, but we need to know everything that happened to you. He's still out there, and we want to catch him before he hurts anyone else."

"Okay." Carolyn looked Leigh right in the eye. "I'll tell you anything you want to know. He threatened to kill everyone in my family if I tried to escape."

Leigh started with her questions. A sketch artist was brought in, and Carolyn did an excellent job of describing her abductor. The longer hair and beard were a surprise to Maxwell. The last time he'd seen Belanger, he looked like a young man ready to head off to boot camp.

"He reminded me of Kurt Cobain. He looked grunge."

They had the make on the car.

Leigh asked about routes.

"We stayed mostly off the main highways. He said we were going to Plattsburgh, New York. That was the story I was supposed to use if we were questioned."

Leigh asked her where she'd escaped. How long she'd wandered in the woods. Carolyn was unsure how long she was in the woods. "It felt like forever."

They were able to determine she'd escaped in the late afternoon until the snowmobilers found her. The names of those kids were added to the list of witnesses needed to be interviewed. With the crime scene in Syracuse secured, Special Agent Ferguson was reassigned to take over that task. He was on his way down.

Carolyn McIntosh was the perfect witness. She was able to give them a workable time and travel line. They had determined that the Highwayman had a six-hour head start on them, which was disconcerting.

Maxwell said, "Carolyn, I've been chasing this guy for a while. No one has been as close to him and themselves as lucky as you are. Did he talk to you about anything other than the story about going to Plattsburgh?"

She looked up, eyes searching, and said, "He didn't talk to me about much other than to make threats. But he would slip in and out of a state. Like he was drunk or on drugs. Do you know what I mean?"

"I think I know what you mean. But could you explain it to me?" Maxwell said. "Just so there's no confusion."

"He would mumble to himself sometimes. Like he was thinking out loud or talking to himself or someone."

"Did you hear what he said?"

"After he killed his friends, he swore a guy's name. Fucking Gusa. Or something like that."

So, Gusa was the catalyst, Maxwell thought. "You said it was like he was on drugs. How do you mean on drugs? Was he slurring his words? Acting drunk? What?"

Carolyn bit her lower lip. "I had a friend, back home, who I went to school with. His name was… I guess it doesn't matter… He ended up addicted to crack. He tried to get off it. He was even clean for six months. Then, one day he just started again. He tried to hide it, but his body language gave him away. He was preoccupied with the need, and even when he tried hanging with me and my friends, we could see it in his eyes. The need to find and score. He'd nod and smile in all the right places in a conversation, but his eyes were looking for a way out. A way to score. Anyway, Lance had that look. And he mumbled to himself like he was conversing, arguing with someone else."

"Like another personality?" Maxwell leaned in.

"Maybe. It was like he was getting crazier, the farther down the road we got. Sometimes he looked at me with hungry eyes."

"Do you mean he wanted you in a sexual nature?" Leigh interjected deliberately.

Carolyn shook her head. "He never made any advances. I don't think he has a sex drive. Because I was so scared I would've done whatever he wanted."

"You told him you're pregnant?" Maxwell was looking through the notes Bentley had taken. "You hoped that would garner some sympathy?"

"Yeah."

"Did it?"

"Not at all. I think if I really were pregnant, he would've had no problem killing me. He was cold-blooded, like a reptile. He often seemed emotionless, except when he was taunting me."

"Taunting you? How?"

Carolyn recounted the rituals of sharpening the machete and the hatchet while she lay tied up in the car. She believed he did this on purpose to terrify her.

She was right.

The interview wrapped up.

Maxwell got on the phone to Boyden and arranged to have Carolyn McIntosh escorted home by a state trooper on a red eye out of Buffalo Niagara International Airport.

Also, as a precaution, police surveillance was assigned to her family home until the Highwayman was apprehended.

Maxwell doubted that he would make good on his threat and go after Carolyn's family. They were south, and the Highwayman was heading north. But probably not to Plattsburgh. If he'd learned anything from Lance Belanger, it was that he could not be trusted to tell the truth.

Outside, Bentley and Perkins smoked together while Maxwell, Halsey, Leigh, and Ogden stood upwind.

Halsey said, "He could be anywhere now."

"Could be, but he'll know the car is a liability when she's found," Maxwell said. "He'll want to dump it and get a new ride. That'll slow him down some." He paused and muttered, "Getting a car is going to involve another abduction, but more likely a murder."

"I'm getting pretty sick of following this asshole's breadcrumbs," Halsey complained. "We got a 'Plan B,' Max?"

"He's going north."

"Yeah, but where?" Halsey looked at Maxwell and shook his head. "Sorry, just sick of looking at bodies."

"We all are," Oggy said.

Maxwell didn't answer. He knew their options. They either waited for a sighting or another body to turn up. He could only hope for the former. "He's going to need money sooner or later."

"Maybe he's carrying a bunch of money with him," Perk said. "He kills someone else, takes their vehicle."

"We've got a good description now. It's being distributed to all police agencies. Something is going to shake loose, and we're going to be there when it does."

"Yeah, unless he changes his appearance again," Ogden said. "Maybe you're right. Maybe it's time to go north as well. Split up and start searching."

They were interrupted by a call from the deputy director, Julian Carswell. "Have you got anything?"

"The girl was a treasure trove of information," Maxwell informed him. "We've got a new physical description, an approximate location where she escaped, along with a timeline. The problem is, he's got a six-hour head start, and we have no idea if he's hunkered down here or crossing the Canadian border."

"Tell me some good news, Max," Julian said.

"The girl is alive, that's pretty good."

"That is definitely one for our side."

"Ferguson is on his way here to handle follow-up with the kids who found her. I think it's time to get on the offensive. If he's moving, we gotta beat him there, and figure out how to ambush him."

"Any idea where 'there' is?"

"I'm working on it."

"I got a call from your friend in Bucharest."

"Datcu?"

"Those hard drives are going to mean a lot of cases, right here in the good old USA."

"Have they made arrests?" Maxwell asked.

"Not yet, but it sounds like we may be chasing down a lot of evil people once the Romanians hand over what they have. They've assigned a new prosecutor to the case, apparently a real bulldog who has made it his focus to wipe out organized crime. Just a second, Max." Julian covered the phone, speaking to his secretary. "Yes, Patti, I know. My anniversary is tomorrow. I'll get a gift." Then he came back on with Maxwell. "I have a meeting this afternoon. Keep me advised through Boyden, unless you apprehend him. Then call direct."

"No pressure there," Maxwell said.

"Really, I thought there was plenty. Do whatever you have to do to take this creep down. The clock is ticking."

"I'll keep you advised."

***

CHAPTER 23 – NOBODY HERE BUT US CHICKENS

1

18 November 2008

De Jong Farm

Lance spent the evening getting ready for the trip the following day. He found keys for the truck. A shotgun, a Beretta 92S semi-automatic 9 mm, and a .22 rifle. He also found three boxes of ammo for each weapon. He set the shotgun and the Beretta on the kitchen table and left the .22 in the closet where he found it. He searched the house.

Every room was painted in flat, eggshell white, and they had old photographs hanging or sitting on antique furnishings. There was even a black dial phone on the wall in the hall outside the kitchen.

The house was typical, sort of.

The farmer was a bad boy.

The master bedroom was like stepping into a time warp. It was ornamented with furniture starkly contrasting the rest of the house. In the center of the room sat a king-sized bed with a large, red leather headboard decorated with black buttons and edged with silver studs. The bedspread was black, the pillows red leather. Encasing the entire thing was a canopy of wrought iron adorned with black and red curtains. And hanging from single hooks were whips, paddles, and a myriad of restraining devices. On opposing sides of the bed was a throne chair and loveseat covered in the same buttoned red leather as the headboard.

"Stylish," Lance said, impressed with the design of the room. He entered and looked at every corner. On a bookshelf, neatly stacked, were more magazines; there were also DVDs depicting male on male dominant-submissive. He walked over to the bookshelf. "I guess your wife wasn't digging the lifestyle," he said as he picked up and tossed each item down. Then he found the photo albums. There were five of them stacked at the bottom of the bookshelf.

Each was bound in identical red leather. Lance had never seen any like them, and assumed they must have been a custom order. He picked them up, set them on the loveseat, and sat down beside them.

Before picking the first one up, he glanced around the room and pondered what made this guy any different from Gimpy Norris. Norris had dabbled in BDSM before becoming a killer. Or rather, before Lance made him a killer. Lance thought about that line, and why some didn't cross it. He looked around the room at the hanging shackles and handcuffs. Then he opened the first photo album.

By the third page, Lance was positive that Perry De Jong wasn't a serial killer, but wasn't sure that if he'd lived, he wouldn't have become one. The photos in the leather-bound albums were sadomasochistic. De Jong was the dominant, his multiple male partners submissive. This was clear from the many poses that included a fitted collar, ball gags, muzzle, and leashes.

He flipped through all the books, just then absorbing that De Jong might have wanted to fit him with a collar. He laughed, and then he thought about how the farmer had looked at him.

"Fuck that," he said and closed the photo albums.

He stepped up to the hanging shackles. There were eight sets in total. Four were medieval shackles suited to a 17th century dungeon. The other four were handcuffs of varying length. All had keys inserted into the locks. That was convenient. He removed two sets and placed them down on the night table. Beside them sat a picture of the farmer.

Lance looked at it and got an idea.

He took the picture and carried it out of the bedroom, down the hall, and into the kitchen. He checked the clock on the wall. It was 9:45 a.m. He looked down at the body splayed out on the floor, meat cleaver still wedged in the larynx. He thought about the line he'd crossed that night in early May of 2000. When he decided that fantasy simply wasn't enough and dove headlong into the abyss. He'd been anxious, but his mind had been made up. The murders of the woman and her child had been fledgling and served him no purpose other than learning to be more careful with future killings. It was a learning process, really, and he'd learned from those two murders. Then he burned it all down. From there, his vocation had been relatively successful.

"Until everything fell completely apart," he spat through clenched teeth. He knew now that the plan had been doomed from the moment he tried to expand and bring in help. When he thought about it, he wasn't any different from any expanding business. As a sole proprietor, he was fine, but he counted on others to hold up their end. *And they hadn't.* He was where he was because of the incompetence of others. *Norris in that goddamned truck stop. Steel shooting his mouth off, stirring a palace coup.* Larry and Dusk would have turned on him sooner or later. He was sure of it and he had only one regret. He should have taken that bitch Carolyn into the woods and cut her up.

"And you," he said, looking down at the farmer's body. "You degenerate fuck. You thought you were going to cuff me? Walk me around like a dog?" Lance's face became hard as he lined up and kicked De Jong's lifeless body in the testicles. "And what? Fuck me in the ass!" He kicked again. "I don't do submissive, you dumb fucking hick!" And again. "I'll show you what I do. You'll fucking see." Spittle flew from his mouth. He could feel himself pulling back, the monster taking over.

He didn't resist.

2

Under the nocturnal cloak, he moved the body out of the house and into the poultry barn. He did this by dragging De Jong, after hooking his arms beneath the farmer's armpits. He pulled the body backward through the house with an ease that gave him a sense of invincibility.

It just felt too easy.

He went out the side door, down three steps, and followed the left side of the dual tire tracks made by the wheels of the Taurus. He was intoxicated, not from liquor or drugs, but from the thing that controlled him. That drove his obsessions and overshadowed his thinking. One moment looking out from behind gray eyes and next watching from afar. He heard someone grunting as he advanced through the snow, yet had no idea those grunts were his. He felt the steady pulse of his heart in his temples. That was real, no matter his vantage points to reality.

There were distant shouts of anger.

"I don't do submissive, motherfucker!"

The barn's man-door flew open. The foul aroma of chicken shit permeating from the upper layer of scratch first swathed, then glazed the smell receptors in Lance's nose.

The structure was split between the bird housing and a feed storage area, separated by a wooden fence dressed in chicken wire. At the center of that indoor fence was a swinging gate that was kept closed to keep the birds from getting into the hundreds of feed bags piled against the north wall.

Should have stayed the course, his other insisted.

"Now it's all fucked up," he agreed.

Miraculously, the cleaver remained lodged in the farmer's neck when Lance lowered the body down onto its back. He floated over him in a daze. There was numbness in his hands… but still, fingers unfastened buttons… limbs pulled free of shirt sleeves and pant legs.

Then he was naked, a monster unveiled from its dark cloak. He scanned the room, amid clucks and purrs from the tenants of the structure. On the south wall of the barn hung a myriad of available tools, including a sickle, a hatchet, and even a chainsaw.

But he wanted the machete.

Without thought, he left the body and marched out into the snowy night. The cold hardened his skin into clay and shrank his new erection to an acorn. His bare feet sank into the abrasive snow as he marched down the side of the barn to the car.

He popped the hatchback, removed the blade, and walked briskly back to the poultry barn. By the time he reached the door, the snow felt like bottle glass grinding beneath his soles. When he stepped into the barn, the straw beneath his feet only intensified the discomfort.

Why the fuck didn't I leave my clothes on? he wondered.

No answer came.

He made his way back to the body, machete twisting left, then right in a gyrating motion. He knelt by the body, set the machete down, and removed the meat cleaver. He then arranged the arms and legs in an appropriate pose as he undressed the corpse and staged it for the next phase. Embedded deep into the dead man's spine and now bent over, the nail file stayed where it was.

He raised the blade.

First the head.

He moved counterclockwise, severing the right arm and leg, then the left leg and arm. In the absence of a beating heart, there wasn't much blood. He pulled each appendage to its appropriate place, doing his best to relive the rituals of past murders. Trying to imagine the pleading and begging. Seeing the emptiness that would settle into their eyes as the last bit of life was pushed out by a failing heart. This was a consolation prize for the monster. An appetizer to temporarily sate the growing hunger to kill.

It wouldn't be enough.

3

18 November 2008

Franklinville, NY

That evening, a decision was made for Halsey and Ogden to start north by vehicle. The starting point would be from Carolyn McIntosh's presumed location of escape in the Great Valley region. Halsey had pushed the idea.

At first, Maxwell was skeptical. "That's gonna be a real long shot."

"It's better than sitting around waiting for the next body to turn up," Halsey argued. "You said it yourself, Max. We don't know if he's already at the border or ten miles away from here."

The debate ended there, in the hotel lobby.

They gathered in a bar and grill called Halford's, pushed two tables together, and sat down. The waitress was a good-looking young lady in her twenties, wearing a long-sleeved white blouse and black slacks. She had blond hair that fell to her shoulders. Perkins had a double Jameson, Halsey ordered a shot of Jose and a beer, while the rest ordered a beer.

Once the drinks arrived, they unfolded a map and got down to it again. Leigh hovered over the map and said, "If he's going to make a run for the border, the question is where?"

"He said Plattsburgh to the McIntosh girl," Perkins said.

"I'm sure that's a misdirect," Maxwell said. "He wants us to think Plattsburgh. He's going to go somewhere closer." He looked at the others, gauging if they agreed. "The state cops and the border people are going to have their guard up at all crossings. So, Plattsburgh is covered."

"Why do you think he's going somewhere closer?" Leigh asked.

"He's compromised now. He's gotta get across that border, or he will be caught. That's inevitable. Caught or killed. Plattsburgh doesn't make a lot of sense. In New York state, it's the farthest crossing from where he was. There's plenty of eyes up in that area. He wants a remote location where he can be incognito. But he's also on the run, and it doesn't make sense. Plattsburgh is too far away. There's plenty of unprotected border that is closer."

"Did the family own any property in that region?" Ogden asked and suddenly silence. All eyes were upon him. "Has someone checked into that?"

"Shit," Maxwell said. "We've dug into Belanger's family. But you might have something there, Oggy."

Ogden smiled.

"I'm going to get someone moving on that." Maxwell left the table to put in a call to Boyden. He told her to investigate if the Belanger family might have an interest in a specific place in upstate New York or even Ontario or Quebec in Canada. "Old property, anything."

"You think he'll be moving toward the familiar?" Boyden asked.

"Possibly."

"Anything else?"

"No, just keep your ear to the ground. We're under the gun here, Linda." Maxwell sounded tired and frustrated to his own ears. "If he doesn't need to get money, he might wait until he's across the border. I'd prefer to grab him on this side."

"Well, it would be easier to get a needle into his arm," Boyden said.

"No, I'm not thinking about that. I just don't want it to turn out like the Ng case." Maxwell was referring to serial killer Charles Ng, who had been an accomplice to Leonard Lake in the murders of as many as twenty-five people, including two toddlers. Lake had killed himself while Ng fled to Canada in 1985. "It took six years to get him extradited. I don't want that to happen with this case."

"I understand," Boyden said.

"We need to figure out where he's going. Try and find something, Linda. Dig into his past, family acquaintances. We've gotta stop him before he finds a way across that border."

"I'll get right on it."

Maxwell thanked her and ended the call. Before he wandered into the men's room to relieve himself, he saw Perkins getting up.

Must be smoke time, Maxwell thought.

After finishing his business, he stepped out, and saw Perkins up at the bar with a cell phone to his ear. The bartender, who also happened to be doubling as their waitress, was making him another double.

Maxwell moved up to the bar and pulled out his wallet to pick up the tab.

Perkins waved his hand at Maxwell and shook his head. Then he said, "Yes, hon. I'll be careful."

Maxwell heard the woman respond, "Take it easy on the booze, Lonnie. I don't want you getting your ass shot off."

Perkins smiled, "No worries there, hon. They don't shoot at the skinny cops."

"Hilarious. I love you. Be careful."

"I love you too, hon."

Maxwell ignored Perkin's protests and paid for his drink. He pulled out his credit card, handed it to the waitress, and said, "I'll take care of that, and the bill for our table goes on this when we're done."

"You're not done?" she asked.

"Not yet."

They ordered a pepperoni pizza and had another round, continuing their talks into the night. Strategizing the Highwayman's next move, pausing to tell the odd anecdote or joke, and the evening ended in anticipation of the morning.

4

19 November 2008

Ellicottville, NY

The airport wasn't an airport at all. It was a landing strip used by a local crop duster, but it was enough to accommodate the charter flight Boyden arranged out of South Dayton, New York, to pick them up.

The twin props on the Cessna 421 idled as the charter of three boarded. Maxwell, Leigh, and Perkins were heading to upstate New York to coordinate with the New York State Police. Another state, new territory, new cops. Carolyn McIntosh's escape made the Highwayman a New York problem now.

Maxwell was meeting with an investigator named Geoff Matlock from the Bureau of Criminal Investigation, BCI for short. They took their seats on the plane and looked out at Ogden and Halsey, who stood in front of the rental car, a 2003 Buick LeSabre. The aircraft idled up and the pilot turned it on the dirt strip, sending up swirls of dust into the morning air. This pushed Halsey and Ogden back into the vehicle as they watched their associates depart.

"What do you think?" Halsey asked.

"I think it's going to be for nothing. He'll get picked up in a Dollar General or taken down by a state trooper," Ogden said.

"I'd take that," Halsey said.

"So would I," Ogden agreed.

They would have, but that wasn't what happened.

When the plane was up and gone, they drove south on US 219 until they hooked north on NYSR 98 at the Great Valley. They drove right past the De Jong farm and Lance, who was readying himself for travel.

5

He was dressed in the farmer's bib overalls, taking in the reflection looking back at him. "My name is Perry De Jong, I got a farm on the south side of Franklinville," he said to the reflection that didn't look like him anymore. He'd cut his hair, thinning it considerably on top to match the photo of De Jong. He still looked younger than De Jong. He thought about this, and it came to him.

Dirt.

He went over to the woodstove, ran his fingers through the soot, and dirtied his face. He smeared the ash under his eyes and rubbed. He held up the mirror with his right hand; in his other hand was De Jong's driver's license. The skin below his eyes seemed grayer, and he thought, *maybe,* and said again, "My full name is Perry Alden De Jong. I'm forty-three. I was born on May 16th, 1965, in Horseheads, New York."

He cut his eyes back between the license and the mirror.

Not exactly, but close enough. The main thing was that he didn't look anything like he had when that little bitch got out of his clutches. This angered him, but only momentarily. He'd fed the monster as best he could last night and tethered it away.

He hoped.

De Jong had even done him a small favor by loading a piece of farm equipment into the back of the pickup, likely for repair or sale. Lance had no idea which or what it was. But it provided a cover story should he need it.

"Yeah, I'm just taking this farm doohickey thing up to my cousin in…" Lance stopped mid-sentence. "Ah shit, I better find out what the hell it is." He went into the living room, where De Jong's laptop was sitting at a corner desk. He moved the mouse and had to close the browser which was, unsurprisingly, on a BDSM hookup site. Apparently, De Jong didn't think of leaving an open browser as being indiscreet.

He opened a browser and found Google Images. He typed in a search for plows and tillers, and was surprised how many different images came up.

After scrolling through four pages, he found something very similar to the one on De Jong's tractor called a disc harrow, and decided that it sounded more credible than doohickey.

He took one last look in the mirror, then gathered up the guns, his machete, and what few belongings he had with him. Outside, he loaded them behind the seat of the pickup. He had one last thing left to do. He went back to the poultry barn and entered.

Inside, he marched past the star-fished body of the farmer and opened the gate separating the chickens from their feed. They cowered from him at the other side of the barn. He knew they wouldn't come if he stood there, so he turned and left.

Lance got into the truck, stole a glance in the mirror, and got going. When the pickup was up onto the road, the farm behind him, the chickens were drawn toward the open gate and the body of their dead master.

***

CHAPTER 24 – HAYWIRE

1

19 November 2008

Leicester, NY

Halsey and Ogden stopped at gas stations and convenience stores along the route. They didn't stop at every place, just the ones where there looked to be lower security, mostly "Mom-and-Pop joints." The kind that didn't have closed-circuit television.

This had been Halsey's idea.

"He'll probably avoid bigger places like Sheetz or 7-Eleven. Too much risk," Halsey said, his voice less than confident. It was like looking for a needle in a stack of needles. But that was police work at its roots, countless hours spent following blind leads and asking questions of people who could offer little or no help. They were pushing bush, like hunters driving their prey toward standers. Except their prey could have been long gone.

They had been to five places already that morning, three gas stations and two convenience stores. The people they questioned all watched the news and knew who the Highwayman was, but none could offer anything of substance.

Now they were sitting in a little diner on the edge of town with their noses stuck in menus. Ogden had suggested the place for breakfast. They could get a bite to eat, show a few more pictures, and ask a few more questions. They were settled into a booth next to the front window that looked out on the eroding parking lot and a line of cars and trucks. Their eyes came out from behind the menus to scan the lot and the highway for a Taurus.

"I think I'm going to have the Big Rig Breakfast," Halsey said.

"Oh yeah." Ogden checked Halsey's choice. The Big Rig consisted of three eggs, four slices of bacon, two farmer's sausages, home-style hash browns, three pancakes, and a selection of rye, brown, or white toast. "Where the hell you going to put all that, Bobby?"

"Investigating is hungry work, my friend."

Ogden laughed. "You're an asshole, Halsey."

"Oggy, why would you say such a thing?"

"I'm out running three days a week; I try not to eat to excess, and I gain weight if I miss a day of exercise or eat nachos and drink the odd beer. You, on the other hand, can eat whatever the hell you want and don't gain a pound. That makes you an asshole."

"Takes one to know one, Chartrand." Halsey closed his menu.

The waitress was a pretty redheaded girl not more than seventeen; both cops guessed her to be the owner's daughter. They were almost right. She sashayed up to the table and took her place, pen and pad at the ready. "Can I take your order?"

Her nametag read: Amy.

Halsey ordered the Big Rig, with an extra order of white toast. Ogden had two poached eggs on whole wheat toast. The girl smiled as she took their order. She'd heard them talking.

Halsey glanced at her nametag and said, "Hey, Amy, is this a family place?"

"Yes," she replied. "My grandpa and grandma own it."

Ogden pulled out his shield and set it on the table. "We're here for a bite, but could you ask your grandparents to join us after we eat?"

Amy's eyes darted back and forth between them. "I thought you were cops." Then her face brightened. "Sure, I'll tell them. Are you after him? The Highwayman, I mean?"

Halsey said, "We need to talk to your grandparents."

She frowned. They weren't going to tell her.

Ogden interrupted. "We'll need to talk to you too, Amy. And anyone else who works here."

"Oh, okay… There's Clive who does the dishes, too."

"We'll need to talk to Clive as well, but let's keep things quiet. We don't want to upset your breakfast rush. Go and talk to your grandparents. Tell them about us, but only them. Okay?" Halsey was firm.

"Sure." She refilled their coffee and wandered to the kitchen with their order.

"Think she'll keep her mouth shut?" Ogden asked.

"Amy seems like a smart cookie. She probably won't post about us on Facebook until she gets home." Halsey looked at the swinging door to the kitchen. The face of a man with gray hair appeared in the window; he was staring at them. Then a second face joined him, a woman in her late fifties. "I think she just told her grandparents." Halsey raised a hand and waved.

The woman smiled and waved back.

The man smiled as well.

At the order window where the waitress placed their bill, another face appeared to check them out, an African American kid who looked around eighteen. Halsey wondered if Amy and Clive had something going on. "It looks as though Clive has been informed as well."

"She's efficient, at least." Ogden sipped his coffee and turned to look. "You know, partner. I think we should've waited until after we ate."

Halsey laughed. "Yuh think?"

Clive didn't wave. He gave them a nod instead.

The plan was to follow the Finger Lakes region through Geneseo and up onto US 20. From there, they weren't sure. Maxwell had told them that the state cops would have them on speed dial if they found something or apprehended Belanger. But the route was theirs to choose.

"I feel like we're swimming around blind," Ogden complained.

"We are," Halsey agreed. "But it's better than sitting around doing bugger all."

"Yeah," he agreed. At least they were doing police work now, instead of waiting for the Highwayman to dump another body. Sitting around accomplished little and Halsey didn't really dig Maxwell's investigative technique. He understood there were different styles of police work. It just wasn't his. Maybe they should have stayed in Pittsburgh. It wasn't really their case anymore; it was the FBI's now. They were calling the shots.

"Hopefully, they pick the asshole up in a checkpoint," Halsey said. "I miss the Iron City."

Ogden lifted his coffee cup and clinked Halsey's. "Amen to that, partner."

The looming faces in the windows withdrew and fifteen minutes later, Amy returned with their breakfast. She set a large oval plate in front of Halsey, the homemade hash browns piled mountain high, looking over a scene of eggs and cured meats. The pancakes came on a separate plate.

Ogden looked down at his poached eggs on toast and said, "This is utter bullshit." Then he stole a piece of Halsey's bacon.

"Hey, get your own."

Amy giggled. "Can I get you anything else?"

"We're good." Ogden folded the bacon over and bit into it. There was a sweet hint of maple and brine. His tongue rejoiced. He crunched down and said, "I need to go for a run."

"Finish breakfast first." Halsey stabbed his fork into a sausage and began cutting it. "You'll get less on your shirt."

Amy laughed again. "Okay, well, if you need anything."

"Thanks, Amy," Halsey said. "Soon as we're done eating, ask your grandparents to come out and join us. After that, you and Clive."

"Okay," she said and headed back to the kitchen.

2

Grandpa and Grandma were Kyle and Samantha Lacey. They switched places with Halsey and faced each other in the booth.

"I've been watching all the reports, it's all over CNN. Do you think he's been up this way?" Samantha asked.

"We don't know," Halsey said. "We're stopping in along the way, hoping to find someone who might've seen him."

"I haven't seen him," Samantha said. "I must have seen that photo of him at least a couple hundred times on the news. It's all they're talking about."

"We have an updated photo. Also, a picture of a car," Ogden said, and set them down on the table. "Take your time and look at these, please. See if you recognize anything."

There was silence as both looked at the pictures. They didn't look at each other until they were both done. Then Halsey put down the third picture, the one that had been circulating on the national news networks.

"Yeah, I recognize that one; but the first? Nope. Doesn't ring a bell," Kyle Lacey said and turned to his wife. "What about you, Sam?"

"I haven't seen him," Samantha agreed.

Ogden said, "I would like you folks to look hard at that second picture. Burn it into your mind. If you see him or the car, call the police."

They both nodded.

"We will," Samantha said.

Halsey sighed, then did his best to smile. "Thanks. Can you send Clive and your granddaughter over to sit down with us?"

When Clive and Amy sat down, she looked over the photographs first. She hadn't seen anyone that looked like the man they showed with the long hair. The same went for the Taurus wagon. "I'm sorry."

Clive looked a little harder but could offer nothing. Ogden gave the kids the same speech about burning the photo into their minds. Inside the diner, others stole glances at the two men and the kids at the table, but when Halsey or Ogden glanced their way, they averted their eyes.

"We better get down the road," Halsey said.

"Yeah, we'll grab the bill, Amy," Ogden said.

"My gram said it's on the house."

"Oh no." Halsey already had his wallet out. "We need to pay for our meal."

"My gram said, 'Catch him.'"

Halsey turned to Ogden, shrugged, and back to Amy, "You tell your grandparents, thank you very much." He pulled a ten from his wallet and passed it to the girl. "I can't let them cover our tip."

"Oh no, I…" Amy started.

"Oh yes you will," he said, and placed it into her hand.

Halsey seemed distracted for a moment, his eyes diverting past Amy. He was looking around the room, checking out the patrons.

Amy said, "Thank you."

This brought Halsey back. "No, thank you, the Big Rig was delicious, and I'm sure I'll probably die of heartburn later on, but it was worth it." Halsey put his wallet away and for a second, his gun was exposed as the jacket he wore swept across his hip.

Amy's eyes went right to the gun.

Although it was politically incorrect to say so, the women Halsey met usually got turned on at the sight of a gun. This girl was young, far younger than anyone Halsey might show an interest in.

He couldn't relate to the shit young people were into. Their music was rap and electronica. He liked classic rock, believing that if an artist couldn't play a musical instrument or wasn't backed up by a chorus of musical instruments, they weren't an artist. He also didn't understand texting.

"Why the fuck would you send someone a text when you've got a perfectly good phone in your hand?" he would complain to Ogden, but in all honesty, he was eventually sucked into that one.

3

Sitting two booths over, the man in the bib overalls, wearing a battered black and tan denim hat emblazoned with the word KUBOTA across the front, picked at his breakfast and listened intently. He recognized both cops, more so the one named Ogden. That was because he'd been the spokesman in Pittsburgh. Lance had watched those newscasts closely, noting the names of the investigators. And here they were, having breakfast in the same restaurant as him.

Lance could hardly believe it.

When they rolled into the parking lot and entered the diner, he almost panicked. Then they sat down, while he considered getting up and heading out the door, jumping into the pickup, and motoring the hell out of there. But he'd already ordered breakfast, and that would have looked strange. He didn't want to stir attention.

So, he stayed.

What if Maxwell walks in? he thought. *Would he recognize me?*

He adjusted his hat, lowering the brim.

And as they ate, he eavesdropped, gleaning what information he could. There was small talk, about home, about Ogden's family, and they joked back and forth. When breakfast was finished, they spoke with the old couple, and then the waitress, and the black kid. Fear bloomed in his belly. He'd had his hat off when the girl came up and took his order. She'd made eye contact with him. Seen his face. When they showed the pictures to the old couple, it dawned on him that the waitress might recognize him when the array was shown.

I've gotta get out of here!

But he couldn't. These two cops might be stopping for breakfast, but they were on the hunt. Likely, they were both attuned to the stirring of prey. Any sudden action would draw their attention. And then that word dawned on him.

I'm the prey, he mused, and pushed his bacon around on the plate.

Having gone from hunter to hunted, Lance still couldn't comprehend what his victims felt as he washed them down and prepared to take their lives. He couldn't identify, for they were unaware, they hadn't become aware they were prey until it was far too late. They may have been hunted, but they were unknowing participants until it was too late.

Where is Maxwell? he wondered and surmised, *he's probably two highways over on a different track.* This angered him slightly. If he were to be hunted, it should have been Maxwell instead of these two errand boys. He'd even left Maxwell a message after shedding his final skin and exposing himself to the world.

Come and get me!

Now he was the prey? They might have thought so. But for the Highwayman, the predators who sought him dined unwittingly among the sheep. And him?

I'm a wolf in sheep's clothing.

This made him feel better.

The cops were wrapping up with the black kid and the waitress. No one had seen him, not even the girl who had taken his order. She'd looked right into his eyes. But she didn't recognize him. At least not today. Some faint resemblance might dawn on her later in the day, prompting her to mention the farmer who was two booths down. It was possible.

But is it probable?

Damn right it was probable, and up until a year ago, he wouldn't have thought twice about tying up any loose ends that might lead to his arrest. He was at a crossroads. He could wait for the cops to leave and then, when the girl finished her shift, he could track her, hit her on the head with a crowbar, *like Bundy*, and take her into the woods for processing.

I'm better than Bundy.

He could do that.

Or he could go with the original plan.

Shadow these two cops as they worked their way north. Have a little fun before breaking off the chase. Maybe send Maxwell a note once he was over the border and tell him about these two lackies.

Dear Agent Maxwell, I sat two booths down from a couple of your crack investigators before I tailed them and...

The cops were getting a meal on the house. This was followed by the waitress protesting, then accepting the tip the younger cop offered. This, while the black kid made his way to the back to the kitchen.

Sorry little buddy, dishwashers don't qualify for tips.

The younger cop looked his way. This jolted him, and he dug into his eggs with his fork and shoveled a heap into his mouth. Then he began chewing while picking up the *Batavia News*. He was careful not to obscure his face, staring down at the headline on the front page that was not about The Search for the Highwayman, but Drive Your Tractor to School Day in Pavilion, New York.

He took a sip of coffee, trying hard to look interested in the story on the second page, which was about a guy who liked to photograph fire hydrants all over the state. He forced himself to read it as he shoveled more eggs in.

He felt the younger cop's eyes scan over him.

He wanted to bury his face in that paper. Hide from those seeking eyes. But instead he gave the cop a look, like someone who develops an awareness of being watched. He glanced in the cop's direction, if only momentarily; it was enough to nullify the searching eyes. But not enough to draw interest.

The cop turned his attention back to the girl.

Imagine what would happen if I killed them, he thought.

It would be like kicking a hornets' nest.

There are police all over the place. If I shoot one, or even two of them, that will bring even more cops. Pissed off cops resting their gun hand on their holster. Looking to save the courts the cost of a trial.

Nope, probably not a good idea.

But that didn't kill the idea altogether.

4

Lance followed them for sixty-two miles. They stopped three times, at a local grocery in Ashantee, at a gas stop in West Bloomfield, and a restaurant called Barb's just east of Canandaigua, New York. Lance followed his hunters through two checkpoints. Surprisingly, he didn't suffer much scrutiny. At the second checkpoint, the cop remarked that his equipment needed to be secured better, but neither asked for identification.

It didn't really occur to Lance that the two cops he was following were slowing him down. Every time they stopped, he would move up the road and find a place to wait. When they passed, he would fall behind about a mile. For Lance, this was a game; he was enjoying shadowing them. He drew a sense of power from it, the same he'd gotten after abducting the FBI Agent, Lewis Ash, from his home in Roanoke, Virginia.

Later, after everything went completely fucking haywire, he would wonder if it was the attraction to the peril that lured him into this dangerous game of cat and mouse.

But that was later.

***

CHAPTER 25 – OFFICER DOWN!

1

19 November 2008

Commander Briefing

New York State Police, Troop B

Gouverneur, NY

Two hours later

They had just assembled for the briefing with several detachment commanders from New York State Police. They came from as far out as Plattsburgh and Star Lake. Also in attendance and introducing Maxwell was Superintendent Daniel Oldman of the NYSP. When the superintendent came in, the room came to order.

"Please, stand easy, gentlemen." Oldman made his way between the folding chairs perched on by mostly troop majors, but also a few lieutenants and a captain from the Bureau of Criminal Investigation. They were all here, the brass from every detachment in Troop B., ready to catch the elusive Highwayman before he killed again or escaped. Oldman took his place at the podium.

"Good morning, gentleman, I am about to turn you over to Special Agent in Charge, David Maxwell. He is the lead investigator on the Highwayman task force. He is going to give us a brief so that we can bring this matter to a close in the most expedient manner possible. We have a rabid killer out there that needs to be apprehended. The key to bringing this to an end will mean full cooperation." Oldman paused. The room was still. He turned his head toward Maxwell and nodded. Maxwell nodded back. "All right, let's get down to it." Oldman stepped aside, and Maxwell took his place at the podium.

"Good morning. Thank you for attending." Maxwell introduced his team, then he went through a quick PowerPoint projected onto a white screen and giving background on the Highwayman's cross-state killings. He didn't have to get too deep into it. Boyden had furnished all commanders with a brief before the briefing, which they had all studied. After running through the history, he addressed strategy. "We have investigators coming from the south, following from the last known point of contact." He used a laser pointer and circled the Great Valley region where Caroline had escaped. "We think he's coming north." He traced the laser slowly up the map. "He has hidden assets in Canada, and we believe he is going to try and cross at one of the less protected areas."

The BCI captain raised his hand.

"Yes, sir?" Maxwell motioned with his hand.

"How sure are you that he's going north?"

"That's a good question. Belanger has been moving on a northeasterly heading since we picked up his trail. Most of his movements have been by secondary highway, state routes. He's steering clear of the interstates. It is our thought that he will try and cross the Saint Lawrence River into Ontario."

"Have you contacted Homeland Security and Canada Customs?"

"We have, and they will be standing guard. But we hope that he doesn't get that far, with the help of all of you." Maxwell clicked and the three pictures Halsey and Ogden were showing around as they came north came up on the screen. "He regularly changes his appearance. Before Carolyn McIntosh's escape, we were working under the assumption that he had short hair, military brush cut style, but McIntosh informed us that Belanger had long hair, almost to his shoulders, and a beard."

Then questions came from different commanders, but all were investigative and strategic. "Do you think he dumped the car?"

Maxwell replied, "We're considering that. But the car has not turned up, and there is a statewide BOLO on it. Belanger does not know that Carolyn McIntosh survived and can identify him."

There was plenty of talk about plausible crossings. Major Gordon Crow, from the Massena detachment, offered up the Long Sault Islands as a foot crossing while the river was still frozen enough to walk on. "Plenty of smugglers use this area to get guns into Canada."

Maxwell noted it. "We think that's his plan. The folks on the border will be watching, but it's a lot of real estate to cover."

"I'll set up some roving patrols in the area for anything suspicious," Crow said.

"We can do the same up in our zone. There's no water to cross at the border," said a Lieutenant Bob Strauss with the Ellenburg troop. "There's plenty of unprotected wood line up there as well."

"Yes," Maxwell said and tried to make eye contact with every one of the commanders. "We need your help. We don't want any more victims, and we don't want him escaping into Canada."

The superintendent took to the podium, wrapping up the two-hour briefing with a pep talk to the troops, and they began to disperse. That's when Maxwell felt his phone vibrate. He reached into his pocket and saw he had a text from Bob Halsey. He swiped the screen and was surprised and a little skeptical to see the text: OFFICER DOWN!

"What the hell?" he thought maybe it was Halsey was clowning around. Maybe about shitty food on the road. But

that was only for a second. Sending an "Officer down" via text was tantamount to yelling "Bomb!" in an airport. No way Halsey would mess around like that. "Shit!" He turned to Leigh and Perkins. "Come with me."

They followed him out of the briefing room and down the hall.

"What is it?" Leigh asked.

"Halsey just sent me a text." Maxwell showed it to her.

The color drained from Leigh's face. "Oh my God."

"What are you gonna do?" Perkins asked.

"Call him back," Maxwell said, and brought the phone up.

Leigh said, "Don't!"

"What? Why…"

"He might be under fire, might be hiding! Don't call, text him."

"She's right, Max." Lonnie nodded.

"Grab me that BCI captain," Maxwell said. Perkins sprinted over and plucked the captain from a group of small talkers. They were coming back. "Michelle, get us a ping on Halsey's phone."

"What's up?" the BCI captain asked. "One of my team members texted me an 'Officer down.' I'm going to text him back. We need to pinpoint his location ASAP." Then Maxwell typed: Is it safe to call you? and pressed send.

They huddled over the phone.

The others came to see what was going on.

The hall filled.

Maxwell was holding his breath.

2

19 November 2008

US Route 20

25 Miles west of Auburn, NY

Two Hours Earlier

Ogden spotted the pickup truck as they drove and initially hadn't considered it suspicious. He'd traveled enough highway, and it wasn't unusual to see the odd traveler on and off during a journey. That was not uncommon. But they had been stopping irregularly, and he'd spotted the pickup behind him four times, even after it had passed when they pulled off to look for witnesses at the gas stops and restaurants. Something about the truck felt wrong.

"Partner, I think we're being tailed," Ogden said.

Halsey looked up. He'd been studying the notes from the last round of questions, looking for something. "What?"

"The gray pickup behind us. It keeps popping up." Ogden eased off the fuel a bit, and the truck began to close the following distance. "I'm going to slow down. I want you to run the plate."

"Okay." Halsey pulled out his phone. "You sure you're not just being paranoid?"

"I don't think so, Bob. Maybe? What the hell else we got to do? Get a hold of your pal in Stolen Vehicles and ask for a favor."

Halsey brought the phone up to his ear and called.

Meanwhile, Ogden eased up on the accelerator to fifty miles an hour, and the pickup crept up on them, roughly five hundred yards behind now.

"What's the plan?" Halsey asked.

"I'm going to pull off, and you're going to get his tag." Ogden flipped on his right-hand turn signal, easing the vehicle onto the shoulder. The pickup kept coming.

Ogden watched the driver's side-view mirror and caught the daytime running lights of the truck just behind the clear message: Vehicles are closer than they appear. "Here he comes."

"I'm ready," Halsey said.

Then *whoosh*, the truck passed.

Halsey got the tag and said it out loud.

"That's it," Ogden said. "Call it in." He put the vehicle in drive again and got back onto the road.

Halsey called it into the Pittsburgh Police Department and waited for them to run it.

"Give me five," the sergeant in charge of stolen vehicles said. But he only took three, and that was long enough for Ogden to catch up with the truck and start following it.

3

"Why are they pulling off?" Lance said under his breath as he pulled past them. "Did they make me?" He shot his eyes up to the rearview in the truck and into the windshield of the car the cops were in. The cop in the passenger seat was looking right at the back of the truck. Then he saw him bring up a phone.

Calm down, he thought.

Then out loud he said, "They probably just pulled over to take a call."

He kept driving — fighting the urge to increase his speed — heart jittering in his chest like an uncalibrated jackhammer. He studied the rearview mirror. They were staying put, and then the road curved and they were gone. But that did little to quell the tightening anxiety in his chest. If they hadn't made him, it was time to break off the chase.

The road straightened, and still there was no sign of them.

Lance let out a gasp.

Nothing.

"Enough of this tomfoolery." His voice was thick with panic.

Then the vehicle appeared behind him, closing quickly.

"Ah, fuck." Lance reached for the bag containing the pistol and shotgun. "What the fuck was I thinking?"

They were about one hundred and fifty yards behind the pickup when Pittsburgh came back with the tag. "Belongs to Perry De Jong, Rural Route 23, Franklinville, New York. He has a fuel tax exemption for dyed gas. Must be a farmer."

Then the cell service dropped. "Shit." Halsey set the phone on the dash. "The call was dropped."

"What did you get?"

"Owned by a farmer from Franklinville, New York."

"Did you get a look at him?"

"No, I was getting the tag."

"I did. Briefly."

"And?"

Ogden smiled. "He looked like a farmer from Franklinville, New York."

Halsey laughed. "Well, that was fun. Do you want me to tag every vehicle on the road?"

Then the pickup gunned it and began to run.

"Holy shit," Ogden said. "Call it in."

Halsey looked at his phone. "No signal."

Ogden pushed down on the gas pedal, and they began to pursue. "Keep checking!"

"I am," Halsey said, holding his phone up. But he was wondering about the odds of probability. He was thinking they had probably spooked someone carrying a package of meth or maybe a stolen vehicle. But the Highwayman? He didn't think so. "You think it's him, Oggy?"

No service.

"I don't know, Bob." Ahead the truck was weaving on and off the shoulder, kicking up dirty slush. "I'd say whoever he is, he knows we're cops and doesn't want to be stopped. You got a signal yet?"

Halsey shook his head.

"Well, we got nothing better to do."

"Yeah."

They were closing the distance in the rental. Then the pickup jammed on its brakes and swung off the highway onto a secondary road. When the driver did this, he cut the corner too tight, and the right rear tire of the truck clunked down over a culvert and bounced. The tailgate fell open, but the driver was able to right the vehicle and keep going. The secondary road was only paved for seventy yards and then it turned into gravel.

Not wanting to make the same mistake, Ogden got on the brakes and took the corner wider. The turn was safer, but the force of gravity slid Halsey forward and left, lynching the seatbelt against his shoulder. The phone fell out of his hands onto the floor, and he reached for it.

"Whoever the hell the driver is, he doesn't want to be stopped. I'd say we've got a pretty suspicious farmer."

Halsey was leaning forward, trying to get the phone off the floor mat, restrained by his seatbelt. Below him, gravel pinged off the undercarriage of the car. The road was washboard now, the suspension rattling like a chain gun. "Oh, for crap's sake!"

Ogden couldn't hear him. He was trying to keep the car from bouncing right off the road. Worse, the snow dust from the pickup was blinding him. He tried to center the car on the road, but it was swimming all over the place like a spawning fish dodging river rocks. They were blinded by snow dust. A stone from the pickup was catapulted from a tire and smashed into the driver's side windshield, leaving a quarter-sized crater of chipped glass.

Halsey finally sat up, unlatched his belt, and went down onto the floor, scrambling for the phone. That was when there was a bang. They had collided with something big, but Halsey couldn't tell, he was trying to right himself after the jolt. Suddenly, they were bouncing right, and the vehicle began to reel over into the ditch. Before impact, he heard Ogden yell, "Bob, hang the fuck on; we're gonna crash!"

Then *bang*!

The airbags exploded, and the snow dust swirled around them in three competing vortexes. Halsey tried to lift himself, pushing against the passenger side airbag. When he finally did crawl back onto the seat, he saw Ogden. He was slumped over the wheel, eyes open.

"Oggy?" Halsey reached for his gun. He didn't know what they had hit or why. He reached over and gave Ogden a slap on the cheek. "Oggy, snap out of it."

Ogden turned his head to look at his partner, and suddenly he was blown back behind a crimson mist. There were two shots. One went through the airbag, catching Ogden in the throat. The second bullet went right into the center of his chest, cutting through his heart and killing him instantly.

Then two more shots came through the passenger side of the windshield. Halsey ducked and waited; shards of glass rained down on him. Halsey listened, heard the rustling of the shooter. He brought up his weapon, blindly squeezing off fifteen shots through the windshield in that direction.

Then the bullets came again.

Crack! Crack! Crack!

Halsey was readying himself to return fire when two more shots came through the windshield, and he was hit. He suddenly couldn't speak, and before he realized he'd been shot through the cheek, the second bullet caught him just below the left collarbone. It felt like a red-hot poker had impaled him and had he been left-handed, he would have dropped the gun.

Jesus Christ!

He couldn't look at Ogden. Didn't want to see that his longtime friend and partner had had his ticket punched. Oggy had a wife, two adult kids, and four grandkids. This was crazy. The world had been turned on its head.

The only way to stop the shooter was to continue the gunfight, but he would have to waste a bit of ammo. He brought the gun up, this time pushing toward the passenger door. Halsey pushed the passenger door open and brought the gun up in the shooter's general direction and squeezed off ten more blind shots. Then there was silence.

Halsey could feel himself slipping. He was losing blood.

Can't stop yet, he thought, and grabbed a fresh clip and switched it out. He was going into tunnel vision, through a smoldering white-hot pain that threatened to send him spiraling out of control and into the abyss.

Halsey, get your shit together.

He didn't need to chamber a round. He brought the gun up and squeezed off a burst of nine shots out into the fading day. He heard the footsteps crunching in the snow, but couldn't see. He only knew that they were running away. Or at least he hoped they were. Seconds later came the sound of the truck revving its engine and driving off.

Halsey found the cell phone in the center console, where it had bounced out of his hands. He picked it up, checked for service. There was one bar. Then he looked at his dead partner and thought, *ah shit, Oggy. This wasn't supposed to happen.*

Sorrow ran bitterly through his veins.

In the aftermath, it occurred to him that he might die next to Ogden, and that almost suited him. He didn't want to look into the eyes of Oggy's wife, Evelyn, or the eyes of their kids and the grandkids. He didn't want to think about the grief and misery that would come.

Slipping again, he closed his eyes.

Bob Halsey's world faded to black.

5

Lance was running back to the pickup; he was out of ammo, but he was pretty sure he'd hit both cops. He was overdosing on the terror and exhilaration. That was making him shake, but also giving him a high of sorts. He'd heard the bullets whizzing by when the cop in the Buick fired back. The proximity to such danger was like a drug, exciting; he wanted more, but then the slide on the Beretta stuck open. He was out of ammo. More bullets whizzed by, one barely an inch from his ear, and he decided to withdraw to the truck.

He rounded the back of the pickup and perused the now empty box. The farm doohickey had fallen out, and the cops had collided head-on with it, mangling the front of their car and causing them to crash. He thought about reloading, going back down into the ditch, and finishing the other cop. He moved around to the driver's door and thought about it for a second more.

There were even more shots from the mangled Buick, and that decided it. It was time to get moving. He was down to hours and still had plenty of roads to cross. There might even be more cops coming. They could have called in to Maxwell or the state cops. That did it. He jogged around to the back of the pickup and closed the tailgate.

Then he jumped in and turned the key, to which there was a grinding sound. He realized the truck was still running. He put it into gear and swung around back toward the highway. If the cop was still shooting at him, he had no idea. He pushed down on the accelerator. The wheels spun, sending up fresh plumes of dirty snow, and he was off.

"Count that as one of the dumbest ideas I have ever fucking had!" He stole glances between the rear and side-view mirrors.

Nothing.

Then he laughed. "But fuck me, that was... Fucking yeah!"

He was back on the highway. Trying to get his bearings, trying to fight off the desire to reload and go back.

No, no, no, can't do that.

But it didn't matter, not in the elevated state he was now in. He wasn't thinking about Canada or what he would do when he got there. He just wanted the fix. A little killing to feed the monster. Was that so much to ask?

Fuck, Lance! The cops will be coming!

He remembered the cop raising the phone to his ear, staring into him, his expression sterile, and yet a fire burned inside him and the other cop. They were hunters. And he was their prey.

"Not anymore," he said. "Not anymore, fuckers!"

We gotta move—gotta move—gotta move!

"I'm moving."

6

Two Hours Later

Halsey awoke to Ogden calling out to him, "Are you with me, Bobby?"

Leave me alone, Oggy.

"Wake up! I'm serious, partner."

You're dead.

"Yes, I am. And if you don't do something, there are going to be more dead people. Get to it!"

Get to what?

"Call it in, partner."

Halsey snapped back, eyes focusing, mind clearing, and there was the body of his friend and partner. Bob Halsey choked and brought up his hand to wipe the tears. The snow was drifting on the dashboard below a windshield that now resembled a glass spaghetti strainer. Outside, a new storm brewed. The light had drained from the clouded sky and snow began to fall again. Faintly, Halsey heard Oggy. "Call it in, partner."

Did you notice? I got a hole in my face.

Halsey reached down onto the seat and grazed the cell phone with the tips of his fingers. It spun at first, then he hooked it with the nail on his index finger. He lifted it.

"Call it in, Bobby." Even fainter.

He had one bar.

Bob Halsey held the phone, opened the contact list, and scrolled until he found Maxwell's name. He touched his finger to the screen and left a bloody fingerprint on it, but it was enough to bring the text prompt.

He typed: `OFFICER DOWN!`

He could feel the warmth of his own blood leaking down his breast, but nothing on his back. The bullet was still in there, he assumed, and it was probably a smaller caliber. If it had been a .45 or a hollow point round, he would be dead, or at the very least, disfigured far worse than he was now.

He stared at the phone.

My days of charming the ladies are probably over.

He gaped at Ogden.

What the fuck, Oggy.

Oggy didn't reply. Oggy was gone, his slumped body an empty vessel. *Oggy is off to wherever his consciousness went.* This thought made Halsey want to cry, but he couldn't. If he wanted to live, he would need all his strength. Never mind the bullet hole in his face, which would have made weeping excruciating.

Halsey was floating inside something, but nothing he would have ever thought possible. Be it shock or some altered state—like a voyeur dream—disconnected by a layer of disbelief. But worse than not being able to cry for his dead friend, was having to compound that loss inside his own head as he lay bleeding.

I called it in, partner, he thought, fading for now.

Then the phone chimed.

A text message from Maxwell

It read: `Roger OFFICER DOWN. Can I call you? Can you talk? Are you in immediate danger?`

He stared at the message. He didn't want to tell them it was Oggy. Didn't want his wife, Evelyn, finding out on *the news*. He would tell them when they got here. He thought he heard Oggy say, "That'll be pretty obvious."

Halsey lost it.

Despite the hole in his face, he let out an agonizing, mournful cry. It rippled through his left cheek like rotating tiny shards of broken glass soaked in bleach. He brought his other hand up to soothe it but stopped short, palm hovering beside his cheek, knowing it would just cause more discomfort in the singing nerve ends. On the upside, he only had one bullet hole in his face. That itself had been nothing short of a miracle. As best he could reconstruct, the bullet had entered through his mouth, missing his teeth and tongue completely, and exited his right cheek.

He looked down at the phone and thought, *oh yeah.*

He started typing.

Halsey sent: Dnager Unkknown. Cannt talk. Shot in face.

Maxwell: Where are you?

He wasn't sure, exactly.

Halsey: PING MME!

Maxwell: Already on that! Hang in there, Bob, the cavalry is coming

Halsey: Hurry

And before Maxwell could respond.

Halsey: Ogs gone. Don't know how long before I bleed out.

Bob Halsey felt himself slipping. He gasped inward and shuddered. He leaned back. Heard the phone chime, but it was slipping from his grasp, falling away, darkness coming.

Maxwell: Hang on. Keep talking. Don't go to sleep, Bob! We are coming!

But Halsey was gone.

***

CHAPTER 26 – CONSPIRACY OF SILENCE

1

19 November 2008

US Route 20

West of Auburn, NY

Lance was four miles out of Auburn when he passed five state police cars with lights and sirens going the other way. He slid his hand below a jacket on the seat, used to shroud the weapons. He touched the cold metal of the shotgun, tracing his right palm over the wood stock, and his index finger found the trigger guard.

Just in case.

The Beretta lay next to the shotgun, still empty. He needed to refill the magazine. Before they passed, he expected them to come to a screeching halt and block the road. Saw himself halting the truck, reaching for the shotgun, and inevitably, they would empty their magazines into him.

He was already a cop killer, but he wondered if Lewis Ash really counted. After all, Ash had been a retired FBI agent, on the outside of the brotherhood.

Not a real cop anymore.

But these two were real cops, and he'd shot the hell out of them. He was sure he'd killed at least one, and he'd hit both.

Blood was in the water now. Every cop in the state would be gunning for him.

Then it occurred to him.

I gotta get a new ride. ASAP!

Ahead, he could see the town now, another two cop cars coming. These weren't state cops, though, they were local.

Maybe they didn't call in the plate?

He didn't really believe that. He just knew that there was now a need for a replacement vehicle, and he had to get rid of this one. He would have to do something extremely drastic. But he couldn't just go on a shooting rampage. They would be all over him in no time at all. He tried to think. If there was another farm, he could hurry in, kill whoever was there, and take their vehicle. It wouldn't be the same as going to that farmer's home and hanging out. And as he clearly understood, most farmers had guns, never mind he was running out of highway with Auburn fast approaching.

2

Southeast of Pulaski, NY

Maxwell, Leigh, and Perkins rode aboard one of the NYST Aviation Units Huey IIs. They were headed in the same direction as the cruisers coming out of Auburn. They had pinged the towers. Halsey's phone gave them a general area, but Perkins had remembered seeing a sticker on the rental that gave them an advantage. The label read: THIS RENTAL CAR IS GPS TRACKED.

Leigh had the coordinates in a matter of minutes.

State and local police were rushing to the scene from all directions. They would get there first, but what was left of the posse wouldn't be far behind.

The atmosphere inside the chopper was a cauldron of conflicting emotions. Perkins was quiet, brooding, looking outside, but not really. His constantly changing facial expressions indicated a man who was distracted. He was, of course, thinking of those two Pittsburgh boys. They had grown on him.

Leigh sat across from him. She'd really liked Oggy and even had a bit of a shine for Halsey. Also, he was a potential train wreck. Now, Belanger had not only killed Lewis Ash, but Ogden and possibly Halsey. She shook her head. When did it stop? Was this going to be her career as an FBI agent? Always getting close to and then burying her friends? The thought enraged her. It was bullshit!

Total bullshit!

Leigh glanced first at Maxwell, and then Perk. Neither returned her wandering gaze, tied up in their own beleaguered thoughts. That was when she decided she was done playing by the rules. If she could get close enough, without witnesses, she fully intended to put Belanger down like the rabid dog he was.

3

Across from her, Maxwell sat board stiff, blood boiling, coursing through him like venom. This had been his call. He'd brought the cops along and had agreed to them bringing up the rear. Now they were probably both dead.

This wasn't the first time he'd lost someone he worked with. He and Julian Carswell had come up with another agent, named Fred Hammerstein, "The Hammer" for short.

They were a tight-knit trio, kicking in doors on raids, tailgating with beers wherever they felt like parking their drunk asses. Work hard, play hard; that was their motto. They felt like cowboys, invincible, out to conquer the world. And then one day, a neo-Nazi named Joshua Gormley ended Fred "The Hammer's" life by shooting him in the throat.

Maxwell shot Gormley dead, but not in time to save their friend.

Both Maxwell and Carswell held Fred's hand as he slipped away.

And here we are again, Maxwell thought. *My call. I got these boys killed.* He felt the same as everyone inside the helicopter. He didn't know if Halsey was dead, but now it was more personal than ever. If they were both gone, the hunt had to continue.

They had to stop him! This had to end!

Maxwell didn't realize his teeth were clenched so hard that the muscles in his cheeks had become rigid and hard-packed contours beneath the skin. He turned his eyes back on Leigh. They both turned toward Perkins, who was drawn from the window into their trio. Their eyes blazed with fury, hunters swept up in a tide of blood and revenge. No words passed between them, but the rage in their eyes was uninhibited. They each knew what the other was thinking. Collectively, within the angry spheres of their eyes, a conspiracy was brewing, but it was one that would never be spoken of.

4

19 November, 2008

Off US Route 20

25 Miles west of Auburn, NY

The first to reach the car was a trooper named Morty Rickman. He stopped his cruiser on the side of the highway and wary of tromping on a crime scene, he plodded cross-country on foot. He came shotgun in hand, safety off, eyes darting in every direction for a shooter, crunching through the snow, thinking that his choice of entry might have been a mistake. He was panting, and the anxiety was crushing his chest, but when he saw the dead cop behind the wheel, his training took over.

Behind him, sirens wailed.

He moved around the car, shotgun at the ready, holster unclasped, perusing every potential ambush point he could think of. As he made his way up the side of the car, he continued to scan for danger. He looked in on the cop in the passenger seat. He was slumped forward, his jacket soaked in blood. He had a hole his right cheek big enough to park a kid's matchbox toy car in.

The sirens were getting closer.

Trooper Rickman kept scanning, moving along the passenger door. Then he was at the front of the car, looking—scanning—looking for danger. There weren't a lot of hiding places, and by the time he was in front of the car, he began to think he'd missed whatever happened here.

Then from behind, there was a gasp, and he heard something like, "Ease on." But what Bob Halsey was trying to say was, "He's gone."

Rickman let out a frightened squawk that would have made his peers laugh their asses off. It was a warbly sound, like something coming out of a goose having its neck rung. He brought the gun around, and then up toward the sky when he saw the barely conscious Bob Halsey staring at him.

"Oh my gosh." Morty moved and opened the door. "You're alive?" Morty felt sudden guilt for not checking his pulse. "Hang on." The trooper went back to his cruiser to retrieve the first aid kit. When he returned, he started checking Halsey over for other wounds.

5

Halsey had a twisted half smile on his face; he wanted to say more. Tell this kid in the Smokey the Bear outfit that they'd been shot up by a farmer.

Or was it the Highwayman? he thought. *Yeah, Highwayman. Had to be.* But he was weak, and the two words he'd uttered incoherently to the kid had been difficult enough. He felt like he was balancing on a skyscraper ledge. As the blood drained from him, it took his balance, his vision, his ability to hold on. If he lost his balance entirely and went off the ledge, there would be permanent darkness.

He had to hang on, but he was losing consciousness, and the fading of incoming sirens, accented by the steady rhythmic *whump* of what could only be a distant helicopter, was fading. He lowered his head. He needed to rest awhile, see what was gonna happen.

He could hear the trooper calling him by the wrong first name, "Hang on, help is on the way." But it was muted, staticky, on another channel, and he was slipping.

Take a rest, partner, Ogden whispered inside his head.

Bob Halsey didn't respond, even in thought. He was tilted forward, eyes trained on the dashboard, following the grooves in the fake leather.

The chopper was coming closer.

The kid was holding his hand and had applied compression bandages to Halsey's shoulder and cheek.

"Talk to me, John," he said. "They're bringing a bird. It's okay. You're gonna be okay."

Then the dashboard began to melt, its skin smoothing into a blur. The contours of the glove compartment melted into what was quickly becoming one-dimensional.

By the time the chopper was on the road and the trio was moving, heads down, beneath the prop blast, Bob Halsey was gone, but he had a pulse. And somewhere between the nightmare world where his best friend was dead, his newfound friends were coming to save him from the darkness which threatened to swallow him forever, Bob Halsey found his balance and maintained his place on the ledge.

There he stayed, holding on for dear life.

There were local and state cop cars piled up on both sides of US 20. The highway was now closed, and there were more coming from north, south, east, and west. Fourteen officers of mixed uniform were on the scene to help and to hunt for the perpetrator of a crime against one of their own. The Highwayman had indeed kicked a hornets' nest, making it personal. The collective mood in the group was nothing less than rage and thoughts of revenge.

Maxwell took control of those officers.

"We've gotta get him in the chopper," Maxwell barked. "He's lost a lot of blood."

"Syracuse is closest," Morty Rickman said. "You could have him there in ten minutes."

Two Auburn cops were carrying a military stretcher down to the scene. They were running through the snow double time.

Perkins called to Maxwell, "We'll get the chopper floor clear."

He and Leigh were moving. Two New York State troopers followed without being asked to help. When they got back to the chopper, Perkins said, "Wind this whirlybird up, Caps. And find us the closest, best trauma hospital you can."

Behind them, Maxwell and his crew were loading Halsey onto the stretcher and covering him with blankets. By now, an ambulance had arrived along with a male and female paramedic. They put an IV in Halsey's arm and gave him some whole blood kept in the ambulance. Trooper Rickman had found a medic alert bracelet on Halsey's wrist when performing first aid. Along with an alert about an allergy to codeine, it also had his blood type. The female paramedic plugged the hole in Halsey's shoulder and applied a dressing to his face. The face bandage was done on the fly, while they carried him toward the bird. They were on either side of the stretcher, more cops than necessary attached to that stretcher, not just wanting, but needing to contribute.

This was one of their own.

Halsey remained unconscious.

7

Then they were in the air with a new passenger, the female of the two paramedics, riding along, bound for the best hospital in the region, Upper University Trauma Center. She held the IV, monitoring Halsey's pulse; it was weak, but she thought it showed some improvement. Probably the blood helped.

Her name was Mary Vargas, a short, stout, strong woman with a determined, weathered face.

Maxwell pegged her at about forty-nine years old.

She hung over Halsey, who was now cocooned in wool blankets. She turned to Perkins and said, "Hey, Slim Jim, can you grab the IV bag for a minute? I want to clean up the dressing on his face."

Perkins looked shocked, even a little indignant, but he took the IV, and held it while Vargas went about checking Halsey vitals and making sure the dressings were secure. He shifted his gaze from her to Leigh and Maxwell, and then said to the paramedic, "Name's Lonnie, not Jim."

Both Maxwell and Leigh let out a burst of off-balance laughter, and then they frowned in shame until the medic smiled and said, "Yeah, whatever, Slim, just keep that bag elevated so I can keep your friend alive."

Then Perkins smiled and said, "Sure thing, sister."

That brought weaker smiles back.

"Two minutes," the pilot called.

When they landed on the roof, a team of nurses and doctors were already waiting to assist. They pulled Detective Bob Halsey from the chopper, angels of mercy coming to the aid of the watchmen who keep them safe.

Maxwell followed carrying Halsey's bloody coat, cell phone, and wallet, along with his detective's shield. His gun had been taken in for processing, because of the shootout. When they got to the elevator, there wasn't enough room for all of them.

One nurse said, "You'll have to take the stairs."

"What floor?"

"Main floor," the nurse called.

Their shoes clomped on the stairwell, echoing against the walls of the switchback corridor they were descending. This was coupled with the erratic breathing of two men and one woman as they descended, even skipping the odd step.

And kept going.

When they reached the main floor, they crashed through the door into the hall. There they saw the elevator open and their friend and colleague being brought out to the waiting trauma team. The person in charge was a slim woman in blue scrubs. Maxwell knew this because she was barking orders.

A nurse approached and asked, "We're getting your friend in to assess the damage from the gunshots. Do you know his blood type?"

Leigh said, "He has a medic alert band on his wrist."

The nurse looked back. "Check his wrists."

Another nurse called, "AB negative."

"That's rare," the nurse said. "I don't suppose…"

"I'm AB negative," Perkins said.

She waved to him. "You, let's go."

Then Perkins was gone to give blood while Maxwell and Leigh found themselves sitting side by side, silence heavy between them. They were in the worst possible place. Time was dragging, they had nothing to do but wait. But Maxwell didn't want to wait. The hunt was down to hours, and he needed to get in front of the Highwayman.

Maxwell turned to Leigh, and she looked back.

He whispered, "We're going to have to move."

She said, "I know. Soon as Lonnie gets back."

"Agreed. Hopefully dumping some of his blood won't slow him down."

"He'll just augment with cigarettes."

Maxwell let out a short bark of laughter, and then his expression became serious. "We're going into it now. This asshole isn't afraid to shoot it up with cops. From this point on, I want you to know that whatever happens out there, I have your back. Same goes for Lonnie."

"Whatever happens?" Leigh asked.

"Whatever happens," Max said. "I have both your backs."

"Same goes here, Max," she said, and thought, *I've just been sworn into a blood oath.*

"Let's go find Lonnie."

Five minutes later, they were standing in a room with him. They talked about leaving. "I don't want to," Maxwell said, "but time is in short supply. I want to deal with this asshole if I can."

"Deal with the asshole," Perkins said. "Yeah, I need to get my heart going a little faster. Get the blood pumping. Michelle, would you mind…"

"Perk, what would your wife say?" Michelle shot back.

"In pursuit of justice and all." Perkins grinned.

"How long is this going to take, Perk?" Maxwell was looking at the half-filled bag, trying to figure out how much time had already passed.

"Probably another thirty minutes," Perkins said.

Maxwell pulled out Halsey's phone and looked at it. He read the text messages they'd shared, trying to consider where it was that Halsey had lost consciousness. Then he closed the text box and checked the phone history. The last number called happened in/around the time of the ambush.

Maxwell brought his own phone up and dialed the number. It rang once, then twice, and then someone picked up and said, "Auto Squad, Sergeant Major speaking."

"Sergeant Major…" Maxwell started.

"I'll stop you there, by telling you this isn't a Monty Python skit. I am a sergeant, and my last name is Major."

"Sure, okay…"

"Now, who are you, and why are you calling me on Bob Halsey's phone?"

Maxwell explained that both Ogden and Halsey had been shot, but the notification was still pending for Ogden. "You gotta keep this to yourself, Sergeant. I got some people setting up with your command. But for now, it's hush."

"Bob gonna live?" Major sounded angry.

"He's in surgery, another of our team is giving blood. Bob and he share the same rare blood type. We don't know his status yet. He was shot in the face and shoulder. I need to know why he was calling you. Did you run a plate for him?"

"I did. I still got the check somewhere here. Hang on."

Maxwell heard Major shuffling around on what he presumed was a desk. He listened to what sounded like a jar of pens tip over, followed by Major saying, "Shit." Then there was ruffling paper and, "There you are." He came back to the phone. "The plate they ran belongs to a 2007 gray Chevy Silverado 4X4, registered to a Perry De Jong out of Franklinville, New York. He's got a farm tax exemption. Bobby asked me to run the plate."

"What did he do when you came back with it?" Maxwell asked.

"He laughed like it was a dead-end," Major said.

"That's it?"

"Yeah. I was busy. We cut the call short."

"How long have you known Bob Halsey?"

"I stood up for him at his wedding. That would be ten years ago, I knew him probably three before that. Thirteen sounds about right."

"Halsey was married?"

This turned Leigh's head.

"Yeah, they divorced about seven years ago, and then she got cancer. It was a late diagnosis, so it took her quick. Even after the divorce, Bob went to the hospital and stayed with her every day. They never had any kids. He still loved her, even though she was the one who left. Her name was Katharine. Beautiful woman. Everyone called her Kate."

"Thank you, Sergeant. We gotta get on the trail."

"You're welcome. Good luck on the hunt."

***

CHAPTER 27 – CARGO VS. PROCLIVITY

1

19 November 2008

State Route 34 South of Hannibal, NY

Lance was pushing hard, scanning the roadside, looking for an opportunity, and one just happened to appear on the shoulder of the highway. An old Volkswagen Bug was sitting beside the road, its driver standing in front of the car, smoking a cigarette. The vehicle was, in fact, a 1968 Beetle, the same year and make that serial killer Ted Bundy had used to stalk and kill his victims. The only difference was, this Bug wasn't cream-colored. It was midnight blue. Lance wasn't sure on the year but made the Bundy connection immediately.

Could be risky, he thought.

He considered this, albeit quickly, and concluded that if he didn't do something, the cops would be on him. He had to get a new ride. The car on the shoulder was approaching fast. He reached down and touched the shotgun.

Here we go.

Brandy Jones was smoking outside the car because her domineering sister Wilma insisted that she do so. She had her butt plunked down on the hood of the car, drawing in on a freshly lit Pall Mall. The car pissed her off, almost as much as Wilma. Wilma, who had a BMW and an Escalade, agreed to let her use this car, but not those cars. Instead of zooming up the highway in style, she was puttering along in a go-cart that sounded like a sewing machine when you punched the accelerator. Even worse, the thing didn't have heat. Her sister had tried to explain the heating system, which consisted of stupid handles that did nothing.

No goddamned heat.

From behind, she heard an approaching vehicle. She took another drag off the cigarette and exhaled, ignoring the vehicle approaching from behind.

"I'm not trusting you with my Beamer," Wilma had said.

She took another drag and blew the smoke out.

The approaching vehicle was slowing, its engine growling in protest, frozen rubber humming on the roadway. Brandy still didn't look back, focused on Wilma and the no-heat bullshit. The Beetle was only one of Wilma's toys. She had a Harley, collected electric guitars, owned a house with a pool in Binghamton, New York, and a villa with an ocean view in East Hampton. Wilma was a lawyer who had decided that she liked girls better than boys, divorced her rich husband, and pretty much got half of everything.

Rich bitch, she thought. *Never had to work for it.*

Another drag off the cigarette.

Vehicle slowing behind her.

Exhale.

Then the vehicle was stopping. She glanced back over her left shoulder, looked at her half-smoked cigarette. The pickup truck made a full stop fifteen yards behind her own vehicle. Brandy sighed and crushed out her smoke. "Oh craps, now what does he want?" she mumbled under breath.

Better hit the road.

She made her way around to the driver's side of the car, and was about to open the door when the truck door opened and the driver, who was dressed as a farmer called, "Excuse me, can I ask you a question?"

She stared back, puzzled.

A question?

Then he came around the truck door, and she saw the shotgun in his right hand. His eyes were blank, focused on some purpose alien to her. Brandy began to fumble the door handle as her mind screamed. *Oh, my God! Oh my God!*

He was coming fast.

She yanked the door open and jumped into the car, slamming the door and locking it. She reached for the ignition and realized that the car key was in her jacket pocket next to the pack of Pall Malls.

"No! No!" Brandy jammed her left hand into her pocket, fishing around, and then she heard the two hard raps on the driver's side window. Metal on glass.

Then…

"Open the door, or I'll blow your fucking head off!"

Brandy froze, turned to see the man standing there with the barrel of the gun trained squarely on her face.

"I mean it!"

She pulled her hand out of her pocket and brought it up onto the steering wheel.

"Last chance," he growled and steadied the weapon. He was huffing and puffing, but not from being out of breath. It was fury. "Open the door, you fucking cunt, or I'll kill you right here and now!" Bits of spittle dotted the window.

Brandy turned her head and looked out the windshield. She unlocked the door and he pulled it open. What happened next was bizarre.

"Get out here!" He pulled her from the car with his left hand, cradling the gun with the right. Brandy felt the doorjamb scrape against her back, and then she was close enough to kiss him. He looked up and down the road to see if anyone was coming. Then he hauled on her.

"Come with me."

"No, please! Don't do this," she begged.

"Shut up! Shut up!" He had her by the arm, pulling her toward the front of the car. "Get your keys out!"

They were in front of the Beetle.

She dug her hand into the pocket, found the keys, and clutched them in her fist. "You can have the car. Please don't hurt me."

At this, he laughed and said, "Open the trunk."

"Oh no, please. You can have the car, please…"

He brought his free hand up and placed it over her mouth, hard. "One more word and you're dead. Don't talk. Don't cry. Don't make a sound." His hand squeezed her mouth. "One word and you are fucking dead! If you understand this, give me a nod."

Brandy nodded.

"Good. Now open the trunk."

A single terrified tear spilled over her eyelid and tracked down her cheek. She got the keys out and opened the trunk.

He took another look around and said, "Get in."

Brandy did as she was told and climbed in. She looked up at the man holding the gun. He gazed down upon her, a predatory expression on his face. He said in a calm but dangerous tone, "Now, do as you're told and stay quiet. If you do that, I might let you live."

Then he snatched the keys from her hand and slammed the trunk on her.

19 November 2008

FBI Headquarters

Quantico Virginia

Under the direction of Special Agent Linda Boyden, the team contacted every relative on both sides of Lance Belanger's family. Most were distant and couldn't offer much in the way of information.

Boyden entered the small office where two male agents, named Grimshaw and Hicks, were winding down what appeared to be a fruitless search. Hicks hung up his phone. "Apparently, Belanger's father was even more estranged from his own family than his in-laws," he said. "These people don't know shit about the comings and goings of their kin."

"So you're out of leads?" Boyden asked.

"Pretty much," he said, adding, "Weird goddamned people."

"All right take a break," Boyden said, disappointed that she would have nothing to report to Maxwell.

"What was that you said?" Grimshaw asked the person he was talking to. He scribbled something down on a pad and nodded. Boyden leaned in for a look. Written on a steno pad was the name: Robert Hawkins. Then he wrote: Belanger family Atty. "Really? You have that?" Grimshaw said, and, "Yes, that would be great." A second later, he jotted down the number. "Thank you for your help."

"Who is Robert Hawkins?" Boyden asked.

"Family lawyer. According to Lance's uncle, Robert Belanger, the father used to go hunting or camping in upstate New York. But he was never along on those trips, he and his brother were estranged," Grimshaw said.

"Any reason given?" Boyden asked.

"None," he said and added, "but I ran Robert Belanger through the database, and he's on the sex offender registry. He was caught in an internet sting that targeted people making, sharing, and distributing child pornography."

"You're kidding," she said. "I wonder if the uncle got at Lance Belanger when he was a kid."

"I guess we can ask him when we catch him."

Boyden said, "Give me the number, I'm going to call the lawyer myself. Good work, both of you. Keep digging. We just got word that they've stabilized Halsey."

"That's encouraging," Hicks said.

"Yeah, it is." Boyden took the number and went to her own desk. She punched it in and waited. The lawyer might be a dead end, but she wanted to follow this lead.

The phone began to ring.

4

New York Route 34

28 Miles North of Auburn, NY

He was making distance now, but the VW was cold inside and didn't have a lot of guts. He figured he had five hours of driving left to do. The cargo in the trunk had remained quiet while he transferred what he needed from the truck into the car. He heard on the radio that one of the cops was dead, and another was in critical condition.

So, one had lived, and he was sure that they'd called in the plates. He didn't have a lot of time. There was nowhere to hide the truck, so he just left it on the side of the highway and popped the hood. Sooner or later, they were going to find it.

Five hours is a long time, he thought. *And I am a fugitive of the law. They're going to be coming hard and fast. Guns drawn, wanting to spill my blood in retribution.*

This made him smile, rather than frown in worry. The plan had been a disaster. From Gusa to Norris to the three morons he'd picked up on the web. A failed experiment with reprobates, but it hadn't been a total failure. He was the most wanted man in America right now. He'd killed a hell of a lot of people, and if he could get across the river into Canada, he could go dormant.

Just for a while, until the heat cools off.

Then he could move again. Maybe up to Montreal and when the media and the cops mellowed, he could try and get over to Europe. He liked Europe. The old countries there had a network that fed into the darkest desires people imagined. He would fit in well there.

Just gotta drive for five more hours.

The cargo in the trunk was quiet.

Ah, yes, the cargo. I'll have to do something about that.

5

Over the next hour and a half, he drove up through Weedsport and into Hannibal, then caught NY 34, and pushed west toward Palermo. No one paid much attention to the puttering dark blue 1968 VW. This gave Lance a sense of superiority to the lawmen and women who hunted him.

But it was false. The hunters were determined, and no matter what Lance thought, they were unyielding in their mission. By the time he reached Palermo, Perry De Jong's farm was being overrun with investigators. A BOLO had been issued for the truck, and a state cop found the pickup on the side of the US 20 only minutes after the lookout was issued. The investigators were behind him, gathering evidence, making their case, doggedly sniffing the air for any scent that would get them closer.

He didn't know this, but knew they were in pursuit. Had to be. But he was only hours away from escape.

"Fucking yeah!" Came out of him in a voice he'd only heard internally. The monster that he'd cultivated and tethered like a dog was now crawling beneath his skin, moving behind his eyes, looking out and bellowing in psychosis. "Feels good," he—it—they roared over the puttering of the Bug's engine.

The snow was starting again.

"That'll keep them busy."

He stepped on the gas pedal, testing the road, pushing the Bug five miles over the speed limit. The car fishtailed slightly and his heart jumped, so he backed off. Then he thought about the cargo and knew he would have to make a stop somewhere and deliver it. It would be fun to take her all the way to Hopson's Point, leave her in the woods for Maxwell to find.

But she was a liability.

He was feeling that insatiable need again. The cops and the farmer hadn't been enough. The smart thing to do would be to take her into the woods and put the gun against her head.

Quick, clean, book, saddle, and go!

Where had he heard that?

Killing with a gun wasn't the same. Lance needed the control that came with total dominion. With ritual, with terror, and yes, with blood. Blood was important to Lance. It was what carried the spirit, if there was one, out of the physical and back to the earth. Blood and terror; they had to be scared, had to know what was coming.

He thought back. There had been plenty of blood, and if he'd stayed the course, he wouldn't be the focus of a national manhunt.

"Bullshit," he cussed. "Maxwell was coming. The FBI has Gusa. They would've swooped in and arrested me sooner or later!" So, he decided to throw the dice. The plan had always been to go to Pittsburgh with the others. But the number was supposed to have been five, not four. Norris was supposed to be included in that project.

Poor Norris. Lance felt a tug of nostalgia.

Then…

"Yeah, poor Norris and his goddamned fucking knife," he snarled. "And poor Larry and Dusk, but not Steel, he was a turncoat, and let's not forget poor fucking Wendy and her bastard kid!" He looked down, saw his knuckles whitening on the wheel.

Am I losing my mind?

Ignoring the question, he said in a calmer demeanor, "Just gotta get to Hopson's Point." The monster pulled back from behind his eyes, not wanting to engage in psychology. It wanted blood, and it would again take drippings from the master's table. Lance refocused, loosened his grip slightly on the wheel, felt the ache in his knuckles, and he felt himself coming back. He whispered to the withdrawing monster, "Once we get across the border, we can go anywhere."

Nonsense. They'll be looking for us there too!

Lance fell silent.

Then he heard a faint sound, barely audible over the sputtering engine. He eased up on the gas, shook his head, focusing on the sound.

"Please, let me go," the cargo whispered faintly. "Please, I want to go home."

Lance ignored the pleading, choosing instead to stare out into the lake effect snow that was thickening. There was a northern wind too, sending torrents of white spinning out across the road. That was good, it would keep his pursuers busy, and he was going to have to make a stop. He needed to deliver the package, and still was in conflict about how. Below the car seat was the machete he'd sharpened for Carolyn.

He reached down, grazing the handle with his index finger, and thought about the blood.

"Please…"

"Soon," he said, but not loud enough for her to hear.

6

FBI Headquarters

Quantico Virginia

Boyden didn't get through to Robert Hawkins immediately. She got his male secretary, who said that the lawyer was in a meeting with clients. He informed Boyden that he would have Hawkins call back. Which he did, forty-five minutes later.

"How can I help you, Agent Boyden?" Hawkins inquired.

Boyden thought, *this guy sounds really familiar.*

"We're reaching out to everyone who has had a connection with Lance Belanger," Boyden said. *Where have I heard this guy before?*

"I was not friends with Lance Belanger. He was simply the son of my client. What do you think I can do for you?" Hawkins asked.

Boyden puzzled momentarily.

She recognized his voice, or thought she did.

But from where?

Then the light bulb went on. Boyden remembered the anonymous tip that had brought Maxwell to Belanger's door in the first place. There was something distinct about that tip. The caller had been a male, but he sounded educated, and a little pompous. But what stuck out for her was the word he'd used.

Proclivity, she thought, and recalled the tipster's exact words. *"I was told that he had a proclivity for torturing little animals when he was younger."* She'd listened to that call only three days ago while circumventing digital and written evidence in the Highwayman file. She was almost sure that the man she was talking to now was that caller. It wasn't just the pompous manner of Hawkins' tone that zeroed her in on the anonymous call. He had a way of breathing. He reminded her of an old black and white television show she used to watch as a kid called *Alfred Hitchcock Presents*. At the beginning of each show, Hitchcock would come out and present a new story for viewers, and it was his breathing that she could always hear. Like Hitch, between sentences and sometimes words, Hawkins took in oxygen in gasping gulps. However subtle, it could still be heard, early development of a fat man's death throes.

"Lance Belanger was not your client, his father was?" Boyden asked.

"No, he was not. I took care of his father's estate after the fire killed Lance's parents," Hawkins said. "Again, I'm not sure how I could help, but I might have a legal issue with discussing my dealings with the estate. I'd have to consult my associates to make sure I'm not jamming myself up."

Boyden decided to drop a hook and see if Hawkins would bite. "It was you, wasn't it?"

Hawkins said, "Huh?"

"You said, 'I was told that he had a proclivity for torturing little animals when he was younger.' That was you, wasn't it, Mr. Hawkins? Wasn't it?"

Hawkins said nothing.

"You had a feeling about him, didn't you? You-"

Hawkins cut her off. "Agent Boyden, I don't know what you're talking about. I certainly want to help you, but there could be legal ramifications."

"He's killed thirty people, Mr. Hawkins. He's wanted for the murder of an FBI agent, and a Pittsburgh Police detective. He's on the run, Mr. Hawkins. Please, stop thinking about your career. We think he may have abducted someone, and we need to stop him before he kills that person too."

Hawkins said, "Agent Boyden, I am going to take a leap of fate, and ask if you have a personal cell phone."

Without missing a beat, Boyden said, "Yes, I do." She recited the number to him. "I'm going to step out for a smoke. Can you call me at that number?"

"I won't be calling you," Hawkins said. "Not without consulting with my associates. But take your phone with you when you go for that smoke. You never know who might call."

Boyden said, "I'll do that."

Hawkins hung up.

She brought up her FBI cell phone and sent Maxwell a text.

Boyden: I might be onto something. Keep your phone handy.

Maxwell: Will be departing Syracuse Trauma shortly. Keep me advised!

Boyden: Will do.

Boyden grabbed her cell phone and cigarettes and marched down to the smoking area. Her heart was thumping, exhilaration rising in waves.

"It's him," she said aloud.

Five minutes later she was standing outside, an unlit cigarette in one hand, her cell in the other. She wasn't alone in the designated smoking area. Three people were standing in a scrum, puffing on smokes about fifty feet away.

Then her phone rang.

"Hello," she answered.

It was Hawkins again. "Agent Boyden?"

"Yes, who is this?" Boyden turned her back on Agent Crabgrass and the other smokers rolling their eyes at the cloak and dagger bullshit, but if it greased the wheels with a pompous lawyer, so be it.

He responded, "I'd rather not say. What specific information are you looking for?"

"As you probably know, we have a federal warrant for Lance Belanger. As you are also probably aware, he's wanted for the Highwayman Murders as well as the Kirkland Island Massacre."

"Yes, I am aware of those things."

"Was it you who called it in back in September of 2007?"

He ignored the question. "We both want the same thing, Agent Boyden."

"Do we?"

"Please ask your questions."

"We were informed that the Belanger family used to vacation in upstate New York. A source informed us that you might know something about that. Did you vacation with the Belanger family up there? Can you give me any information to help us bring this killer to justice?"

He hesitated.

"Sir, I think you tried to do the right thing earlier. In fact, it was your call that got us next to Lance Belanger. I think you want to do the right thing here."

"I do," he said, then pulled in another gulp of air. "My former partner and Wallace Belanger used to do a fishing junket up there two or three times a year. In Massena, New York, they'd… Most times, it was a good old boys thing. Fishing and drinking. No women allowed."

"Did he take Lance along?"

"According to my former partner, not if Wallace could help it," he said in a sarcastic tone. Then, "Yes, he was on a few of those excursions, but he rarely went out with them to hunt or fish." Hawkins took another deep gulp of air, an edge of apprehension in his voice.

"Where exactly did they fish and hunt?"

"The firm representing Wallace had a retreat on Long Sault Island at that time. It's gone now. The flooding took it a few years back. But Lance Belanger was up there."

"Lance Belanger didn't like to hunt or fish?"

"Clearly, he liked to hunt. He had a proclivity for it. Just not the type of game they were hunting."

"Do you think that Belanger would remember the place?"

"Yes, he would remember it. One trip for sure."

"What do you mean?"

"Wallace found a dead cat hanging behind the cottage after they came back from fishing in the Saint Lawrence. It had been a neighbor's cat. Wallace beat the shit out of Lance for it, he was really intoxicated."

"Were the police called?"

"No. Perhaps they should have been?"

"Well, is there anything else you can offer? Anything that might pinpoint Lance Belanger's location?"

He thought about it. "I don't think so."

"Thank you for your honesty."

"He's a monster. You need to take him down."

"We're working on it."

7

19 November 2008

New York State Route 3,

Near Sackets Harbor, NY

The snowfall increased immensely with the passing of each hour; winds began to rise, building drifts across the highway, transforming into snow squalls, turning into an all-out storm. Weather forecasters on WVCR out of Loudonville, New York, warned that more "lake effect" was on the way. For the second time that early into the winter, upstate New York, Pennsylvania, and Ontario, Canada, were going to be feeling the wrath of Old Man Winter.

Lance didn't care, he'd made good time. He was now only a couple hours from his destination. Soon he would be walking into a new life. To add positivity to his situation, the cargo in the trunk had stopped begging and now only resorted to frail, intermittent weeps.

The car was an icebox. He couldn't find a heater control on the dashboard and scolded himself for this. But then, he imagined it was even colder in the trunk, and that made him smile. He would have to deal with that.

Sooner rather than later.

***

CHAPTER 28 – CHAUNCY AND CHEATER

1

19 November 2008

US Route 11

South of Richville, New York

Bob Chauncy was loaded down with 53,000 liters of aviation gasoline. AvGas had a higher flashpoint than regular gasoline, making it even more volatile. Chauncy serviced five local airports in the region, filling their small tanks after drawing his fuel from the refinery to the south.

After the weather went for a shit, he'd made up his mind that as soon as he got into Richville, he was shutting it down. They could wait for their fuel. He was northbound on Route 11 and driving along at forty miles per hour, in the middle of a bunch of other fools who should have parked their vehicles. Behind him, a flatbed was following his tracks and the tracks of those ahead of him because it was the only visibility.

"How are you doing up there, Tanker Yanker?" asked a voice over the CB radio.

He took in the side mirror. Behind him, there were at least nine sets of headlights. Behind those, he saw the Freightliner pulling a large piece of tarped machinery. Chauncy picked up the handset. "Plugging along. That you behind me?"

"Is so," the driver confirmed.

"What you hauling?" This sounded like "hawlin'."

"I got a locomotive engine on board."

"Oh, that looks like fun. Did you tarp it in the storm?"

"No, as luck would have it. Where you headed?"

"I got a bunch of stops. But I'm shutting her down in Canton. They don't pay me enough to play in the snow with a bunch of idiot four-wheelers."

The driver laughed. "Don't I know it. Nobody pays enough anymore."

"Yeah." Chauncy shifted the eighteen-speed up a gear, which dropped the RPMs lower. He always ran one gear too high in the snow. It was harder on fuel, but lessened his chances of spinning out. "Can you believe all these idiots out here? Don't people pay attention to the weather channel?"

"Did we?"

Chauncy laughed. "What's your name, driver? Mine's Bob."

"Nice to meet you. My name's Norm, but my handle is 'Cheater,'" the driver said.

"Nice to meet you, Cheater," Chauncy said. "So, which is it?"

"Which is what?"

Chauncy laughed. "Why do they call you 'Cheater?' Women or logs?"

"A little of both," Cheater said.

"Where you headed, Cheater?"

"I think I'm going to follow you into Canton and shut her down. They're predicting that there might be some freezing rain on the way, and I don't play in freezing rain."

"Me either. I might grab a bite up in Canton. You interested?"

"Absolutely. I'll just keep following your tracks. It's always nice to have someone leading the way when the weather's shitty."

"Well, let me tell you something, Cheater. I lost my perspective on the road ten minutes ago. For all I know, we could be heading into a farmer's field."

"Watch out for cows, Bob."

"Even the cows aren't stupid enough to be hanging out in this crap. But if I pass one, I'll let you know, my friend." Chauncy looked in his side view again. The vehicles behind him were bunched up, barely a car length between them. *Idiots,* he thought.

"Apparently, you're leading a parade."

"Yeah, a parade of dummies. You see how close they are?"

"Yeah, I'll back her off," Cheater tittered.

"Not you…"

"I know, I'm kidding." He was laughing again, and Chauncy thought he would enjoy sitting down for a meal with this new fellow traveler. Then freezing rain began to beat against the window. It sounded like sizzling bacon, snapping and crackling, sealing all in a clear case of ice. "Ah shit, guess what?"

"Yup, I'm starting to get it back here too."

"Come on… Canton."

"Ditto that."

Death came riding a pale horse, emblazoned across its nose, Peterbilt, below that in the grill a lighted cross. Chauncy had seen trucks like this before, evangelical Christian drivers spreading the word of scripture on the highway. Chauncy called them "Vampire Hunters." Earning their way into Heaven, saving one sorry soul at a time. Apparently, this southbound driver was in a hurry to get to the great gig in the sky, because he was driving too fast for the conditions. When he hit the sheet of ice beneath the snow, the drive wheels on the Peterbilt began to kick out from under the trailer and rather than get off the fuel and straighten the truck, the fool behind the wheel stepped on the accelerator and tried to pull out of an imminent jackknife.

Chauncy took his attention from the side-view mirror and saw the truck crossing the line and coming straight at him. The seconds of his life counting down from four, he only had time for a single thought.

Head-on with a goddamned Vampire Hunter!

The nose of the Peterbilt burrowed straight into the middle compartment of Chauncy's Super B tanker, and there was a momentary sigh before the explosion. The driver, who had been TRUCKING FOR JESUS, was already dead. The lacerated aluminum from the tanker's skin sliced the block off the engine, cutting the cab, and slicing the driver in half.

What ensued was utter chaos.

The AvGas ignited immediately, exploding upward, then raining down like napalm onto the highway and following vehicles. One after another, they piled into the back of Chauncy's trailer, and then the pup trailer exploded. Shrapnel went in every direction while the dry van cut the tops of more vehicles unable to stop on the glazed asphalt.

Cheater managed to avoid colliding with Chauncy's tanker, and every other burning vehicle, by turning his rig into the ditch in a controlled crash. He was still watching the road when his rig flopped on its side, and all he could think about was his time in the military and driving the infamous Highway of Death in the first Gulf War. He could hear them crunching against each other. The explosions felt akin to artillery and airstrikes. And there was that all too familiar smell.

Burning flesh.

2

25 Minutes Later

US Route 11

13 Miles Southeast of Canton, NY

Roughly thirty-five miles from his destination, Lance was puttering along at a little over 35 MPH. He couldn't go any faster, the roads were windblown and greasy, never mind that visibility was abysmal. On the radio, the state police were considering shutting all highways down until the storm relented, but that had little bearing on his plans. He was close. All he had to do was get across the river.

Inside the nose of the car, there was only silence. He hadn't stopped to take care of that business and wondered if he should at all. He was so close.

Why mess it up now?

But Lance's mind was buzzing with white noise, a prelude to the all-out psychosis that took him before each kill. The buzzing was the sound of insanity before the monster was untethered and allowed to take over. Except the monster was no longer tethered, it moved freely inside him, quarreling with the rational, the prudent, the caution. Like a hungry infant, it only knew that it wanted to be fed.

"She's probably freezing to death anyway," he said.

We need to look. Why waste it?

The snow pounded against the Beetle; the crystallized wind lifted and shoved the little car all over the road. But Lance held it straight, away from the sloped shoulder falling to a ditch.

He supposed it wouldn't hurt to pop the hood and confirm whether she was dead. If she was, he could just close the forward trunk, and that would be the end of it. But if she was alive? What then?

Stab her with the machete.

More buzzing in his head.

Stabbing her would be good. A metaphorical "fuck you" to the hunters, and one more for the Highwayman body count. He leered maniacally, looking on, straining his eyes to see what was ahead.

He knew he was close to Canton, and hoped he wouldn't meet any more cops, but thought there would probably be another checkpoint in his future.

And as if on cue, he saw the pinpricks of blue and red lights flicker through the snow and wind. "Oh shit." He reached down and touched the reloaded pistol he'd hidden under a coat on the passenger seat.

3

Over South Edwards, New York

New York state was being pummeled from Buffalo to Rochester right up into the Thousand Islands. They were twenty miles south of Palmerville, New York, when the chopper pilot, Troop Sergeant Jack Meaford, said to his observer, Troop Corporal Deanna Ackerman, through the headset, "Dee, if this gets much worse, we're going to have to put down somewhere before we completely lose visibility."

"Pretty milky out there, Jack," she agreed.

The others were wearing headsets. Ackerman had set them up to listen in as they flew. She spent extra time with Maxwell, as he had a working boom on his headset. "Just flip that toggle, and you can speak to us in the front," she told him, and they were up in the air.

"Grab my chart, Dee, looks like we're flying treetop to treetop."

She reached down and pulled out their flight plan.

Maxwell looked at the others. He might have protested, but the ride in the chopper was getting rough, and collectively he, Leigh, and Perkins shared in the fear that they might be going down every time the craft shuddered in the winter blow. Strapped in, Leigh held onto the side of her seat, knuckles white.

They all wanted to be on the ground.

Maxwell started to speak, and realized nothing was going through. He saw Ackerman pointing to the intercom's toggle lying in his lap. He shook his head, feeling stupid, then flipped the toggle. "Where would you put us down?"

Ackerman was still looking over her shoulder at him from the cockpit when the pilot replied, "Maybe Palmerville Airport if I can find a good landing spot. If not, I'll try for Canton, but I gotta tell you, it'll be risky. If we go down…"

"Okay, if you need to put it down in Palmerville, do what you gotta do," Maxwell said through his headset. To Leigh, he yelled over the prop blast, "We're going to need a vehicle. See if you can get onto the state cops from Gouverneur just in case we have to land in Palmerville."

Leigh brought out her phone and checked.

"No service," she yelled back.

Maxwell looked at his own phone. He had an incoming text, but the phone hadn't received it. His cell phone was blank, the words NO SERVICE gawking at him. He looked at the bars on his phone. A single bar flickered on and off, interrupting the NO SERVICE message.

The text was from Boyden.

He opened her previous text, gaping at it, waiting for what was to follow: I might be onto something. Keep phone handy.

Give us something, Linda, Maxwell thought.

Perkins pulled out his phone. "I got nothing."

Ackerman interrupted with, "Service will get better the closer we get to the ground."

"Come on," Maxwell said, lifting the cell up over his head, waving. "Come on, God damnit!"

Then there was a chime, and the text from Boyden came through: He's going to cross at Long Sault Islands. Call me ASAP!

Long Sault Islands, he thought. He remembered looking at it on the map. He brought his eyes up to meet Leigh and Perkins. "He's going to Long Sault Islands."

"Uh, no…" the pilot started.

"Not you," Maxwell interrupted. "Our suspect."

"Please turn your intercom off when talking to the others, Agent."

Maxwell was still holding the toggle. "Sorry. How long to Palmerville?"

"Maybe five minutes. If I can find it." There was an edge of distress in the pilot's voice that pushed all three of them into an elevated state of anxiety.

"Keep trying for the troopers," he told Leigh and added, "You too, Lonnie. I'm going to keep trying for Boyden."

The aircraft pitched right, and the body shuddered against the beating wind and snow. Maxwell looked out the window, and realized the pilot's description of flying in milk was spot on.

All he could see was white.

"Dee, I'm bringing her down low. Watch for obstacles."

"I'm watching, Jack," Ackerman said and nodded to Maxwell. "Make sure you guys are strapped in, it could get really bumpy."

Maxwell heard her, but he was thinking, *obstacles?*

Across from him, Leigh said, "I've got a signal." And she began speed-dialing Troop B of the New York State Police. Looking down at her phone, she saw the word, DIALING, but it only pulsed.

The pilot looked back, but only momentarily. What he saw was Perkins and Leigh holding up their phones. Then he shifted back to his main concern, flying the bird.

Then, as if a switch had been flicked, all three phones came to life at the same time. "Got it," Leigh said, and Maxwell's phone began to ring.

"Get a map up of Long Sault Islands, Perk, let's see if we can figure out where he's crossing," Maxwell called, then put his phone to his ear. "Hello, Linda. Tell me you got more."

"No banking transactions yet."

"What about Long Sault Islands? How did you find this out?"

"When Belanger was a kid, he used to vacation up there with his father and a couple work associates, both lawyers."

"They had a cottage there?"

"Yes, but it's gone. The river took it in a flood."

"Do you have coordinates on this?"

"Yes, I'll send them to your email, and I also included satellite images of the area. To me, it looks like a whole lot of land and trees. No structures, but I'll leave that to you. Maybe you'll see something I don't."

"Well… Ah, shit…" First, Maxwell felt the butterflies in his stomach, then he was suddenly jerked sideways and the phone tumbled from his hands. It bounced off the floor just out of reach.

Going down, he thought.

He hadn't even processed that his fellow passengers were also being thrown around. Leigh's phone was knocked from her hands, but she tipped it upward with her index and middle finger and managed to catch it. Perkins didn't drop his phone, but he hit the back of his head against a steel hand bar protruding from the side of the fuselage.

Caught in a downdraft, the Huey II plunged like a stone for almost twenty feet. Then it nudged hard to the right and back left, as the pilot fought to bring it under control.

"Hang onto something, folks," the pilot warned through the intercom. "I'm going to try for Palmerville. Two minutes until we're on the ground."

Maxwell unlocked his seatbelt, scooped up his phone, and brought it to his ear. "You still there?"

"Yes, what was that?" Boyden asked.

To Boyden, Maxwell suddenly sounded pissed off. "We're in the middle of another damned snowstorm, and it's getting too dangerous to fly. We're setting down in Palmerville, Linda. Leigh is trying to arrange transport. Can you get onto the Ontario Provincial Police? Don't pull any punches, tell them about Long Sault Islands, and that they should start setting up just in case he makes it across the border."

"Wouldn't we get onto the Mounties?" Boyden asked. "They're federal."

"The OPP has a much larger presence. Those are the guys that are going to be best utilized. Coordinate with the RCMP and Homeland Security, but we'll get the fastest response from the OPP."

"Okay."

On Leigh's phone she heard, "New York State Police, Troop B, Corporal Douglas speaking. How can I help you," The Duty NCO said.

Then Leigh said, "Yes, my name is Special Agent Michelle Leigh. I'm aboard a state police Aviation Unit helicopter out of Rochester. With me is the lead FBI investigator on the Highwayman case, Special Agent in Charge David Maxwell. It looks as though we're putting down in Palmerville, New York, due to bad weather, so we need a vehicle to that location fast!"

Douglas responded to this with, "I hate to tell you this, Agent Leigh, but you guys are on your own for the time being. We just had a major accident involving two tractor-trailers, and one of them was a fuel truck. Cars are burning, and there's possibly as many as people dead, maybe more. Everything is on fire. And it isn't just the cars and the semis, Agent Leigh. The highway is burning."

Leigh shook her head. "We're chasing a suspect. We need your support."

"I understand that, but we had to reallocate our resources so that nobody else gets killed. There are survivors. They take priority over one fugitive."

"Oh, for fuck's sake," Leigh blurted.

"I'm sorry, as soon as we can send a car, we will."

"Is your troop commander available?"

Now Corporal Douglas sounded irritated. "No, he's dealing with a tanker full of jet fuel that blew up. Right now, our priority is this accident. If I can get you a car, I will, I just don't have one available right now."

She could feel Maxwell's eyes drilling into her. He might not have been able to hear the conversation over the prop blast, but she was sure he understood. She shook her head and handed the phone to him.

"Hello," Maxwell said. "This is Special Agent David Maxwell; I am the field commander. I just want to confirm that you have nothing you can give us?"

"Not at this time. We have a small disaster to deal with. If I can get a car, I'll get back to you."

While Maxwell made his case to Douglas, Perkins brought up a map of Long Sault Islands and was looking at the closest locations to the border. He traced the route with his eyes. If he hadn't already, Belanger was probably going to cross east of Massena. There, a three-mile hike would take him into Ontario, Canada; half of it was across the river.

The chopper shuddered again and banked. Everyone held on this time, and it leveled out. Both the pilot and observer were scanning the ground. They might have been over Palmerville, but they couldn't see it.

Maxwell handed the phone back to Leigh and mouthed, "Shit."

She nodded.

Then Maxwell reached down to touch the intercom toggle, and found he'd left it on. "Troop Sergeant Meaford?"

"Go ahead, Agent Maxwell," the pilot said.

"We have no support vehicle for Palmerville."

"I heard. You really should turn that toggle off."

Maxwell smiled. "Yeah."

"There's a big accident. It's all over the Troop channel. Lots of folks dead. But there's good news, Agent Maxwell. At least for you."

"What's that?"

"We can't land here anyway. Visibility is zero."

"So, now what?" Maxwell expected they might be rerouting to Canton.

"I believe you were about to suggest something, Agent."

Maxwell looked at the others. They were going to lose the Highwayman - if they hadn't already. This was their last, best bet. He took in Leigh and Perk, covering his mic boom. "You up for this?" They nodded; even Ackerman. He said into the intercom, "What are the chances of you getting us to Long Sault Islands?"

"I don't believe in chance, Agent. But if everyone here acknowledges the risk, then I'm willing to try and get you there," the pilot said.

"Let's do it," the observer said.

"Okay, let's do this." The Huey II disappeared into the flat fading daylight, its occupants hoping that they would catch up with their prey before he vanished again. They were roughly sixty miles from Long Sault Islands.

4

NY State Route 310

Outside Madrid, New York

Lance was still shaking his head. With Canton in his rear-view mirror, he still couldn't believe it. There were police cars, two of them, but for some reason, they left the checkpoint and ran right past him, heading south with lights and sirens going.

"What the hell," he mumbled.

He kept going, right through Canton, and got off US Route 11 onto NYS Route 310. Strangely, he realized he still had his hand on the gun when he made the highway change.

Lance looked for a radio station, turning the dial until he heard a radio announcer saying, "Not good, folks, state police and Emergency Services have got their hands full down on Highway 11, just south of Richville. There's a multi-vehicle pileup, and this includes three tractor-trailers. If you want more information on this, check in at the New York State Police website. And finally, a warning. The storm isn't supposed to ease up until early tomorrow, folks, and state cops are urging everyone to stay off the road. Now, how about a little 'Sympathy for the Devil' by the Rolling Stones?"

Lance laughed and turned the radio all the way up. He continued at roughly 30 MPH, the little Bug sputtering along, hitting an occasional finger of drifting snow, sending up an exploding plume of white powder.

He was going to make it. Everything was on his side now. The storm, the accident, even the dumb bimbo who was sitting there puffing away in front of the VW. He figured he was about a half an hour from freedom.

5

Ten miles to the east, a state police Huey II, was flying on a parallel route ten miles to the east and had already passed Lance Belanger.

If they didn't crash, they were going to beat him.

***

CHAPTER 29 – THE RIVER

1

19 November 2008

NY State Route 31

Hopson's Point

Somehow, whether by fate or just dumb luck, Lance made it to the crossing just south of Hopson Bay on the Saint Lawrence River. The snow was still coming down, cutting across the land in merciless squalls that battered the Beetle as it puttered up the road. Anticipation filled Lance now. He'd almost made it. Just another mile, then he would be doing some walking in the storm, across the ice.

That was okay.

He'd taken enough warm clothing from the farmer's house, minus the gag balls. He grinned at this. In his rearview, he saw vehicle headlights stabbing through the absence of color that was now being drained by the darkness. And of his cargo? He would have to leave her. There wasn't any time, the storm was perfect cover for crossing into Canada, and he needed to take advantage of that.

"Just too chancy," he said. "I've got to take advantage."

But oh, how he wanted to.

He passed by a kayak and canoe rental place. His heart was pounding with anticipation. He dared to pick up the speed to 40 MPH. It would be cold out there, and he would need to be resolute and walk briskly. He had gear, a backpack containing the last of his money. He hadn't counted it, but there was already several thousand in Canadian cash mixed with the American dollars that had dwindled since Pittsburgh. But he had enough to get him the things he would need and reestablish himself. He had the identification as well for Wilson Rogers. He thought about the guns and machete. Carrying all of that across the river along with that heavy bag would be taxing. He would have to leave everything but the handgun.

Ahead, he spotted the place and realized the game was almost over, and it was looking very much as though he would be the victor. The Volkswagen Beetle puttered toward its final parking spot.

2

20 Minutes Earlier

Long Sault Islands

It had been the ride from hell, but navigational skill and a little luck got them to the island. The only issue was where they would land. The storm was in full force, and soon the light would be gone from the sky.

"The Ontario Provincial Police are going to pitch in, but they're catching the storm as well," Leigh had said when she called it in almost forty minutes before.

"Goddamned storm." Maxwell stared out into the darkening sky.

Perkins was turning his cigarette pack over on his knee, deep in thought. Maxwell guessed Perk was jonesing for a smoke. But the mood inside the fuselage was electric. While the pilot and observer conversed, looking desperately for a place to put down, Maxwell, Perkins, and Leigh shared one thought.

This was it.

If the Highwayman made it into Canada, the hunt would no longer be theirs. He would be picked up by someone across the border, and then extradition hearings would begin. The Canadians wouldn't just hand him over. Not with the possibility of the death penalty. They would eventually get him back, though. No country wants to care for someone as despicable as Lance Belanger.

But they would be cheated of trapping him after what he'd done. The people he'd killed, including cops. And that's what they all were, cops. Lewis Ash was dead. Oggy was dead, Halsey wounded. All of them were thinking about this. All of them wanted a piece of that takedown. Even Perkins, who didn't know Ash, and had only got to know Bob Halsey on the chase. But every one of these dead men were brothers, and the FBI agents he shared this harrowing helicopter ride with were now a part of his journey as a homicide detective. He knew that if they weren't killed, they were now lifelong friends.

"There," the observer said, pointing to a spot.

The pilot said, "Yeah. We might just be able to do that." Then over the intercom, "Agent Maxwell, you're going to get your wish. We found a spot to put down on Long Sault."

"Thank you, Troop Sergeant Meaford," Maxwell said.

"Don't thank me yet," the pilot said. "We still gotta get this bird on the ground."

"Do what you have to."

They were all looking through the windows, scanning the gray for something, some sign that the Highwayman was out there, Maxwell most of all. They would have to hope that some power greater than them would bring that together. There were so many obstacles and variables working against them, not least of all, the weather; finding a man in that weather on the ground was a long shot.

But it's all we got, Maxwell thought.

But it wasn't. There was something else. Maxwell hadn't felt it since he and Cole Abraham visited Belanger at his home in Lawrenceville, Pennsylvania. He could smell the prey he sought. Not in the literal sense, but a feeling ran through him, sharpening his senses, bringing up his heart rate. Maxwell was a hunter, he felt a weird sixth sense when he closed in on his prey and right now, he was sure that he would be meeting Lance Belanger face-to-face.

Then from the rear of the aircraft came a crack and a bang, and the chopper quaked to an unnerving mechanical sound that clunked and clanged, vibrating behind them. Then they went into a spin.

"I clipped something with my tail rotor," the pilot said, and then he said something else, causing his three passengers to lock eyes, processing the words. "Hang the hell on! We're going down."

Then they were spinning.

The G-force pulled them back against their seats.

Maxwell turned to the window, trying to see where they were going to crash, and then he heard Lonnie say something foreign to the situation.

"This just became a smoking helicopter," he said and opened his cigarette pack, shaking out two, three, four smokes onto the floor before he was able to snatch the fifth and stab it into his mouth.

"Are you kidding?" Leigh said.

"You guys want one?" Perkins held up the pack. "I ain't dying without a smoke."

They were gyrating like a tetherball. After dropping ten feet, the aircraft stopped as if held back by invisible wire, but it was really the skill of a seasoned pilot trying to slow their descent and turn a crash into a hard landing.

From the cockpit Maxwell heard the pilot say to his navigator, "Did someone just light up a cigarette in my aircraft?"

Perkins took a drag.

Leigh held on.

Maxwell braced himself.

The pilot worked the stick and rudders, fighting for control.

Then Deanna Ackerman said, "There!"

3

East of Hopson Bay

Lance pulled the car onto a service road that led to the Saint Lawrence River. Two hundred yards to the river was what he guessed. It wasn't plowed; the Beetle got stuck partway in, and he stopped trying to rock it out after a voice inside his head warned, *time to get moving.*

He began to unpack his gear. He removed the shotgun and flung it into the snow. It disappeared below the fresh powder. The machete followed suit.

Let them look for that.

Then he put on the heavy winter jacket he'd taken from the farmer and stowed the gun inside his right pocket. He pulled on a balaclava and hoisted his small knapsack onto the roof of the car. He tried to make the distance to the island, unable to distinguish through the looming gray. Soon it would be dark, and that was all the better.

Time to go.

Lance slung the knapsack over his shoulder, was about to step off, and he thought about the cargo. He stopped, sighed, and placed his pack down. He moved to the front of the Beetle, put both hands on the slope of the hood, and brought the balaclava up, exposing his face to the abrasive bite of snow crystals. He leaned down, cupped his right ear with his hand, listening for something. He didn't have time.

"Are you dead?" he whispered. "If you're not, I want you to give Maxwell a message for me." He leaned in, his lips almost on the paint, and said, "You're alive, but only because I decided to spare you. You're a parting gift for Special Agent Dave Maxwell. All you have to do is give him a message for me. You tell him I won. Can you do that for me?"

He listened.

For a whisper, a whimper, a tap of acknowledgment.

Nothing came.

"I won." He asserted. He got up, grabbed the bag, pulled down the balaclava, and started for the river, leaving the car and its cargo for his pursuers.

When he reached the frozen river, he tested the ice, uncertain if it would sustain his weight. He pushed with his foot in a few spots, even jumped up and down until he was confident it would hold him. Then he moved across the frozen water, pushing toward the growing silhouette that awaited. The snow continued to blow, and the crossing was difficult. Drifts ebbed out across the ice as high as three feet, and he slogged up and over them, listening to the crack and complaint of the river as things flowed below its crust.

As he neared the island shore, he wondered what Canada would be like. Would it suit his needs when the killing started again?

"Because it never ends, Agent Maxwell," he muttered to himself. "The game never ends. Lewis Ash learned that. And maybe one day when you're looking back on this case like that broken old man, maybe I'll pay you a visit."

He was gonna make it.

The island, a leaden specter turning charcoal, waited.

4

Long Sault Islands

They didn't die when the chopper hit the ground. It was a hard crash; Perkins felt the vertebrae in his neck and back compress. Leigh was slammed against Perkins, and

Maxwell felt like he'd been kicked in the left butt cheek and thigh. The pilot was injured when they impacted, his right ankle broken by the rudder control he'd used to save their lives. The Huey II had suffered severe damage as well. The skids broke the initial impact, and when they gave, its belly sustained the remainder, sending shock waves up through their seats. When the props dipped into the ground, great clods of snow and dirt kicked up from the earth along with shrapnel from the blade tips. Then those five seconds of utter terror passed, and the drama began to relent. The mechanical groans and growls eased, the reality of being static sinking in, all to a slow *Whup! Whup! Whup!* of the prop turning, slowing, easing.

And then crisp silence.

The pilot took off his helmet. "Is everyone okay?"

They sounded off,

Ackerman: "I'm okay."

Leigh: "Yes."

Maxwell: "I'm good."

Lonnie Perkins: "Well, that was a barrel of fucking monkeys." The cigarette in his mouth was broken, dancing on every syllable. "Listen, Caps, thanks for getting us down, but I think I'll drive from now on."

There were a few smiles.

"I think my ankle's broken," Meaford said.

Maxwell's head began to clear.

He wanted to get on the hunt, but they had to make sure everyone was okay. Patch up the pilot's ankle and make sure they kept him safe. They grabbed a first aid kit. There was a chunk of bone protruding from just above Meaford's ankle. Leigh fashioned a donut out of a cloth dressing and placed it over the protruding bone, then wrapped it in gauze. Both she and Maxwell had advanced trauma first aid training. After they elevated the pilot's foot, they began to talk about what came next.

"You can't walk on that, you'll have to stay here," Maxwell said. "I think we should leave your partner here to take care of you. Just in case Belanger comes stumbling through here."

The pilot unholstered his Glock. "I can take care of myself. Deanna, you should go with them."

"I'm not leaving you, Jack," she said.

Maxwell interrupted. "I don't doubt that, but I want you to have a backup. The three of us are going out there to see if we can find him. If we spook him out of the woods, I want your back covered."

The pilot nodded. "You be careful out there."

"Yeah," Ackerman said, unholstering her own piece.

"We'll call you by name if we come back."

"Okay."

"Don't shoot us."

"We won't," the pilot said.

"If someone else comes… use extreme prejudice." Maxwell put a hand on his shoulder.

"I will."

"Now show us where the hell you think we are."

The observer grabbed the chart, and she put them somewhere downriver of Hopson Bay, a nook of trees surrounding them. They were in a small land harbor obscuring the crashed chopper, but not fully enveloped. Perkins used the map he'd saved on his phone and figured that if he was right on the distance, that either Belanger had or would cross just northeast of them. They were still in New York state, but the river that ran around both sides of the islands enveloped them in a sort of no man's land between countries.

"Half a mile," he told them. "It's the shortest distance across the ice."

Maxwell felt the pull. "We've gotta get moving."

"Get going, then," the pilot said.

"Get him," the observer said.

Then they were on the move.

The trio trekked east, toward the south shore, taking their last shot, spread out in an ill-shaped arrowhead moving a hundred yards apart, Maxwell at the tip. Leigh was toward the shore and Perkins moved to the north. All felt the biting cold, the gun steel through their poorly suited gloves. The snow brushed their shins, but the island sheltered them from the worst of it. The forest dragged the bottom of the storm, stealing the momentum of its winds and offering some relief. Less than a mile away, a lone figure was coming right at them, oblivious of their presence, but nonetheless lethal.

5

Leigh and Lance were less than twenty feet apart when both realized that they'd come face-to-face. Leigh was scanning the ground for tracks, the tree twigs for breaks, any sign that someone had come through, but she was too damned early, and now before her, a man with a knapsack, a heavy overcoat, and a ski mask stared dumbly.

She saw realization dawning in his eyes, an expression changing from confusion to epiphany.

Leigh had her gun down; she too was slow in processing the situation, first thinking that the man in the ski mask might be someone else from the island. But then she knew, saw the emergence of realization behind the mask, his hand digging into his pocket, and it was coming out. She looked for cover and dove behind a tree, yelling, "Gun!"

The unfolding seconds of frozen time played out like a movie, one frame at a time. Leigh elevated her own weapon, still off-balance. She saw his gun come up, as she aimed hers at the center of his visible mass. She never heard the report when he fired at her first.

Releasing half of the breath she'd instinctively taken, Leigh squeezed the trigger, thinking, *never anticipate the shot.*

Sight trained on his mid-section.

The shot should be a surprise.

There was a click, hammer striking primer.

Then something made her flinch.

Crack!

The slide came back, metal against oily metal, discharging the spent cartridge and chambering a fresh round. Leigh felt something sear across the skin on her right cheekbone, just below the eye. She could smell gunpowder. She re-aimed her gun.

Her shot had gone wild, missing him.

"We're coming!" a voice yelled.

He was about to shoot again, swiveled his head in the direction of the voice. Then he saw the woman taking aim, arm shaking, and he turned and ran.

Crack!

He was moving as she had, into the trees over the rise of snow from which he'd come. Heading for cover. He cut left toward a tree. She was sure she'd missed him. Then his left elbow exploded into a crimson mist.

"Ahhhhhhh!" he screamed, like an infant feeling real pain for the first time in his life. His left arm, unhinged, swung at an obscene angle as he cradled it with his right, hunched over like a football player. He got behind a tree.

I'm hit, Leigh thought, and pulling off her glove, she brought her left hand up to her face. She touched the area gingerly, fearful she could make it worse. Her heart was drumming in her ears to the steady ring of having fired without hearing protection. She could barely hear her own voice.

"Shot," she said. She pulled her fingers away. Tiny dots of blood. It didn't hurt too much. Mostly it burned, and that's when she grasped that the bullet had just grazed her cheekbone, taking with it a three-inch-long landing strip of skin and cauterizing the wound.

It was superficial. But it had been close.

Too close.

She suddenly felt cold inside, and she began to shake uncontrollably. Her gun hand was vibrating like she'd just contracted Parkinson's disease. The tremors became quakes and then she was losing all control, overdosing on the dump from her adrenal gland. She tried to steady the gun, one hand with the other. The voice inside her head decreed, *I could have died. Too close. Way too close!*

She was shaking, face contorted, understanding that she, the proverbial moth, might have indeed flown too close to the flame. The question was, would she be drawn to its lethal light once more?

Gotta focus. Gotta focus!

She tightened her grip, trying to steady herself.

But it's so damned hard. I don't know if...

She closed her eyes, took a breath, and heard the voice of her mentor. *"Michelle! Get your goddamned head in the game!"*

She opened her eyes and began to control her breathing.

It wasn't real, Lewis Ash was dead, but he was goddamned right.

The tremors eased some.

6

Over the rise and behind the tree, Lance began tending to his own wound, trying to stop the blood that was milking from the unhinged appendage like a broken copper pipe. Tears cascaded down his cheeks, running into his mouth, while he let out strangled, hiccupping moans that were guttural and incredulous. The fucking bitch had blown off his elbow!

Fuck me, fuck me, fuck me!

He shrugged off the knapsack he'd been carrying. Put the gun beside it. He needed something to stop the flow of blood. He didn't want to think about how much he'd already lost. He unsnapped the cover and snatched a t-shirt from inside. He bit down on the shirt like a shark and tore it open. Every movement was draining him. He held one end in his teeth and wrapped it in a loose-fitting knot above the wound. Then he took three deep breaths and yanked! It slowed the flow, but not without grating the splintered bone against splintered bone, awakening shoots of pain that first glowed fiery hot, then rushed like California wildfire up his arm.

He screamed again and fell back against the tree, hot tears running down his twisted face. He shivered against the blackening pain that rolled through him. He thought he might pass out. Then he heard them coming. Knew he had to get moving. Three more quick breaths and he picked up the gun, his hand trembling. Pointed blindly around the tree and without aiming, squeezed a bunch of shots off. *Crack! Crack! Crack! Crack!*

All the while shrieking against the agony.

Three more deep, quick breaths. Calmer but numb, like Novocaine was replacing the blood he'd already spilled, and this brought rage. *The fucking bitch shot off my goddamned fucking elbow.* He didn't have much time. He would have to get moving.

Gotta move, he thought. *Gotta get across the river!*

Then, through ringing ears, he heard,

"Get down!"

"Who's firing?"

He fired again twice.

Crack! Crack!

He stumbled from behind the tree, then up and over the crest into the snow.

Nobody got a shot off.

7

For Maxwell and Perkins, the bullets came like angry hornets buzzing between the trees. One clipped a branch, inches from Perkins' head. They were only a combined fifteen yards from Leigh, who had her head down, when they hit the deck. Maxwell went down on his face, holding up his gun hand and sliding on the other right into a fresh mound of snow. He pulled back, shook the cold powder from his face, his gun hand still up, checked his weapon, and scanned the woods for the shooter.

The shots had stopped.

Maxwell called Leigh, "You okay?"

"He's hit! Gone over the rise."

Maxwell caught Perkins' attention. Leigh was between them. He mouthed, "Cover me, Lonnie."

Perkins nodded and scanned the area where he believed the shooter had gone. But it was dark and the trees were charcoal stands against the gray of night. The snow helped with that, defining the storm currents that whistled through the trees.

Maxwell got up and bounded forward, and in seconds was beside Leigh. He saw the wound on her cheek, which looked like a freshly applied strip of war paint. He didn't ask, but started feeling around her. "You hit anywhere else?" He gingerly ran his hands around, checking, looking for the wet warmth of a bleeding wound.

"Just the cheek, Max," she whispered. "But I got him in the arm. He's hurt bad."

Maxwell stopped checking her. "You sure?"

"Yeah."

Then Perkins was there. "You okay, Michelle?"

She said, "I'm good."

"Good, because I can't donate no more blood. I'm tapped." Then he smiled and winked at her. "By the way, nice shooting, girl. Not bad for a government employee."

"You okay to move?" Maxwell asked Michelle.

Michelle stood, ignoring what she'd just been through, giving all the answer that was needed.

"Okay," Maxwell said, and scanned the tree line. He saw tracks in the snow, gone back the way he'd come. Twenty feet ahead and ten feet beyond that, to the right of the snow path, there were black ichor stains in the snow. *Blood trail,* he guessed.

Perkins was the last to speak. The grin was what earned him the nickname "Perk." It was purely coincidence on the name, according to one staff sergeant in LPD. It was the smile that perked you up. Everyone loved Perk. He was positive, humorous, and supportive. But in every man or woman there is darkness, where wrath waits to be collected and dealt. The smile on Perkins' face morphed into a grimace. He was ramrod straight, a tower of rage ready to strike out.

"I've about had enough of this running through snow shit," Perkins said through gritted teeth. "Let's go get this little Pennsylvania peckerwood."

Maxwell guessed he was probably out of smokes as well.

The trio got moving.

8

Lance stumbled through the knee-high snow, his left elbow, or what was left of it, pulled against his chest. The throbbing was akin to a funeral drum. He was running, listening to his heart pounding in his temples, each breath a gulp of air followed by a succession of gasps. And…

It hurts, oh fuck a duck in the mouth with a shotgun, it fucking hurts!

But he kept going, looking behind him, seeing the blood trail in the snow. Not wanting to acknowledge that it was his. But it was, and his steps were getting shorter.

Who else is out here? More cops, FBI? Maxwell?

There were more. Lance knew that for sure. He heard distant voices calling to each other, and now they were close, getting closer.

He would have just run out onto the river to try and make a break for it, but across the frozen Saint Lawrence searchlights floated between the trees, beams cutting across the ice.

More hunters, waiting on the other side.

He heard a woman call, "Max! Blood trail!"

Max? Maxwell? Come and find me.

"This way," another man called.

Was that Maxwell?

He didn't think so. The man sounded like a Kentuckian; he had the same twang in his voice as Norris. Then he could hear their feet crunching the ice crust above the snow, along with twigs snapping, and there was even a wheeze of panting.

He was three hundred yards from the shoreline, squirting blood into the snow like a cow's teat during heavy milking. He smiled despite himself. Had he learned that lingo out at that faggot farmer's house?

Fucking DNA everywhere. And that made him cry-laugh.

"I hear something," said a new voice, one that he was sure was Maxwell. And he thought they couldn't be fifty feet behind him. But he was running out of steam, his fuel tank pissing crimson all over the snowpack.

Lance stopped, listened, and then took in the frozen river.

More lights floated on the opposite shoreline. The Ontario Provincial Police had delivered on their promise, unbeknownst to the stunned and slowing Lance Belanger. They were searching for him. He would be better off if the

Canadians caught him. He knew this. They didn't have a death penalty. He could fight extradition, but...

But I don't have the strength to make it across the river.

And he didn't. The blood loss was draining his resolve. How much blood had he lost? *A fucking lot!* Was it enough to kill him? Maybe not, but his legs were becoming stumps of clay, and he was beginning to feel nauseous.

Getting shot sucks.

He giggled.

They were closer.

He had the dark. It had always been his friend, the cloak beneath which he hid and moved. But the dogs of law enforcement were coming without relent. The scent of his bloody wound was bringing them. They were gaining ground, and he was losing strength. Lance trudged on, his fingers tingling, and something hard bounced off his knee.

He'd dropped the gun.

He kept going, each step a little harder. His mind rode a carousel of memories. Of murder, of compulsion, of arousal, but no love. Love was so foreign to his psyche, mirrored only by contempt.

He stumbled, almost fell over.

Heard his other say, *it was a good run.*

How much blood loss before he passed out?

I should know this.

Then it was too much. He felt himself going to his knees. To his left there was a tree big enough to hide behind. He moved to it. Once there, he leaned his right side against the trunk and slid down onto his ass.

He was losing it. The gloating "I won" echoed far off in the past. But not so far, really.

It was a good run, the voice said again.

"Yeah, it was," he agreed.

They were coming.

Maxwell was in the lead, with Leigh in the middle, Perkins bringing up the rear. Maxwell's eyes darted between the thickening blood trail and the woods ahead, moving at a curt walking pace, pushing against the snow clumsily, waiting to take up firing positions.

Maxwell saw the gun on the trail and snatched it up.

Is it the only one?

Then he heard mumbling.

Maxwell stopped, raising a hand for the others to do the same.

He was about to say something when he heard, "Agent Maxwell, this is Lance Belanger."

Maxwell followed the broken trail with his eyes. It stopped fifty yards ahead. To the left, he saw clouds of breath coming from behind a tree trunk. Maxwell readied his weapon and said, "I know."

"How?" Lance took in a painful breath.

"How what?" Maxwell asked.

"How… did you find me?" Lance was slipping.

"That's what we do."

Lance let out a mournful laugh. "I guess."

He gave Leigh and Perkins a glance, waved them right and left. Then to Lance, "What are we doing here, Lance?"

Leigh and Perkins began to creep out on either side, ready to flank him. "Is that Agent Leigh with you? She's not a very good shot."

"Lance, you've lost a lot of blood. I'd say a couple of quarts."

"Tell me… about… it." He let loose a giddy desperate laugh.

"I have your gun. You need to throw out any other weapons and give up."

"Okay," Lance said.

"Okay, what?"

"I'm… I want to surrender. I give up."

Maxwell kept his gun ready, putting Lance's gun into his pocket. He nodded to the others and they began to move in, weapons trained, fingers pressed against triggers, eyes and ears searching, listening.

"You got any other weapons, Lance?"

He laughed again. "I… I wish."

Five feet away now, Maxwell kept the gun on the edge of the tree bark. He watched the labored vapor clouds form and dissipate with each breath. Then he moved around to find Lance looking up at him, a grimacing smile painting his face.

"Keep your hands where I can see them."

Lance raised his right hand. It wore a glove of red. His left arm was mangled, twisted over palm up, the left forearm only attached by shredded muscle and skin. He moaned then. "This is the best I can do."

Then Leigh and Perkins were there, holding firing positions. Maxwell began patting Lance down. Body, arms, legs, he searched his pockets. All the while, Lance mumbled to him.

"I have so much to tell you, Agent Maxwell. So many secrets to share." He stared out into the woods, past Maxwell, who continued his search. "When I get better. We can do sessions. You'll have so much…"

Silent, Maxwell didn't look to the others.

"This will make you a celebrity, like John Douglas and Robert Ressler."

"I've been after you a long time," Maxwell said. "But there aren't going to be any sessions. If you've got something to say, you might want to say it now." Then he looked back at Leigh and Perkins, wishing they weren't there. Their presence made what he would do next even more difficult. "Time isn't your friend, Lance."

Maxwell reached down and loosened the makeshift tourniquet on Lance's arm. The blood began to flow faster now, further staining the snow deep red.

Lance saw something in the trees, a silhouetted figure. *Who is that?* His vision was blurring, the distant silhouette was fuzzy, and he wondered, *Is that Norris? Or Death?* He drew back from the looming figure. Looked down at his elbow, and then back up at Maxwell.

"I guess we aren't that different after all."

"You're wrong about that."

Lance lowered his head, losing strength, barely able to bring his eyes up to meet Maxwell. But the pain was also seeping out. "Not so different at all. Except my church is black and hollow, like my soul."

"You're running out of time," Maxwell said. "Is there anything else?"

"Yes," Lance said.

"What's that?"

Lance whispered then, inaudible to the others, and just barely for Maxwell, who heeded the words as each breath became shorter. Each sentence was fragmenting. Then there were gaps. Leigh and Perkins came closer. Maxwell listened fixedly, like a confessional priest to the damned, but he offered no paradise nor redemption. Maxwell had no church or belief in a higher power. He burned Lance Belanger's final words into his mind. It was all he was going to get. Then Lance's eyes washed out, stilled, and he sounded afraid. "Oh my God, they're coming."

Then nothing.

The Highwayman was dead.

***

# CHAPTER 30 – AFTERMATH

1

The subsequent investigation into the shooting death of Lance Belanger was ruled as justified thanks to the corroborating testimony of Louisville P.D. Homicide Detective Lonnigan Perkins and FBI Special Agent Michelle Leigh, backed up by FBI Special Agent in Charge David Maxwell.

All three testified that Belanger raised his Glock and took aim at Leigh, superficially wounding her and that she fired a single shot in return. Belanger fired five more shots at them, then fled, dropping his gun, and taking shelter behind a tree where he bled out.

Before expiring, Lance Belanger confessed to the murder of Wendy Birrell and her infant son, Patrick. A call was placed to retired Detective Hayward about the killings and two more dots were connected. That cold case would need to be reopened.

The helicopter pilot and the observer got a message out to state police and within hours, a rescue crew came with snowmobiles, two stretchers, and lots of New York cops. Belanger's body was loaded onto the second stretcher. The pilot was brought back and hospitalized. He was also being subjected to a disciplinary hearing for crashing the helicopter, but Julian told Maxwell he would intervene.

While the rescue was underway, a state conservation officer came across an abandoned Volkswagen Bug. As he investigated it and prepared to call a tow truck, he heard something. One word. "Help."

He opened the hood and, in the trunk, found a woman curled up inside. She was in the fetal position, frozen but alive. He lifted her up and carried her to the back seat of his pickup, cranked the heat, and threw his coat over her. Ten minutes later, driving far too fast for the conditions, he delivered her to Mountain Medical Services in Massena. They were able to get her core temperature up, but she lost three toes on her right foot and one on the left to deep frostbite.

There was little question of the justification within the news media; except for a couple alt-right conspiracy internet podcasts.

One, called *Ragecity Tonight*, claimed the entire Highwayman saga had been created by the FBI as a para-military exercise to both chump and embolden a public whose opinion of the FBI was faltering. The hosts of the show, Stan Winter and Derek Merriam, also believed the moon landing was faked and that the New World Order was running the whole show.

"It's Ruby Ridge! It's Waco! It's Oklahoma City all over again," Winter pontificated. "We are being corralled, people, and the Highwayman Project is just the beginning."

"So, you believe the entire thing, right from the word go, was orchestrated?" Merriam patronized.

"Yes."

"From the beginning?"

"Absolutely. Come on! Who kills fifty-two people and makes it almost all the way into Canada? This was a coordinated effort by the Canadian and American governments. Their own version of a black op, but on American soil."

"Yeah, it does look bad. That one agent, the one that got killed…"

"Lewis Ash, and he was executed by FBI's hierarchy. Disposed of, man! Thanks for your service. The FBI has no loyalty to anyone. The execution of Lewis Ash demonstrates that clearly."

No one with a brain took them seriously.

But then, there were plenty of brainless idiots out there.

2

Maxwell returned to Quantico. He had plenty of work to do, and now cleared of the Belanger death, he wanted to get down to it on the Gusa hard drives after finishing up the investigation and filing his final report on the Highwayman case. That couldn't be done without the coordination of state police in Pennsylvania and New York, and the Louisville and Pittsburgh Police Departments. Never mind INTERPOL and Bucharest or the other smaller departments he would have to work with to get the evidence and conclusions drawn up into a final report that would give *War and Peace* a run for its money. Thank God, Belanger hadn't made it across the border. That would have doubled the work.

Maxwell didn't feel any guilt about Belanger. He believed he probably would have died anyway. But there was regret. Not being able to study him in a controlled environment might mean that there was more they didn't know and had lost.

But had they? Belanger confessed to the Birrell murders.

He would have died anyway, he thought. And all he'd done was expedite the inevitable. But Maxwell wondered if he hadn't sold his soul to the Devil. *Doesn't that just make it easier the next time?*

Would there be a next time?

The blood was on his hands. Perk and Leigh hadn't intervened, but he was the one who made the call, and that was his to carry. Regret, yes, that he'd involved them in this, but he shed no tears for the disgusting human being that was Lance Belanger.

Maxwell attended Detective Ogden Chartrand's funeral. Also in attendance were Perkins and Leigh, and Halsey was brought by ambulance to a wheelchair and was set up beside Oggy's wife, Evelyn, who was flanked by her adult children and grandkids.

Leigh pushed the chair.

Both Ogden and Halsey were awarded the Medal of Valor, Ogden posthumously. It was a sorrowful event, but also inspiring in how the family of law enforcement comes together when one of their own has fallen. The police came from California, Boston, and even Canada and Mexico to show their respect.

After the eulogy, political speeches, and an honor guard gun salute, Chartrand Ogden's family and friends dropped fresh soil onto the coffin. During this, Evelyn Chartrand sat and looked on, clutching her grandchildren's hands, a folded American flag in her lap.

She was last to stand. She didn't say her goodbyes before the audience. She said to the onlookers, "Thank you for coming out to say goodbye to Oggy. I'm now going to ask that everyone give my family and me a private moment to say our own goodbyes."

No one replied, so she added, "I will meet all of you at the reception."

The officers and dignitaries began to disperse. Leigh was about to push Halsey back to the waiting ambulance. He was still weak. But Evelyn said, "Bobby, I'd like you to stay a minute, if you can. You're family."

"Yeah, I can stay," Halsey slurred, cheek still pinched by fresh stitches. He wanted to stay, he had unfinished business.

A few minutes and everyone else was gone.

Halsey looked at the grandkids, tears welling up in his eyes. They began to cry. "Come here, boys," Halsey said, barely able to hold back weeping himself.

They came to him, eyes gleaming from endless tears spent.

They took Halsey by each arm, cuddling their heads on each bicep. Halsey felt it in his shoulder but pushed the pain away. He'd promised Oggy he would take care of his family if something happened.

"Who are you going to take care of if I kick the can?" he'd asked Oggy during a bull session that involved copious drinks of the alcoholic variety.

"I'll take care of your girlfriends, Bob." Oggy winked.

Halsey had laughed.

Now?

Halsey said to Oggy's ghost, *"I'll take care of them."*

And from that promise, Halsey drew something. He would have purpose once again, something he hadn't had since the death of his wife. He even pondered giving up drinking but hadn't committed yet. He took Evelyn's hand. "I promise you that as long as there is breath in my body, I am here for all of you."

She leaned in and kissed his forehead. "Thank you, Bobby. He loved you, and so do we."

That was more than Halsey could take. He dropped his head and began to cry. Evelyn consoled him some, taking comfort in an embrace made awkward by his injuries.

Then they took turns saying their goodbyes.

First Oggy's widow, then the kids, the grandkids, and then Bob Halsey.

Leigh and Maxwell watched from a distance.

Halsey reached into his pocket, removed the small medal case, and opened it. He plucked out the Medal of Valor and whispered, "I'll take care of them, Og. I promise." Then he dropped the Medal of Valor into his partner's grave. "You take care of that for me."

Evelyn Ogden saw him drop the medal but said nothing. She simply waited until he was ready and pushed him up to meet the others.

Leigh returned to the Pittsburgh field office. There, she was assigned a new lead investigator from the Pittsburgh Police Department for the Kirkland Island portion of the Highwayman investigation; until Halsey could return, was the indication.

Belanger might have been dead, but there were months, possibly years, worth of investigatory work to be carried out. The replacement homicide investigator's name was Hunter Kay. Kay was a thirty-year-old veteran of the Pittsburgh PD, and he was extremely efficient. But he wasn't Oggy or Halsey. The investigation continued; the individual pieces of evidence obtained were into the tens of thousands, and they were still collecting.

Leigh realized that in the hunt for the Highwayman, they had outrun the collection process and tedious investigation. Leigh felt something about the Belanger shooting, but she wasn't sure it was guilt. Her part in it was justifiable, and she didn't judge Maxwell for speeding up the process.

She did ponder whether Lewis Ash would have approved.

You weren't there to protest, Lew, she thought.

She did that a lot, talking to Ash's ghost, but never getting a response. Sometimes when she was alone, away from everyone, she even spoke out loud. Leigh didn't have any religious convictions. It was a form of therapy, she supposed.

In her off time, she visited Halsey in the hospital, until he was released into physical therapy, and eventually back to his apartment. Then she started eating dinner with him and keeping him up to date on the investigation. They talked about other things; non-cop-shit, Halsey called it. Movies, music, likes and dislikes, food. As weeks became months, they grew closer, a sexual tension growing between them that neither knew how to move on.

One night, when they were alone at his place, he finally asked, "What happened out there on the island, Michelle?"

She sipped her third glass of wine and replied, "We took down a rabid animal."

Then she leaned in and kissed him.

Where it went from there is a much longer story.

4

Perkins returned to Louisville and resumed the lead on the investigation into the murders at the KT Ironworks and that of Amelia "Pigtails" Hill.

Maxwell returned a week after that with Special Agent Evan Ferguson. There were meetings with the Louisville PD chief, a slim man named Sullivan. Long Sault Islands came up in those discussions and both Maxwell and Perkins were adamant that Belanger had given them no other choice.

"You've created a lot of paperwork and publicity for me, Agent Maxwell. I have to be able to explain to the bureaucrats that letting Detective Perkins go with you was the right thing to do," Chief Sullivan said.

"It was the right thing to do. I owe both Leigh and Perkins my life," Maxwell replied.

The chief smiled.

Perkins did not, studying Maxwell.

Maxwell continued, "If not for Agent Michelle Leigh and Detective Perkins, I might not be standing here today. The Highwayman would have gotten away."

It was a half-lie, but one worth telling. He, Perkins, and Leigh were a threesome now; they had a secret that could never be told, but it was also a secret worth keeping.

The toughest person to deal with was Lonnie Perkins' wife, Ashley, who was unbending that her husband wasn't allowed to leave the state on anymore crazy FBI manhunts without her expressed permission. Throughout this, Maxwell listened after Lonnie abandoned him, going outside for a smoke.

"I promise to come to you first," Maxwell told her.

"You better, Agent Maxwell."

"Call me Max."

5

And if Lance Belanger had survived, he would have been happy to know that he'd achieved the celebrity status he so desperately sought. The news cycles, blogospheres, and even groupies gave Lance Belanger what he'd coveted from the moment he surrendered to his darkest desires.

He became the focus of documentaries, true-crime articles, and books, and there was even talk about a biographical series being pitched to HBO based on a New York Times bestselling true-crime novel. The book was called *Hunting the Highwayman,* written by Horace Montillo.

Lost to the media frenzy were the victims, who were only presented statistically, further fanning the flames of the Highwayman's notoriety. He was infamous, but the truth was that he would never be remembered the way he'd wanted. In the end, he was just another face in a sea of horrible faces. He would never be as big as Bundy, Gacy, Dahmer, or any other who had achieved rock-star status in serial murder. He was what Jim Morrison would have called a face from the ancient gallery.

One among thousands.

Later in the year, the FBI also published *The Highwayman File*, an evolving training manual intended for use by the people who actively hunt the monsters that walk among us.

And what of Andrei Gusa? Outside Bucharest, Romania, in a private meeting, Alexandru Vladimirsku was being briefed by his brother, Grigore, one of three underbosses in the Vlad crime family.

"I have information that Andrei Gusa is not dead," Grigore said.

Alexandru's eyes widened, his body stiffened, and he said, "Not dead?"

"The suicide was a ruse. Our sources have indicated that Andrei Gusa is in the United States, alive, under FBI protection."

"You're sure?"

"Yes."

"This is bad! Very bad!" Alexandru shook his head, worry lines creasing his pale forehead below the thick brush of dense, silver hair that topped his head. "This has to be taken care of, Grigore!"

"It will be, Brother. I am reaching out to our contacts in America, but the price will be heavy."

Alexandru lifted a glass filled with Russian vodka and stared through the drink, as if some answer lay in the liquid. "Grigore, if Andrei Gusa sees the inside of a courtroom, the price will be even heavier. Whatever it takes. Spare no cost."

"I would like Negrescu Assassni," Grigore said. The Negrescu Assassni, "Negrescu assassins" were three ruthless cousins who would carry out almost any job for a price. "They have contacts in America, they would be most effective."

"Contact them!" Alexandru sipped his vodka, swallowed, and frowned. "I don't care who you or how any you have to kill, I want Gusa dead!"

"I will call them and make arrangements."

***

EPILOGUE – ICE CREAM MEN

1

Eighteen Months Later

Ypsilanti, Michigan

On a mid-summer morning at 4:00 a.m., the kid working behind the counter at the 7-Eleven didn't know what to make of the two old dudes. They were alike in many ways; both were scruffy looking, both had unkempt gray hair and half-grown beards. They even looked about the same age, around fifty-ish. But they could be in their forties, he supposed. He'd had the odd tweaker in during the overnight shift, and most of them looked twenty years older than they were. But these two guys? He didn't make them as drug addicts.

There were physical differences. One was a long, lean man with weathered skin pulled taut around his skull and cheekbones like worn leather. The other was pudgy but similarly weathered, sporting a truck driver's belly. Etchings in the corners of his eyes told of hotter climates than the sweltering summer humidity of Ypsilanti, Michigan. There were more agreements in their demeanor than not.

They wandered the store. First the chip aisle, two bags of salt and vinegar, then the pop fridge, two large bottles of Mountain Dew, and finally the lay-down freezer where they plucked out two drumstick ice cream cones.

During this time, another guy, ordinary looking, maybe forty, wandered in and entered the washroom. By the time the bathroom guy came out, the two old dudes were up at the counter paying for their items.

Who buys ice cream at 4:00 in the morning? the counter kid thought. And it appeared that the bathroom guy might be thinking the same as he was puzzling over their ice cream as well.

It was strange, but he'd seen many strange things after dark that bred immunity to the crazy nocturnal patrons who came and went. But these guys felt different.

The thin old dude paid for the items, and while the kid was waiting for the order to ring through, he bagged the items up. Once the purchase had cleared, the thin man nodded to the fat man, and the two exited the store.

The bathroom guy stepped up to the counter and said, "That was weird."

The kid smiled and nodded. "Yeah. Ice cream for breakfast."

They looked through the glass windows as the two others got into opposite sides of a beat-up white Chrysler minivan. Thin man driving, fat man passenger.

"Maybe they just put down their bong and needed some munchies," the bathroom guy said.

"Yeah," the kid agreed, smiling. "Maybe."

The van sat idle for a few minutes, the old dudes getting ready for travel. Seatbelts on, muted chit-chat, and then it came to life. Headlights beamed through the window, shining on the two voyeurs inside the store. For a moment, the kid, the bathroom guy, and the two old dudes shared in a fleeting glimpse. It was broken after only moments when the van reversed, backed out of the parking spot, exited the lot, and disappeared down the road, its oddball occupants gone forever from the lives of the two onlookers.

Both watched the darkness, contemplating the oddity, and finally the bathroom guy said, "Give me a pack of Pall Malls."

"Sure." The kid turned, snatched a pack up, and scanned them.

The bathroom guy paid and exited the store.

2

They drove northwest, drinking Mountain Dew and listening to *Coast to Coast AM* on the radio. The fat guy's name was Oliver Thorne. He unwrapped his ice cream and bit into the hard cone. Simultaneously, he handed the thin guy, named Karl Holly, his ice cream and said, "You want me to unwrap it?"

"Nah, I got it," Holly said and took the cone. Resting his wrists on the steering wheel, he peeled the wrapper and tossed it into a makeshift garbage bag between the bucket seats.

"Maybe we should've gotten three of each," Thorne said.

"Waste of money," Holly said.

"I suppose," Thorne agreed.

They had North Carolina accents, both from Charlotte, both far from what they called home. "Maybe you oughta check," Holly said.

"Once we're on the highway. I don't want to be seen without my seatbelt."

"Good point."

Thirty minutes later they were on Interstate 275, pushing their way northwest toward Plymouth. Thorne unlocked his belt and turned to lean between the bucket seats. On the floor in front of the rear passenger bench was a heavy wool blanket draped over a motionless lump. He pulled it back to reveal an unconscious woman.

She was young, early twenties, blonde, her mouth duct-taped, eyes closed, and there was a thread of dried blood that had trickled from one nostril over her lips onto the shiny gray tape.

Holly had hit her in the back of the head with a tire thumper, which looked like a miniature wooden baseball bat. The thumper had been stolen off the catwalk of a rig at a Flying J on the same day they abducted her. That was late last evening near Wellington, Pennsylvania. The thumper wasn't in the car anymore. After wiping the blood away with a rag soaked in windshield washer fluid, he'd disposed of it in a rest stop trash can. The same rest area where they'd found her dozing in an unlocked, rusty Honda Prelude.

She was their catch for the night.

"It'll be light soon," Thorne said.

"Where we gonna take her?" Holly asked.

"I got a place in mind," Thorne replied.

The highway beckoned.

***

AFTERWORD

Hello there! If you're reading this, then it means you have indulged me by reading a story that has spanned over eight hundred pages of two novels, and for that I thank you. It was never my intention to write something this big, indeed not a story spanning two books, but here we are again.

Writing a book is a strange process, and I believe that in my fifty-four years, I've only scratched the surface of all that could be learned from the practice. Right now, I'm sitting in my basement office, hiding from the thirty-plus days of rain that has pummeled the province of Alberta from the beginning of summer into almost the end of July. As the rain beats against the window three feet above me, on the right, I'm pondering what to write or if I should say anything at all.

Isn't the story enough? Do they really want to hear my musings?

Perhaps not.

But nevertheless, here I am and, presumably, here you are, so let's talk about the Highwayman series, and what I would like to do with it.

There were questions about Lance Belanger and whether he would be the anti-hero of a book series like Dexter Morgan or John Cleaver. The answer to that was and is "No." But that doesn't mean that there aren't new and different stories that will stem from the Highwayman. There are just so many interesting characters to draw from. Perk, Max, Leigh, Ferguson, and even the late, great Lewis Ash.

Highwayman is just the starting point of what I hope will be a marathon of stories that will become Highwayman Book Three, Book Four; and from there who knows?

But whether there are more Highwayman books is up to the readership. If you want more, I will give it.

First, I must make a confession; I'm not doing it just for you. Honestly, it's for me too. The characters from these two novels call to me every day, demanding to be heard, sending messages that sound like something a delusional person might hear. Sometimes it's the ghost of Ash, or Perk, or Leigh, or Maxwell. For me, these characters are quite real, you know, drawn from a collage of personalities that have come in proximity to the part of my brain that collects and compiles tidbits of information. From them, a mental picture will form to a backdrop of sounds.

Maybe a distant scream in a secluded place.

Soon words will begin to form sentences, sentences paragraphs, chapters and... Or maybe I'm on my way into the city, and I stop at a 7-Eleven that is not in Ypsilanti, Michigan, but a place called Morinville, Alberta, and I see two old dudes picking up snacks of ice cream, Mountain Dew, and it's like 3:00 a.m.

I ask myself a question, "Who the hell buys ice cream at this time of the morning?" That thought gets stowed for a quiet moment where it will manifest into an idea.

And then the madness begins again.

Thanks for tagging along.

I hope to see you next time.

MJ Preston
20 June 2019

ACKNOWLEDGMENTS

A novel of this size is a massive undertaking. Getting a project like this to print does not happen without the knowledge and input of several people. I would like to thank the following people for their help in getting this book to print.

Karen "Stormy" Preston – If not for the understanding and support of my best friend and life partner, I am doubtful that, at this stage in my life, I would have written as much as I have. Being the partner of an aspiring writer with a day job means having your time together parceled out even more. She has always understood my passion to write and was willing to sacrifice our time together so that I could pursue it.

Patti Holycross – Patti served as a beta reader, research assistant, and a general butt-kicker. She was instrumental when it came to keeping my facts straight. Her help with this project has been immeasurable. I can't thank her enough. The fact that she volunteered to help me with this book speaks volumes about her character. She remains a constant reader, and I consider her a true friend.

Dan Hunter – A retired lawyer, Dan's insight and suggestions helped me navigate the murky waters of the American legal system.

Philip Perron – Who suggested over a beer that I write this. Philip has always been a staunch supporter of my work and a good friend.

Kevin M. Sullivan – Research for this project included dozens of books, documentaries, and other source material about serial killers and the people who hunt them. While all the source material was fascinating, one book was a standout. *The Bundy Murders: A Comprehensive History* by Kevin M. Sullivan provided a template for the madness of the Highwayman Killer.

WildBlue Press – Steve Jackson, Michael Cordova, Ashley Butler and so many more who have worked to bring *The Highwayman Series* to life in print, digital, and audio.

*For More News About M.J. Preston,
Signup For Our Newsletter:*

http://wbp.bz/newsletter

Word-of-mouth is critical to an author's long-term success. If you appreciated this book please leave a review on the Amazon sales page:

http://wbp.bz/foura

Thrillers You'll Love From WildBlue Press

HARD DOG TO KILL by Craig Holt

Stan Mullens is an American mercenary in the Congo who is sent into the jungle to track and kill a former colleague. Stan discovers that his victim hasn't done anything wrong. And as he struggles to survive, he is increasingly drawn in by the man he is supposed to kill. Ultimately Stan has to choose between old loyalties and new friends.

wbp.bz/hdtka

HUNTER by James Byron Huggins

In yet another experiment to extend human life, scientists accidentally unleash a force that might well be a terrible curse. Now an infected creature is loose in the Alaskan wilderness, and the America military is forced to ask the world's greatest tracker, Nathaniel Hunter, to locate the beast and destroy it before it reaches a populated area. **wbp.bz/huntera**

16 SOULS by John Nance

On takeoff from Denver during a winter blizzard, an airliner piloted by veteran Captain Marty Mitchell overruns a commuter plane from behind. Bizarrely, the fuselage of the smaller aircraft is tenuously wedged onto the huge right wing of his Boeing 757, leading Mitchell to an impossible life-or-death choice.

wbp.bz/16soulsa

BORDERLAND by Peter Eichstaedt

When a prominent land developer is brutally murdered on the U.S.-Mexico border, it's not just another cartel killing to journalist Kyle Dawson. The dead man is his father. Dawson, a veteran war correspondent, vows to uncover the truth.

wbp.bz/borderlanda